A MOST UNLIKELY LADY

DARCY MCGUIRE

Boldwood

First published in Great Britain in 2025 by Boldwood Books Ltd.

Copyright © Darcy McGuire, 2025

Cover Design by Head Design Ltd.

Cover Images: Bella Howard and Shutterstock

A CIP catalogue record for this book is available from the British Library.

Paperback ISBN 978-1-83603-562-6

Large Print ISBN 978-1-83603-561-9

Hardback ISBN 978-1-83603-560-2

Ebook ISBN 978-1-83603-563-3

Kindle ISBN 978-1-83603-564-0

Audio CD ISBN 978-1-83603-555-8

MP3 CD ISBN 978-1-83603-556-5

Digital audio download ISBN 978-1-83603-557-2

This book is printed on certified sustainable paper. Boldwood Books is dedicated to putting sustainability at the heart of our business. For more information please visit https://www.boldwoodbooks.com/about-us/sustainability/

Boldwood Books Ltd, 23 Bowerdean Street, London, SW6 3TN

www.boldwoodbooks.com

To my fierce, wild, wonderful daughters Makielah and Meguire. And to Derek, my forever.

1

Ivy Cavendale leaned back in her chair and stretched, nearly missing the distant scrape of a door shutting along the corridor outside her room. The candle glowing on the desk flickered in a warm draught as sweat trickled down her back, tickling her spine.

'Those little devils. Surely, they wouldn't try sneaking out.' Ivy spoke to a scrappy little tabby cat curled on her lap – the orphanage's newest member and her constant shadow. She hadn't named him. It didn't seem wise. Not yet. Not until she knew he would stay. His only reply was a rumbling purr.

'A lot of help you are.' Ivy raised her pale brows at the tufted ball of fur and couldn't stop her smile until a loud bang had her heart knocking hard against her ribcage. Olivia had warned her to be vigilant. The children were prone to testing new mistresses. They probably took one look at pale, thin, wide-eyed Ivy and thought they could run riot over her.

Another thump echoed down the long hall.

'Right. This won't do. Something must be done.' She slammed the quill down on the parchment where neat rows of script listed supplies needed, tasks to be completed, and funds required.

They must understand who is in charge. I am not someone with whom to trifle.

Which was a real problem. As Ivy was very much someone with whom to trifle. She much preferred to tuck tail and hide than face any kind of conflict. Even one involving small, parentless children.

'Well, not any more. You promised Olivia you could handle being the headmistress of All Souls Orphanage. This is your first night. You will not fail before you even start. You don't want to go back to Aunt Gertrude's, do you?' Ivy was painfully aware she was arguing with herself. Out loud. In an empty bedroom. But if she didn't bully herself into action, no one would.

'What would the duchess say? After all the time and effort she's put into teaching you how to protect yourself, only to discover you were frightened off by a few orphan children, for heaven's sake?'

The duchess would have quite a lot to say if she knew Ivy had taken up Olivia's offer for work. Especially since Philippa expressly told Ivy to stay well away from Lady Olivia Smithwick, Marchioness of Brightmore, when Ivy first broached the topic of accepting the headmistress position that came with room, board, and a small income.

That's hardly the point, is it? Philippa doesn't know Olivia. She might be the Duchess of Dorsett, and she might work for the Queen, but that doesn't mean Lady Philippa Winterbourne is right about everyone all the time.

'Yes, exactly.' Well, at least Ivy agreed with herself on one point. 'Stand up right now, open that door, walk down the hall, and sort out whatever mischief is going on.'

She nodded her head and scooped the kitten up, plunking

him unceremoniously onto her narrow bed where he stretched, circled three times, then resettled on her pillow, his green eyes glaring at Ivy for such unprecedented rudeness.

'Sorry, kitten. But I must go and do something about that racket.'

Oh dear. What if the noise isn't the children?

Fear, familiar and paralysing, wrapped icy fingers around her ankles, holding her in place.

If it wasn't just impish children trying to sneak out a window or raid the larder for a midnight snack, Ivy was the only adult in the orphanage. The only person standing between her twenty-seven charges and whatever monsters might be lurking in the darkness.

'Even more reason to make haste! Those children need you. Don't stand here like a weak, useless ninny. Take the pistol if you must. You are not a scared little girl any more, so stop acting like one.'

Ivy looked to the unimpressed kitten for his agreement. He blinked, yawned widely, then put his head on his front paws and began to purr.

'Marvellous. Not even the bloody kitten believes I can do this.' Wrestling the pistol out of the side drawer of her writing desk, she exhaled a shaky breath and pushed open her bedroom door.

The orphanage was arranged with the sleeping quarters upstairs on the eastern wing, classrooms and library downstairs in the centre, and the dining hall and kitchens on the far west side of a rambling mansion once belonging to the Duke of Kilmare. Lady Olivia Smithwick and her Committee of Concerned Ladies for Community Betterment – a charitable group of wealthy ladies who organised and funded this venture – acquired the building through an impressive combination of flattery, flirtation, and a passionate appeal to the new duke's sense of patronage. It didn't hurt that he was in financial ruin and couldn't afford the upkeep of such a large, derelict mansion. Especially in the unfashionable neighbourhood of Islington. Thankfully, their new little charges held no such standards and were quite happy to sleep in rooms where water might drip from the ceiling during a heavy downpour, or mice were apt to skitter through the walls, searching for errant crumbs.

'We just need more donors. And if anyone can charm gentlemen out of their coin... and possibly much more, Olivia will do it,' Ivy muttered to herself as she picked her way down the hall in the dark, not wanting to alert the children of her arrival.

And far better her than me. I'd rather pluck out both my eyes than charm a gentleman out of anything.

The noise was coming from three doors down. Five young ladies were supposed to be sleeping soundly in that room. The children were housed in rooms of mixed ages, allowing the older children to lend a helping hand to the younger ones with little tasks like readying for bed. At thirteen, Sarah Turner was the oldest girl in room number three where the sounds of scuffling hastened Ivy's feet. She considered Sarah one of the more serious children, often seen with a ratty book under her arm and a worried frown tugging her lips down. Hardly the kind of child who would allow mischief to occur amongst the younger girls in her room.

Fear's bony fingers crawled up Ivy's spine, wrapping around her ribs and tightening in a painful squeeze. She clenched her jaw, forced air through her lungs, and pressed her ear against the smooth oak grain, trying to make out any voices. A wavering light glowed from the crack between the door and the floorboards. Someone had lit a candle.

The timbre of harsh words was too low to be any of the girls. A man was in there. Maybe more than one.

'Bloody hell. Bloody hell. Bloody hell.' She repeated the whispered curse like a mantra, willing the fear to release her lungs so she could scream if necessary. For all the good it would do. No one was near to help her except more orphaned children.

So, that leaves just me. Dear Lord. We are doomed.

She was no hero. But as one wasn't currently available, Ivy would have to make do.

She shoved open the door, her eyes wildly searching the room for any figure larger than herself. The pistol she gripped followed her gaze in a crazed arc.

A young man in the clothes of a gentleman with the snarl of a feral beast stood in a half-crouch, his arm raised to protect his already bleeding head. Serious, bookworm, no-nonsense Sarah swung a fire poker at him. The young man grabbed the poker before it could crash into his skull again and pulled hard, tugging Sarah off balance. She dropped the weapon and stumbled forward. Before he could retaliate with a swing of his own, Ivy aimed the pistol just over the man's shoulder. She pulled the trigger, hoping to embed her bullet in the wall and scare the lunatic senseless. A deafening bang caused the young girls to scream as Sarah pressed her hands over her ears and dropped to the floor in a protective ball.

Acrid smoke and the sour scent of sulphur filled the room.

'Fucking hell!' the man bellowed as the poker clattered to the ground. He pressed his hand against his shoulder. Though his coat was black, and the sputtering candle flickered in the wind from the room's open window, Ivy could see thick crimson blood coating his fingers. The bullet had missed the wall and found a home in his right shoulder.

Bother. I always pull to the left.

A stupid, dull thought to have at such a time. Ivy couldn't let her mind spin away into panic or she would be no good to the girls. This man was still a threat, even as blood seeped through his fingers.

Footsteps sounded in the hall. Sarah slowly rose from her crouch, her attention fixed on the wounded man. Children spilled out of their rooms, seeking the source of such a terrifying bang.

'Stay back, children.' Ivy spoke in a commanding tone she barely recognised. She felt the press of little bodies filling the doorway behind her. 'Sarah, look at me, dear.' Her voice was calm and firm when everything inside her quaked.

Sarah turned away from the man, her owl-like eyes huge. Her chin quivered, but she pressed her lips together in a determined line.

Brave, sweet girl. I will keep you safe.

But there wasn't time for softness, not when they clung to their courage like flotsam in a stormy sea. 'Take these girls into the hall. Get them away from here. Now.'

Instead of following Ivy's command, Sarah turned to a red-haired girl, only a head shorter than herself. 'Margaret, lead the others out.'

The girl gulped in a sob.

'Now!' Sarah fairly screamed.

Margaret's gangly legs poked out from a too-short night-gown, and freckles stood in stark contrast to her pale skin. Tears tracked down her cheeks, but she gripped the nearest girl's hand, and the rest followed suit, forming a wavering chain of white cotton dresses as they skittered along the far wall, scurrying out of the bedroom like so many weeping ghosts.

'You too, Sarah.' The last thing Ivy needed was one of her charges being hurt by a wounded, deranged fool of a man.

Sarah crouched down and reached for the fire poker, dragging it across the floor and picking it up, then taking her side by Ivy. 'I won't leave you, Mum. Not with 'im 'ere.'

Someone jostled in behind her. A gangly young lad Ivy remembered from earlier in the day.

Henry something-or-other.

He had gotten into a scuffle with one of the other boys in the schoolroom. Stuck in the vulnerable state between man and boy, he had height but no muscle and was comprised mostly of sharp elbows and knobby knees.

'I'll protect you both.' Henry's voice squeaked on the last word.

Wonderful. A girl with a poker, a boy with delusions of grandeur, and a lady quaking in her half-boots. I'm sure the three of us will strike fear into this blackguard's heart.

But there was no time to succumb to her doubts. Taking the poker from Sarah, she lifted it in one hand, holding the expended gun in the other. 'You two stay behind me.' And like magic, they followed her orders without argument.

The man's gaze flitted from Sarah to Henry and back to Ivy. Lurching forward, fresh blood seeped from the wound in his shoulder. He bellowed a curse and stumbled to his knees. His face went a ghastly pale green, and Ivy wondered if he was going to heave up his accounts all over the moth-eaten rug. She and her charges shuffled away from him and closer to the door.

'Bloody fucking hell,' he gritted between clenched teeth.

'Watch your language, sir. There are children present.' Again, a rather stupid thing to say, but Ivy wasn't thinking clearly. 'Come any closer, and I shall brain you with this.' She shook the poker like a sabre and took another step backwards. Sarah's small hand pressed against her back, guiding Ivy toward the door while Henry crowded her right side.

Bless them both.

'You stupid bitch.' The intruder's eyes were red-rimmed, his lips twisted into a vicious snarl. 'You shot me.'

'And I'll do far worse if you try to hurt these children.' Rage filled Ivy with false bravado. Not at the insult – it wasn't the first time she'd been called such nasty names, and they hurt far worse coming from someone who was supposed to love her unconditionally than a stranger invading her home. It was the thought of this brute violating any child under her roof that incensed her. These boys and girls were already far more experienced in pain and trauma than anyone deserved. 'I'm locking you in this room and sending a runner for the constable. I can reload my pistol in exactly two minutes. Unless you pick this lock faster than that, my next shot won't be to your shoulder.' She had cleared the door frame, and before the man could react to her words, she dropped the poker and slammed the door shut. Shaky fingers scrabbled for the keys tied around her waist, and she clicked the lock tight seconds before the handle jiggled violently.

'You'll pay for this, you...'

Ivy ignored the shouted insults and turned to face the rabble of children crowding the hallway.

Good heavens.

She desperately wanted to collapse to the floor in a spineless heap, but there simply wasn't time.

I shot a man. In the shoulder.

It was nonsensical. Ivy Cavendale did not shoot frightful men. She ran from them, screaming like a banshee the whole way. Yet, here she stood, the gun still smoking by her side, and twenty-seven pairs of eyes looking to her for instructions.

Oh my giddy aunt. Right. Well. Best pretend I know what the hell I'm on about.

Ivy pulled her shoulders back, tipped up her chin in a manner her best and bravest friend, Millicent Drake, often adopted when facing off against adversaries, and focused on Sarah. 'Please take the children to the kitchen and see what you can find there. I shall come to you once this is sorted.' She had no idea what 'sorted' meant in this situation, but there wasn't time to think about the myriad problems facing her. Instead, it seemed prudent to keep issuing orders. 'Henry, how quickly can you run?'

'Faster than a whip, Miss Cavendale.'

As the daughter of a duke, even a murderous, dead duke, she should be addressed as Lady Cavendale. But titles seemed rather silly after having shot a man.

'Excellent. Run as fast as you can, find a nightwatchman to come immediately.'

'Head toward Islington Green. The watch house is there. You're sure to find one of 'em wandering about.' Sarah nodded sagely.

'I know where to find a watchman.' Henry scowled at the girl before turning back to Ivy, his expression becoming earnest once more. 'I won't let you down. I swear it.'

Sarah rolled her eyes, then turned and started directing the children toward the kitchen. Later, when Ivy had time to process the evening, she would need to think on why poor Sarah Turner was able to face such terrifying events with unmitigated calm. But not just now.

'Hurry, Henry.' Ivy wasn't sure how long her captor would be content to sit in a locked room and bleed all over the floorboards.

Henry nodded once more and took off like a sprint racer.

Hurrying back to her room, she found the box where she kept extra bullets, gunpowder, and cleaning supplies for her pistol. Hastily reloading, Ivy returned down the now-empty hallway to stand outside her captive's door.

We need servants. Even just a few. Children shouldn't have to run for the nightwatchman when an intruder has violated the safety of their home.

It was an oversight. An expensive one, but worth the investment, even at the cost of other amenities, like candles. And coal. And the wages of a certain headmistress. She could easily make do with just rent and board. For now.

The man had stopped yelling curses and was deathly quiet behind the door. His silence was more ominous than the angry shouts.

Dear God. What if he's lost too much blood? What if he's dying right now? If he dies, it is my fault.

Or this could be a ploy to get me to release him.

Perhaps she should open the door just a crack. To ensure the man didn't need medical care. She bit her lip, and her silly, soft heart won out. Crouching low, she pressed her eye against the keyhole. She could make out the window, open to the night sky, curtains billowing in the summer breeze. But nothing else. Her stomach rolled unsteadily.

If the man did die, would the magistrate press charges, even if her actions were in self-defence? The beau monde would no doubt condemn her as the daughter of a mad duke following in her father's footsteps, but vicious gossip was something she could handle. A hangman's noose was quite different. Even if she didn't end up in Newgate, she could find herself in a sanatorium. But if he wasn't dying and she opened the door like a fool, innocent children might pay for her stupidity.

'No. I have my pistol. He wouldn't be rash enough to risk certain death.' Unless he was confident she posed no threat. After all, Ivy was only a slip of a woman, shaking like a leaf now the children didn't need her to be fearless. Hardly someone to intimidate a man desperate enough to break into their orphanage.

She dithered – something Ivy was particularly skilled at doing – and ran through every possible outcome. At the very worst, if the man did overpower her, the children were safe in the kitchen. Henry was fetching the constable. It was only herself at risk, and surely her life wasn't worth that of another's, even a scheming, terrifying toad of a man.

'I won't live with his death on my hands,' she muttered. Then louder, 'You, there. I have my pistol at the ready. Don't do anything foolish. I just need to make sure you aren't dead. If you could say something to assure me you are still alive, it would be greatly appreciated.'

Silence greeted her.

'Come now, let's not be peevish. Even a groan will do.'

Still nothing.

'Drat.' The curse seemed hardly vile enough, so she tried again. 'Damn.' Yes. That was better. Far more worthy of a pistol-wielding lady.

There was nothing for it. She couldn't, in good conscience, let the man die. Rattling the keys loudly, she pushed the correct one into the lock and twitched it back and forth without actually unlocking the door. He didn't grab the handle and try to open the door. In fact, he didn't do anything.

Most likely because he's lying in a pool of his own blood, dying. From the hole I created in his shoulder.

'Bother.' She forced out a long breath, then clicked the lock and jumped back, pointing her pistol at the door. Again, nothing happened. He didn't wrench the door open. He didn't come lurching out, covered in blood and screaming profanities.

The silence mocked her pounding heart. Leaning as far away

from the door as possible, she pushed down on the handle with the tips of her fingers, the other hand resolutely pointing the pistol where she imagined his head might emerge. The click of the latch was remarkably loud over her ragged breaths. She pushed the door inwards and leapt back, making sure he wouldn't be able to grab her hand if he lurked by the wall.

Nothing. No leaping madman. No bleeding corpse on the floor. Just an empty bedroom. The night breathed a fragrant sigh through the window. Ivy carefully entered the room, swinging the pistol to the shadowy corner at her left, then her right. The room was glaringly bereft of bleeding miscreants.

Ivy let a choked sob escape as she lowered the pistol. The intruder was gone.

2

Commissioner Edward Worthington, Duke of Landbourne and secret spy to Queen Victoria, squinted at his pocket watch before pressing the heels of his hands against his aching eyes. It had been a long, hot, sweaty day, and he should have gone home hours ago, but the Metropolitan Police didn't follow business hours, so neither could he. Edward dragged another report across his desk and wished Constable Dearing had better penmanship. With a disgusted grunt, he pulled out the detested reading glasses he kept hidden in a drawer and settled them on his nose. They were a glaring reminder of his susceptibility to the ravages of time.

I haven't reached my fourth decade. Yet.

But it wasn't far off.

A swift knock preceded the head of his secretary poking into his office. The painfully thin man sported an equally slim moustache that could have been pencilled on. His dress was impeccable despite the late hour. His brown coat buttoned neatly, snowy cravat tied in a simple knot, and waistcoat showing no signs of wrinkles or wear. Edward wondered if the man used lacquer to attain such a severe hair part.

Swiping the dreaded glasses off his nose, he covered them with the poorly written report.

'Yes, what is it, Reading?' His beleaguered secretary didn't deserve such a curt tone. It wasn't Reading's fault Edward was making no progress on his latest mission. Finding the Devil's Sons – a reprehensible brotherhood of lords – and bringing them to justice. They had been orchestrating a flesh ring, preying on innocent country girls who came to London to interview for positions as housemaids. The young women were drugged and shipped across the Channel in caskets. Upon arrival, they were forced into the worst kind of prostitution with no power to refuse the twisted requests of the lords who bought them.

It was Edward's responsibility to ensure the titled gentlemen responsible for these crimes were found and received the Queen's justice. A far swifter and more brutal sentence than anything Prime Minister Russell or the House of Lords would decree. Not that Edward could admit his affiliation with the Queen and her rebel band of vigilantes to anyone but Reading. His secretary had been with him far too long to maintain such secrecy.

'As always, your manners set quite an example, sir.'

By rights, Edward should be addressed as 'Your Grace', but he had put a stop to such nonsense the moment his uncle's title was thrust upon him eight years prior. He was never meant to inherit, but his cousin had always been a rash fool with more confidence than wit. In an ill-advised phaeton race, Cousin Cecil overturned his carriage, thus ending his short life of excess. Edward became the newest Duke of Landbourne, which was a bloody nuisance.

He was proud of his work as Commissioner of the Metropolitan Police. It was a title he had earned through years of hard work and dedication. A stark contrast to the dukedom, which came from a stupid choice made by his pompous, infantile bully of a cousin.

Edward never wanted the responsibilities of a dukedom, and he couldn't marry so there would be no heir. Putting the fantasy of love aside long ago, he had poured himself into his work, fighting for justice. He wasn't about to give that up for the fussy life of a bloody duke. So, he found worthy stewards for his five properties and continued as though nothing changed, including how his staff addressed him.

'Why are you still here, Reading? It's past midnight. Go home to your... cats.' Edward returned his attention to the report in front of him.

Reading had been working for Edward since his first day at 4 Whitehall Place fifteen years prior. He was quick, resourceful, and thorough to a fault. He was also the closest thing Edward had to a real friend. But that didn't stop their constant sniping at each other.

'I was just leaving, sir. But a report has come in. About *her*.' Reading's ears tinged red at the tips.

Edward didn't have to ask who 'her' might be.

Lady Ivy Cavendale.

A woman who rubbed against him like a scratchy wool jumper. Irritating, but also quite warm. He had several men assigned around the clock to keep an eye on her. Highly unusual behaviour for a man who never showed interest in any woman and certainly not a disgraced wallflower like Miss Cavendale. Reading was far too professional to question his superior's judgement. But his ears told another story. The man couldn't look at a street doxy charged with vagrancy without turning completely crimson, let alone imagine his employer showing unprecedented interest in a certain young woman.

He's wrong. They all are.

Despite the whispers circulating Scotland Yard about their stone-hearted leader's sudden attention to Lady Ivy Cavendale – a pale, haunted woman whose father made the papers last year for a very suspicious murder/suicide including his son – Edward's focus on Ivy had nothing to do with anything as insipid as romance or altruistic as charity.

It's the selfish hope of absolution for my unforgivable sin. But nothing can save a man guilty of murder. Not even seeking justice against the Devil's Sons which is what I should be focusing on, not her.

The sadistic group of lords were led by three men known only as the Snake, the Wolf and the Crow.

One of the leaders, the Snake, had already met his fate, but the other two were infuriatingly hidden by the men serving them. Edward and Lady Philippa Winterbourne were charged by the Queen to uncover the identities of the Wolf and the Crow, capture them, and hold them accountable for their crimes. It was a challenging mission that should consume all of Edward's focus. Yet one word from Reading shattered his concentration.

Which is completely unacceptable.

'I assume you mean Lady Ivy Cavendale.' The pale-eyed, lithe woman floating somewhere in the shadows of Edward's mind. Hovering like an ethereal creature, insubstantial yet impossible to dispel.

'The very one, sir. I know you were informed earlier today of her sudden move to the orphanage in Islington. A rather odd place for a lady of quality to live.'

Edward grimaced. He should have informed Philippa immediately of Lady Ivy's move to the All Souls Orphanage, but there hadn't been time between reading reports, meeting with the constables from various boroughs, and establishing the crimes most worthy of the Prime Minister's private investigators. He planned on sending a note to the Duchess of Dorsett the next morning. After all, how much difference could one day make?

A whole bloody lot of difference if something has happened to Lady Ivy.

'Spare me the commentary, Reading, and get to the point.'

Reading tugged on a crimson ear and swallowed, his Adam's apple bobbing like a buoy in the waves. 'Right. Yes. Well, the nightwatchman reported a young lad came tearing out of the orphanage not more than an hour hence. Claims they've had an intruder.'

An electric current of alarm thrummed through Edward. He sat straight in his chair, the report in front of him forgotten. 'Intruder? What bloody intruder?'

Philippa is going to eviscerate me. I can't fail her. Not again.

Yes. That's why his heart beat an erratic tattoo against his ribs. Not because he was worried about Ivy Cavendale.

Why would I care about her fate? I hardly know her.

His concern simply stemmed from the ill-advised promise he'd made to the duchess months ago. It was right after the masque ball held by Lord William Renquist. The first night he met Lady Ivy Cavendale, and one he wouldn't soon forget.

She'd kept to the shadows that night. Hiding. Not realising her efforts to evade notice only drew Edward's sharpened focus more tightly in her direction. Seeking hidden truths buried in the darkest of lies was the one talent Edward possessed. And something about Lady Ivy Cavendale piqued his interest like a hound scenting the fox.

He'd hardly had time to think about his awareness of her that night as he was more concerned with capturing Lord

Gartling, an esteemed member of the House of Lords from one of the oldest lines of bluest blood. A man also known to his sick brotherhood as the Snake. One of the three leaders in the Devil's Sons. The dead one. Philippa ensured the man faced immediate justice with a well-placed bullet to his chest after he attempted to murder Lord William Renquist's maid, Penny. She was now Lord William Renquist's wife in a scandalous wedding between a maid and her marquess that the beau monde still tittered over.

When the dust settled on that night three months ago, Philippa had surprised Edward with a visit to his home the next day at the unseemly hour of eight in the morning. His butler almost swallowed his tongue when called upon to host someone of such esteem with no notice. Thankfully, Edward was dressed, breakfasted, and on his way out of the door. He delayed his departure because no one rescheduled with the duchess.

'I need you to do me a favour.' She refused to sit in the rather dusty parlour Edward never used. She stood with her spine ramrod straight next to his leather couch, rubbing her index finger against her thumb in a clear sign of agitation only her closest confidantes would recognise. Sunlight illuminated her morning gown of wine red so dark it was almost black. Her lips had been stained a colour to match. Shocking when the Queen dictated a natural face to be the comeliest option. But Philippa defied even Queen Victoria. She was stunning with her raven-black hair twisted into an intricate mass of curls and braids, the strands of silver only highlighting her beauty. Her sharp eyes, bluer than a fathomless sea, could cut through any man sharper than a blade. High cheekbones, skin that seemed to defy the years Edward knew were matching his own at nine and thirty, and a figure many young misses would cinch themselves breathless to achieve all combined to create more than just a woman. Philippa was a force of nature. It was no wonder she had captured his heart so long ago, when they were still children.

But she had never been enamoured of him. A fact his youthful pride couldn't accept. And so, the brash fool that he'd been made an irreversible mistake. One causing them both immeasurable harm.

Don't think of it. Not here. Not now.

His feelings for Philippa no longer smouldered with the passion of romantic love. Those flames died long ago and, in their place, grew respect of the highest order and an unpayable debt. So how could he possibly refuse her favour? Even one that ran so counter to his own desires.

'It came to my attention at the masque that Ivy has developed a friendship with someone I don't trust.'

Even now, months later, Edward remembered his reaction to Philippa's announcement. Alarm threaded through his nervous system with a healthy dose of denial. 'What on earth does Lady Ivy Cavendale's friendships have to do with me? I neither know the woman nor care to know her.'

Balderdash!

Even after only one meeting, it was impossible to deny his interest in the mysterious woman.

Philippa strode closer to him, close enough for him to note the fine lines fanning from her cobalt eyes. 'She is an innocent who has suffered much. More than you could possibly guess.' Which only increased Edward's growing curiosity. Something he was positive Philippa intended.

Damn her ability to play me so easily. Just as she did when we were children.

'Protect her, Edward. You owe me this after failing to protect —' But Philippa couldn't say her name. And Edward understood. It was a blade between them, cutting away their shields and exposing raw wounds neither wished to admit. Philippa continued as if she'd never stumbled. 'I don't trust Lady Olivia Smithwick. Her newly developed friendship with Ivy is highly suspicious. What could a woman like that want with someone as socially irrelevant as Ivy?'

'I doubt Lady Cavendale would appreciate your assessment of her.'

'I am not assessing Ivy's worth. It is immeasurable. I am simply stating her position in the beau monde. A station based neither on her merit, intelligence, or abilities. Society is a poor judge of character. Which is my point, if you would only pay attention. Lady Olivia Smithwick has captured the beau monde's regard and is basking in that power. So why would she waste her time considering Ivy as a viable friend? Her motives are corrupt.'

Shrugging, Edward refused to lend credence to Philippa's claims. 'Perhaps she appreciates the same qualities in Lady Cavendale which drew you to her.'

She snorted, a decidedly unduchesslike sound that reminded Edward painfully of the Philippa he knew from his youth. 'Doubtful. Ivy thinks Lady Smithwick is just a harmless, wealthy member of the beau monde, devoted to charitable causes. But she's wrong. I've been around enough liars to recognise the shape and scent of one, even across a crowded ballroom. Lady Olivia Smithwick is deceiving the beau monde, her husband, and Ivy. But she isn't fooling me.'

Edward had noted Philippa's reaction to Lady Olivia Smithwick at Lord Renquist's ball. While Edward had limited dealings with Lady Olivia's husband, the Marquess of Brightmore, he was a respected member of the House of Lords. Lady Olivia had only newly returned from the Continent, where it was rumoured her husband banished her at least ten years prior for cuckolding him. Unfaithfulness might earn a woman like Olivia Smithwick a certain tarnished notoriety, but she hardly posed a threat to Lady Ivy Cavendale's already ruined reputation. Still, Edward long ago learned the imprudence of doubting Philippa Winterbourne.

If Lady Olivia Smithwick had caught Philippa's interest, it did not bode well for the newly reinstated marchioness. More often than not, members of the peerage who gained Philippa's notice met an early, unfortunate, and well-deserved end. Which made Lady Olivia's friendship with Lady Ivy Cavendale most concerning. And a confounding puzzle. The two women couldn't be more opposite. Lady Ivy Cavendale dissolved into a crowd like mist while Lady Olivia Smithwick drew people's eyes as surely as a sparkling firework in the midnight sky. And yet, it was quiet, pale, private Lady Ivy Cavendale who plucked at Edward's curiosity like a violin string sending vibrations through his bones. And this was the exact reason he should stay away from the woman.

'What can I possibly do? Wade into the murky waters of female friendships and make Lady Ivy's connection with Lady Olivia a crime?' Edward tried to keep his voice calm. Steady. Free of any inflection. After only meeting Lady Ivy once, he already found his thoughts diverted. And he could afford no distractions in their mission.

'Don't be an idiot. I need you to keep an eye on Ivy. Make sure she is safe. You have hundreds of men at your disposal. Surely you can spare a few.'

Damnation!

The one woman he meant to avoid at all costs was the exact woman Philippa was asking him to watch closely.

'Are you trying to punish me? Is that what this is?'

'Trust me, Edward. If punishment were my aim, you'd already be bleeding from multiple wounds.'

Lady Ivy Cavendale carried secrets with her. Of that, he was certain. Mysteries he had neither time nor reason to explore. But Edward could never resist such enigmas. He was compelled to seek out hidden truths, even if those revelations caused immeasurable harm.

Even if they end in an innocent's death.

Perhaps that was why Philippa lowered herself to such depths. Requiring help from Edward only because she knew it was the last thing he wished to do. The Duchess of Dorsett hated him with acidity potent enough to burn the skin from his bones – an enmity Edward certainly deserved – but she wasn't cruel. Generally.

No. It is as difficult for her to ask me a favour as it is for me to grant her one.

She had stood in his dusty parlour all those months ago, her lips pressed tight together, her eyes flashing with fire and something even more terrifying. Fear. An emotion rarely seen in the duchess. Which was enough for Edward to place a rotation of his most trusted men on alert, noting the comings and goings of Lady Ivy Cavendale. And after three months of listening to their reports, he still knew infuriatingly little about the reclusive woman.

She mostly kept to her aunt's house, only venturing out to visit Philippa weekly or take tea with her closest friends, Lady Millicent Drake, Lady Hannah Killian, and the newly married Lady Penny Renquist. She did not promenade in Hyde Park. She did not visit the pleasure gardens of Vauxhall. She was not invited to the balls held at Almacks. She didn't even venture out to Harrods on Borough High Street to window-shop. Which made Reading's announcement earlier that morning of Ivy moving into the All Souls Orphanage highly unusual but not nearly as alarming as his newest report of an intruder.

Narrowing his gaze on his secretary, Edward forced any weakness from his voice. 'Has she been harmed?'

'Quite the contrary. She shot him.'

'Bloody hell.' Edward stood from his desk, strode to the hook holding his greatcoat, swept it over his shoulders, and nearly knocked Reading over as he strode past. He walked into the summer night with one purpose: finding Lady Ivy Cavendale.

* * *

Ivy was desperate for a cup of tea. Laced with a strong dram of whiskey. She blamed Philippa. Before meeting the duchess, she'd never imbibed anything stronger than ratafia – and then only a sip at a ball to cool her parched throat. But now, Ivy had developed quite a taste for the harsh burn and corresponding warmth of smoky spirits. It would be just the thing to chase away the deathly chill shaking her hands. Hands shackled together with heavy, metal manacles.

'It's unnatural. That's what it is. A woman. With a pistol. You could have done some real harm.' The constable, a young man with spotty skin and nary a wisp of facial hair, loomed closer to Ivy. She refused to lean back against the chair. A chair the idiot constable had dragged into the centre of the library. She hated being in the centre of anything, but especially someone's attention. Constable Spotty Skin stunk of pickled eggs and sardines. But she wouldn't show him fear. Even if it tickled along her nerves like a thousand spider legs. She must be at least five years older than the man, though he spoke to her like she was a particularly silly, stupid girl.

At least the children are back in their rooms. Safe and sound.

The last thing she needed was for her young charges to see Ivy shackled in cuffs, shaking with fear as an arrogant, young fool of a constable accused her of being nothing more than a hysterical woman.

'Yes. Well. He did break into the room of five young girls. Perhaps the one guilty of harm was the intruder.' Ivy's voice shook, and tears threatened.

I will not cry.

If only her voice were stronger. If only *she* were stronger. But she had learned the danger of men in positions of power early in life. The ones meant to protect were often the most dangerous. So she spoke in whispers when she wanted to shout until her throat hurt.

Don't. Don't be weak in front of him. He'll only attack.

'Allegedly. This mysterious disappearing man *allegedly* broke into the room,' the constable said, looking over at the night-watchmen. 'Bleeding girl. Can't believe a word she says. Delicate creatures, ladies. You put them under stress, roles of leadership like this, it's no wonder she's gone loony, making up stories. These poor children need a man here to keep their heads out of the clouds. A headmaster who won't let fancy run free. Not some barmy bit of skirt, filling their minds with wild tales of a Spring-heeled Jack leaping into windows.'

The watchman winked at the constable and nodded, his gaze flitting to Ivy as his lips tilted in a sly smile. He leaned against the door, crossing his arms over a thick chest. 'Me dad always said there's nothing more dangerous than a spinster putting on airs. She probably saw the wind in the curtains and imagined a spectre in the night.'

The constable nodded, his sharp chin cutting through the air. 'Too many of them penny dreadfuls. Rotting poor girls' minds. It's a wonder we let them read at all. Too much thinking is dangerous for a woman's weak constitution.'

Enough!

'If I was wrong, then it seems rather daft of you to put me in shackles for shooting at nothing. Do you think my imagination conjured the blood splattered all over the floor? Or my poor, delicate brain somehow convinced twenty-seven children that wind and curtains lurched across the floor with a poker, screaming profanities? Mayhap my fragile constitution is to blame for the broken window in Sarah's room. Or her recollections of the man trying to bash her head in. Or Henry's testimony, who stood next to me as the man nearly—'

The crack of the constable's hand across her cheek startled Ivy into silence. She'd never been hit before. It was shocking. And painful. Sharp. Hot. Infuriating. Her head snapped to the side. But she didn't shatter. She didn't break. Oddly, her fear crystallised into something hard and bright in her chest.

How dare he?

The question in her mind was spoken with Philippa's crisp diction, but she quite agreed.

Returning her gaze to the constable, she raised her brow. Before she could give words to her thoughts, the man disappeared. One moment, he stood in front of her, his arm raised. The next, he was thrown into a wall with a terrifying crash.

Dear Lord. Another intruder. This one is even more angry than the last.

It was a nonsensical thought. But so was the vision of Constable Spotty Skin crumpled on the floor as a large man slammed his fist into the poor man's face. His nose made an audible crunch as a wave of blood flooded from it. The brute attacking the constable didn't stop. He continued to rain blows as Constable Spotty Skin covered his head with his arms.

The attacker was turned away from Ivy, so she couldn't see his face, but she didn't need to discern his features to know he was a beast. A madness washed over her as terror turned into rage.

What is wrong with these men?

The nightwatchman was no help. He had uncrossed his arms but just stood there, wide-eyed, watching the violence unfold.

Again, it was left to Ivy to do something.

Really. I am not the right woman for this job.

But no one else was going to come to the constable's rescue. Letting the anger fill her voice with strength, Ivy stood from her chair. 'Stop it. This instant!'

The man froze.

Well. That's something, then.

Twice in one night, Ivy had issued orders with no expectation of those orders being followed. Twice, she had been surprised.

His back expanded and contracted with huge breaths. He was tall. At least a head taller than her, and Ivy was not short. He was also frighteningly large. His back stretched the beautifully tailored jacket he wore to its limits. Wide shoulders, thick arms, powerful fists covered in blood and clenched at his side. When he slowly turned to face her, Ivy took a startled step backwards.

'Commissioner Worthington.'

It can't possibly be the commissioner.

The few times she'd seen the man, he had been the picture of a calm, cold, controlled gentleman. And yet, she would recognise his features anywhere. Aristocratic nose, high cheekbones, sharp jaw. His raven hair, usually combed to perfection and sprinkled with silver at the temples, fell over his brow in shocking disarray.

Probably from all the exertion required when beating a man.

The very idea should have sent Ivy scurrying from the room like a terrified church mouse. She did not appreciate conflict, physical or otherwise. At least, she hadn't. But Philippa's influence over Ivy must be extending beyond her new appreciation for whiskey. She had been training with the duchess since Millie's wedding nearly six months prior. At first, it was solely to improve her skills in self-defence, but most recently, Ivy had begun to enjoy the combat. As her skills improved, so did her appreciation of the form and athleticism required to overcome an opponent. There was a gratifying sense of power derived from landing a well-aimed punch or hitting the centre of a bullseye with her pistol.

Of course, she wasn't sparring with a man. Maybe that helped. While Philippa was a skilled and intimidating combatant, she was still a woman. And someone Ivy knew would never really hurt her.

The lessons had become a bright spot in Ivy's week. Surprisingly, she was rather good at fisticuffs with her lean body, steady hand, and stubborn determination to continually improve. She had no hope of becoming as fearless as Hannah or as courageous as Millicent, but at least she could keep herself safe without putting others at risk. Tonight had been the first time she was called upon to use her skills, and while the whole ordeal was horrifying, she was quite proud. She hadn't fallen apart. Yet.

'Lady Ivy. Please accept my apologies.' Commissioner Worthington executed a curt bow. His voice, rough and dark like summer thunder in a midnight sky, was in complete opposition to his words and demeanour. One never would have guessed the commissioner was pummelling a man with his bare fists not moments before.

Except for the flash of fire in his eyes. The vibrations of violence in his tone. The blood on his swollen knuckles.

Good heavens.

'I rather think you owe your apologies to the constable.' She glanced at the man who was trying to roll into a seated position with some help from the nightwatchman.

Commissioner Worthington didn't even look at him. 'He hit you.'

'Yes. Well.' Ivy was suddenly very aware of the commissioner's proximity to her. She took a tentative step backwards. 'Not nearly as hard as you hit him. I am fine, Commissioner.' She lifted her joined hands to touch her cheek.

'Dear God. He shackled you as well?' Commissioner Worthington turned to the constable, who flinched away. 'Keys. Now.'

The man fumbled in his pocket, shakily pulling out a ring of keys.

Commissioner Worthington snatched them from the quaking man. 'Return your uniform. You are dismissed.' His voice was a menacing growl sending skittering nerves down Ivy's spine.

'Sir! She was being disrespectful.' The constable looked wildly at Ivy as though she might agree with him. Ivy pressed her lips into a firm line, and the constable's eyes narrowed, hatred twisting his bleeding mouth into an ugly snarl. 'The damn bitch claims to have shot an intruder. She's clearly ma—'

Before he could finish his sentence, the commissioner leaned so close to him, Ivy feared he would smash his forehead into the constable's and knock the man senseless.

'Leave. Now. While you still have the use of your legs.' It wasn't the words. It was that voice, darker than the Devil's soul, sucking the air from Ivy's lungs.

Her knees turned to jelly, and she sat heavily on the chair. How the constable didn't melt into a puddle of fear, she would never know. He might have been an unmitigated ass to hit her, but he was far braver than Ivy. He held the commissioner's gaze for a full second before dropping his head and turning away.

'Yes, sir.'

'You, go with him.' Commissioner Worthington glared at the watchman, whose mouth fell open before he snapped it shut, nodding silently.

Ivy watched both men disappear through the doorway then wrenched her attention back to the commissioner. He was facing her, his dark eyes unreadable in the wavering candlelight.

I'm all alone. With a man I hardly know.

Fear reawakened, skittering cold fingers over her neck, freezing her lungs with a frigid breath.

He prowled closer, the keys clinking in his hand. Gone was the gentleman she'd first met at Lord Renquist's ball, and in his place was something else. Something primal and angry and terrifying. It didn't matter that Commissioner Worthington was a respected member of society. Or that he worked with Philippa. It didn't matter that his actions toward the constable were to protect Ivy. Or that he wanted to free her from the shackles biting into her wrist. Only one thing mattered.

She was alone. With a powerful man. In the middle of the night. The fear she carried with her as close as her own skin skittered through her mind, chasing out every rational thought.

'Please. Don't come any closer.' Gone was her commanding tone. In its place was the whimper of a wounded creature. Ivy was a fool to think she could protect herself against a man like Commissioner Worthington. Despite her training, her newly developed skills, and her fleeting rage, she was still just a fragile, weak, vulnerable woman in the presence of a far more formidable predator.

3

The molten rage burning in Edward from the moment he walked into the library and saw his constable smacking Lady Ivy froze in his veins like raindrops in a frigid wind. He stood completely still. The terror in her gaze was something Edward knew well. He'd seen it in countless victims during his fifteen-year career. Whatever caused her to transition from fearless protector to frightened prey mattered less than what he could do to reassure her she was safe. But the desire to uncover her secret hurts and vanquish those responsible for them washed through Edward like a rogue wave.

Not now. Later.

'I won't. Not until you tell me.' He kept his hands in front of him and crouched down on his haunches, making himself as small as possible. 'When you're ready, I want to unlock the manacles.'

Ivy's wide eyes darted from his face to his hands where the keys glinted in the dim light. She swallowed, her elegant throat constricting. Blonde hair, so light it was almost silver, fell around her in a shroud. While her skin was always pale, it looked porcelain in the candle glow save for the red mark of the constable's hand. Her wide mouth was pressed tight together. She was stunning, but fear tightened her features into something fragile. Edward was keenly aware of how easily this strong woman might break if he wasn't careful.

'I'm not going to move any closer, Lady Ivy. When you're ready, reach out your hands, and I'll get you free of those.' He held his breath. Waiting.

A tear tracked down Lady Ivy's cheek, and she dashed it away with her shackled hands before sniffing. 'I am not crazy. Or stupid. A man came in here and was going to harm the children. I swear it.'

Edward nodded his head slowly. 'I believe you.'

Ivy took a shuddering breath. 'You do?'

She didn't believe him. And why should she? He had done nothing to gain her trust barrelling into her home and beating a man like some lawless barbarian.

'Yes. I would like to hear what happened. But not while you're in those.' He nodded to the cuffs.

Lady Ivy swallowed, then pressed her lips together. 'All right.' She held out her pale arms. Something inside Edward's chest cracked. She was terrified, but she reached out anyway. 'You may u-unlock these. Please.' She sniffed loudly, her cheeks and neck becoming stained in blotches of crimson. It was akin to watching paint bleed onto canvas, and Edward was mesmerised, curious what patterns might emerge.

He carefully wrapped one hand around her forearm to hold it steady, noting how she stiffened, her shoulders hitching closer to her ears. Her skin was warm and petal-soft in his rough palm.

He fit the key into the lock and turned it. The click was deafening in the quiet room but not as loud as her breaths. Pulling the metal open, Edward helped free her right wrist before repeating the process with her left. Peony and rosemary surrounded him, a unique blend of sweet and earthy. He pulled the scent into his lungs, not wanting to exhale. Pale-blue veins created a network of trails beneath her skin. He traced one with his finger before he could think better of it.

Lady Ivy inhaled a sharp breath. He glanced up, and her crystal eyes were almost eclipsed by black pupils. In another woman, he might assume it was desire. But passion wasn't causing the pulse at her throat to beat so wildly. He pulled his hand back.

'Forgive me. I wanted to ensure you were not harmed. If shackles are fastened too tight, they can create sores,' Edward lied. He never lied. But how could he admit the spiderweb of vessels carrying blood throughout her body was as beautiful as a butterfly's wing? Delicate and vital? He had reached to touch it with the same thoughtless wonder as a child reaching for open flame.

I'm going mad. It must be fatigue. When did I last eat? What nonsense is filling my head... spiderwebs and butterfly wings.

'I am unharmed, Commissioner. I assure you.' Gone was the commanding tone of the woman demanding he stop beating the constable. With no one to protect, Lady Ivy lost her courage. A warrior attempting to slip into the shadows. Yet one more contradiction to add to his list.

She rubbed where his finger had danced over her skin. The spray of colour painting her neck and chest grew darker. 'May we postpone your interview until the morrow? I find myself overwhelmed.'

He should respect her wishes. Let her hide away as she seemed determined to do. But something within him rebelled. She expected to be treated like a weak, broken creature because so many viewed her as such. But just as Edward could sense a lie in others, he could sense the truth in her. When she commanded him earlier in such a demanding tone, he did not question the veracity of her nature. Not as he was doing now. 'Truly? You seem far more in control of yourself than most would be after experiencing such traumatic events.'

She stood from her seat and stepped behind it, putting the chair between them. A meagre shield, but something, nonetheless. She gripped the back of it, and he had no doubt she would lift the thing and use it as a weapon if he came any closer.

Overwhelmed, indeed.

'I assure you, I am quite beside myself, sir. A woman's constitution is not meant for such violent acts. I can understand why your constable had trouble believing me. I hardly credit it myself. I'm sure I couldn't fire that weapon again if I was forced to.'

'It is ungentlemanly to contradict a lady, but I find in this instance, I must. You forget, Lady Ivy, I know your friend, the Duchess of Dorsett. If Philippa has taught me anything, it is the vicious nature of women. They are far more fearful creatures than any man I have encountered, myself included. And they are far more deserving of respect than most men display.'

'Yourself included?' she fairly whispered before pressing her wide mouth together in a tight line.

'I certainly hope not, Lady Ivy.'

'Then respect my request, Commissioner Worthington. Allow me to retire. I cannot think clearly and will be of no further use to you this evening.'

Damnation. I walked right into that.

Edward stepped back and bowed. 'Well played, Lady Ivy. How can I question you now without declaring myself a cad?'

Lady Ivy didn't respond. Instead, she tapped her forefinger

against the chair and dropped her chin, her eyes fixed on a spot directly in front of her feet.

He fought a smile. 'I concede to your demands. A reprieve for tonight. But I shall return tomorrow afternoon. And I must insist you answer my questions then.'

'As you wish, Commissioner.' She kept her gaze down, refusing to face him. The diminutive wallflower, easily overlooked, easily forgotten.

But not by me. I see you, and I am determined to uncover your secrets.

'Until the morrow, Lady Ivy.' He bowed sharply and forced himself to turn and walk away.

* * *

Lady Olivia Smithwick was a striking woman. Her hair was as fair as Ivy's but contrasted Ivy's smooth chignon with an untamed style highlighting her unruly curls. The wild waves coiled into a loose twist, and a waterfall of spirals framed her high cheekbones. Bold eyes – as green as Ivy's kitten – missed nothing, and her lush mouth drew the attention of every man in the room. When there were men in the room to be distracted by such a singularly beautiful woman. Thankfully, this particular room was blessedly free of men. For now. But the threat of Commissioner Worthington's commanding presence loomed.

It was one of the reasons Ivy invited Olivia to join her and was in the process of imploring her to stay for the commissioner's interview. No one noticed the paler, softer, far less dramatic Ivy when Marchioness Brightmore walked into a room. Ivy had scrawled a hasty note to Olivia early that morning to request her assistance instead of Millie, Hannah, Penny, or Philippa for this very reason. Commissioner Worthington was sure to be distracted by the flirtatious, charming Lady Olivia.

The last thing I need is for his notice to capture me.

She had felt just so the night before. Arrested by the commissioner's dark gaze. Imprisoned by his firm hands as his rough fingers traced over her skin.

What kind of touch creates such sparks and fires in one's blood? It is unaccountable.

And yet, when she escaped Commissioner Worthington the night before to curl in her single bed with the kitten purring against her belly, it wasn't fear that caused her hands to tremor. It was something else entirely. Something quite unnameable. She couldn't dispel the fizzing heat washing through her veins nor acknowledge what it might mean. She had been frightened at first, but then it changed into something else. When he held back instead of pushing forward, talked of respecting women, brushed his hand over her arm so carefully. A breathless kind of curiosity bloomed.

Desire.

No. Not that. Never that. Ivy had long known she wasn't like other women in that department. Her father made sure any interest she might have in the opposite sex was completely squashed by fear and revulsion. While her childhood friend, Millie, spent their younger years dreaming of passionate romances with handsome men, Ivy preferred to imagine a life of safe solitude. Her father had broken that part of her. Lord Cavendale secretly and systematically amputated any interest Ivy might have in male company.

'Once you are wed, your husband will take you any way he wishes, little Ivy. And as often as he pleases. How I envy him that privilege.'

Ivy swallowed down the bile threatening to rise, refusing to remember the details.

He's dead now. Gone forever.

But it didn't ease the bubbling hatred simmering in the centre of her soul. It didn't stop the impotent anger that only found teeth and claws when she sparred with Philippa. It didn't dispel the terror of a little girl trapped in her father's twisted fantasies.

She pulled her focus back to Olivia. She was talking about something, her expressive eyes flashing in the early-afternoon sunlight as they sipped tea in the one room of the orphanage forbidden to the children. The front parlour. A space designed to entertain wealthy matrons interested in donating large sums of money or offer a reprieve to the tutors engaged in educating the children so they might enjoy their morning and afternoon tea on the well-padded, if not slightly faded, settee. She wondered what the parlour might think, knowing it was also perfectly designed for conducting interviews with the Commissioner of Scotland Yard when a certain headmistress was accused of either shooting an intruder or simply being mad. If rooms had thoughts about such things.

Wondering about the opinions of a parlour is probably not the best way to prove I am sane.

'Did you hear me, Ivy? Are you well? You've gone quite pallid.' Olivia's shell-pink morning dress was hemmed with seed pearls along the neckline, drawing attention to her alabaster skin. Ivy could easily imagine Olivia as a carved statue of some Greek goddess were she not so animated.

First the parlour has opinions, now my friend is a stone statue. Evidence of my mental acuity is not exactly running abundant.

Ivy tried to smile and failed. 'I'm sorry, Olivia. I must have been lost in thought.'

'Are you worried, dear? Don't trouble yourself about the commissioner. I know how to handle men like that. I'm only sorry you had to—'

Before she could finish her sentence, the Duchess of Dorsett swept into the room.

Oh dear.

Philippa was resplendent in a blackberry gown overlaid with ebony lace. Rubies and onyx gemstones dangled from her ears and more wrapped around her neck. Her hair was piled into a complicated twist of curls and braids. She did not hesitate at the door but instead strode forth as proud and terrifying as an avenging angel to stand directly in front of Olivia.

The contrast of Philippa's dark magnificence against Olivia's ivory perfection was breathtaking.

Commissioner Worthington won't have time to interview me while investigating the double homicide that is sure to take place between Philippa and Olivia. This is all my fault.

Ivy never told Philippa she had taken the position Olivia offered to her. In part, because Philippa had expressly forbidden her to do so, and in part because it was thrilling to make a decision completely on her own with no one's permission or approval.

Philippa strongly disliked Lady Olivia, though her reasons for such vehement emotions were opaque. She only alluded that she had suspicions about the woman. When Ivy had pressed her on the matter, Philippa refused to elaborate. While Ivy trusted Philippa implicitly and the duchess' intuition was rarely wrong, in this instance, Ivy knew Philippa's judgement was flawed.

Olivia had been nothing but kind and thoughtful in her interactions with Ivy. She sought her out at the few social events Ivy attended and sent her an express invitation to join the Committee of Concerned Ladies for Community Betterment, an organisation Olivia presided over as chairwoman and whose commitment to charitable acts on behalf of children was gaining notice within the beau monde and parliament.

While the idea of helping others, especially the most vulnerable and needy members of society, drew her with a magnetic force difficult to resist, Ivy had initially declined Lady Olivia's invitation. She had been shunned by the beau monde when her father, in a fit of apparent insanity, had murdered her brother. Society believed he then killed himself, although Ivy knew the truth of the story. Still, the peerage wanted nothing to do with a young lady tainted by such evil blood. Ivy feared any assistance she could offer Olivia and the Committee would be outweighed by the negative impact of Ivy's reputation. Olivia would not accept Ivy's written refusal and effusive apology, instead paying her an unannounced visit at Aunt Gertrude's modest townhouse in Paddington. Ivy had tried to explain everything. Painful as it was to speak about, Ivy put forth in no uncertain terms that including her in any venture would only invite gossip and speculation.

But Olivia waved a gloved hand and flashed her white teeth in a brilliant smile. 'We can't choose our family, Lady Ivy. We certainly can't control their choices. I don't care what your father did, what your brother did, or how low you have sunk in the eyes of the beau monde. I need a kind, brave, courageous woman to help me protect London's most vulnerable citizens. You are the perfect candidate. If your only objection is fear your reputation might damage our success, let me assure you, the beau monde has plenty of fodder from my own actions and that hasn't hindered our endeavours a whit. Put your mind at ease on that score. Won't you please help?'

How could Ivy refuse such an offer of friendship and a chance to do something useful with her life? And how could a woman of Olivia's altruistic conviction be guilty of any serious crimes? It was the only time Ivy disagreed with the duchess. The true measure of their friendship would be whether Philippa embraced Ivy even after she went against her wishes.

I suppose today is the moment I find out the strength of Philippa's regard for me.

Though Ivy certainly hadn't planned for Philippa to discover her partnership with Olivia like this. She was going to explain it all to Philippa at their next training session. After she had spent a few days at the orphanage and gained some confidence in her new post.

So much for careful planning. And now my subterfuge will end in murder.

'I should have known I would find you here.' Philippa's cobalt eyes flashed like a blade in sunlight. 'Exactly what do you think you are doing subjecting Lady Ivy Cavendale to such danger?' She held a jewelled fan in her hand and leaned over Olivia, pointing the fan like a sparkling dagger.

Olivia's eyes widened for a fraction before her mouth curled in a cold smile. She stood, forcing Philippa to take a step backwards. 'I'm sorry. I don't believe we've been formally introduced. I am Lady Olivia Smithwick, Marchioness of Brightmore.' She inclined her head in the most infinitesimal bow, a direct insult to the duchess who outranked Olivia and deserved a curtsey at the very least. 'You must be the Duchess of Dorsett. I've heard so much about you, although I must admit, I thought you were younger, Your Grace.'

Oh. My. Lord. Olivia has a death wish.

Philippa raised a single black brow as a rare blush washed over her cheeks. 'And I expected you to be far more intelligent. Pity. So rarely do I meet an adversary worthy of my time and energy. I had such high hopes for you, but I find myself disappointed.'

Olivia was almost eye level with Philippa. She leaned closer, her full lips pursed in a scowl. 'Give it time. Grand ladies such as yourself often overestimate their skills and underestimate the prowess of their opponents. I shall enjoy proving you wrong, Lady Winterbourne.'

'And I shall enjoy crushing you beneath my heel, Lady Smithwick.'

'Lovely. I'm so glad you both finally get to meet. Perhaps we can put away our threats long enough to discuss the intruder who visited last night and devise a solution to ensure the children are safe from further threat.' Ivy tried very hard to keep her voice from wavering. 'Or I can let the two of you battle to the death, and I shall sort things out on my own,' she murmured.

Philippa swung her head around to face Ivy. 'You should have told me.'

Damnation.

The disappointment in Philippa's gaze was enough to level Ivy. She hated disappointing people. Especially those she respected and cared about.

'I know. I should have told you I was taking a position as headmistress. I knew you would disapprove, and so I stayed silent. I was a coward.'

'Don't bully her,' Olivia hissed, stepping away from Philippa to reclaim her seat.

'A duchess does not bully. She expresses her opinions with conviction, and those who disagree eventually realise they are wrong,' Philippa threw back. Looking at her seating options in the small but cheerful parlour, she took a wing-back chair near the low table, as far from Olivia as she could sit without leaving the room entirely.

'Of course I would have supported you in finding useful work, Ivy. I just would have insisted you do so with reputable partners.' Her gaze cut across to Olivia.

Ivy jumped in before Olivia could offer a rejoinder. 'Philippa, how did you know I was here?' Ivy knew Philippa had informants everywhere, but she doubted any of them would waste time keeping tabs on Ivy.

A knock sounded on the parlour door, saving Philippa from having to answer. The young lady they hired to help with daily chores poked her head into the room.

'There's a gentleman at the door. He says he's here to speak with you, Mum. Looks like a right tight-arse if you ask me.'

Ivy's cheeks coloured as a large hand pushed the door further open. Commissioner Worthington spared a withering glare at the scruffy maid. A tall, thin man with an almost invisible moustache and beautifully pressed jacket trailed behind the commissioner. He carried with him a smart leather satchel.

'I'd say she's got that very close to bang on.' Philippa nodded at the young lady. 'Very astute. Come in, Edward. We've been waiting. Who is this?' She stared pointedly at the thin man whose ears turned an alarming shade of crimson.

Commissioner Worthington. He must have told Philippa I was here. The squealer!

'My secretary. Mr Reading. Do not frighten him off, Philippa. He poses no threat to us.'

The commissioner's familiar address with someone as lofty and powerful as a duchess was shocking. Ivy wasn't privy to the exact relationship Philippa shared with Commissioner Worthington, but she gathered they'd known each other since childhood and that their feelings for each other were complex and contradictory. Commissioner Worthington's shuttered gaze gave very little away, but the stiffness in his shoulders bespoke of something... interesting.

I am not interested in anything about the commissioner.

Her heart gave a curious thump, out of rhythm and rather resonant. No doubt it was brought on by Ivy's nerves at having to recount the events of the prior evening.

'It's comforting to know your rudeness extends to all manner of people and isn't solely focused on me, Your Grace.' Olivia stretched her full lips into a wide smile, like a cat baring its fangs at a rival.

Philippa tilted her head slightly as if an insect stung her neck, but she resolutely ignored Olivia's sharp barb. Her focus remained firmly on Commissioner Worthington. 'I believe you have come to speak with Ivy. Shall we begin?'

Commissioner Worthington looked first at Philippa, then Olivia, before finally resting his gaze on Ivy. His intense regard unsettled her, making Ivy unaccountably aware of useless details. A fly buzzed lazily against the windowpane to her left in the stuffy room. Sweat trickled a slow track between her corseted breasts, tickling her skin in a most excruciatingly distracting manner. Prickles of awareness, like sparks of fire, burned behind her knees and under each arm. Perhaps she was going to faint. She desperately wished for a cold cloth to press against her forehead. Looking at the commissioner's shoes, she noticed they were scuffed and dusty from the street.

'We shall not commence this interview.'

Ivy jerked her head up. 'Pardon?'

Commissioner Worthington's square jaw flexed; his dark-blue eyes were still fixed on her. 'I said *we* shall not commence this interview. *I* shall interview Lady Ivy Cavendale. Reading will stay and take notes. Everyone else will leave.'

Philippa and Olivia stood at the same time, both speaking over each other.

'I most certainly will not,' Philippa commanded.

'What a witty jest,' Olivia flattered.

'This is no jest. It is a police investigation. I will not have Lady Ivy Cavendale's testimony brought into question because I allowed a duchess and a marchioness to interject their thoughts and opinions at will.' Edward turned to Philippa. 'You know it must be done this way. I need you to trust me.'

Philippa? Trust a man?

Hardly! It is one of the few ways we are alike.

But unaccountably, the duchess tipped her head down in a subtle acquiescence.

'Fine. I shall depart. But I expect to speak with you later, Commissioner. I will see you tomorrow, Ivy, for our weekly meeting. Nine o'clock, sharp.' She noticeably ignored Olivia.

'She is needed here.' Olivia's flirtatious tone hardened as she turned from the commissioner to face the duchess. 'Ivy's timetable is not yours to command.'

'Nor is it yours, Lady Smithwick.'

Ivy had the unaccountable feeling of being a rag doll pulled between two unruly girls. She turned her attention away from the commissioner to focus on the ladies doing battle over her. 'Actually, it is mine.'

The commissioner made a noise similar to a sharp laugh, or perhaps it was only a cough.

Olivia and Philippa turned as one to face Ivy, and her courage faltered. She softened her tone in an effort not to offend either woman. 'I am not needed at the orphanage at nine in the morning. The children will all be hard at work on their lessons with both tutors to supervise them. My weekly meetings with

Lady Winterbourne are important to me, and I will not sacrifice them.'

Olivia's green eyes hardened. 'Certainly. We did not discuss the details of your work here, but I wouldn't want you to abandon all your personal pursuits, nor is it necessary. That would be cruel of me, and unlike some, I am not a creature who rejoices in the discomfort of others.' She tipped her chin up, a small smile playing on her generous lips at the implied insult to Philippa.

'One is left to wonder exactly what kind of creature you are, Lady Smithwick.' Philippa thwacked her fan against her skirts and continued before Olivia could reply. 'I will take my leave.' She turned her back to Olivia, nodded at Commissioner Worthington, and sailed out of the door without a backward glance.

Olivia's mouth tightened. 'Never in my life have I met a more arrogant, rude, horrific woman. I don't know how you endure her friendship, Ivy.'

Having nothing to say that would appease Olivia, Ivy remained silent.

'It was a pleasure meeting you, Lady Smithwick, but as we are on a tight schedule, I must ask that you also depart.' Commissioner Worthington's gravelled voice sent shivers along Ivy's skin.

'Of course.' Olivia batted her lashes at Commissioner Worthington, but unlike every other man Ivy had observed interacting with her friend, the commissioner seemed completely unaffected. 'It was a pleasure meeting you, Commissioner. I do hope our paths cross again soon.'

The crimson stain on Reading's ears travelled down his neck as he shuffled his feet.

Commissioner Worthington merely nodded.

Olivia swept across the floor, pulling Ivy into a brief hug, where she brushed her lips against Ivy's cheeks in an airy kiss. 'Remember, you needn't say any more than is absolutely necessary. If you need me, send word. I shall keep my carriage at the ready.'

Ivy forced her wide mouth into a smile. 'I will, Olivia. Thank you.' Though how her friend could help Ivy endure the next hour was impossible to imagine.

Once Olivia took her leave, Ivy awkwardly gestured to the various mismatched chairs. 'Please, make yourselves comfortable. I can make a fresh pot of tea if you wish.' She desperately hoped they would take her up on the offer if only to give her a few moments to collect her thoughts.

'Your maid cannot do this for us?' Reading asked as he settled himself on the shabby settee and unbuckled his satchel, pulling out a tablet of paper, quill, and pot of ink. He placed the ink on the table.

'No, she helps with the cleaning and some of the cooking, answers the door if she is near the entry at the right time, but we haven't the funds for any proper house servants. It's no trouble for me to refresh the pot.' Ivy bent to pick up the tray of tea things, but as she turned, Commissioner Worthington stepped closer, blocking her path to the door. He reached out a large hand and took the salver from her, his fingers brushing against her own.

The fizzing sparks were back. Starting at her fingertips and rushing up her arms in a maddening spiral of sensation.

Stiffening her spine, she clenched her teeth tight.

'We are in no need of tea, Lady Ivy. Please. Sit. Let us begin.' His eyes were the deep blue of a bottomless pond.

Ivy looked at her options and was unaccountably flummoxed. She had been sitting on the settee, but Reading sat there now, taking up far more space than his thin frame needed. The wing-back chair Philippa recently vacated was behind Commissioner Worthington and not easily accessible. Out of options, she took the chair Olivia had been using, an Eastlake armchair with battered wooden legs and a lumpy seat. At least this meant the commissioner would have to take Philippa's seat on the opposite side of the room unless he wished to crowd Reading on the settee.

Ivy sat on the edge of the chair. Folding her hands neatly in her lap, she clenched her fingers together to hide the trembling.

The commissioner turned to the chair behind him, but instead of sitting in it as a normal person might do, he picked the thing up with frightening ease. It was not a light piece of furniture, yet the man lifted it by both arms as though it weighed nothing, strode around the table, and placed it gently down in front of Ivy. They were so close, their knees would touch if she didn't scooch back in her chair.

Eyes wide with alarm, Ivy did just that, scrambling back until her back pressed against the velvet padding.

'This is much better, don't you think?' Commissioner Worthington's firm mouth stretched into a tight smile, vertical creases framing his mouth.

Ivy was momentarily distracted by the harsh lines of his cheekbones and jaw contrasting with much softer lips. His teeth were straight and white, an uncommonly attractive feature in any gentleman. He had a freckle just beneath his left eye. For a mad moment, she was tempted to rub her thumb over it to test its texture.

Alarm thrilled through her veins as she clenched her fingers even tighter.

4

Edward knew his proximity unsettled Lady Ivy. But he also knew people found it harder to lie when they were flustered. Not a kind thing to do, but he wasn't a kind man. He was the Commissioner of Scotland Yard. It was his mission to determine truth from falsehood. That was the only reason he sat so obscenely close to Lady Cavendale, leaning forward with his elbows on his knees. Not because it brought the scent of peony and rosemary into his lungs. Not because he could discern the faint sprinkling of caramel freckles across the bridge of her proud nose. Not because this close, he could watch her pale skin transform into a crimson sunset as her peculiar blush painted speckled patterns across her throat, disappearing into the high-necked pale-blue morning gown she wore.

I want to be close to her to better detect the truth. That is all.

He had to stop his eyes from rolling at the blatant lie.

'Let's start with what first alerted you to an intruder.' He kept his voice even, noting how Ivy's chest rose and fell rapidly. If she did not calm down, he feared she might faint. And then he would be forced to hold her in his arms, press a cold cloth against her forehead, whisper comforting words into the delicate shell of her ear until she regained consciousness.

Nonsense! I am the Commissioner of Scotland Yard. I don't whisper comforting words into women's ears. Reading is a much better candidate for such nonsense.

Though the thought of Reading holding Ivy sent a wave of itchy heat through him. Edward forced his focus back to Ivy. She was struggling to find words.

'There is no need to rush, Lady Ivy. Take your time. It might help to close your eyes, take a few deep breaths, and let your thoughts drift back to last night.'

Lady Ivy pressed her wide mouth together, breathing deeply through her nose and holding it for, by his count, at least five. The action seemed to bolster her. 'No. I don't think I shall close my eyes, Commissioner Worthington. I prefer to keep a careful watch on the happenings around me.'

'Is that what you do in the shadows of a ballroom, Lady Cavendale? Keenly observe the beau monde in their mad antics without ever being tempted to join?'

Damnation.

The question had nothing to do with his investigation. But Edward had first noticed Ivy at the Marquess of Stoneway's masque ball because of her tendency to slip quietly into the shadowed corners of every room she inhabited. Her clear desire to remain unnoticed struck him as singularly odd. She was beautiful, young, intelligent, and healthy. She was also single, and her circumstances would be greatly improved by a fortunate match. Not that every young woman wished for marriage, Philippa certainly never had and for good reason, but what was Ivy's reason? It tickled at him like a stray hair in his collar.

While he was here to determine who invaded the orphanage, he couldn't deny he also wished to gain a greater understanding of Lady Ivy Cavendale. Perhaps if he could untangle the contra-dictory nature of her actions and spirit, she would cease to claim his thoughts in such an alarming manner. Because despite her tendency to withdraw, Ivy Cavendale was a fierce fighter. Edward knew this in the marrow of his bones. So did Philippa, or she wouldn't have taken the woman under her tutelage. Yet she acted like a meek, demure milksop of a maiden. It made no sense.

'What relevance does my behaviour at balls have to do with an intruder climbing through the window and terrorising the girls within, Commissioner Worthington?'

She had him there. He blinked, refused to glance at Reading, whose ears were no doubt flaming beacons of moral outrage, and reassembled his thoughts.

'Merely trying to determine your character, Lady Ivy.'

Ivy's pupils dilated. 'Ah, yes. Trying to determine if you can trust a woman whose bloodline is steeped in madness and murder. Perhaps I am victim to the same evil that claimed my brother and father only last year.' He didn't miss the convulsive spasm of her throat as she nearly choked on the word 'father'. 'Is that your aim in asking such an inconsequential question? The answer is simple. I am shy. And the edges are safer than the centre, Commissioner.'

Edward knew of Lord Cavendale's death. And his son, Alfred. Philippa and the Queen kept him well informed. He was also privy to the whisperings among the beau monde of Lord Cavendale's more perfidious inclinations. One hoped a man drawn to such disgusting sexual depravities would keep his twisted affections away from his own children, but Edward had seen all manner of sins in his time as commissioner. Is that what plagued Ivy so grievously? Had her father—

His mind recoiled from the idea even as his investigator's

instincts smelled the metal tang of truth. If that were the case, he needed to proceed with the utmost care. Such hidden wounds were unpredictable and could bleed anew at the slightest provocation. He had seen first-hand the damage women sustained and how it could twist and poison their lives. But he had also witnessed the resiliency of what society deemed the 'weaker sex'. He knew 'delicate' ladies could show more endurance, courage, and fortitude than any of their male counterparts. Edward's respect for women was forged in painful experience, and he would never again doubt their ability to recover from the most devastating injuries.

'A shy woman brave enough to stand off against an intruder?'

Ivy shook her head. 'Not brave. Just desperate. There was no one else to protect the children. I had no choice.'

'You could have run. Or stayed locked in your room.'

Ivy clicked her tongue and tapped her finger against her skirt. 'Only a monster would have abandoned these children.'

'Then I know a great many monsters, Lady Ivy. Dancing in ballrooms, eating ices at Gunter's, promenading along Bond Street.'

'What about leading Scotland Yard?' She sucked in a breath and glanced over his shoulder, breaking their eye contact.

She didn't mean to ask that. But she wants to know if I can be trusted. Because she doesn't trust men.

The image of Lord Cavendale flashed in his mind, a hazy picture of a kindly-looking gentleman from some long-ago event. Edward imagined ploughing his fist into the bastard's ingratiating smile. Over. And over. And over.

'Please forgive me.' Her low voice was barely a whisper. 'Of course you aren't anything of the sort.'

Edward wanted to reach out and run his finger down the length of her petal-pale cheek. He wanted to offer comfort and sanctuary. Which was impossible. He had no comfort to give. And a man condemned to solitude knew nothing of sanctuary.

So, he gave her what he could: honesty. 'I've made monstrous decisions in my past. Not intentionally, but what good are intentions when it is action that determines one's destiny? Intentions cannot reverse time. But actions cut so deep a soul is cleaved in two.'

'You admit to being a monster?'

'In truth, I believe we all have the capacity to become fiends. To let the darkness seep in a little at a time until one day, we have been sucked so deep into the quagmire, we've forgotten what it is to stand in the sunlight. We recoil from its warmth.'

Ivy refocused on him, her ice-blue eyes holding him frozen. 'If that is true, then we are all doomed,' she whispered.

Edward softened his mouth into a near smile. 'Ah, but there is another side to this coin of humanity. You see, I also believe we have the courage to stand up against insurmountable odds. To sacrifice our own happiness, safety, and fortune to provide succour for others. To learn from our mistakes. Grow from even the most grievous sins. Become better versions of ourselves, even if we are irrevocably flawed. Like men who devote their lives to pursuing justice for innocent victims. Or women who stand in front of vulnerable children and refuse to abandon them for their own safety.'

'So we are beasts and beauties combined?'

'Some of us are more beautiful than others.'

A sharp cough came from Edward's left.

Ah, yes. Reading. Thin little compass of morality.

But he was annoyingly right. Edward should never have let the thought escape. He should never have had the thought in the first place, no matter how true it might be.

Of all the women in Edward's acquaintance, Lady Ivy

seemed the most resistant to flattery of any kind. And he had no
desire to woo her with pretty words. Understand her, perhaps.
Unravel the tangle of contradictions comprising her person,
most certainly. Determine the best course to ensure her safety,
decidedly so. But to embark on any path more intimate was
completely out of the question. Men like Edward did not deserve
the affections of a woman like Ivy Cavendale.

'I've taken us off-track.'

'I'm not sure we can even see the track from here,' Reading
muttered from the settee.

Edward's withering glare was wasted on the man as he
refused to look up from his parchment.

'Perhaps we should get back to the questions, Commissioner.
Unless you have what you need?' Her reasonable request only
highlighted the foolishness of his earlier comment.

An odd hollow ache in the vicinity of his chest thrummed an
answer.

No. I don't have what I need. Not even close.

Terrible time for self-revelations when he was in the middle
of an investigation.

He tried to focus on her question. 'I apologise, but we still
have much to discuss.' Leaning back in his chair, he noted her
body slowly softening with his diminished proximity. 'Do you
recall what time it was you first became aware of an intruder?'

Over the span of a half-hour, Lady Ivy walked him through
the course of events precipitating her firing a pistol. Reading
interrupted them once to resharpen his quill, at which point
Lady Ivy asked to make a fresh pot of tea for herself if no one
else.

She settled the tea tray on the low table, avoiding Reading's
pot of ink, and poured a dish for each of them. Edward noticed
the economy of her movement and a certain fluidity in her joints

betraying her gentle breeding. Though her fortunes had drastically diminished with the loss of her father and brother, she carried herself with the poise and polish of a fine lady trained for entertaining the bluest of bloods in the beau monde. Edward wondered if she lamented her changed circumstances from high-born lady to headmistress of an orphanage. Something told him she did not.

'I must ask you once more to describe the man's dress. You say he wore the clothes of a gentleman. But there are a myriad variety of gentlemen. Did he seem like he was flush? Down on his luck? A dandy?'

Ivy paused in sipping her tea, drawing her pale brows down in concentration. 'I hadn't thought about it, but you are right. Let me think... His coat was of a modern cut and despite the efforts of his activities, did not show excessive wear. His hair was styled in a modern way.' She closed her eyes and scrunched up her nose in an expression Edward absolutely did not find adorable. 'His boots were of fine quality. Based on their shine, I would wager they were newly purchased this season. He did not have the clothes of a dandy, but certainly, I wouldn't find him out of place at White's or escorting a lady to Almacks for a ball.' She popped her eyes open, the pupils contracting and contrasting against the singular shade of blue. There were no striations of brown or gold in her irises. Just a thousand hues of ice with a darker ring of sapphire around the edges. Stunning. 'I would say he presented himself in dress as a rather well-to-do gentleman, though his words and manner were far from genteel.'

Edward had lost his place. Again.

Perhaps I should comment on her fine eyes next. I could really throw Reading into a tizzy.

Instead, he used the excuse of claiming his tea and taking a sip to regain some equilibrium. 'What age would you place him?'

Ivy pursed her lips and blew out a breath. 'Well, certainly younger than you, Commissioner.' Was that a spark of mischief in her voice? The left corner of her wide mouth tipped up.

'Are you teasing me, Lady Ivy? Hardly fitting for such a proper headmistress. Or a finely bred lady. And you are both, are you not?' Edward kept his tone light and allowed himself a smile.

Another sharp throat-clearing from the settee.

Ivy glanced at Reading, her spine stiffening before she refocused on her teacup, all traces of levity gone. 'I just mean to say, he was neither a lad fresh from his books nor a seasoned gentleman. Perhaps in the mid to latter part of his second decade.'

Edward would gladly have thrashed Reading for ruining the shimmering moment of *something* between himself and Lady Ivy. He struggled to keep the growl of frustration from his voice. 'Would you recognise him if you saw him again?'

Ivy's mouth trembled for a moment before she hardened it in a determined line. She nodded her head in a jerky motion. 'I hope never to see that blackguard again. But if I did, yes. I would recognise him. Of course I would.'

Edward rested his elbow on the arm of the chair, then leaned his chin on his palm. For a moment, he took her measure. She was thin, her lean body almost boyish with its lack of curves, and yet she wasn't weak. Even covered from neck to wrist to boots in blue cotton, her simple gown couldn't conceal the supple strength of her arms. Her movements betrayed the kind of fluid grace attributed to jungle cats or birds of prey. He hadn't asked Philippa about her training sessions with Lady Ivy, but he would wager the woman excelled at sparring. Clearly, she was a decent shot. And despite her very real fear of facing off against an unknown intruder, she hadn't faltered. When the moment called for action, instead of slipping into the shadows, she had thrust her body between innocent children and the monster who would destroy them.

Courage. Valour. Wit and winsomeness to boot. She would make an admirable addition to the Queen's Deadly Damsels.

A silly name Millicent Drake had given to the Queen's secret force, intent on investigating crimes for the crown. But the idea of Ivy working with him to find this intruder wasn't silly.

While she was obviously uneasy speaking to him about the past night's traumatic event, she had not stumbled in her retelling. Her low voice had remained calm and factual even while her hands were at first clasped so tight, her knuckles had gone completely white. Many fine ladies would fan themselves in a frantic frenzy, burst into tears, claim the vapours, or embellish their story to highlight their own bravery; Ivy did none of these things. She remained calm. Logical. Systematic. All traits men rarely assigned to women, yet qualities they showed as often as their masculine counterparts. She would make an excellent partner in his investigation.

He hardened his lips against a smile. She would never agree. Not if he put it to her so baldly. So, he would try a different tack. Provoking her.

'After hearing your account and looking over the reports from the children, I believe you confronted an intruder last night, Lady Ivy.'

Instead of blessing him with a smile, she frowned. 'You've decided I'm not mad, then? What a relief.'

Edward's lips twitched. 'Indeed.'

Lady Ivy Cavendale had an unusual tell when she was irritated. She tapped her index finger three times against whatever surface it was near. She had tapped her delicate digit three times against the chair when he insisted on interviewing her the night before. She did it again against her skirt when he moved his seat in front of her to commence their interview not an hour earlier. And she was tapping now, against the rim of her cup.

Tap. Tap. Tap.

An angry little finger when she fought so hard to keep the rest of herself still.

'So now you believe me, what are you going to do? This man was intent on nefarious acts. What is to prevent him from coming back another night?'

'Excellent point, Lady Ivy. Neither you nor the children will feel truly safe until we apprehend him.'

'Exactly so.' She nodded.

'I have two directives. To capture this man and make him face justice while also keeping your orphans safe.'

'So, what is your plan to apprehend this villain?'

He leaned forward again and noted her back stiffening once more, though this time, she did not shift away. 'Not my plan, Lady Ivy. *Our* plan.'

'Pardon?'

'It's quite simple. You will join forces with me. After all, you are the only one who can recognise him. You said so yourself.'

Ivy placed her teacup on the table, stood, and crossed her arms over her chest. He rose as well and noted how the top of her head would fit perfectly beneath his chin. A rather idiotic thing to observe about a person.

'I simply thought you were asking if I could identify him, not suggesting I actually join you in seeking the man out. I am not like Philippa or any of the other women you—' She stopped abruptly and turned her head to Reading, who merely dipped his pen in the inkpot and held it poised and ready over the parchment.

'Don't fret. You can speak freely in front of Reading. He is aware of my particular association with the Queen and the duchess.' Edward had few intimate friends, and it spoke volumes that he counted his secretary as one of his closest confidantes. Especially considering he paid the man.

Ivy parted her lips and looked from Edward to Reading and back again. 'He knows?'

'Yes,' Edward said.

'About everything?'

'I am a vault of secrets, Lady Cavendale. You might not trust many, but you can trust me.' Reading lifted his head for a brief smile, his ghostly moustache catching a glint of sunlight and shimmering like sweat on his upper lip.

Apparently, the man's horrendous taste in facial hair charmed Lady Ivy because, after a moment of thought, she actually returned Reading's smile with a tentative one of her own. Edward was not disgustingly jealous.

When she turned back to Edward, her smile hardened. 'I am not like Philippa or Millie or Hannah. I'm not like Penny. I don't race into danger. I run from it.'

Edward strode closer, standing right in front of her. He ducked his head to meet her gaze. 'No. You don't. You didn't. Not when it counted.'

She stepped away, but not before he recognised the sudden flare in her eyes. Fear? Desire? Anger at being contradicted?

'I told you. I was desperate. Terrified. I'm no hero, Commissioner Worthington.'

'None of us are, until there is a need. When those children were being threatened, you became a hero to meet their needs. And I need your help now, Lady Ivy.'

* * *

Commissioner Worthington was as mad as a march hare. No wonder Philippa held such dislike for the man. He was pushy. Arrogant. Rude.

And he might have called me beautiful.

Which only confirmed his mental infirmity. No man thought Ivy was beautiful. And she wanted to keep it that way. The confounding thump of an errant heartbeat rattled her reasoning.

This is lunacy.

The commissioner was actually proposing she join him in hunting down an intruder. She could only imagine what Philippa might say on the subject.

She would tell me I can do this. Because she's just as foolish as the commissioner when it comes to her faith in me. Well, I can't. That's all there is to it.

'I can't help you, Commissioner. You have the entire force of Scotland Yard at your command. Not to mention the Queen's Deadly Damsels. What do I have to offer that you don't already have?'

'As I previously stated, you know what he looks like. That makes you integral to my plan.'

'What plan?' She tried to keep her voice even, but anxiety, fear, and frustration were making it difficult.

Reading looked up from his parchment. 'Excellent question, Lady Ivy. Please do explain your plan, sir. Just so I can ensure I record it accurately, of course. Not because we doubt the veracity of your thoughts.'

Bless you, little whisper of a man.

Ivy had never had a male ally. She would not have guessed to find one in a reed-thin secretary with a silly moustache and wicked wit.

'Everyone is replaceable, Reading.' Edward's clipped words

would have been more menacing if he hadn't delivered them with the hint of a smile.

'Certainly, sir. Even you. But while we are both still here, perhaps you can enlighten us on how you plan to catch this man, protect the orphans, and ensure Lady Ivy is safe throughout the investigation.'

'Yes, exactly.' Ivy nodded. 'Something reasonable, I hope.'

Edward returned his attention to Ivy. 'I'm always reasonable, Lady Ivy. Unless a situation calls for me to be otherwise.'

And what on earth is that supposed to mean?

The commissioner addressed Reading. 'You have brought up three points. For the first, I plan to catch this man through well-planned investigative work. Lady Ivy will join me in looking for the braggart in all the usual places a young gentleman might find himself until we ferret him out. As for points two and three, I shall keep the young urchins and Lady Ivy safe by disguising myself as a manservant and staying here. Until we can be certain the risk is eliminated.'

Reading muttered a curse as the nib of his quill broke. His ears were flaming torches of indignation. 'You can't be serious.'

'You're jesting,' Ivy spoke at the same time.

'Oh, I am very serious.'

'But you are the Commissioner of Scotland Yard. You can't waste your time here when surely you are needed elsewhere.' She winced at the shrillness of her tone. But the idea of sleeping under the same roof as Commissioner Worthington, even with ten doors between them – because she certainly wasn't putting him in a room anywhere near her – caused a strange reaction in her body. Fear, certainly, but not the usual wave that left her shaking and nauseous. It was more like a sprinkling that heightened her other emotions. Emotions she found most confounding. A strange thrill of anticipation. A sparkling fizz of something she couldn't name. And underneath all of it, the warm sense of comfort, like a thick blanket wrapping her tight.

I do not feel comforted by the presence of a man. Especially not a large, powerful, highly infuriating man.

'You are correct, of course. I am the Commissioner of Scotland Yard. A position that comes with the highest level of authority, and if I can be trusted with the safety of London's citizens, then surely you can trust me to keep you and your charges free from harm. Besides, I shall only be sleeping here. When we are not conducting our investigation, I'll spend my time at 4 Whitehall Place lest Reading become despondent with grief at my absence.'

Reading snorted. 'Don't trouble yourself on my behalf, sir. You have to hold some kind of affection for a person to grieve their loss.'

'Which is why I know you would miss me terribly.'

Ivy interrupted their argument, too flustered to care overmuch about manners. 'Well, I still see many flaws in your plan. Assuming I could be of any assistance, which is a dubious guess at best, how do you possibly expect me to join you for the investigation? Most of the locations where young men of the beau monde socialise are strictly forbidden to women.'

The commissioner winked at her. *Winked.* As if that answered any of her queries. 'I've some thoughts on that. But we can go over the details later. We should have plenty of time to polish the finer points this evening once the children have gone to bed.'

It wasn't her heart that thumped this time. Something lower, living dormant and still below her belly, clenched, then unfurled in a rush of warmth.

Good heavens!

Just the idea of sitting with Commissioner Worthington,

wrapped in the intimacy of evening darkness, heads bent close while they reviewed the finer points of his plan. It was all too much.

But what choice did she have? She couldn't stay alone with the children and feel safe. Not now. And if a strange constable was assigned to watch over the orphanage, it wouldn't be any better. At least she knew Commissioner Worthington. As much as one could ever know a person after only a few brief meetings. And Philippa trusted him. That should count for something.

And he isn't asking me. He's telling me.

'Fine. I don't suppose I have any power to refuse, do I?'

'You have the power to refuse me anything, Lady Ivy. Except this.' His soft tone belied the determination in his deep-blue eyes. 'Your safety and that of the children is of paramount importance.'

Why?

She wasn't brave enough to ask that particular question. Though she couldn't argue with him about the children. They deserved the highest level of protection. The commissioner was certainly more qualified to provide that than Ivy. Only a fool would refuse such an offer. Ivy was many things, but she was no man's fool.

'I shall make up a room for you. There are only two boys in room ten and three in room nine. I can shift them all together, and you can take room ten.' It was the westernmost room of the wing devoted to bedrooms and farthest from her own, which was situated at the eastern end of the wing. It was also at the entrance of the hall, so he would be able to hear anyone trying to sneak along the corridor from other areas of the house or sneak out of the bedrooms. That was her main concern. Not creating as much distance as possible between where he would be sleeping and her quarters.

'Please, don't trouble yourself. I won't have much with me and can share with the boys if needed.'

A stifled chuckle had them both turning to the settee. Reading was stoppering the inkwell and carefully placing his things into the satchel. He looked up from his work and raised his brows at them. 'The *Star of Venus* would love to get their hands on that bit of news. The Grand Duke of Landbourne and Commissioner of Scotland Yard to boot, bedding down in a sad little cot he must share with bedraggled urchins. I would wager a month's salary the caricaturist would draw quite the picture of it.'

'Duke. You are also a duke?' Ivy failed to keep the shock from her voice. She should have known the man's pedigree, but really. Who had the time to study Debrett's when there were far more interesting things to read? Like the ingredients of her hair tonic. 'Why does no one address you with your proper title? All this time, I should have been calling you Your Grace.'

For a divine moment, the commissioner's cheeks flushed. He shrugged in a gesture speaking of great discomfort. 'I earned my title as Commissioner of Scotland Yard. I prefer it to anything else.'

The first gentleman I've met who prefers his lesser title because of how he achieved it.

Very few titles were earned unless one did something quite significant for the Queen. Yet the peerage preened about honorifics given to them for no reason other than birth order. Commissioner Worthington's implied message was surprisingly progressive.

What a fascinating man.

No. Men were not fascinating. They were fearful creatures to be avoided. Except now, she would be sharing her home with one. The prospect seemed far less frightening than it should.

Because it's not any man. It's Commissioner Worthington.

And why should that make a difference? A dangerous question indeed. Her logical mind shied away from it like a horse spying something foreign and frightening in its path.

Reading cleared his throat, pulled out a pocket watch, flicked it open, and squinted at it for a moment before staring meaningfully at Commissioner Worthington. Ivy wondered who really commanded whom in this strange relationship of secretary and commissioner.

'Ah. Yes. I suppose Reading, in his subtle way, is implying we should be on our way. I shall return later tonight. Do not trouble yourself with my supper or anything of that nature. I have no wish to be a burden. I can manage my own meals and refreshments.'

Ivy hadn't thought about meeting the physical needs of Commissioner Worthington while he stayed with her. The children received simple, healthful food that a hired cook provided twice a day. Ivy was planning to partake of the same fare, but that hardly seemed fitting for a duke. She knew how her father and brother preferred their meals. Rich cuts of beef or venison. Roasted duck and pheasants stuffed with chestnuts and cranberries. At least six courses, including soup, roasted meat, some kind of fish, seasonal vegetables, exotic fruits, and pudding. Always pudding. Her brother had a notorious sweet tooth. A rogue wave of guilt washed over her for Alfred. While she was closer to her younger brother, Patrick, and grieved him most terribly when news of his death during the war reached England's shore, she hardly wept for Alfred at all and fairly rejoiced at the death of her father. What kind of cruel daughter refused to mourn the loss of her family?

The kind whose father did not deserve a single one of my tears.

Anger, potent and hot, flushed through her veins at the mere thought of Lord Cavendale. And it was a welcome rush of power, so different from the fear she used to feel in his presence. She almost wished he had lived to see what Ivy was becoming. She wished she could have confronted him with her growing confidence. Perhaps held a pistol to his chest. Seen the fear in his eyes for once as he realised he had no control over Ivy. Not any more.

But he is dead and gone. And I will never be able to hold him accountable for his crimes.

His death was a blessing and a curse for Ivy and not something she could ever fully explain to anyone. Not even her dearest friend, Millie.

Commissioner Worthington drew her back into the moment as he stepped closer, reaching for her hand. A common practice for lords and ladies when they took leave of each other. Ivy's breeding demanded she comply. She lifted her ungloved hand, and he clasped her fingers gently. The rasp of calluses catching on her skin created a buzz along her nerve endings, zinging up her arm and landing in the most unusual spots. A sensitive patch of skin just behind her right ear. That secret and newly awakened place below her belly. Left of centre in her chest where her heart thumped once more out of rhythm.

He didn't lift her hand to his mouth, pressing firm lips against her over-sensitised skin. And why would he? Such an action would be completely untoward. But for the first time in her life, she yearned for something quite unnameable. The thought shocked her. She pulled free from his grasp just as he bowed his dark head. He immediately stepped back, clasping his hands behind his back, and trapping her with his dark stare. But she couldn't discern his thoughts in such a careful gaze. They were hidden like cards against his chest.

'Until this evening, Lady Ivy.' He turned and strode out of the door.

Reading nodded at her. 'You will be quite safe with him, Lady Cavendale. He's got the growl of a lion but the heart of a kitten, I swear it.'

Why Reading's words comforted her, she could not say. But there was something soft and kind in the curl of his lips, even framed with the silly moustache. He nodded at her, then hurried after the commissioner, the leather satchel swinging jauntily at his side.

5

The indomitable duchess paid Edward a visit the moment he returned to his office at Scotland Yard, causing him to wonder if she was having him watched. He wouldn't put it past her.

Lady Philippa Winterbourne, Duchess of Dorsett, caused quite a stir in the crowded offices. Such a lofty member of the peerage, a confidante of the Queen herself, rubbing shoulders with common bobbies. Quite the kerfuffle, as his Scottish compatriots would say. But the real disturbance was to Edward's equilibrium.

Edward's office – once a bedroom when the original building was used as a private residence – had been converted into the commissioner's office when Sir Robert Peel took over the building and turned it into the headquarters for the Metropolitan Police. A bookshelf graced one wall stuffed with all manner of reference materials, books for research, and various ledgers. His inherited desk from the previous commissioner claimed the centre of the room. A behemoth monstrosity of dark wood, it was elaborately carved and sported a leather-covered top stained by all manner of things best forgotten. He hated it but didn't have the time, money, or motivation to replace the thing. A large window on the far wall let in bright sunlight and allowed Edward a glimpse of the bustling street beyond.

Reading ushered the duchess in, and she looked dubiously at the hard-backed chair sitting opposite Edward's desk. Instead of sitting, she paced. Her gown of deep purple was overlaid with some kind of black gossamer fabric. Jewels were sewn into the skirt and bodice at varying intervals in the shape of little star-bursts. She looked like a sparkling midnight sky even in the drab surroundings of his office.

'To what do I owe this honour, Lady Winterbourne?'

She paused in her pacing, raised a single eyebrow, and stared unblinking at him for what seemed an eternity. 'You know why I'm here. I asked you to ensure Ivy's safety. Now she's being attacked by unnamed hooligans climbing through windows.'

'It was just one hooligan, and we've no idea what his purpose was in trying to break into the orphanage.'

'Succeeding. Not trying. He succeeded in breaking in. And if it weren't for Ivy, he could have succeeded in much worse.'

Edward rarely saw Philippa flummoxed. 'What has you so worried?'

She shook her head in tight, sharp movements. 'I don't know. I'm missing something and I don't like it. While there's no reason to assume this has anything to do with the Devil's Sons, my instincts are screaming at me that it does. I just don't know why.'

'Perhaps it might help if I knew a little more about Ivy. Her father and brother were mixed up with this lot—'

'No, just her brother.' Philippa resumed pacing. 'Although her father was far from innocent. He was significantly more insidious than his son.'

'Did he ever hurt Lady Ivy?'

'That is not my story to tell. Nor is it one I know from the

source. Just whispers. Insinuations. And my own suspicions.'
While Philippa gave no details, her judicious lack of commentary for certain questions he put forth revealed much.

'Do you believe he abused her?'

Silence.

'Do all men frighten her, or is it something about me in particular?'

Silence.

'Is it wrong of me to include her in this investigation?'

An eye roll accompanied by silence.

'I believe she is stronger than she knows, but I've no wish to push her beyond her boundaries. Am I pushing her too far?'

That elicited a snort. 'Of course she is stronger than she knows. She's been taught her whole life – as most women are – that she is the weaker sex and needs protection. Ironic the people she needs protection from are the same ones reminding her only they can provide such safety. Why are so many men such horrific examples of hypocrisy?' Philippa finally stopped her pacing, snarled at the chair for sins Edward couldn't begin to fathom, then carefully sat as if the thing might collapse under her insubstantial weight.

Edward dared not answer that verbal trap disguised as a question. Instead, he asked another. 'Am I making a mistake, Philippa?'

For a moment, the duchess froze, her cobalt eyes holding his as she rubbed her thumb against her index finger in an endless circle. 'If only you'd asked me that question twenty years ago.' He didn't miss the sharp edge of her voice. Nor could he plead ignorance as to why her words cut so deep.

'I shall never forgive myself for her death, Philippa. I take full responsibility.'

'And what good does that do?' Philippa shrugged, her blood-red lips hardening in a firm line. 'Living in perpetual self-punishment doesn't bring her back. It doesn't ease my grief or your guilt.'

Edward felt each word like a cudgel smashing into his soul. Because she was right. 'If there was a way to fix my horrifying decision, to go back in time and undo the wrong I committed, I would do anything, give anything, to rewrite our history.'

'I know. But you can't. No one can change the past, Edward. We can only try to move forward. I have hated you for so long. But I grow weary of this loathing. It only ever takes, and I no longer wish to feed its endless hunger. I don't believe she would want us to be forever at odds.'

'She loved us both. Of that, I'm certain. Even if one of us was most undeserving of her love.'

'No one is truly deserving of love. And we are also all deserving. It is one of life's greatest dichotomies.'

'Does this mean you forgive me, Philippa?' He would never forgive himself, but to earn Philippa's exoneration was a boon he never expected. Hope was a dangerous light as apt to burn as illuminate.

Philippa speared him with one of her more effective stares. 'Let's not get ahead of ourselves, Edward. Protect Ivy. Find this man and discover his purpose. Ensure this has nothing to do with the Devil's Sons. Do for Ivy what neither of us could do for *her*. Then we shall talk of forgiveness.'

* * *

During Ivy's restricted activities as a proper lady of the beau monde, time moved at a painfully slow pace. She could only needlepoint cushions, paint plates, and practise the pianoforte – an instrument for which she held no talent – for so long before her brain started leaking out of her ears. But she was swiftly learning this was not the case for working men and women.

The afternoon and early evening flew by in a rush of activity. Upon Commissioner Worthington's departure, the children were released into the yard to partake of the beautiful summer sun and fresh air for an hour. As headmistress, Ivy was in charge of supervising them, and she found the task equal parts entertaining and exasperating. After the seventeenth time reminding young Billy Banks it wasn't polite to tug on Margaret O'Hara's hair, no matter how red it might be, she was more than ready for the children to return to the house and work on various household chores.

She spied Sarah Turner standing next to a bedraggled hydrangea bush and wandered over to check on the girl.

'Hullo, Sarah. Are you well?'

Sarah had a book pressed tightly against her chest and a doll tucked under her right arm. The dolly was missing most of its hair and someone had drawn eyes where buttons were once sewn. It looked like a terrifying rendition of an infant.

'Err, that is a lovely little doll you have. Has she a name?'

Sarah shrugged. 'She's not real, Miss Cavendale. There's no point in giving her a name.'

Ivy thought of the kitten doubtlessly sleeping on her pillow at that very moment. As it was real, she really must find a name for the ball of fluff. 'Sometimes, we pretend things are true to practise what it might be like when they become reality.'

Sarah's light-brown eyebrows pulled low over her grey eyes. 'That doesn't make any sense, Miss Cavendale.'

Because I have no idea what I'm saying, Sarah.

'Why aren't you playing with some of the other girls?'

Sarah hugged her book tighter. 'I'm too old to play, Miss Cavendale.'

Ivy's heart cracked as she put a tentative hand on Sarah's arm and squeezed. No child should feel too old to play. 'Not even for a bit? Perhaps we could play a game together. When I was young, I used to love to look at the clouds and come up with creatures they might be, adventures they were having in their cloud kingdoms. Will you try with me?'

Sarah squinted at the sky dubiously. 'That sounds silly.'

Ivy smiled at the girl. 'A little silly doesn't harm anyone. Come on.'

Biting her lip, Sarah looked up once more. 'Well... I suppose that one looks a little bit like a rabbit, but with wings.'

'Ohh, a flying rabbit. And where do you think he's off to?'

'She,' Sarah corrected.

Ivy nodded. 'Right. Of course. Where do you think *she* is off to?'

They discussed the adventures of the flying rabbit until Ivy realised it was long past time the children returned to the house and started on their chores.

With the help of Sarah, Ivy ensured each little person had a task they were capable of completing. Some assisted with laundry, others cleaned the large home, and several helped the cook prepare the evening meal. Henry, a few of the older boys, and one little girl with adorable blonde pigtails worked in the yard with the lone gardener they could afford to employ.

The favourite jobs were rotated amongst the children along with the less enjoyable tasks. While Ivy was new to supervising, Olivia had assured her the children understood the system and only needed monitoring. Remarkably, it all went rather well.

When Olivia came to Ivy with the idea of running the orphanage, both women were of a like mind. They wished All Souls to operate differently than other institutions. Education and training were top priorities. Finding apprenticeships or positions in a field of interest for the children was the main goal of the Committee of Concerned Ladies for Community Betterment. To this end, the morning hours were spent educating the younger children while the older boys and girls attended apprenticeships. The afternoons were devoted to healthful physical activities and chores, and the evening was meant for resting and reflection. The children seemed to appreciate the opportunities they were given and completed their chores with minimal squabbles.

Ivy wondered if shooting a man on her first day of work might have been a useful strategy for earning some respect. The few times she needed to intervene in an argument or scuffle, a sharp look and a few reminders of how respectful young men and women should behave seemed to silence the children into wide-eyed obedience. She didn't think it was her commanding presence that inspired such immediate positive responses, but she wasn't going to question her good luck.

In the midst of it all, Ivy was able to help Henry and his bunkmate in room ten move their few belongings into room nine. His doe-eyed devotion to Ivy worried her a bit, but he wouldn't hear a whisper of complaint from his friend which made the transition much smoother than Ivy anticipated.

Evening arrived in a mad rush of young people flurrying from task to task. Their supper included a lively cacophony of young voices, clattering plates and spoons, and the satisfying exhaustion resulting from a day of productivity. Ivy wasn't sure she'd ever felt such contentment. Until she remembered their new house guest would be arriving sometime that night.

She wished with a fervency bordering on desperation to visit Millie for a cup of tea and some comfort before her fateful evening with Commissioner Worthington. Of all Ivy's friends, Millie had known her the longest. While Ivy never told her of the troubles she had with her father, Millie was a bright woman with sharp powers of observation. She might not know, but she certainly suspected. It would be such a relief to finally tell her friend everything and ask for advice about living with a man.

Living *with a man. Ivy Cavendale. How is this happening? And not just any man. The Commissioner of Scotland Yard.*

He inspired something far more dangerous than the habitual fear she'd grown accustomed to managing. Commissioner Worthington aroused her curiosity. While fear kept her cautious, watchful, and safe, curiosity was another matter entirely. It was a known killer of cats and ladies alike. Something Ivy should squash immediately. If she only knew how.

Only a coward would retreat to her room instead of waiting for the commissioner to arrive.

I can live with being a coward. I'm exceedingly good at it.

When the last child was tucked into bed, she rushed into the kitchen to make a small pot of hot chocolate with a dash of whiskey for good measure. A forbidden treat, but one she was willing to sacrifice new ribbons and fripperies to purchase. When she lived in her father's house, she was only allowed the rich beverage on very special occasions. He showed excessive concern over her figure and complexion, believing the chocolate might ruin both. So, Ivy was allowed one cup on her birthday and Christmas.

Upon leaving his house to live with her aunt, she was determined to have a cup of hot chocolate whenever she pleased. Her father left her a small inheritance, but it required excessive economy if she wished it to last for her life's entirety. And she did, as the only other option would be marrying. It was another reason why Olivia's offer was so appealing. The position came with free room and board and a small income. But even without her new position, Ivy would budget ruthlessly to afford her treat. Hot chocolate was much more than just a delicious drink. It was a symbol of her autonomy. With her father's and brothers' deaths, she had less wealth, less standing in the beau monde, and certainly less companionship. But she would never have less hot chocolate.

After such a trying day, she planned on climbing into her narrow bed, snuggling the kitten, sipping her cup of dark delight, and becoming engrossed in a penny dreadful. The ghastly stories should frighten her into sleeplessness, but there was something about the fanciful violence that made her feel incongruently safe.

She poured her steaming chocolate into the little pot already holding a dram of whiskey and took the tray through the grand entry toward the stairs.

Far too grand an entry for an orphanage.

Towering columns led up to a painted, albeit faded, ceiling. A sweeping staircase, wide enough to fit ten large men, teetered unevenly upward. Papered walls displayed darker squares, rectangles, and ovals where pictures once hung. But it was the marble floors echoing ominously with each step she took that Ivy truly despised.

The front door flew open and Commissioner Worthington entered.

Oh my!

He looked nothing like the neatly presented gentleman Ivy knew.

'Drat,' she muttered, almost dropping the tray carrying her precious pot. A crime she would have held against Commissioner Worthington for the rest of his days. She froze, words spilling from her mouth before she could stop them. 'What are you wearing?'

Scruffy breeches hung loose on his muscular frame, hiding the shape of his thighs.

Not that I've noticed his thighs. Or that I want to notice them now. I couldn't care less if the man has tree trunks for legs. Let him wear silly pants that hide the hard lines of muscle running along his—

Forcing her eyes away from his legs, she took in a battered waistcoat of once green material that was now a greyish brown. Under that, the commissioner wore a plain spun linen shirt, unbuttoned at his neck. No starched collar. No cravat. Just an intriguing peek at the hollow of his throat.

Dear God. Is that chest hair? Just there, where his shirt buttons?

She was no idiot. She knew men had hair in places women did not. But she never imagined she might see Commissioner Worthington's body hair.

The very idea! I wonder if it covers his legs as well...

No. She would not permit her gaze to wander south again. All the air was mysteriously sucked from the room and Ivy struggled to draw in a deep breath.

Commissioner Worthington stretched out both arms, displaying himself proudly. His inky hair was mussed, his shirt-sleeves rolled up to mid-forearm, revealing more intriguing black hair sprinkled over his arms and lending credence to Ivy's theory that it must also cover his lower extremities. 'Do I not look like your common working man, hired by the kind ladies of the Committee for Community Betterment to be a general dogs-body for whatever needs doing?'

Ivy opened her mouth but found no words. Nothing about him looked common. He was intimidating in the proper clothing of a gentleman. But dressed in the casual garb of a normal man, his distinctive features were highlighted to an obscene degree. A strong brow, Roman nose, firm lips, sharp cheekbones, and the shadow-beard painting his hard jawline.

The clenching was back, low in her belly. And the rush of heat as though someone pulled aside the curtains inside her body and let in the summer's sunlight. An echoing thud in her chest resonated in her bones.

What is wrong with me? Mayhap I'm catching the ague. Or this is the beginning stages of consumption.

She couldn't check her forehead for fever as she was still holding the tray with her pot of chocolate and a teacup.

'Did you not hear me, Lady Ivy? Or have I missed the mark? Reading said it was the perfect disguise, but I never know with that man if he is just trying to hornswoggle me.'

'No, you look just... um, well. You look perfect, Commissioner.'

'Please. We are going to be seeing quite a lot of each other. You can't keep calling me Commissioner. Especially not when I'm dressed like this.'

Ivy's face grew warm. Her cursed blush, a horrid stain erupting with the slightest provocation, was likely spreading over her neck. She hated being so easily unsettled. And he would know it. Of course he would with her neck looking like it was covered in an unsightly rash. 'I certainly can't use your Christian name.'

Commissioner Worthington's eyes grew wide. 'Heavens, no. The very pedestals of propriety might crumble before us should you presume such a familiarity.'

A strange, bubbling giggle tried to escape her mouth, but she clamped down hard.

I will not simper in front of this man.

The painful thump in her chest was back.

'Only, I don't think we need be quite so formal, do you?'

Did she? Think they should be formal? A thousand thoughts

raced through her mind, but not one of them answered his question.

'Erm...' she dithered.

'At least not when it is just the two of us,' Commissioner Worthington continued as if she'd contributed something meaningful to the conversation.

Struggling to regain her composure, Ivy clenched the tray so hard, she wondered if she might break the wood. 'What do you suggest?'

'Would you call me Worthington? Only when no one else is about. And only if you are comfortable with that.'

Worthington. Such an innocent combination of vowels and consonants, and yet she could almost taste them in her mouth, as decadent and addictive as her hot chocolate.

'Perhaps. I shall consider it.'

He nodded. 'Of course.' His clever gaze dipped down to her tray. 'Is that hot chocolate?'

Instinctively, she turned away, hiding part of the tray from him as if he might take it.

Laughing, he put his hands up in mock surrender. 'I won't steal your precious treat, Lady Ivy. My sister was mad for the stuff when she was a girl.' He stiffened and pressed his mouth together.

Ivy quirked her head to the side. 'You have a sister?'

'Had.' One word spoke volumes when paired with the flash of anguish in his eyes. The lines in his face instantly deepened.

Grief. She knew that emotion intimately. Loss. Sorrow. All the feelings one experiences when someone they love is ripped away. She felt the fierceness of it when she was only a child of eight and her mother died. A pain too big to fit inside her body, and yet she stuffed it there with determination because it was all she had left of the woman who loved her with nothing but gentle touches, warm smiles, tight hugs. Worthington carried that same agony and, while his body was much bigger than hers, it still wasn't big enough to contain it. She saw it pushing out of him like a ropey vine.

She would have to be a true skinflint to deny him a little of her chocolate. And while Ivy was many terrible things, she wasn't selfish. Dipping her chin in a sharp nod, she turned back toward him. 'I'm sure I can find another cup. If you'd like some, that is.'

The small smile creasing his cheeks was so sad, Ivy felt compelled to reach out to him. Offer some kind of comfort. Which was impossible.

I'm carrying a tray, after all.

'I wouldn't dream of depriving you, Lady Ivy. Perhaps we should postpone our planning of the investigation until the morrow. You've had a long day. And I find myself in need of rest.'

A pang of disappointment cut through her before she remembered to be relieved. 'Yes, that would be... I mean to say, I am rather weary. Err, well. I hope you find your rest. If your room is not as it should be, you need only let me know.'

He nodded. 'Is it just up the stairs?'

'Oh. Of course. You haven't had a chance to explore the house. Please, follow me. All of the rooms are on the eastern wing. The western wing has more rooms, but we've left those largely untouched for now.' Turning, Ivy hastily ascended the stairs, not looking back to see if he was following her. There was something incredibly intimate about guiding a man to her bedchamber. Or at least, the hallway leading to her bedchamber. Ivy refused to think about it any further. She couldn't. All the particles of her body might fly apart if she did, releasing her soul to rise into the night air like mist and dissipate into eternity.

When she reached the second floor, she made a fast right

turn. Her swift steps matched her heartbeat as she counted each footfall. Sometimes, frightening tasks were best done quickly. Seven long strides from the stairs to the hallway. Four more to room number ten. She turned partly and noted he was close behind her. Close enough that she could discern where his neck turned from golden honey to pale eggshell. 'Your room is here.'

'And yours?'

Ivy's shoulders tightened.

'Should there be any trouble, I would need to know where you are. Only for that, Lady Ivy. I swear it.'

He was right, of course. And she was being ridiculous. A silly, missish girl when, in fact, she was nearing her third decade. 'I'm at the end of the hall. The last door on the left. Goodnight, Commissioner Worthington.'

Spinning tightly on her heel, she did not wait for his response.

6
_____

Edward's first night at the All Souls Orphanage was long, uncomfortable, and taught him several important truths.

Truth one: a cot designed to hold young children was not a comfortable bed for a large man. His legs hung off the end and, every time he moved, he feared the whole thing would collapse. At some point in the evening, he'd given up, laid the blanket on the ground, and slept on the hard wooden floor. It was a vast improvement.

Truth two: sleep was impossible when his mind kept wandering back to Lady Ivy Cavendale. She was clearly unnerved at the idea of sleeping in such close quarters – if one could call a long hallway with at least nine rooms between them full of seven and twenty young people close. But there had been a moment. When he spoke of his sister – a shocking thing to do as he never spoke of Liza – Lady Ivy's eyes softened from wary mistrust to painful understanding. And then she offered him some of her hot chocolate. A treat he would guess she rarely shared.

Everything about her was a contradiction. Vulnerability

paired with thick, high walls of protection. Courage coupled with intense fear. Curiosity combined with hesitance to step into the unknown.

When the first pink light of dawn crept through his window and landed squarely on his face, Edward accepted there would be no more sleep for him. Instead, a cup of hot coffee and whatever food he might be able to rummage in the kitchen was his best option. He re-donned his workman's clothes and, without the benefit of a washbasin or mirror, crept down the stairs to the kitchen. A brass tap and Belfast sink were tucked away in the scullery. Edward made use of the sink and a cake of soap to splash water over his head and scrub his face in abbreviated morning ablutions. The freezing water stole air from his lungs and sleep from his mind. An effective tool for waking oneself up quickly. He finger-combed his hair into some semblance of order but would need to return to his home to properly dress and complete his toilet before going to work.

Will Reading be more upset by my late arrival or coming on time with the bedraggled appearance of a beggar? I shall try both methods over the next few days to see which annoys him more.

It was the small pleasures in life that made it worth living.

Edward was contemplating all those small pleasures as he put the kettle on to boil. He had brought with him a small bag of coffee beans. It was doubtful the orphanage would carry such luxuries in their pantry, and he refused to start his day without the drink.

If it's good enough for Queen Victoria, then it's damn well good enough for me.

Humming a bawdy tune that would cause poor Reading's ears to burn red with embarrassment, he didn't hear Lady Ivy until she cleared her throat primly.

Spinning, Edward was certain his own ears burned with a

blush to be caught mid-melody for such a rude song. But surely a fine lady such as Ivy Cavendale wouldn't know the words to the 'Lass of Islington'.

'Are you looking for a cellar to rent, Commissioner Worthington?' Lady Ivy's crystal eyes sparked with mirth.

Damn. She does know the words.

One more contradicting fact that piqued his curiosity and stirred something far more dangerous within him.

She seemed to realise what she was truly asking as the double entendre of 'cellar' from the song hung between them. The intriguing splash of crimson spreading over her throat saved him the burden of being the only one blushing. 'Forgive me. I didn't mean to imply you were, that is, I was just... Drat.' She gave up and spun around, presumably to leave, but Edward lunged forward and caught her arm, turning her back. His instinctive move to keep her from escaping brought them within a few inches of each other.

Instead of stepping back, as he should, or letting her step back as he expected, they both remained frozen, nearly touching one another. The air between them grew impossibly thick. Edward still held her arm. The lean muscles tensing beneath his fingers confirmed his suspicions. She might be slight, but she was strong. Yet another fascinating contradiction to add to his list. He couldn't stop his mind wondering what she looked like naked, all supple skin and long lines, sleek like a cat and just as likely to swipe at him with sharp claws as purr with pleasure. He traced down her arm slowly before brushing his fingers along the heel of her hand and finally breaking contact.

She was dressed for the day in another one of her simple blue gowns. Her fair hair, like the gossamer strands of spider silk, was tied in a neat twist at her nape. The neckline of her dress was high, but he didn't miss the rise and fall of her small, corseted breasts beneath the cotton. Such a delicate shift of cloth, innocuous, innocent, and yet completely captivating. He wondered if the firm flesh would fill the centre of his palm. If she would cry against him when he rubbed a thumb over her nipple. Small breasts, in his experience, were just as delightful as full ones, holding equal mysteries as he learned what best pleased the woman to whom they were attached.

'Please, don't leave.' His words were rough with absolutely unacceptable desire. Something he ruthlessly denied himself. Something he refused to unleash on any woman, especially one who clearly held no interest in him.

Over the course of his adult life, he'd engaged the services of several professional, discreet women to sate his physical needs when they became unmanageable. While he respected those women, found them attractive, and in the case of the last, Delilah, developed a close friendship, he never allowed himself more than mutual sexual release. In fact, as soon as his relationship with Delilah deepened into a connection eclipsing tupping, he ended that part of their arrangement and never sought out a replacement.

He made a vow to himself so long ago, the night his world ripped apart.

The night I destroyed her.

Others had paid most dearly for his sins, and he promised never to allow himself the kind of joy found in one's mate. Impersonal sexual relief was one thing, but affection? Companionship? Love?

Never.

Because a man with my sins doesn't deserve to find happiness in another. Eternal solitude is a fitting punishment.

But Ivy's sweet, earthy scent – one more intoxicating contradiction – tempted him to forget his past and his promise. His body grew tight. Grinding his teeth together, he did the impossible. The inevitable. He stepped back.

Lifting a shaky hand to run through his mess of hair, he willed himself to regain control. 'I mean, will you stay and speak with me? About the investigation.'

Whatever affected him seemed to have equal power over her. She looked behind her, the pulse in her neck beating madly as skin and tendon pulled tight. He wanted to lick her, just there, and feel that pulse upon his tongue.

Impossible! I have no right to indulge in such intimacies. Nor would she wish me to do so even if I could.

But still, his mind wandered down dangerous paths.

Heaving a sigh Edward couldn't begin to decipher, Ivy turned back to him. The blush staining her neck created two rosy spots on her cheeks.

If I pressed a kiss there, would her lashes brush over my mouth like the wings of a moth?

An absurd, whimsical thought. Edward was not an absurd or whimsical man. He was logical. Feet firmly placed on the ground. Devoid of flight or fancy.

Would her pale skin glow in the moonlight?

Enough! I don't give a flaming fig about skin glowing in the moonlight!

Except now he couldn't help but wonder if hers would.

'The children don't come down to break their fast until half past eight. Cook should arrive in another half-hour, but we have a few minutes of quiet if you'd like to bring your coffee into the parlour?'

'Would you like some?' he offered.

She wrinkled her nose.

Like a wood sprite.

Nonsense. Like a normal woman.

'No thank you. I can make some tea. I'll be with you in a moment.'

'I don't mind talking in the kitchen.' He pulled up a stool to the scarred wooden table and blew on his steaming coffee, hoping the rich scent would clear Ivy's fragrance from his head.

She pressed her lips together. Perhaps she was hoping for a moment of solitude to gather her thoughts.

Terribly unfortunate. But if I'm off balance, then it's only fair you should be as well.

'So, tell me, Worthington, what master plan have you concocted to find this nefarious gentleman who crept through the window of my orphanage?'

Edward sipped his coffee.

Yes. Focus on the investigation.

Savouring the bitter taste of his morning brew as much as he was going to savour her reaction to his plan, Edward returned his cup to the table. 'We are going to attend a ball together. Tomorrow night. The Widow's Ball.'

He expected surprise. Perhaps some trepidation. The Widow's Ball, after all, was a notorious affair just this side of completely scandalous. Certainly no place for innocent young misses or marriage-minded mamas of the beau monde. This fete was reserved for rakes, widows, and married members of the peerage looking for more than just a staid evening of measured dance steps and watered-down ratafia. It would be full to bursting with blue bloods seeking a darker kind of adventure. The perfect place to hunt a man willing to sneak into a bedroom full of young girls and wreak unknown havoc.

And the last place Lady Ivy would wish to be.

A fact he realised far too late.

'The Widow's Ball?' Her fair eyebrows flew high enough to almost disappear into her hairline. 'Are you mad?'

Edward wasn't used to his plans being questioned quite so baldly. Generally, people nodded and hopped to. Even Reading, with his sharp wit and dry humour, kept any doubts he had to thinly veiled statements of pseudo-support rather than openly dismissing Edward.

He straightened his spine, rising to the full six foot five inches that intimidated all but Philippa. 'Not quite. It is the perfect place to search.'

Ivy was seemingly unimpressed by his commanding presence. She rolled her eyes. 'It is the perfect place to feed every gossip in the beau monde! I may be a gently bred miss who prefers the walls of ballrooms to the dance floors, but even I know what happens at the Widow's Ball.'

Don't ask. Take the high road. Be a gentleman, for God's sake.

'What happens, Lady Ivy?' Something about her inspired a need in him to provoke. Pull her from her shadows. Nettle her into matching his fire with her own.

Never one to tempt or tease, something about this woman pulled at the darker side of Edward. The side he kept tightly contained beneath the veneer of a respectable gentleman intent on seeking only justice. She invited him to do the one thing he never did: play.

He couldn't stop the gravelled wickedness in his tone or the wild hope that she might describe any one of the decidedly improper activities taking place at a ball designed for devilish deeds.

Her throat worked in a strangled swallow. 'What does not happen at that bacchanalian celebration? Even my... father, who was hardly a saint, refused to allow my brothers to attend.' There it was again. The nearly choking sound as she stumbled over any mention of her sire. Her pale skin whitened further, and

Edward no longer wanted to tease Ivy. Instead, he ached to shield her. Protect her.

'I will not allow any harm to befall you. I swear it.' *It is my duty, after all. That is all this is. Dedication to my role as Commissioner of Scotland Yard.*

She lifted a hand to sweep away a strand of hair escaping her neat knot. 'I can keep myself safe. That is not what concerns me.'

'What is it?' A desperate need for her to share her fears with him filled Edward with longing he'd not known since his youth.

She looked over his shoulder, then at the table, then to her fingers before finally tipping her chin up and staring at him. 'I have nothing to wear to such a fete.'

Edward held her gaze. She was lying. Her fear had nothing to do with gowns. But she wasn't ready to trust him with her truths. Fine. He could wait. 'That will never do. I shall send word to Philippa. The Duchess of Dorsett has every modiste in London at her beck and call. Surely, she can have a dress for you by tomorrow evening.'

Her eyes, so clear and expressive he fancied he could fall into their depths like a great adventurer exploring an iceberg's crevasse, widened in alarm. 'What about your reputation? The entire beau monde would fly into a fervour at the very idea of the respectable, powerful, eligible Commissioner Worthington squiring poor, plain, sad little Ivy Cavendale to an event as scandalous as the Widow's Ball.'

His thoughts recoiled at such ill-equipped descriptors. Proud, certainly. Serious, most assuredly.

Beautiful.

Not that he noticed, but yes, exactly. Her own opinions about herself were blatantly false.

'You're hardly little. I'd wager you're taller than a quarter of the gentlemen at White's.' As soon as the words emerged, he realised his mistake. Of all the points to contradict, her height was perhaps the least complimentary.

Her brows came down like a guillotine. 'Pardon?'

If he ever questioned whether Lady Ivy Cavendale was capable of shooting a man, the harsh edge of her words would put to bed any of his doubts. In fact, if she had her pistol handy, he was fairly certain she might point it at him and pull the trigger as easily as another young lady poured a dish of tea. His only consolation in mistakenly focusing on her height was the anger he inspired. He found it vastly superior to the fear plaguing Ivy whenever she mentioned her father. A man Edward desperately wished to revive from death only so he could send him back to hell himself.

'I don't mean to say... You have a very lovely figure.' *Damn.* He hadn't meant to speak so plainly.

'Pardon?' This time, she said the word with the same confusion one might feel if they were told their skin was green or their limbs were made of pudding instead of flesh and bone.

'I just mean your height and slender form are incredibly pleasing.' *Not better.* He literally bit his tongue.

Breath exploded from her in a shocked burst. 'Pardon?'

She has certainly illustrated the vast meanings held in one word.

'I'm only saying your description hardly merits the many appealing facets of your total person.'

Shut up. Just shut up now before you completely bury yourself.

But he didn't shut up. He kept going. 'I can't see why anyone would question my interest in you.'

Flaming feathers on a phoenix's arse. Did I just admit to being interested in her? A woman who would rather watch me be pickled in vinegar than grace my arm at a ball. Marvellous.

Ivy tapped her finger against her skirts. He could actually see the woman gathering her thoughts back together like one might collect pieces of shattered pottery. 'I can think of at least twenty reasons to start. The first being that you *aren't* interested in me.' She glared at him, and if a woman could will a statement into reality with nothing more than focused desire, his attraction to her would shrivel up and die as surely as a salted snail. 'But never mind. Leaving aside the undeniable stir we might cause attending the Widow's Ball together, what exactly do you hope to gain from flouncing around a dance floor with me?' Her tart words belied a deeper emotion that her expressive skin could not hide. The wine-red stain seeped up her neck. Did it also slip lower? Painting her pale breasts with patterns he could trace with his fingers or tongue?

Not helpful.

Unaccountable nerves created a jitter through his system. He couldn't remember the last time someone made him feel anxious. While his plan might not be the pinnacle of investigative brilliance, it was a starting point, and he needed her to trust him. He'd wager Lady Ivy Cavendale trusted very few men, if any.

With good reason, no doubt.

But not all men were such horrific monsters. While Edward knew he deserved no kind of pleasure in the arms of a woman, a fossilised piece of his soul cracked at the thought of Ivy never knowing the joy such intimacy could evoke because of whatever past pain she suffered. It seemed a horrific crime that someone as undeserving as Edward knew the heights of physical pleasure, while Ivy was trapped in...

Fear.

If only he could show Ivy that some men could be trusted. At least in this.

But does she even want that?

He was determined to find out. And if she did wish to

explore such desires, a shimmer of something bright and warm erupted in his chest at the thought he might be the one to earn her trust. To help restore a piece of joy that had been stolen from her.

What a load of lies I tell myself to justify breaking my vow. She might deserve to know pleasure, but I hardly deserve to be the one who shows her.

Because with Ivy Cavendale, it wouldn't just be tupping. It could never just be tupping.

Forcing his mind to return to his plan, Edward bought himself time by taking another sip of coffee. 'You said the man wore the clothes of a gentleman. And he was young, so mayhap he is an eligible lord looking for a bit of fun. While sneaking you into White's or Boodles isn't impossible, this is a far easier place to start. A man willing to cross the boundaries of law and propriety by breaking into an orphanage is exactly the kind of young buck sure to seek an invitation to the Widow's Ball. And despite your fears about my reputation, I have been seen in far worse places than a private ball.'

'Have you?' Her arch look rivalled that of Philippa. He wished the duchess could see her protégée now. She would be immensely proud.

Shrugging an answer to her question, he continued. 'If we don't see him there, we can try a ride along Hyde Park or stroll down Bond Street, but this is our best chance.'

'Ah. I see. Your brilliant plan is to escort me around London during the height of the summer season in hopes of not being noticed?'

'Yes. Exactly.' He nodded, grateful that she was finally being reasonable.

'Brilliant,' she hissed, her tone communicating the exact opposite. Turning from him, she plucked the kettle from the hob and shook it. Finding the contents lacking, she stormed out of the kitchen. He heard the tap running in the scullery. Before he could follow her, she was back, her skirts billowing around her legs as she strode to the hob and plunked the full kettle down. Bending over, she pulled open the stove and fed it a few sticks. He *did not* notice how the fabric of her skirts pulled tight across her bottom. While her limbs were lean and her lines were sleek, her arse was lush and full. His fingers twitched at his side as his body grew tight. How would it feel to grip her narrow hips and pull that firm bottom flush against him?

Delicious. Sweet. Perfect.

Again, not helpful.

7

First, Worthington made a ridiculous proposal about escorting her to a ball.

Not just any ball. The Widow's Ball.

A place no innocent young lady belonged.

But exactly the kind of place a scurrilous lord might be. And am I really so innocent?

She didn't feel innocent. She felt itchy and restless in ways she'd never before imagined.

Perhaps I'm allergic to something in this house. The bed sheets. The soap. A certain Commissioner of Scotland Yard.

Then, he pointed out her height, a fact she was acutely aware of as most men hated looking up to any woman, but most especially a woman like Ivy Cavendale. Not that Worthington had any worries there; the man was as tall as a giant oak tree and just as strongly built.

I don't care how strong he is. Or tall. Or well proportioned.

He called her plank of a body *desirable.*

Of all the stuff and nonsense.

The last thing Ivy needed was the interest of a man like Edward Worthington.

Only, what might happen if I did capture his interest?

Not a thought worth entertaining. But for the first time ever, it filled Ivy with more questions than fears. Which was unaccountable.

The very idea of attending a ball with him – dancing within the frame of his powerful body, feeling his hands on her skin, letting his scent infiltrate her senses – created a slow burn low in her belly that spread out, getting trapped in highly inappropriate places. The backs of her knees, the hollow of her throat, the apex of her thighs.

Fear. That was what she should be feeling. That was what she always felt when imagining dancing with a lord of the beau monde. His body too close. His breath too hot. His hands too demanding. But that was not what she felt when she imagined Worthington's chest close enough to her own she could feel the heat of him. His breath skating over the delicate skin of her neck. His hand pressing against the small of her back as their bodies moved together along the strains of a stringed quartet.

I'm ill. This is some kind of strange fever.

But the ache she felt wasn't like that of the ague. This was something new, something entirely different from anything she had experienced before. She found it equal parts frightening, frustrating, and fascinating.

She always viewed men as terrifying beasts best avoided. Her father had explained in excruciating detail all the ways a man could use her. Would use her. All the ways *he* wanted to use her. Though he never went further than lingering touches that stained her skin like invisible bruises. Because her virginity was far too precious. He couldn't very well sell her to the highest bidder if she was already ruined.

Her father told her night after night if he let himself give in to her temptations, if he allowed himself to sample what she so blatantly offered, the beau monde would know his daughter was damaged, dirty, and devious. It would reflect poorly on him to have harboured such sin within his household. So, he invaded her mind instead of her body and created a black darkness there with claws that slashed, teeth that sunk into her imagination and ripped her innocence asunder, threats of what was to come that kept her huddled in the shadows, desperate to evade any notice from the gentlemen seeking out biddable wives. While her body remained innocent, he painted shame over her soul in heavy brushstrokes.

When he died, she rejoiced and hoped the fear would die with him. But the black monster invading her mind still lingered. Ivy worked furiously to ensure she would never need to marry. It was why she used such economy with her money. It was why she first started working with Philippa to learn skills of self-protection. It was why this tingling new awareness of Worthington was so unexplainable.

Watching her closest friend fall in love a few months after her father's death, indeed, accidentally interrupting Millie and Lord Drake in an intimate moment, only confirmed the damage her father had exacted upon Ivy. Like amputating a limb, only he had cut off any normal desires she might have for another. She could never look at a man the way Millie watched Drake. The love and need in her friend's gaze, a fire burning so bright it singed anyone near them, was impossible for Ivy to imagine ever harbouring within her own heart. It was mystifying.

So what is this confounding curiosity whenever Worthington is near? Why do I look at him and wonder what it might feel like to have his fingers brushing over my skin? His lips pressing against my own? Why do I ache in places best forgotten?

When she had stumbled upon Millie and Drake so many months ago, his head had been buried between Millie's thighs. At the time, Ivy reacted with abject horror and a desperate need to protect her friend from such unseemly ravishment. A ravishment from which Millie most adamantly wished *not* to be rescued. Ivy couldn't understand how her friend so willingly submitted to such demeaning behaviour. But now, as she stood in the kitchen of the orphanage, alone with a strong, powerful man wearing the clothes of a commoner and the manners of a gentleman, she wondered.

I need to speak with Millie. Immediately.

Gripping the handle of the kettle tightly, she squeezed until her knuckles whitened and her body cooled slightly. She turned from the stove and narrowed her eyes. 'I cannot attend a ball with you tomorrow night. I'm expected to be here, watching over the children.'

'Find someone else to cover for you.'

She threw her head back and laughed. Because finding someone willing to take on the responsibility of seven and twenty children was such an easy task. 'I don't have anyone else to ask. I have very few friends, and they all have responsibilities.'

'What about Philippa?'

Dear God. He really is an imbecile.

'You expect me to ask Lady Philippa Winterbourne, the Duchess of Dorsett, personal confidante to Queen Victoria, to leave her mansion in Belgrave Square and spend the night in Islington with a house full of urchins whilst I frip around the Widow's Ball on your arm looking for some nameless lord?'

'Yes. Exactly.'

Ivy shook her head and bit back a foul curse no lady would ever utter. 'No. It's impossible. This is my responsibility. Not hers.'

'Your safety is *my* responsibility. As is that of the children here. If we don't find this man, you are at risk. So are they. Trust me. Philippa will understand.'

'Why?' The question plagued her. 'Why is my safety of any interest to you at all?' She was of little import. The commissioner could easily assign someone else to this case. Anyone else. She certainly didn't merit the time and energy of a man as lofty and important as the Commissioner of Scotland Yard and a duke to boot.

Madness.

'Why not, Lady Ivy? Why are you unworthy of protection?'

Her throat became tight. In a horrible moment of vulnerability, tears threatened. She shook her head, unable to answer.

He took a step closer and reached out, his fingers tracing along the line of her jaw. The rasp of his calluses was surprisingly pleasant. She understood now why her kitten arched his back and purred whenever she stroked him.

The very thought sent heat to her cheeks and sucked the air from her lungs. In an attempt to restore oxygen to her body, she was enveloped in the scent of rich coffee and a spice she couldn't quite place.

Jamaican pepper.

'You deserve far more than mere protection, Lady Ivy.'

Oh dear.

The perplexing feeling of some heretofore unknown organ within her body unfurling, tingling, growing hot and wet and needy was simply overwhelming. Placing both hands on Worthington's solid, far too fascinating chest, she pushed him back.

Space. I need a great deal more space. And air. In my lungs.

A very cold cloth to place against her very hot skin wouldn't go amiss.

But as she held his gaze, his words lingered.

What do I deserve?

Every fibre in her being wanted to ask, but she couldn't force the words from her lips. Because even as her body ached, her mind recoiled. She didn't want his attention. Or protection. Or interest.

'Men look at you and only want one thing, little Ivy. The pleasure they can take from your flesh. And what pleasure you will give them.' Lord Cavendale's strained voice reached her in the darkness as his hand moved in a frantic rhythm.

Ivy swallowed down the bile and forced the memory from her thoughts. He was dead and gone. His power over her should be at an end. But she couldn't stop her hands from shaking.

Worthington's dark-blue gaze sharpened as if he could see her memories, hear her thoughts.

What if he knows?

Impossible. No one knew. Not even Millie. It was her darkest, sickest secret, pushed so far down into her depths, it created her foundation. A broken, twisted thing upon which nothing could be built.

And that's where it must stay.

'Are you well, Lady Ivy?' The concern in his voice wrapped around her, threatening to dissolve the shields she meticulously constructed.

No.

'Of course. I am fine. Just astounded at your ridiculous plan.'

Edward's firm mouth tilted in a grin not quite reaching his eyes. 'You mispronounced resplendent, Lady Ivy.' He turned, picked up his coffee, and paused at the door of the kitchen. 'When you meet with Philippa today, tell her our plan. If she is unable to assist us, I have several constables with young wives who would happily volunteer their time. Send me word at Scotland Yard.' He nodded politely, as if his hands hadn't just moments ago been touching her, as if his words hadn't been tearing apart her carefully built walls of protection, as if his very presence hadn't been wreaking havoc on her senses.

Smug bastard.

Yes. Thank God for the anger that rushed in, replacing the mystifying need for something... more. Anger, she could understand. Anger, she could hold without fear of being burned. Anger, she could control.

She returned her focus to the kettle. 'Tea. What I need is a strong cup of tea.' Anger and tea. Elements that could rule a kingdom or contain the fears of a woman on the edge of becoming something entirely new.

* * *

Edward strode into his office at 4 Whitehall Place and slammed the door shut. Impotent rage boiled in his blood. Lord Cavendale might be dead, but that didn't change the fact he was an insipid, evil, loathsome bastard. Edward would give a great sum of money to turn back time and find the wretched, diseased man long before Ivy ever drew breath. He would dismantle him one piece at a time, ensuring his vile appetites would never touch his defenceless daughter. The sins of men against women were a cruelty never failing to astound Edward.

'I noticed you finally arrived and in a great temper. That should make our work today far more efficient.' Reading entered, a folder in his elegant hands.

'Not now.' Edward's black glare should have sent the man running. Any other person would have tucked tail and hidden far away.

Reading stepped closer.

Contrary, smug wisp of a man.

'I have new information that might pertain to the Devil's Sons. Perhaps you would care to drag yourself out of your snit for a moment to review these files.' Reading placed the folio on Edward's desk and retreated a step, clasping his hands behind him.

'These are financial records.'

Reading nodded. 'Well done, sir.'

Edward bit back the sharp retort wanting to burst free; it would only be a waste of air. If Reading weren't so good at his job, and one of the few men willing to stand up to Edward, and remarkably skilled at research, and possibly Edward's only friend, he would have dismissed him by now.

'These are Lord Smithwick's financial records.'

'Quite.'

Suspicion flared. 'Who directed you to look into Smithwick's finances?'

Reading's ears flushed crimson. He had the decency to look away. Because Edward knew the man couldn't lie straight to his face. 'I don't recall.'

'Bollocks! Did Lady Winterbourne put you up to this?'

'She may have mentioned some suspicions she held about Lady Olivia Smithwick.'

Edward shut the file. 'I don't understand what Philippa's obsession is with Lady Smithwick, but this is beyond the pale.'

Now who isn't being honest?

Edward had several good guesses about Philippa's focus on Lady Olivia Smithwick. The marchioness was stunning. Her pale beauty a dramatic foil to Philippa's dark magnificence. In all the years he'd known Philippa, he'd never seen her look at a woman the way she looked at Olivia Smithwick on the night of Renquist's ball. Except for once, a very long time ago. He'd wager it was far easier for Philippa to be suspicious of Lady Olivia than admit her attraction to the woman.

Because she is a stubborn fool who refuses to live her life.

Pot. Kettle.

And now he was arguing with himself. Reading would have a field day if he knew.

Focus on the conversation, man! 'Reading, we have no reason to be investigating Lord Smithwick.'

'We didn't. Until I started investigating him. Now, I'm not so sure. Read the report.' Reading turned to leave but paused at the door. 'Is there a reason you came in here with thunderclouds over your head?'

Edward forced his face to remain a blank mask. 'I've no idea what you mean.'

'Might it have something to do with a certain young lady who is currently acting as headmistress of All Souls Orphanage?'

'Fuck off, Reading.'

Reading nodded sagely as if Edward had told him he was the smartest man in Scotland Yard. 'I thought so. A word of advice.'

Edward rolled his eyes and tugged on his hair, hoping the pain would clear his head. 'As if I could stop you.'

'Precisely. Do pay attention. You have a tendency to ignore me, and that never bodes well for you.'

'If I pay attention, will you promise to leave?'

Reading tsked, then speared Edward with a piercing gaze. 'Tread carefully with Lady Ivy. Trust, once broken, is difficult to rebuild.'

How could the man possibly know where Edward's thoughts had drifted regarding Lady Ivy? He tapped his finger on the file in front of him. 'Have I broken trust with Lady Ivy?'

'No. But someone did. One doesn't need to be as skilled an

investigator as I am to know the lady has been wounded most grievously.'

The black rage Edward had been battling since he left Ivy's kitchen swept over him once more. 'I suspect her father.'

Reading made a clicking noise at the back of his throat. 'Bastard.'

Edward pressed the edge of the file into the pad of his thumb, focusing on that small pain. 'Yes.'

'You like her.'

Damn Reading and his ridiculous intuition.

'The last thing she wants is the interest of a man. Certainly not a man like me.'

Reading crossed his arms over his thin chest. His expertly tailored suit barely wrinkled. 'But you do like her.'

Edward's head felt trapped in a vice. 'I admire her spirit.'

'Because you like her.'

He swallowed his scream and spoke through clenched teeth. 'The kindest thing I can do for her is leave her alone. You said it yourself. Trust, once broken, can't be rebuilt. Even if it wasn't me who broke her.'

Reading narrowed his gaze. 'I never said Lady Ivy was broken. This is my point. You don't listen to me. I said trust was broken, not Lady Ivy. But it can be rebuilt. Slowly. With care and patience.'

'What are you trying to say?'

Rolling his eyes, Reading ran a hand over his barely there moustache. 'Take the time, Edward. You might find she has as much power to rebuild your broken parts as you do hers.'

'I don't have broken parts.'

He snorted. 'You are nothing but a sack of broken parts.'

Edward opened his mouth to refute the man, but what was the point? He was right. Not that Edward would ever give him the satisfaction of admitting it. So instead, he changed tack. 'How could I possibly rebuild Lady Ivy when you clearly stated she wasn't broken?'

The infuriating secretary tilted his lips in a smile. 'So, you were listening.' He turned and paused at the entrance to Edward's office. 'There is no honour in living a half-life. How long will you punish yourself?'

Any other man would suffer his last breath for delving so deeply into Edward's pain. But Reading was Edward's only friend. He could hardly afford to kill him in the middle of Scotland Yard.

'Get out.' He spoke quietly, amplifying the threat in his words.

Reading pressed his lips together in a tight line. Edward knew he wished to say more, but he was too smart to risk breaching the boundaries he'd already pushed. Instead, he shut the door softly behind him just as Edward threw a glass paperweight at it. The resounding bang and resultant shatter of glass did nothing to ease his self-loathing.

'Forever,' he spoke to the empty room. 'I will punish myself forever.'

* * *

Ivy tried to ignore the boning of her corset as it dug cruelly into her ribcage. Philippa had outdone herself. She glanced down at the drastically plunging neckline of her midnight-blue evening gown resplendent in silk and lace. It was a daring colour, far darker than anything Ivy traditionally wore, and the contrast against her pale skin was dramatic. Crystals were sewn into the material like starbursts that only further called attention to Ivy's exposed flesh and highlighted the unique hue of her icy eyes.

What am I doing? I am a wallflower. I disappear into the crowd. I do not stand in the centre of a room and attract attention.

She refused to cast up her accounts in front of the assembled group of ladies sitting in her parlour, but more air in the room would be much appreciated as she couldn't seem to draw a full breath. She couldn't believe the women she once thought of as her closest friends had somehow coerced her into wearing this dress.

Witches. All of them. They cast some kind of spell over me, and I lost my wits.

It was the only explanation for the madness of the past forty-eight hours.

When Ivy had arrived at the duchess' Belgrave mansion after her meeting with Worthington the day before, she wasted no time in retelling Philippa the ridiculous plan Worthington had concocted. Instead of the outrage she expected to see from her patron, Philippa had narrowed her eyes and ordered her butler – a stuffed shirt with the military posture and disdainful face of a ruling despot – to bring around her carriage. Sending servants off in all directions to deliver notes to Millicent, Hannah, and Penny, all three women had abandoned whatever plans they had for that day to convene at Madame Collette's esteemed shop. The modiste only catered to the beau monde's creamiest of the crop. Ivy would never dream of wearing anything designed by the highly sought-after dressmaker who was booked out a full six months in advance.

When Philippa strode through her doors, the elegant French woman abandoned the young miss she was fitting much to the bluster and loudly voiced protests of her mama. Philippa arched a brow at the matron, effectively quelling the woman's outrage, while Madame Collette assigned one of her 'most talented protégées' to finish the young lady's wardrobe.

She swept the duchess and her entourage into a private room, and once the parameters of need were established, the afternoon rushed by in a whirl of satins, crepes, cotton, and velvet. It was decided that Ivy's shape would best be set off by simple lines, decadent fabrics, and a silhouette far more daring than Ivy would ever dream of wearing. The rest passed in a blur that brought her here, to this moment in her parlour, awaiting Worthington to escort her to the Widow's Ball with the same amount of enthusiasm she imagined condemned men awaited escort to the hangman's noose.

'Delacroix has done a wonderful job with your hair, Ivy. You look ethereal.' Philippa sat in the parlour, her left eyebrow raised dramatically as she admired the work of her talented lady's maid. She held a steaming cup full of mostly whiskey with a dash of tea. Millie sat next to her, and Hannah claimed the wing-back chair. Penny sat on the other side of the low table, fidgeting in her fresh green satin gown with lace appliqués along the bodice. Ivy would wager the once maid, now marchioness wasn't yet used to wearing the copious layers of cotton, linen, silk, and overly restrictive corsetry of a lady. Ivy could commiserate as she futilely attempted a deep breath, the whale boning only digging deeper.

Millie gave her a reassuring smile. In all the flurry of activity, Ivy hadn't had a chance to speak with her privately. She desperately wished to confide in her friend about the wild thoughts and rogue feelings overtaking her normally reserved person. Just the thought of Commissioner Worthington seeing her so exposed raised a cacophony of emotions within her she could only examine with the help of her dearest friend.

Fear, of course. Anxiety. But more troubling, a certain breathless anticipation. A tightening need. An unaccountable hope for... something. Though she couldn't imagine what exactly she hoped for outside of her modest décolletage remaining within the insufficient material of her bodice.

'Yes, you look quite beautiful.' Hannah's sharp gaze saw more than Ivy wished to expose. While she hadn't known the woman a full year yet, there was something unerringly trustworthy about Hannah. Her keen intelligence and a certain depth of understanding made her a discerning friend. While Ivy had no desire to share her sordid secrets with anyone, she instinctively knew Hannah would neither judge her nor think any less of Ivy for the sins she'd endured. Indeed, Hannah's own dubious past would allow a certain empathy for Ivy. What a rare gift to have such friends. Ivy was luckier than most.

The silky strands framing her face brushed whisper-soft against her cheek. While she only had a cracked oval mirror in her room no larger than a dinner plate, she was vain enough to have spent far more minutes than necessary staring at her reflection after Miss Delacroix pronounced her ready. 'Quite beautiful' was a stretch for a pale woman with a nose too large and mouth too wide, but she did look altogether... different.

Will Worthington notice?

Did she even want him to notice?

Yes.

The answer came before she had time to censor it. Nerves bubbled like sparkling wine in her belly.

'I'm not sure how we're supposed to conduct any kind of investigation with me in this dress. Can you imagine the gossip that will ensue?' She refused to show her nerves.

Hannah tsked. 'I know you are used to staying on the edges of society. I am always more comfortable in the shadows as well, Ivy. But a wise woman once told me when one is surrounded by jewels, even a diamond can fade into the background.' Hannah shared a silent communique with Philippa.

'I don't understand.' Ivy had lost her wits right along with her modest neckline and desperate need for self-preservation because Hannah's words made no sense.

'I think she means that when one is attending a dance like the Widow's Ball, the best way to disappear is to look just as you do tonight, Ivy,' Penny spoke softly.

'Like a wanton?' She heard the hysteria in her own voice.

I suppose I shan't be hiding my nerves. So much for putting up a brave front. This is why I belong in the shadowed corners where it is safe.

Millie rose from the settee and walked over to where Ivy paced. She placed a calming hand on her arm. 'You will do wonderfully, Ivy. You are smart, and brave, and beautiful.' She pulled her close, pressing a kiss against her cheek. 'And if Worthington does anything you do not wish, I will use him as target practice until he's more full of holes than a pincushion.'

Ivy's garbled laughter barely escaped her tight throat. How fervently she wished for a few moments alone with Millie to spill out her questions. Her worries and hopes.

Before Millie resumed her seat on the settee, she leaned close, whispering words only Ivy could hear. 'And if there are things you *do* wish for him to do, that is also perfectly fine, Ivy. I promise all will be well.'

How can she possibly know what I wish when I hardly know myself?

And how was it that Millie could unerringly understand exactly what troubled Ivy without Ivy speaking a word of her confusion?

Because she is my best friend. And the best of friends know what is needed.

'You are ready for this evening, Ivy. Your skills in defence and attack are far greater than you give yourself credit for, and if you need assistance, Edward will protect you. Of this, I'm certain.' Philippa's cobalt eyes flashed with an undiscernible emotion. She pressed her crimson lips together and rubbed her index finger against her thumb in an endless circle.

'Of course. I shall be fine,' Ivy lied through clenched teeth.

'You have your pistol?' Hannah asked, her own hand patting the pocket where she kept any number of weapons.

Ivy nodded. Madame Collette hadn't so much as blinked when Philippa insisted pockets be sewn into Ivy's full skirts. A muff pistol pressed against her right thigh while the reassuring weight of its twin balanced her left side.

'And you are going to take a dagger in your reticule; one never knows when it might come in handy.' Millie released one of her throwing knives from the cleverly hidden strap on her wrist and flicked it in the air. Ivy watched it spin up and then return to earth. Millie caught it easily by the hilt with a satisfying thwack.

Ivy held out her jewel-encrusted purse: a throwback from the height of her debutante days. 'Yes. Right here.'

'Don't forget a hatpin is handy in a pinch. Though I don't suppose you are wearing a hat tonight.' Penny's brows drew down in a frown. 'Still, almost anything can be a weapon. Your wits being the most effective of them all.' Her gaze lingered on Ivy. While they were newly acquainted with each other, it didn't stop the concern spilling out of Penny's voice. Once more, Ivy acknowledged her luck in finding such fierce female friends.

While none of them said it, they were all worried. They knew Ivy was the most timid of them. Scared, wounded, frightened, and more likely to run for the shadows than stand and fight. She hated conflict. But for once, their collective concern grated on Ivy's nerves, as did her own insecurities. She wasn't some weakling. She had been training with Philippa since

Millie's wedding. Well over six months ago. When the intruder broke into poor Sarah's room, Ivy stood against him, shot him in the shoulder, and not once did she shrink back from his fearsome presence no matter how terrified she might have been.

I can attend this stupid ball with Commissioner Worthington. I can find this blackguard and ensure he never threatens the children under my care. I can do for them what no one did for me.

A wave of nausea rolled through her belly.

Dear God. What am I doing?

A knock sounded. As Ivy was the only one standing, she tried to walk calmly through the front entrance. Her pale hand shook as she reached for the handle and opened the door.

Edward stood on the front step half in shadows, half illuminated by the flickering lamplight. Gone were the clothes of a working man. Instead, he wore an expertly tailored black suit. His white cravat was tied in a simple barrel knot, but it drew her eye to his throat. He'd freshly shaven, and a gust of wind brought the scent of soap, Jamaican spice, and coffee. Her fears dissipated in the heat of something else.

Attraction. I'm attracted to him.

Once more, Ivy found it difficult to breathe.

But I'm not capable of such feelings.

The warm rush of awareness washing over her skin and making her lips and fingertips tingle begged to differ.

Lamplight glinted in his eyes, and she caught a flash of something raw and needy before he blinked it away.

'You look quite lovely.'

She hadn't admitted until this very moment that she wanted him to like her in this dress. Which was stupid. Glancing down, she was horrified to see the splotchy crimson blush staining her exposed décolletage. She pressed a hand over her chest.

'Don't.' Worthington stepped forward, the heat of him

touching her like a caress. 'You've nothing to hide, Lady Ivy. I did wonder if...' As if realising he was about to expose a secret meant to stay hidden, he snapped his mouth shut.

'Wondered what?'

He cleared his throat, his eyes straying up to her hairline instead of holding her gaze. 'If Philippa would be able to find you a gown in the time allowed. She has outdone herself.'

Liar.

If only she could divine his thoughts. But perhaps it was better she didn't know. Stepping back to allow him entrance and create much-needed space between them, she remembered her manners. 'Thank you.'

Philippa, Hannah, Millie, and Penny emerged from the parlour.

'Ah. I see you found several women willing to step in for you this evening. How lovely.' Worthington raised his brows and clasped his hands behind his back, rocking on his heels.

Philippa narrowed her eyes and smacked her ever-present fan against her skirts of burgundy and midnight silk. 'Ivy explained your plans. It's clear you haven't adequately prepared for her absence from the orphanage, so we have all agreed to share the responsibility. While you two are hunting down the intruder, someone needs to be here protecting the children. Who better than the Queen's Deadly Damsels?'

Edward's well-shaped mouth curved in a smirk. 'I'd hardly call you a damsel, Philippa.'

'But I am most certainly deadly. Be careful, Edward. If anything happens to Ivy, you'll be answering for it.'

An unspoken message passed between the duchess and commissioner. Ivy glanced at Millie, Hannah, and then Penny. Based on the similar expressions of curiosity each woman wore, it was clear none of them knew what secrets Philippa and

Worthington shared. Her interest in the commissioner deepened. Perhaps she was not the only one with demons in her past.

Worthington gathered Ivy's coat from where it hung near the door and helped her put it on. For a brief moment, she felt the heat of his breath on the back of her neck and shivered, but then he stepped away.

Oh my.

This was going to be a long night.

'We shall be off. Are you all staying tonight?' Edward looked at each of the women in turn.

'No. I am.' Millie's flaming-red hair shone like a beacon even as she twitched a blade free and palmed the weapon. 'Drake will be joining me later. We'll be staying in your room, Commissioner. I hope you don't mind.'

'Given the size of the cot in that room, I have my doubts either of you will find enough space to lay flat, let alone sleep.'

Millie's wide smile lit up the entryway. 'I had some of our men bring over a bed. We shall leave it for your use.' She winked at him. In any other woman, it might be flirting, but Millie was so obviously in love with her scarred major general husband, the gesture was a simple extension of friendship.

The commissioner responded with a grateful smile. Ivy belatedly wondered how he had fit himself on the cot she provided the night before. He hadn't spoken a word of complaint, but based on his relieved expression, he must have been terribly uncomfortable.

'Drat. I didn't think of that,' she muttered.

Worthington offered Ivy his arm, easily smoothing over the awkward moment. 'I've slept in far less comfortable accommodations.' He spoke softly so only she heard, then to the group, 'We shall wish you all goodnight. I will bring Ivy back when our investigation has concluded and return to my own house this evening confident in the knowledge you and your fine husband will be protecting the children tonight.'

Millie smiled her thanks, and the other women offered their wishes for a successful hunt, which felt very odd. Ivy had been on fox hunts before, but hunting a man was altogether different.

Before she could process her nerves about spending the evening with Worthington, they were snugly tucked into his sporty barouche and bumping their way toward Widow Lovemore's grand mansion in Mayfair to attend the Widow's Ball.

8

Philippa should be thrown into the dankest cell in Newgate. Surely she dealt in deals with the Devil to contrive a dress for Ivy that was so wholly distracting. The duchess was punishing him. There were countless reasons for her to do so, but he would bet it was because she knew he was entertaining lascivious fantasies about Ivy.

The insufferable woman is always right. One day, someone will prove her wrong.

But it would not be this day, and it would not be Edward.

Ivy Cavendale was quite possibly the most beautiful creature he'd ever encountered. She stood next to him, her hand protected in the crook of his elbow, her lithe figure shining like a beacon of hope in a sea of debauchery as they surveyed the crush crowding the dance floor at the Widow's Ball.

Though it was still early, wine and spirits flowed heavily as titled lords and ladies left their staid rules of propriety at the entrance to Widow Lovemore's lavish ballroom. Panels of crimson and cream silk draped the walls. Innocence contrasting with heady desire. It was Widow Lovemore's theme for the evening. Red and white roses – no doubt costing the wealthy widow a small fortune – filled vases and bowls throughout the spacious room, lending their heady scent to the miasma of beeswax, body odour, and cloying perfumes. The large French doors lining the west side of the ballroom had been thrown open, welcoming revellers onto a palatial courtyard. Torches lit pathways into the garden beyond where any number of activities could be embarked upon with some degree of privacy amongst the ornamental trees, artfully designed hedges, and whimsical fountains and lawn sculptures.

Although the patrons of this particular ball weren't overly concerned with privacy. The widow had placed chaises longues, large wing-back chairs, love seats and various other pieces of furniture along the edges of the ballroom in darkened corners and alcoves. Several were already occupied with writhing bodies. It was the one ballroom where a wallflower might find herself in far more peril sticking to the shadows than dancing a waltz on the chalked floor.

Edward followed Ivy's gaze as she watched Lord Twining – a gentleman cresting his fifth decade and a highly respected member of the House of Lords – lead his wife and another lady to a chaise large enough for three. She turned quickly away.

'Are they not worried about their reputations?' she asked, her eyes firmly fixed on the couples swirling across the dance floor in what might be considered a scandalous waltz for any other event but now seemed quite tame.

'Who would point fingers at them in this crowd?' Edward looked around him at the sea of titled peers engaging in all manner of wickedness. 'The widow has strict rules about her balls. What happens here stays here.'

Ivy swallowed. 'I see.' But based on her wide, blinking eyes, Edward wasn't sure she did see exactly how corrupt the highest echelons of society could be when they were granted the safety of shared secrets. 'What on earth could he possibly be doing with two women? And why would they so eagerly join him?' She glanced at the French doors, squinting into the darkness beyond before pulling her attention back to the couples swirling to a talented pianist playing Strauss. A stringed quartet accompanied her.

Something cracked in Edward's mind as he tried to come up with a suitable answer. How did he explain to an innocent woman all the ways one could find pleasure with a willing partner, or partners in the case of Lord Twining?

Thankfully, she didn't wait for an answer. 'Perhaps we should take a turn around the dance floor?' Ivy suggested.

Edward was never more relieved to dance. He held his arms out in a practised frame. When Ivy hesitantly placed her hand on his shoulder and he slid his fingers around her waist, something shifted into place within him. Like a dovetail joint fitting perfectly into its carved partner. They locked together seamlessly.

Ivy inhaled a sharp breath as Edward closed his hand over hers and swept her into the stream of flowing couples on the dance floor.

The crush was too close to allow much space between them. He flexed his fingers against her waist, shifting her closer as they flew through the intricate steps.

'I haven't danced a waltz in years,' Ivy breathed.

Any response died on his lips as the couple to his right bumped into them, pressing Ivy flush against him. He tightened his grip to steady her, crushing her against his chest. It was impossible to ignore her shape and how sweetly she fit within his arms. Need filled him, hardening his body in ways she would not be able to ignore given their unintended embrace.

Ivy froze against him.

'Forgive me.' Edward cursed his body for betraying him. He leaned back to gauge her expression. Her eyes were wide, the pupils almost encompassing the crystal blue. Her breaths came in short gasps, and she licked her lips even as she stared at his mouth. 'Lady Ivy, are you well?'

'Air. I need air.'

Gripping her hand, he fought through the crowd until they reached the French doors. He sought out a deserted corner against the balustrade. She placed both hands on the concrete half-wall as he placed himself at her back, blocking her from view of any curious eyes. A need to touch her, to comfort, overwhelmed him. He placed a gentle hand on her shoulder as she took large gulps of summer night air.

'Damn corset,' Ivy rasped, refusing to look at him. But neither did she ask him to step away.

'Shall I remove it for you?' He fought for levity in a moment fraught with an undefinable tension.

Her laugh was closer to a gasp as she pressed against the bodice of her gown, no doubt seeking more space. Edward cursed fashionable society for deeming such restrictive clothing necessary for women to wear. For several endless seconds, they stood that way, Ivy struggling for breath and Edward helpless to assist. Eventually, her breathing slowed.

She straightened, forcing his hand to slip away as she turned to face him. 'I am better now. I think it was just the heat and the crowd.'

Clenching his fist at his side, he tried to hold on to the sensation of silken skin against his callused fingers. When he would have stepped back, her gaze once more caught on his mouth. She pressed her lips together as if testing the sensation of pressure. As if wondering what it might feel like to have him exert similar pressure there.

God, woman. You make me ache.

'Lady Ivy, when you look at me like that, I find it difficult not to wonder what you're thinking.' His voice was a dark growl in the night.

The crimson stain he now knew extended along her clavicles and between the fascinating cleft of her small breasts darkened at his words. She opened her mouth, then snapped it closed again.

'Do they frighten you? Whatever thoughts you have trapped in your mind?' Because he would rather suffer the fires of hell than scare Ivy.

'I don't know.'

* * *

Ivy was dizzy. Probably from lack of oxygen as her cursed dress seemed determined to crush her lungs. Or, mayhap, it was spinning on the dance floor in Edward's strong arms.

Worthington. Not Edward.

Possibly it was the shocking image of so many lords and ladies embracing both on and off the dance floor. She looked over Edward's – *Worthington's* – shoulder, and even in the moonlight, she could see a couple pressed against the stucco wall, just on the other side of the balcony. The man's back was to Ivy, but the woman's expression was highlighted in the flickering torchlight. He pressed kisses against her neck. Her eyes were closed, her mouth open in ecstasy as she gripped his hair, guiding him lower. One of his large hands dipped into the woman's neckline, and she gasped. Not in pain or revulsion, but in pleasure.

Ivy ripped her gaze away to refocus on Edward. His bottom

lip was fuller than the top. How would it feel if he pressed his mouth against her neck?

Or touched my breast with his strong hands?

The idea should repulse her. But it didn't. In fact, she found the images floating in her mind impossible to dismiss.

'I've never been kissed by a man.' The admission spilled from her before she could stop it.

Why did I say that?

Edward's dark-blue eyes widened. He licked his bottom lip, the firm flesh glistening in moonlight. Without thought or plan, she stepped closer, reaching up to place trembling fingers against his mouth.

Why did I do that?

He closed his eyes, his expression almost pained as he covered her hand with his larger, warmer one, pressing it more firmly against his lips. In a moment of shocking intimacy, his tongue darted out, and he licked her finger. Now, she was gasping in pleasure.

Why did he do that? And how can I get him to do it again?

She wanted more. And when it came to men, Ivy never wanted more.

'Do you wish to be kissed, Lady Ivy?' His words tickled against the pads of her fingers, and then he nipped lightly.

Yes.

'I don't know,' she said again, unable to voice such a shocking desire as her fingers brushed over his mouth once more.

He wrapped his fingers around her wrist, gently guiding her arm up so her hand rested on his neck. His tightly cropped hair bristled against her fingertips in the most fascinating sensation. He bent his head closer, their mouths almost touching. She breathed his exhalation and tasted hints of mint and aniseed.

He is going to kiss me.

She froze. Need overwhelmed her, but old fears surged, and Ivy was caught between desire and dread. He turned his head slightly, his nose skating along her cheekbone until his mouth hovered near the shell of her ear.

'Will you let me know when you're certain?' he asked. His voice rumbled along her senses like thunder. 'Because I would very much like to be the man who kisses you.'

He stepped back, and Ivy almost fell into him as his solid warmth suddenly disappeared.

Something sharp and insistent pulsed through her blood. A hollow ache clenched low in her belly. Her nipples chafed against the dreaded corset, and the resultant tingles spiralled through her body, creating a hunger for something elusive. Frustration filled her, replacing the earlier fear.

Edward's mouth curled in a wicked smile.

'Bastard,' she hissed, then slapped her hand over her mouth.

'You mispronounced "admirable gentleman", Lady Ivy.' The sparkle in his eye mocked her.

Ivy crossed her arms over her chest, huffing out a breath. 'I'm beginning to understand why Philippa so dislikes you, Worthington.'

'Well, she is usually right. Infuriating as that is to admit. Shall we return to the dance floor, lest people think you lured me out here with less than honourable intentions?' He winged up a dark brow.

Ivy had the urge to smack him. She never felt impulses to hit gentlemen. Avoid them, certainly. Hide from the more aggressive ones, undoubtedly. Ignore them completely, most definitely. But Edward – *Commissioner Worthington* – did something no other gentleman ever had. He provoked her. And when she responded, instead of pressing his advantage, he backed away, forcing her to step forward if she wished to continue whatever game they were playing.

But this isn't a game.

It was Ivy's life. A part of herself she thought missing entirely was emerging from the dark shadows of her past. The thrill of discovery blended with the fear of the unknown. She could still feel the warm, firm pressure of his soft lips against her fingertips. It wasn't difficult to imagine them brushing over her mouth. One word from her, even a nod of assent, is all it would have taken to finally know.

I am such a coward!

He extended his hand to her, and she took it, berating herself for five different kinds of fool.

'I am a patient man, Lady Ivy. I don't mind waiting. And I promise you will tremble with desire, not fear, when you are certain of what you want.' He kept his eyes ahead as his words crept into her soul, lighting fires she never imagined could burn quite so hot.

'What if I'm certain I never want to kiss you... or anyone?' Her voice was an unrecognisable rasp.

'Then we shall remain as we are, though hopefully, you might trust me enough to become friends and not just someone with whom you seek out dastardly gentlemen.'

Men didn't seek friendship with women. The fairer sex were tools men used to gain power through matrimonial contracts, or physical receptacles upon which to slake their lust, or pretty bits of lace draped over their arms to show off as one might with a jewel or bauble. They were never friends because that implied a level of equality few men granted women.

'You wish to become my friend?'

'I do.' Edward's deep voice rumbled along her nerve endings.

'Why?' The question burned in her mind. What possible

benefit would Edward gain by wanting a friendship with her? Ivy Cavendale? A skinny little coward skulking around the edges of ballrooms. Too broken to even look at men and see anything other than monsters.

Except she didn't see a monster when she looked at Edward Worthington.

They re-entered the ballroom before he could answer and almost crashed into Lady Olivia Smithwick on the arm of her husband.

'Ivy!' Olivia was breathtaking in a silver gown with crimson flowers embroidered into the material, becoming larger blooms as they cascaded down the skirt. Her blonde riot of curls was caught in a deceptively simple knot that seemed to artfully unravel and spill over her pale shoulder. 'I never imagined you would attend the Widow's Ball.' Olivia pulled free of her husband's grip and wrapped Ivy in a tight hug. She narrowed her eyes. 'What are you doing here?'

'She came at my request.' Edward smoothly inserted himself into the conversation before Ivy could respond. Claiming Ivy's hand, he squeezed it almost painfully. A speaking look quelled the truthful answer she would have given her friend. It was clear Edward wished her to keep their real goal a secret. Though why she needed to hide the fact from Olivia was beyond Ivy's understanding.

Olivia's gaze flicked from Edward to Ivy and back again. 'Really? I didn't think you would... er... be interested in such events.'

Lord Smithwick reclaimed his wife's hand, wrapping it around his arm and holding it trapped there. 'And how do you know this lady?' He tilted up his chin to better look down upon Ivy.

Where Olivia was strikingly beautiful with high cheekbones,

a full mouth, and porcelain skin, her husband was so very...
ordinary. Neither tall nor short, fat nor thin, his features blandly
regular. The only noticeable thing about him was his mouth. It
twisted in a sour expression as his grey eyes glittered with barely
concealed malice.

'Oh, we met at Lord Renquist's masked ball. Allow me to
introduce you to Lady Ivy Cavendale.'

Lord Smithwick's nostrils flared as recognition tightened his
already sour mouth into a pucker of disgust. 'I knew your father.
They say insanity runs in the blood.' He arched a judgemental
brow.

'If that's the case, then all the peerage would be stark raving
mad, my love. Everyone here has a loony uncle or crazed cousin
tucked somewhere in their lineage.' Olivia's sweet smile
contrasted the seething hatred barely concealed in her gaze.
Based on the slight tick in Lord Smithwick's left eye, Ivy would
bet all of her books that the mad uncle and crazed cousin Olivia
mentioned were both twisted branches in Smithwick's family
tree.

Ivy shot her friend a warning glance. She didn't miss how the
man's grip tightened on Olivia's hand, crushing her fingers until
the tips turned red. But Olivia continued as if nothing were
amiss. 'Lady Ivy helped me with my ripped hem. But I haven't
seen her since the masque.' Olivia gave her own meaningful
look to Ivy.

It would seem everyone wanted to keep their activities secret.
Far be it from Ivy to reveal her friendship to Olivia. Especially
not to a man who seemed capable of all manner of ugly
violence. She wondered if Lord Smithwick even knew the part
Olivia played at the All Souls Orphanage. She would speak to
Olivia on the matter at their first opportunity and offer her
protection if necessary. Philippa disliked Olivia, but surely she

would put her feelings aside and extend sanctuary if the woman were in real need of help.

'It has been months, hasn't it? What a fortunate surprise to see you here.' Ivy pulled out her rusty social skills and did her best to knock off the dust.

'Indeed. What luck you've had in your choice of escort. You're sure to stay safe – even in such a den of iniquity as this – with Commissioner Worthington by your side.' Again, Olivia was communicating far more than her words conveyed. The dart of her eyebrow and slight dip of her chin was a warning to Ivy. *Keep the commissioner close.*

Why? What dangers lurk here?

Or perhaps Olivia was just concerned with Ivy's virtue, for certainly there were lords and ladies present who would not hesitate to take that which she did not offer. The contrast between such predators and Edward was stark.

I am a patient man, Ivy. I don't mind waiting.

His words echoed through her mind, and the unspoken promise to never breach her boundaries echoed through her cavernous soul. Unless she wanted more.

I do want more.

The thought whispered through her like a warm wind in the heart of summer.

'I hardly think the commissioner's activities concern you, my dear.' Lord Smithwick reclaimed Ivy's attention as his gaze darted to Edward. 'There wouldn't be any reason for my wife to note who you attend balls with, would there, Commissioner?'

'None outside polite interest, Smithwick. Something you might wish to practise.' Edward's cool tone belied the insult.

Smithwick narrowed his eyes into slits. 'Come, darling. We should leave before I'm lectured on proper decorum by a man who spends his time with thieves, murderers, and madwomen.'

He flicked his gaze to Ivy. 'Lady Cavendale.' He spat her name as if it tasted bitter on his tongue.

Before she could respond, Smithwick jolted Olivia away. Ivy's friend looked over her shoulder as she was swept into the throng of bodies spinning on the dance floor and gave Ivy a reassuring smile. If anyone could manage a man as cruel and petty as Smithwick appeared to be, it was Olivia. Still, Ivy's heart clenched at the thought of her friend being alone with a man like that.

He is her husband. She is alone with him all the time.

A truly depressing thought and one reason why Olivia may have taken such a keen interest in the orphanage.

'Damn jealous fool. He sent his wife away over a decade ago for flirting with too many footmen, and now he brings her back only to attend a ball designed for such temptations. Half the gentlemen in this room would pay a pretty penny to tup Smithwick's wife, and he is growling over her like a rabid dog.'

Ivy turned to Worthington. 'Are you one of that group?' The sharp question revealed a new emotion burning within her. Oily and thick. Ugly and small. Jealousy.

Edward's gaze clouded with confusion. 'What group?'

Shifting restlessly in her slippers, Ivy noted how they pinched her toes and rubbed painfully on her heels. Why pretty shoes always had to be so damnably uncomfortable was a mystery. But better to focus on the masochism of fashion than the sick feeling crawling up from her belly.

'The group of men who want to t-tup her.' She stumbled over the coarse word.

Edward's lips tilted in a small smile. He leaned closer to her, whispering in her ear. 'First, you lure me onto the veranda, now, you speak of tupping? Lady Ivy, I'd no idea you were so scandalous!'

Heat crawled up her neck, washing over her cheeks. 'That isn't what I meant. I just thought... Lady Olivia is so very lovely, I imagine...'

Shut up, Ivy! Shut up now before you make a bigger fool of yourself than you've already done.

'Imagine what precisely? Wait. No. Don't tell me. After all the wickedness you've managed tonight, I'm not sure my delicate constitution could survive hearing whatever things you might,' he waggled his eyebrows suggestively, 'imagine.'

Ivy gave into temptation and swatted his arm. It was like hitting granite.

Dear Lord, can men be carved from stone like statues?

Edward didn't try to hide his smile. 'Lady Olivia is beautiful, but she is not the woman I think about when I imagine...' His thumb grazed over the delicate skin of her wrist, and Ivy quivered. 'Tupping.'

In a terrifying moment of clarity, Ivy realised she'd taken this conversation too far. Only moments before, she had retreated from kissing; now they were talking about far more dangerous activities. She glanced over the crowd, desperately seeking the right response. Something cool and sophisticated. A flat-out denial of her interest. Some way to back-pedal out of the swamp in which she found herself. Because while she asked the question, she wasn't ready for his answer. She was far too afraid to entertain such ideas. Her father had thrilled at describing the violent act to Ivy while she shook in her bed. The ripping. The tearing. The inevitable screams that would only spur her nameless husband on to greater depths of invasion.

She swallowed hard as bile crept up her throat. 'I do not believe some women are ever capable of enduring such an act of... aggression.'

Slowly, he turned Ivy to face him. It was nearly impossible to hold his gaze. So much emotion swirled in the depths of his dark-blue eyes, not the least of which was anger, though at whom, she couldn't guess. 'I don't know what you've been forced to experience, my lady. One day, I hope you might share it with me. But regardless, I promise you this: you never need to fear me, Ivy. Not now. Not ever. Whether we do nothing more than talk or you demand I worship your body until you are dripping with desire. Whatever we do or do not do, it will all be at your command.'

Several of his words caused her mind to trip and stumble.

Worship my body.

Dripping with desire.

My command.

But Ivy commanded no one. Ever. Such heady power was unthinkable. She glanced away from him, unable to reason when his words rioted through her mind.

A man caught her eye, a grateful distraction from this most confusing conversation. He was moving through the crowd with determined steps bordering on frantic. A man she recognised. Only when last she saw him, he was bleeding from a bullet in his shoulder. A bullet she placed there.

'Oh dear.'

'What?' Edward's eyes searched her face.

'He's here. The man.' She pointed as the gentleman disappeared into the crowd, heading toward the entrance and escape.

Edward followed her finger, his eyes narrowing as he spotted the man exiting the ball. 'Fuck.'

Ivy hardly had time to be offended at Edward's language before he gripped her hand in his much larger one, and they began the arduous task of weaving through the crowd.

By the time they burst out the front door and onto the gravelled drive, the gentleman was turning down Hill Street toward

Berkeley Square. From there, he could head north toward Oxford Street or south to Piccadilly, where it would be easy for him to grab a hack and disappear.

Edward looked at Ivy, then behind him at Widow Lovemore's overflowing party. His dilemma was clear. He couldn't leave Ivy behind, nor did he seem inclined to drag her along with him as he chased down a potentially dangerous man.

So, she decided for him.

It would be impossible for them to get Worthington's barouche from the queue of waiting carriages in time to track where the man went.

We'll just have to leg it.

'Come on, then!' Her hand still in his, she made a mad dash toward Berkeley Square, tugging him along behind her.

It was thrilling to run pell-mell through the streets of London in the middle of the night, air rushing past her cheeks, Edward's warm hand gripped in hers. She felt altogether unlike the Ivy Cavendale she knew. This was a brand-new creature entirely, and someone she preferred to the frightened miss hovering at the crowd's edge.

It became quickly apparent her slippers were just as big a hindrance when running as they were for dancing. She paused, and Worthington's brows rose with concern.

'Are you well?'

Kicking off one shoe and then the other, she grinned. 'I'm grand.' She pulled him once more.

As they turned and came upon the square, they needed to make a choice. Peering down the dark street, it was impossible to know if he had turned onto Davies Street toward Oxford or taken Berkeley to Piccadilly.

'We should each take a direction. I can head north toward Oxford and you south to Piccadilly.' Ivy was breathless, but only because her corset was making it impossible to fully expand her chest.

'No.' Worthington's growl took her by surprise.

'Why ever not? It's the only way to be sure we find him.'

'I will not have you chasing a dangerous man down the dark streets of Mayfair alone.'

Ivy opened her mouth to argue, but he held up his finger to his lips, his head cocked to the side.

'Did you just shush me?' Ivy hissed.

The faint scuffle of feet to her right silenced her as she met Worthington's gaze.

'Piccadilly!' They said in unison before they took off again.

While Ivy was quick, Worthington's height and strength gave him an advantage, and he was slightly ahead of her when he suddenly skidded to a stop at the corner of Charles and Berkeley. Ivy crashed into him, but the man's solid body barely moved. He reached back, putting a steadying hand on her hip but also ensuring she stayed behind him.

Ivy peered around his wide shoulders and saw the man she shot standing with a gun in his hand. The weapon was pointed at Worthington.

'Drat,' she muttered.

9

Edward had other words to say. Like, *fucking bastard*. Or *worthless piece of shit*. And he wasn't sure if those insults should be directed to the man in front of him holding a pistol or to himself for putting Ivy in such danger. Either way, 'Drat' didn't quite cover the depth of his emotions.

'Stay behind me.' He kept his voice low, and his eyes focused on the man in front of him.

'Reach for your pocket, and I'll shoot.' The man's voice broke on the last word, betraying his fear.

Edward's dress jacket left no room for something as bulky as a pistol, so reaching for his pocket wouldn't help in any case, but he kept his hands splayed out in front of him. Cursing himself for a fool, he imagined his favourite pistol, tucked safely away in his greatcoat, hanging in some wardrobe, no doubt, at Widow Lovemore's mansion. They hadn't stopped to collect their coats in the mad rush to capture this fiend. A fiend who now had the advantage of weaponry.

'Hell and damnation.'

Yes, cursing will protect us from this desperate man with a gun. Bloody brilliant, Edward!

Never had he felt quite so useless as facing off against a superiorly armed man with only his body to act as a shield against any bullets seeking to rip through Ivy's fragile body.

Perhaps bluffing will work.

'Listen to me, young man. I am the Commissioner of Scotland Yard. My men are only moments away. If you surrender now, things will go much better for you.' He kept his hand in front of him, like he could hold off the bullets with his flattened palm.

'Bollocks! If your men are so close, why did you drag a lady with you? Why not leave her behind where some of your people could keep her safe?' The man's left hand shook and, with it, the pistol he was holding in a tight grip.

'Because sometimes, ladies can be quite useful in fraught moments.' Ivy pushed Edward's hand away. Before he could stop her, she stepped out from behind him.

Her right arm was extended, a muff pistol clasped in her gloved hand.

'Ivy.' He growled her name between clenched teeth in a warning, but it was no use. The woman was fearless.

'Wh-what are you doing?' The man swung his arm wildly toward Ivy, then back to Edward.

'I thought it would be obvious after our last encounter. I shot you once, though based on your quick recovery, my aim needs work.'

The man involuntarily hitched his right shoulder.

Ivy raised a brow, her mouth quirked in a cold smile. 'Or perhaps my aim was better than I thought. You don't look well, sir. There is a sheen of sweat on your brow. Your skin is white. And even now, your hand is shaking. You should be in your bed recovering, not running around the streets of London trying to shoot innocent people.'

The man shook his head. 'Be quiet!'

Ivy cocked her weapon. 'No. I don't think I will. Put down the gun. Before you see how very loud I can be.'

'I can't fail. Not again. They'll destroy me.' His lip twitched in a spasm.

'Who will destroy you?' Edward asked.

Ivy stepped further away from Edward, deftly splitting the man's targets. While Edward silently cursed her for leaving his protection, the logical part of his brain applauded. The further apart they were, the more impossible it would be for the man to subdue both of them. If he shot Edward, Ivy would be able to level him with her own pistol. If he aimed for Ivy, Edward would tackle him to the ground and smash his face into bloody pieces.

The man stiffened his spine, his gun retrained on Edward, and while he kept his focus there, he spoke to Ivy. 'I don't think you will shoot me, Lady Cavendale.'

Edward's body stiffened.

It was a peculiar thing to face down the barrel of a pistol. While he should have been reviewing his life or recounting his numerous regrets, his mind went oddly blank.

'I'd wager you are right-handed, sir. I'd further guess you can't use your right hand because of the wound to your shoulder. That's why it's tucked so carefully in your pocket. I wonder how accurate you are with your left.' Ivy's voice was admirably calm, although Edward guessed she was not quite as cool as she pretended.

The man swung his gun toward Ivy. 'You bitch! This is your fault. Why were you even there?'

Acting on instinct, Edward launched himself toward the man

with a mighty roar. Before the fool could retrain his aim on the new threat, Edward grabbed the gun, wrenching it from the man's grip and tossing it on the cobblestones.

Ivy screamed behind him as Edward ducked underneath a wild swing from the man. He leapt forward, gripping the man around his waist and tackling him to the ground. The man's high-pitched shriek alerted Edward to the fact he had landed on the man's injured shoulder.

The scream abruptly stopped as the blackguard passed out.

Pulling himself onto all fours over the man, Edward slapped his pale cheek, but there was no response. 'Huh,' he grunted. He'd never subdued a man by simply landing atop him before. But then most of the men he tackled weren't recently shot.

'You idiot! He could have killed you.' Ivy's enraged voice registered as the pounding in his ears slowly subsided.

Pulling himself up from the ground, he turned to face her. The fear he'd kept at bay when the man's pistol pointed at Ivy resurfaced like a wave of lava. 'He could have killed *you!*' he roared, jabbing his finger at her for unneeded emphasis. 'You were supposed to stay behind me.'

Ivy's hair had come free of its pins and fell around her in wild disarray. She was also without her coat. Her chest expanded and contracted in wild breaths that drew his gaze down for a distracted moment.

'I was trying to save you!' She stepped closer to him, fairly vibrating with anger.

'I was trying to save *you!*'

Yes. I'll just keep repeating back what she's already said, only louder. That will convince her that I'm right and she is not.

The man at their feet groaned. They both looked down.

'He needs a doctor.' Ivy nudged him with her bare foot.

Something about her pale toes touching the black fabric of the man's jacket shattered Edward's control. Pulling her into a harsh embrace, he let the warmth of her seep into his skin.

'You scared me.' He whispered the words against the top of her head, tightening his arms around her.

Her whole body went rigid before slowly melting into him.

'You scared *me*,' she replied.

For an endless moment, they stood that way, both breathing hard, both encapsulated in each other's fear and relief.

Scuffling feet alerted them of the nightwatchman's panicked approach. Ivy broke away first, shoving her pistol into some hidden pocket in her skirt.

The next few hours were consumed with ensuring Ivy got home safely with an escort from one of his men, engaging a doctor to meet them at 4 Whitehall Place to assess the man's injuries, and calming down an enraged baron, Lord Augustus Thurston, who came to claim his wounded son.

The man now had a name. Clarence Thurston, second son of Lord Thurston and fresh out of studying Classics at Cambridge. Lord Augustus refused to allow Edward to question his son based on such thin evidence as 'a hysterical young miss falsely identifying his dear boy as some kind of street thug and baselessly threatening him with a gun, which no lady of morals would ever own'. While Edward was clear Clarence would need to submit to questioning, the baron would have none of it.

'I am a personal friend of Prime Minister Russell. I will see to it you are stripped of your position here, your title. Everything!' The baron's face grew crimson with rage. He stormed out of Edward's office and joined his son in a waiting carriage, trundling off into the sunrise.

'Well, that could have gone better.' Reading poked his head

into Edward's office. No doubt the man had been listening to the entire affair from the other side of the door.

'It could also have been much worse.' Edward didn't dare think of what could have happened.

'It would seem Lady Cavendale saved you. How very dashing of her.' Reading feigned interest in a loose thread on the cuff of his sleeve. He wanted a reaction from Edward.

Exhaling a calming breath, Edward looked up and gave him the one thing he wouldn't expect. The truth. 'She is a remarkable woman.'

Reading's sharp gaze flicked to Edward. 'Quite.'

'Did you have a reason for coming in here other than to annoy me, Reading?'

Reading ceased hovering in the door and stepped into the office. He pulled a piece of parchment from the file he was carrying. 'Well, annoying you is always my primary goal, but yes. I did have another reason.' Walking to the desk, he dropped the sealed letter in front of Edward.

'What is this?' Edward turned the letter over to look at the seal.

Head of a crow. Body of a wolf. Tail of a snake.

Edward looked at Reading as everything went deathly still. 'Where did you find this?'

'In Lord Clarence Thurston's pocket.'

Edward raised a brow. 'And what were you doing in Lord Thurston's pocket?'

Reading fiddled with his file. 'Well, the doctor had to remove his coat to check his wound. What was I supposed to do when the letter practically fell out?'

Edward brushed his finger over the seal.

'Perhaps it will help with the investigation.' Reading sat

across from Edward. Placing his file carefully down, he tugged on his vest.

Edward took a letter opener from his drawer and slid it beneath the wax seal, popping it free of the parchment. He opened the paper and quirked his brow. 'It's just columns of numbers.'

FH: LOA: AO: RS: ASO:

1. 13 *2. 10* *1. 8* *2. 12* *1. 10*

2. 12 *2. 11* *2. 10* *2. 9* *2. 10*

1. 9 *1. 10* *1. 13* *2. 10* *2. 9*

1. 15 *1. 12* *2. 13* *1. 11* *2. 10*

2. 13 *2. 9* *2. 10* *1. 12* *1. 9*

Reading took the paper and frowned. 'What do you think it means?'

'It means there's no way to link this letter to Clarence Thurston. That's what it means. Nor does it help us investigate the Devil's Sons.' Edward needed to think. He stood up and began pacing. 'If the Devil's Sons are behind the boy breaking into the orphanage, the danger to Ivy and all the children just increased tenfold.' Fear kicked along his nerves.

Reading nodded.

'The baron will claim the note was never in his son's pocket.'

'True.'

'But without a chance to question Clarence, we can't determine the Devil's Sons' plan.'

Shrugging, Reading heaved out a sigh. 'Quite the conundrum, sir.'

Edward shook his head. 'Not helpful, Reading.'

'I did find the letter.'

'Yes, well done, you. Now, if you could tell me what the hell it means, that would be marvellous,' Edward muttered. He was missing something. A piece to the puzzle that would take him one step closer to hunting down these bastards. 'I need to speak to Philippa. And then get back to the orphanage.' He thought Ivy would be safe after catching the intruder, but if the Devil's Sons were involved, she was in more danger now than ever before. He grabbed his coat from the rack and reached for the door, but Reading stopped him. His long fingers wrapped around Edward's wrist in a surprisingly strong grip.

'It's six in the morning, sir. I doubt the duchess would welcome such an early visit. May I recommend you get some sleep. Change your clothes. Perhaps have a bath.'

'I don't have time for a bloody bath, Reading. She could be in danger right now.' Panic, raw and frantic, rose in his chest.

'Isn't her friend with her right now? Lady Drake? And I'm sure Major General Drake is there. No one is going to attack her with those two as protectors. And, sir, she did a fine job last night of defending not just herself, but you as well.'

'Thank you for reminding me of my ineptitude,' Edward growled, yanking free of Reading's grip.

'I'm merely suggesting you might be more effective in your role with some sleep. Maybe something to eat. And definitely a bath, unless you wish Lady Ivy to associate you with the scent of sweat, damp wool, and mud.' He sniffed pointedly and took a step back.

Edward tentatively sniffed near his armpit.

Reading might have a point.

'Send a note to Lady Ivy. Tell her Major General Drake must stay with her until I can return this evening.'

Reading nodded.

'Send another note to Philippa. Let her know I will be coming round this afternoon to update her on the case.'

'Yes, sir.'

'And Reading.' Edward twisted the handle of the door, pausing in its threshold.

Reading raised his brow, waiting.

'Smug doesn't look good on you.'

Reading's words followed Edward out the door. 'Everything looks good on me, sir.'

* * *

A week passed since Ivy and Edward's encounter with the man she now knew was Lord Clarence Thurston. During that time, things had been rather dull. She should be grateful for the peace, but instead, she found herself twitching with restless energy.

Edward continued to spend his nights at the orphanage, though she was often abed before he came from Scotland Yard, and he left each morning before she'd come down to break her fast. They had precious little time together. What time they did have was focused on new developments in Edward's investigation, but frustratingly little progress was being made. It would seem he'd all but forgotten their conversation at Widow Lovemore's. This was another thing she should be grateful for, but again, she found herself unaccountably agitated.

I was given an opportunity. One I wanted. And I froze. Because of old fears. I'm still letting Father control me from the grave.

She hated that he held sway over her choices even in death.

The bastard deserves to be forgotten. Forever.

Her fears weren't just confined to the burgeoning desires she had for Edward. When he told her about the missive he found in Clarence Thurston's pocket, she had initially been horrified, but as time passed, even that emotion dissolved into an edgy impatience for *something* to happen. An outright attack would be far preferable to the interminable waiting.

Millie, Hannah, and Penny had all dealt with members of the Devil's Sons but Ivy thought she would be far too frightened. Yet now, the very idea of those loathsome men – so like her father – coming anywhere near the orphans she protected created a fire in her belly to sharpen her knives, oil her gun, and stand guard at the gates. Maddeningly, no direct attack was imminent so she focused on the things she could control.

Settling into her routine as headmistress and gaining confidence in her skills at corralling a herd of young people distracted her from the interminable waiting. Her favourite time was reading stories to the children before bedtime in a room that had once hosted grand balls. Now, it echoed with the adventures of Edmond Dantès, the mad passion of Victor Frankenstein, and the gothic glory of Jane Eyre's frightening discoveries. It was a new routine she started at the request of Sarah, though she was certain if the Committee of Concerned Ladies for Community Betterment caught wind of the stories Ivy read to the children, there would be much frothing and fussing over appropriate subject matters.

They can all hang. The children love the stories and have likely seen far worse in their short lives than anything written on these pages.

When she wasn't engaged in such pleasurable activities, her time was spent chiefly in determining ways to stretch their meagre funds far enough to feed seven and twenty hungry bellies. One of the local orphanages in St Giles had sent her an inquiry about whether there were any more beds at her location as they were full to overflowing. The western wing could easily be converted for more children, but there was no point in taking them. She could barely manage the needs of her current wards without adding any more. It was all rather frustrating and provided ample worries to take up her time, making it easy to put much more troubling problems like her growing restlessness to act on any number of ill-advised ventures – tracking down Clarence and forcing him to reveal his secrets or sneaking into Edward's room in the middle of the night and confronting her fears about kissing him – to the back corner of her mind.

Which was why the invitation she received from Olivia two days prior to meet her at Gunter's on this day for an ice while the children were busy with their studies was such a welcome distraction. Ivy's tight personal budget didn't extend to such extravagances, but Olivia assured Ivy in her note this would be her treat. She had a brilliant idea to raise funds for the orphanage and needed to discuss the plans.

Ivy was certain Edward would not want her traipsing across London on her own, even for the temptation of a delicious ice and the hope of much-needed funds for the orphanage. Thankfully, she was under no obligation to ask his permission.

Dressed in a sprigged muslin gown three seasons old, her reticule heavy with a muff pistol and dagger, and a straw bonnet she'd just redone with new ribbons plunked on her head, Ivy stepped out into a bright day and took a deep breath of the summer air, fragrant with dog rose and honeysuckle. She made her way along Upper Street where hackneys were plentiful. Soon, she was tucked away in a carriage smelling faintly of onions, the summer breeze tickling against her neck as she trundled toward Berkeley Square.

The last time she was in the same neighbourhood, she had been chasing a man with a gun.

'Ivy Cavendale, who have you become?'

It was a worthy question, and one she couldn't yet answer.

Gunter's was packed with young ladies grouped together like brightly coloured bouquets, gentlemen in summer suits of white linen or taupe smoking cheroots and laughing too loudly, and young children running to and fro with dripping fingers and sticky faces. Sitting at a table in the corner of the crowded tea shop was Olivia, like a fairy queen in a bubble of solitude amongst so much chaos.

Ivy wove her way through the crowd.

'Ivy. How wonderful to see you. You look beautiful.' Olivia rose and pulled Ivy into a hug, placing a soft kiss on each of her cheeks. 'Please, sit. I ordered us two ices. Elderflower and cherry. You choose.' She gestured to two small *tasse á glace* cups with a scoop of white ice in one and bright red in the other.

'Thank you so much for the invitation, Olivia.' Ivy smiled at her friend. Looking at both ices, her mouth began to water. 'Elderflower, I think. Less chance of staining my dress.' She sat down and pulled the glass of white ice toward her, scooped a spoonful into her mouth, and closed her eyes, savouring the creamy, sweet treat. 'Divine.'

Olivia's blonde ringlets were expertly twisted into an intricate knot with tendrils framing her face. A lavender gown highlighted her full figure while bringing out the pink hues in her cheeks and lips. She looked lovely, but there was fatigue in the lines around her mouth and the carefully concealed bruising beneath her eyes that pearl powder couldn't hide.

Ivy leaned forward, lowering her voice in the loud tea room. 'Are you quite well?'

Olivia stretched her lips wide. She scooped up her own spoonful of cherry ice. 'Of course. I'm splendid and so excited to discuss my new plan with you.'

Ivy was familiar with not wanting to share private affairs, even with close friends, so she did not press Olivia. 'What mischief are you hatching?'

Olivia popped her spoon in her mouth before it could drip on her dress. Taking a moment to swallow her treat, she gave Ivy a conspiratorial wink. 'A fundraising ball held by none other than the stuck-up, thinks-she's-better-than-everyone-else Duchess of Dorsett.'

Ivy's eyes widened. Her mouth dropped open. 'You can't be serious.' Leaning back in the wicker chair, Ivy shook her head. 'She'll never agree to host a ball for you.'

Olivia ate another spoonful of ice. She kept her eyes on the spoon as she placed it carefully next to the glass. 'No. But she might if *you* asked.'

Bloody hell.

'Olivia, I think you grossly overestimate my influence on Philippa.' Ivy indulged in another spoonful.

'We must try, Ivy. The orphanage is in desperate need of funds, and the Committee of Concerned Ladies for Community Betterment can only do so much with the limited pin money we are privy to. Not like a certain duchess who has a veritable fortune at her disposal.'

'Not all titled members of the beau monde are flush with money.'

Olivia sent Ivy a dark look. 'I'm aware. But the duchess is not one of the many titled poor. And more importantly, every lord and lady south of Scotland is tripping over themselves to win her favour. You are her friend. Surely she wouldn't refuse your request to throw a charitable ball, would she?'

Ivy couldn't imagine what Philippa's reaction might be as she'd never dreamed of asking her for something so outlandish. But the orphanage did need money, and the beau monde would follow Philippa's lead like lemmings.

'Can you not ask your husband if he might be willing to host the ball? I'm sure I could get Philippa to attend.'

Olivia almost spit out her spoonful of cherry confection. 'Percy? I dare not ask him for anything. Funding Hyacinth's debut has put him in a foul mood, even though he brought me back from Europe especially to manage the task.'

Ivy had not asked Olivia about her relationship with her daughter. Rumours swirled that Lord Smithwick banished Olivia to Europe for ten years, keeping her separate from the girl. But she could hardly ignore the topic now Olivia mentioned it.

'You must be so excited for her debut.'

Olivia's green eyes misted, and her chin quivered. She pushed away her nearly empty *tasse á glace*. 'Much trust has been broken between us. I am working to regain her faith, but it has not been easy.' For a horrifying moment, Ivy worried her friend might burst into tears in front of some of the beau monde's most vicious gossips.

Throwing her head back, Ivy laughed so loud, she worried she might upend the unsteady café table.

Shocked from her tears, Olivia looked around the room, then back to Ivy. 'What on earth are you—'

'Don't let them see your pain,' Ivy whispered before breaking into another peal of false cheer.

Olivia tried, at first softly and then with more gusto, garnering the attention of several young ladies licking ices and fluttering their fans.

The ladies leaned closer, so Ivy spoke loud enough for them to hear. 'Can you even merit it? The poor viscount caught with his trousers around his knees in the middle of the park while his poor wife tried to shield him with her parasol. His tailor is sure to be looking for a new job before summer is over.' Scooping the last spoonful of elderflower ice, she ate it triumphantly.

The young ladies to her left twittered and gasped as Olivia shook her head, her shoulders shaking. 'An almost unbelievable tale.' Leaning closer, she lowered her voice. 'Thank you.'

Ivy was used to being the woman who received support from others. It felt good to be the one providing help to a friend. 'You might want to wait on your thanks until after I've spoken with Philippa.'

'I'm hoping we can arrange the ball by the end of the month. That gives us two weeks.'

Again, Ivy's mouth dropped open. 'That's hardly any time at all.'

Olivia shrugged. 'She has us to help.'

Ivy snorted. 'Yes, I'm sure she'll welcome your help with open arms. I don't know why you two dislike one another, but it doesn't bode well for a joint venture.'

'It is not I who dislikes Lady Winterbourne. Indeed, I hardly know her. Yet, since I returned from Europe, she has snubbed me at every event we've attended. If you wish to understand the cause of our discord, you must direct your inquiries to the duchess, not me.'

Ivy stood, smoothing a hand over her skirts. 'If we hope to gain her support for this ball, I don't think discussing her feelings about you will help.'

Olivia raised an eyebrow in a look Ivy was tempted to tell her was very similar to her nemesis. 'Fine by me. I don't need to court her approval. I only hope she can put aside whatever petty issues she has to support the children.'

Ivy clutched her reticule tightly, taking comfort in the weight. 'I think she will. I shall visit Philippa immediately. If we are to have this ball in a fortnight, there is much to do.'

Olivia rose, pulling Ivy into another hug. 'Thank you, Ivy. You are a good friend. I don't deserve such kindness.'

Ivy squeezed her shoulders. 'We all deserve kindness, Olivia.'

Olivia released Ivy, painting a bright smile over her face like one might paint a porcelain plate. 'I'm off to meet Hyacinth at the modiste's. Wish me luck. She forbade me from joining her, but she needs to understand I respond to ultimatums about as well as she does.'

Ivy exhaled a long breath. 'It seems we both have challenging conversations ahead. I shall wish you luck if you do the same for me.'

Olivia nodded. 'Good luck, Ivy.'

'Good luck, Olivia.'

Ivy smiled at her friend, then turned and started weaving back through the crowd. She was jostled by a boisterous group of young men, nearly tripped over a little girl with a large red stain on her white cotton dress, and deftly sidestepped a lad as he ran full tilt through the store with a dripping glass of coffee ice. When she emerged onto the street, she sighed with relief until she thought of the task ahead.

'How the devil am I going to convince Philippa to host a charity ball... for Olivia?'

She got no answer from the bustling crowd as she hailed a hackney to take her the short drive to Grosvenor Square. It wasn't until she was sitting in another musty carriage, she felt the crinkle of something in her pocket. Her fingers closed around parchment. As she withdrew the small, sealed note, the elderflower ice curdled in her belly.

Head of a crow. Body of a wolf. Tail of a snake.

The Devil's Sons had sent Ivy a message.

10

It had been a brutal day at work. Edward had called around to Lord Augustus Thurston's house, hoping to convince the man to let Edward interview his son, only to find the house in a state of mourning. Lord Thurston refused to meet with Edward, but the butler informed him Clarence Thurston had an unfortunate accident that morning while cleaning his duelling pistols. The entire house was in a state of shock.

'I spoke with him just before the accident. Delivered a note for him, and all seemed well. He didn't even have his guns laid out.' The butler's face was white, his eyes glassy. Edward knew it was wrong to ask the man questions when he was still reeling from the death of his young master and revealing more than he should, but he pressed forward.

'Do you remember anything about the note you delivered? Anything strange or unusual?'

The butler shook his head, his face clouded with confusion. 'No, it was just a note. From one of his friends, I'm sure, as the seal was familiar to me.'

Edward's heart pounded so hard, he could feel the pulse in

his throat. 'Was it a distinct image? Head of a crow, body of a wolf, tail of a snake?'

'Yes. How did you know?' The butler's gaze sharpened on Edward, his lips hardening into a firm line as if realising he'd said too much. 'You must leave. The family needs their privacy. I insist.' He straightened to his full height – close to a foot shorter than Edward – and waved over a much larger footman.

Edward nodded, retreating to the entrance. 'Of course. Please extend my deepest condolences to the family.'

He returned to his office convinced that the Devil's Sons had claimed another victim. Whatever threat they held over poor Clarence Thurston's head was enough for the man to take his own life.

Damnation! If they are willing to kill a baron's son, how easily might they target the daughter of a dead duke?

Impotent rage boiled like acid. The need to find Ivy and ensure she was safe nearly overwhelmed him. Before he could call back his coach and do just that, Reading approached with a message from Philippa.

'Lady Winterbourne sent a note. She requests your presence post-haste. I wonder if you will get any work done today with all this rushing hither and thither,' he mused.

Edward had no time to engage in verbal warfare with his secretary. He hadn't yet removed his coat, so he simply nodded at Reading, turned, and swept out of 4 Whitehall Place only to have his rage further stoked upon arrival at the duchess' mansion.

The very woman he couldn't seem to stop thinking about sat serenely next to Philippa on her plum settee. He barely had time to register relief before Philippa shattered his calm by handing him yet another note to inspect. This one found in Ivy's pocket with the damning seal of the Devil's Sons and actually signed by one of the remaining two leaders. The Wolf. Just thinking such a dangerous man had been so close to Ivy was enough to shatter Edward's thin shield of control.

Fear washed in and swept away logical thought. 'I cannot believe you left the orphanage on your own and traipsed halfway across London to *eat ices*. I certainly hope the treat was worth risking your life.'

Foolish woman! Has she no idea of the dangers facing her?

The Wolf had been close enough to Ivy to sneak a note into her pocket, and on the heels of discovering Clarence Thurston's 'accidental' death, it was enough to make Edward consider locking Ivy away from harm in some tower. The missive slipped into her pocket could just as easily have been a blade thrust into her belly or a bullet embedded in her chest. The very idea turned Edward's blood to ice and filled his chest with an unholy rage.

Belatedly, he realised she did not know of this increased threat as he had yet to inform them of his morning's discoveries. In staccato sentences full of barely contained frustration, he described his morning visit to Lord Thurston's and was gratified to see Ivy's eyes widen and her cheeks pale. While he despised the thought of frightening her, a little fear could be healthy in promoting caution.

'Dead?'

Edward nodded.

'Do you think he intentionally killed himself because of something in the note he received?' Philippa asked.

Edward nodded once more.

Ivy's delicate throat constricted as she swallowed. 'While I certainly held no fond feelings for Clarence Thurston, I wouldn't wish such a fate on anyone.'

'Do you see now how foolhardy it was to traipse across

London on your own?' Edward asked, confident her contrition would be forthcoming.

Ivy crossed her arms over her chest, anger bringing rosy colour to her cheeks. 'I hardly expected my life to be at risk by joining a friend in a public place.'

'Indeed. A woman should have the freedom to wander at will without risking her life. Blaming Ivy for the threat others pose is an illogical argument. I expect better from you, Edward.' Philippa glared at Edward. Shame licked the edges of his anger.

Ivy glanced at Philippa; her tremulous smile almost broke him. 'Thank you.'

Leaning back on the plush pillows, Philippa raised perfectly arched brows. 'I'm not saying I've forgiven you for joining forces with *that* harridan.'

Ivy exhaled, pressing her lips together. She swung her gaze from Philippa back to Edward before standing. 'Clarence Thurston's death is a tragedy, but one he invited with his own actions. I won't let fear of these men stop me in my pursuits, and I won't apologise for my behaviour today because I've done nothing wrong. I met with a *friend*.' She glared at Philippa for a moment, who responded by thwacking her fan against her palm. 'To discuss a philanthropic venture that would be incredibly beneficial for the *orphans* under my care. An endeavour no one in this room is obligated to assist me with, might I add.'

Philippa rolled her eyes at that.

Ivy continued. 'It is even more imperative we determine what the Devil's Sons are about and stop them. I only wish I had paid more attention to who was around me at Gunter's. Mayhap I could have identified the Wolf, but we are one step closer. Then the commissioner can go back to his life, I can settle into being headmistress without threat to my wards or myself, and you can sit in your beautiful parlour and hate whomever you choose in peace.'

Philippa raised a brow. 'I do not hate Olivia Smithwick. I just don't appreciate being manipulated for my social and financial power.'

Ivy huffed out a dry laugh. 'You do hate Olivia. But you are right. It isn't fair to coerce you into throwing a charity ball if you have no desire to do so. I shall tell her you are disinclined to host. Now. Can we please get back to this note?' Ivy leaned forward and tapped a finger on the parchment sitting next to her teacup.

Edward wanted to tear out his hair. 'Do you not understand the danger is only increasing while you are talking of balls? A man took his own life today because of the Devil's Sons.'

Philippa and Ivy swivelled to him in unison. 'We are quite aware of the risks facing us, Edward. While you froth and foam over their threats, Ivy and I are working on how to eliminate them. Would you care to join us, or should you return to your office at Scotland Yard?'

These women are impossible!

But he was hardly going to abandon them. 'Fine. What charity ball? And how does that have anything to do with this note?'

'It doesn't.' Philippa rounded on him.

'It doesn't,' Ivy snapped at the same time. A flash of something dangerous in her eyes unaccountably heated Edward's blood. 'I am throwing a charity ball with Olivia to drum up funds for the orphanage. That's why I was at Gunter's. Not just to eat an ice.' Her jagged stare could have cut Edward in half.

Well done, Lady Ivy.

It was intoxicating to watch her step into her power, even if her anger was directed at Edward.

'Now that's cleared up, perhaps we can return to the matter at hand.' Ivy picked up the note and read it aloud. '"Danger and death await you if you choose not to heed our warning. Leave Islington now, or you shall share in your family's fate. The Wolf." A bit melodramatic.' But Edward wasn't fooled by the brave face Ivy showed them. He heard the hitch in her voice.

'Perhaps you should stay with me for a while. I can have Stokes make up a bed for you immediately.' Philippa stood and walked to the bell pull, but Ivy stopped her.

Ivy's cheeks went pale even as she straightened her shoulders. 'No. The children need me. I won't run away like some frightened little mouse no matter what everyone thinks.'

'You are no mouse, Ivy. Trust me on that. You can fight. And you will fight. But not alone.' Philippa pulled the decorative rope that would summon her butler.

'And you mustn't venture out into the streets without an escort.' Edward could not allow Ivy to place herself in such vulnerable situations.

Ivy let the note fall into her lap as she looked at him. 'I don't believe you have any say over what I must and mustn't do, Commissioner Worthington. You are neither my father, my brother, nor my husband. My choices are my own.' Her finger tap-tap-tapped against the note.

'Damn it, Ivy. Don't you see I'm trying to protect you?' Edward stood, pacing like an agitated jungle cat. He'd never had to deal with such a restless feeling in his chest. Fear. Frustration. An incessant need to growl and claw at anything or anyone who might get close to Ivy. He felt like some crazed animal, and he hated it. 'You refuse to listen to reason.'

Philippa arched a black brow and followed Edward with her far too astute gaze. 'I wouldn't question a woman's reason,

Edward. We are far more reasonable than our male counter-parts. Though, in this instance, I fear you make a point.'

Edward took perverse joy in Ivy's shocked look.

I am right, sometimes.

'Pardon?' Ivy focused her anger on Philippa, which was a nice reprieve for Edward.

Philippa shrugged a shoulder. 'I hate to admit it, but he is. The Devil's Sons are becoming bolder by the day, and I won't risk your life to prove a point about a woman's right to independence.'

Ivy clenched her teeth. 'This is ridiculous. So, I'm to just stay under lock and key indefinitely?'

'Oh, I don't think it will take too long to flush out our prey. In fact, I have an idea.' Philippa's crimson lips curled in a smile that inspired pure dread within Edward. He'd seen that look before.

'Dare I ask?' He steeled himself for something dreadful.

'We've already caught one of the Devil's Sons' leaders. The Snake. The Wolf has just shown his hand with this note, and once we catch him, the Crow will have nowhere to hide. Powerful men who rule by fear expect to be obeyed. The best way to provoke this wolf into a rash decision is to defy his orders. He wants Ivy to leave the orphanage, but we'll announce the opposite. Ivy Cavendale will become the champion of all orphans.'

The parlour door opened, and a dour-faced butler with the military posture of a general and the disapproving brow of a priest slowly entered.

'You rang for me, Your Grace? Are you in need of your lap blanket? I know older ladies are more susceptible to the cold.' His face remained impassive, but there was a hint of triumph in the way he tilted his chin up.

Philippa and her butler had been waging war against each

other since the duke died over ten years past. It was a rare treat to watch one of their skirmishes, and Edward appreciated the distraction from their tense conversation.

Philippa's mouth crimped at the corner. She exhaled long and low through her nose. 'Don't be stupid, Stokes. Your thoughts must be dusty from lack of use. Do try to focus. There is much to be done.'

'Of course, Your Grace. Done for what?' Stokes kept his gaze focused on the carpet in front of him, the perfect picture of obedience.

'For the charity ball we are going to host, of course.'

Ivy's face broke into an astonished smile at the same time Stokes' lips pulled down in a pained expression.

'And when is this wonderful event taking place?' Stokes could have been asking how long it might take dysentery to kill a person.

'Two weeks. So we've no time to spare. Invitations must be sent immediately. Just think what fun you'll have decorating, Stokes.' Based on Philippa's smile and Stokes' heavy sigh, Edward guessed he wouldn't be having much fun at all.

'Thank you, Philippa! Truly.'

Philippa narrowed her gaze, looking quite fierce. 'Where else would we announce your decision to stay on as headmistress of All Soul's Orphanage indefinitely?'

'May I have the note? I would like to compare the writing to the one we found on Lord Thurston.' Edward stood from the settee and walked to Ivy. She tilted her nose up, her wide mouth pressed together in an expression leaving no doubt in his mind what she thought of him. She was livid.

So be it. Anger is an emotion I know well. Anger I can manage.

It was every other emotion Ivy inspired within him that he found difficult to contain. Emotions best left unexamined and locked away in the dark corners of his soul. But for whatever reason, every time he was in Ivy's presence, those rogue feelings started banging on the walls, demanding attention, fighting to be let free, wanting to run riot through his system like a terrible fever.

Handing the note over with no other comment, Ivy returned her attention to Philippa. 'Olivia will be so thrilled.'

Philippa's lip curled as though she smelt something rotten.

'Is Her Grace's indigestion acting up? Should I instruct Cook to prepare you stewed prunes again?' Stokes' mouth twitched as he rocked ever so slightly on his heels.

Philippa blinked at the man. 'I hardly think you have time to be making ridiculous suggestions when there is a ball to organise.'

'Of course, Your Grace.' Stokes bowed his head in a jerky movement and turned, slowly exiting the room.

Philippa hissed out a disgusted breath. 'I should pension the bastard off.'

'Then who would you practise taking shots at?' Edward asked.

'I'm just so glad you are willing to host the ball, Philippa. Truly. We really do need the funds most desperately.' Ivy stood, and Edward couldn't help noticing how her day dress fell in soft folds. The simple cut highlighted Ivy's long, lean lines. He ached to touch her as he had at the Widow's Ball. To feel her pressed against him.

To lie naked with her.

A shocking thought to have in Philippa's parlour. But once the image crept into his mind, it was impossible to dispel. There was something achingly intimate about two bodies stripped of their shields, sheltering one another, skin against skin.

As if he needed a reminder of all the reasons he deserved no such sweetness in his life, Philippa cleared her throat, her gaze once more on Edward.

'I think it's time you escorted Ivy home. Do try to make sure she doesn't have to save you from any more pistol-wielding gentlemen, Edward. It is your job to protect her, you'll remember.'

Lovely of her to bring up his failure to keep Ivy safe. Just as he had failed Philippa so many years ago. A timely reminder.

Ivy turned her back to Edward, facing Philippa instead. 'I'm sure Commissioner Worthington has much to do without escorting me home.'

Ivy moved to the door, but Edward was faster, catching her hand and pulling her to an abrupt stop. The flash in Philippa's eyes should have warned him, but it was too late. She'd already seen Edward's frantic reaction. Knowing Philippa's quick mind, she would form conclusions far too close to the truth. He dropped Ivy's hand as though it burned him.

'As Philippa pointed out, it is my job to ensure your safety, Lady Ivy. My carriage is outside, and I will happily escort you back to the orphanage. I'm sure Reading will inform me of any pressing matters at 4 Whitehall Place should they arise. In the meantime, there is plenty of paperwork I can accomplish just as easily in my borrowed room at the orphanage as I could in my office. Philippa, would one of your footmen be so good as to run a note to Reading? He can send me my files.' Maybe Philippa would think his concern was merely about protecting Ivy. Nothing more.

'Of course.' Philippa nodded. 'Ivy, I need to speak with Edward alone for a moment.'

Or maybe she will see right through me and cut off my bollocks once Ivy steps out of the parlour.

Ivy looked from Philippa to Edward, then back again. Her brow quirked.

Edward bit the inside of his cheek. He would not be charmed by a woman's brow. It was ridiculous.

'Of course.' But the look she gave Philippa was full of hidden meaning.

What the devil are they discussing? And how do women communicate with each other without saying a word?

It was a trick he'd love to learn.

'We shan't be long.' Philippa took Ivy's hand and squeezed it. 'Edward will meet you in the entryway in a few minutes.'

Ivy did not glance at Edward as she left the parlour. Her anger with him was increasing by the moment, but he refused to feel guilty.

I'm trying to protect her.

He followed Philippa with his gaze as she walked across the room and peered out the window. She stretched the silence so tightly, Edward was sure he could hear the fabric of time tear just a little. But he wouldn't speak first. She called this meeting.

So, she can bloody well start the conversation.

Edward strolled around the settee and tugged up his trousers to take a seat. Folding his hands in front of him, he leaned back and sighed.

Philippa turned to face him and rolled her eyes. 'You won't admit it. So, fine. I shall say it for you. You like Ivy.'

'She is a kind, thoughtful woman. I'm sure a great number of people like her. Yourself included, and you like far fewer people than I do, Philippa.'

Tsking, Philippa turned back to the window, brushing her hand over the thick, woven curtain. 'Don't ruin my opinion of you by being so wilfully ignorant.'

Something in her tone cracked Edward's composure,

allowing scissures of irritation to burn through his shell of control.

'I rather thought your opinion of me was irrevocably destroyed all those years ago. Isn't that what this conversation is really about? Warning me away from Ivy? Reminding me of all the reasons why I will never deserve that kind of happiness? Because trust me, I am aware.'

Philippa left the window and walked to the chair opposite Edward, but she did not sit. Instead, she rested her hand on the back of it. 'Don't be an idiot, Edward. I don't want you to spend the rest of your life in misery. *She* wouldn't have wanted that either.'

'Nor would she want you to spend the rest of your life mourning her. That is why you still wear the colours of a newly widowed woman, though your husband has been dead for more than a decade. Because you are still grieving her. Tell me I'm wrong?'

'I find darker colours to be more flattering.'

'Bollocks! How can you possibly expect me to entertain ideas of love or marriage if you refuse to move forward?'

'Because I lost the other half of my soul, Edward.' Philippa's voice wavered, and tears shone in her eyes in a shocking display of emotion. 'I lost my life partner.'

'And I am to blame for that, Philippa.'

She closed her eyes. A single tear tracked down her cheek as she slowly shook her head. 'I thought that for a very long time. But I was wrong.' Wiping the tear away as if it never existed, she pinned Edward with her gaze. 'It was easier to hate you than forgive you, but I can't find peace within myself if I'm still at war with you.'

Edward slipped off the settee and went to Philippa. 'I don't deserve your forgiveness, Philippa.'

'You're getting it anyway.'

What was the appropriate response for such a stern offering of grace?

A handshake?

Too American.

A hug?

Most definitely not.

A carefully penned note of thanks?

I'm not an eighty-year-old dowager.

'Err. Well. Thank you.'

Philippa rolled her eyes. 'Dear God. I wasn't sure things could get more awkward, but you've managed to find a way. Bravo. Let's never mention this again.'

Rocking back on his heels, relief swept through him. 'Yes, wonderful suggestion.'

'Now, will you finally admit you *like* Ivy?'

As quickly as the relief arrived, it was gone again. Edward exhaled a pained breath. She was incessant. But he couldn't lie to Philippa. 'I do. I like her very much.'

Dear God. I've admitted it.

Something about saying the words aloud gave them power. Like incanting a spell. He felt a rush of energy flow through his body.

Philippa's cobalt eyes flashed. 'I knew it. A word of advice.'

She wasn't asking his permission, but Edward nodded anyway.

'Some fears must be faced alone. Others require the support of a friend. Be a friend to her before you are anything else.'

Damnation. I hate when she is right.

'I'm not sure I'm the kind of friend she needs.'

Philippa tapped a finger against her lip. 'I'm not sure either.' Before he could respond to her encouraging show of confidence, she continued speaking. 'But there is only one way to find out. I wouldn't keep her waiting much longer. If I know Ivy, she'll find her own way home soon.'

'Right.' Edward gave Philippa an abbreviated bow, then walked to the door.

'Oh, and Edward?'

He paused in the door frame.

'I will cut you open and hang you from London Bridge by your own entrails if you hurt her.' Philippa's smile was stunning. 'Fair warning.'

And how does one respond to that? Certainly not a handshake or a hug.

He settled for a nod. 'I would expect nothing less from you.'

11

_____

The carriage ride home was a silent, uncomfortable affair.

How dare he assume he can control my actions? I have lived years of my life under the thumb of my father's wishes. My brother's wishes. Society's wishes. Never once have I been free to make choices based on my own wishes.

But she'd done that today. A simple visit to Gunter's felt like crossing a line. Despite knowing Edward didn't want her to venture out alone, despite society deeming such behaviour brazen, and despite even Philippa disapproving of Ivy's actions because of Olivia's involvement, she made a choice based on her own judgement.

Certainly, a note had been slipped into her pocket. And yes, she might have been in some danger, but danger could find a young lady anywhere. A carriage could lose control on a sunny street in Mayfair, she could slip out of her saddle while riding her horse, fever could sweep through the city, claiming peers and paupers alike.

I can't live my life constantly fearing all the things that might *happen. Past trauma and tragedy have yet to break me. Must I be so afraid of future trauma and tragedy?*

'No,' she said aloud.

'Pardon?' Edward asked.

She shook her head. 'I wasn't speaking to you.'

After a protracted moment, Edward nodded. 'Of course. There are only two of us in this carriage. How silly of me to assume you might be addressing me.'

'Yes, exactly,' Ivy agreed.

And what did Philippa wish to speak with him about?

She wouldn't dare lower herself to ask, though curiosity made it hard to focus on anything else. Forcing her gaze out of the window, she took in the beautiful summer afternoon. The ladies of Mayfair were out in full force, no doubt returning home from their social calls. Ivy determined she would spend the remainder of the carriage ride counting floral hats. A far better pastime than speaking with the pompous ass of a commissioner. And it gave her something to watch other than him during their carriage ride home. Whenever she did look at him, she found her eyes drifting to his mouth, which was neither helpful in maintaining her ire, nor was it beneficial to her overall equanimity.

His lips had firmed into a hard line, and she was not considering how they might feel pressed against her own mouth. Nor was she imagining how his fingers, which were currently drumming a staccato beat on his muscled thigh, might coast over her skin. Ivy forced her gaze back to the window once more and resumed counting.

Twelve hats draped in flowers. Thirteen if I count that debutante with those unfortunate drooping daisies.

The carriage barely rolled to a stop before Ivy leaned over and pushed open the door. Not waiting for the driver to clamber down and set the step, she nimbly jumped to the gravel drive and crunched her way to the front stairs.

If Edward protested, she didn't hear him. Sailing into the orphanage, Ivy refused to look behind her to see if he followed. The children would just be finishing their time in the yard. Ivy made her way through the mansion, letting herself onto the back veranda and gardens beyond. The sound of laughter and shouting greeted her, as did the scent of honeysuckle and hyacinth.

Once upon a yesteryear, Ivy would have been like one of those ladies walking with a chaperone through Mayfair on her way back to her father's house after visiting with Millie. She would be dreading whatever evening activities would be expected of her. Helping her father host a dinner for important lords, dressing for a ball where she would spend the evening dusting the wall with her gown or hiding away in her room, hoping her father would not visit in the darkest hours of early morning.

Now, she was the headmistress of an orphanage and planning an evening of reading to the children, retiring to her clean little bedroom with her fluffy kitten, and disappearing into her penny dreadful while sipping a cup of hot chocolate. Free from fearing any unexpected visitor.

But what about expected visitors? What about invited *visitors?*

Because even feeling frustrated with Edward hadn't dissipated the attraction simmering beneath the surface of her skin. Tension had been building within Ivy since Widow Lovemore's ball, and her argument with Edward in Philippa's parlour only drew the strings tighter. Her anger toward him strangely highlighted his physical appeal. Which made very little sense.

How can a woman want to smack a man and kiss him at the same time?

After their conversation at the ball, Ivy found herself thinking about kissing far more than usual.

That's because I never used to think about kissing at all.

Now, it popped into her mind at the most inopportune times. When she was lying in bed trying to go to sleep. Tallying the weekly budget. Even during their carriage ride home.

And a lot of good all this imagining is doing me.

So instead, Ivy spent the remainder of the day focusing on something that did make sense. Taking care of the children. She didn't see Edward when the girls and boys traipsed in from their playtime to tackle their chores. She didn't see him in the dining hall at dinner when Sarah sat on one side of her and Henry sat on the other, pouring her water whenever her cup reached halfway empty. She didn't see him in the ballroom when she read the children the next chapter of *The Tenant of Wildfell Hall*. Not that she was looking for him. In point of fact, she was glad he wasn't skulking around. The last person she wanted to see was Edward Worthington.

Take your perfectly shaped mouth, strong thighs, smouldering glare, and stupid glossy black hair, ball it up, shove it in your pipe, and smoke it.

When the children were abed and she was bringing her pot of hot chocolate up from the kitchen, the wavering light peeking out from under his door caused her slippered feet to pause.

Should she check on him? Had he even eaten?

It's not my responsibility to ensure he eats. I'm not his mother. I'm certainly not his wife.

The very thought caused a flutter in her chest. A rather fizzing kind of flutter.

Ridiculous. The last thing I want is to be married.

Her heart thudded painfully.

Stupid organ. What could you possibly know about anything?

And now, she was arguing with her heart.

Brilliant.

Lifting her chin, she started to walk away when Edward's door flew open.

* * *

Ivy jumped back, bobbling her burden. With fast hands and determination only melted chocolate could inspire, she managed to right the tray.

'What are you doing?' she hissed, mindful there were twenty-seven children supposedly sleeping. The last thing she needed was to wake them or, more likely, pique their curiosity and have them pressing little ears against the door to better hear the raised voices echoing down the hall.

'I was coming to find you,' Edward hissed back.

'Why? I'm going to bed.'

Edward took the tray from her hands. 'I need to show you something.' He turned and walked back into his room. With her tea tray.

With my bloody hot chocolate. Blackguard.

Ivy stormed after him, shutting the door behind her so the children were less likely to hear her blistering tirade against the thieving scoundrel.

'That's *my* hot chocolate.' She pointed to the pot as Edward carefully placed the tray on his rumpled bed.

There was a decided lack of space for adequate furniture in this room. With Millie's contribution of a proper mattress and bed frame dominating the left side, Edward had managed to squeeze in a small desk and straight-back chair against the right wall. The desk was littered with papers, and a small lamp balanced precariously on the edge.

Ivy cocked her head at the new furniture, momentarily distracted from reclaiming her evening treat. 'Did you take the desk and chair from the schoolroom?'

'Yes. Henry helped me move it in here while the children were completing their chores earlier. Awfully kind of the lad. I didn't think you would mind.'

Ivy shrugged. 'I don't. It's just... Well. I'm sorry there aren't better accommodations for you.'

Why am I apologising to him? He stole my hot chocolate!

Because looking around the small space, it was glaringly obvious that the Commissioner of Scotland Yard, a man holding the title of a bloody duke who had his own Mayfair mansion no doubt replete with servants, a butler, and many fine desks, was sacrificing his comforts. And for what? To protect Ivy? She hardly merited such effort.

'I am quite content, I assure you.' He tucked his hands into the pockets of his trousers, looking every bit a man at ease.

While the man always presented himself as neat as a pin, his room revealed a much more chaotic side to Edward Worthington. His jacket hung haphazardly on the desk chair, books were stacked in leaning piles on the floor, and his boots were toppled over each other, half tucked under the bed. Despite the mess, the entire room smelled of clean linen, coffee, and Jamaican spice.

Ivy belatedly realised an incredibly important fact.

I am alone, with Edward, in his bedroom. And he's not even wearing boots.

Glancing down, she noticed he had remarkably well-shaped toes.

Dancing devils. I just strolled into a man's bedroom and shut the door behind me. What have I done?

Edward must have seen her eyes widen because he leveraged

the one thing that might keep her in his room. 'I promise I shall return your hot chocolate, and you can leave, but first will you please look at something with me?'

'I shouldn't be in here. Alone. With you. You're not even wearing stockings!' She couldn't stop staring at his feet.

'They are only bare feet. It isn't as if I'm without my shirt or trousers.'

The very idea!

Ivy's gaze crawled up his body with the bed behind him as an inspired backdrop. She tried to imagine what he might look like without his shirt and trousers, standing just there, with the backs of his knees almost touching the mattress. Errant thoughts about his black body hair skittered through her mind.

'If you keep looking at me like that, things might get quite a deal more scandalous than merely unstockinged feet.' Edward's voice had grown rough.

Ivy blinked, forcing her focus away from his thick thighs, wide shoulders, and trim waist to look at the floor.

Not the floor! Now I'm staring at his feet again.

She turned away from him completely, pressing a hand against her cheek. 'It is rather warm in this room, don't you think? Perhaps I should open a window.' But to do that, she would need to crawl over the bed as the window was on the left wall.

'I haven't noticed any issues with temperature until now.'

Ivy straightened her spine and turned back to face him. 'Well. It is sweltering.' She tapped her finger against her dress in agitation.

Edward's stern mouth softened. 'Would you prefer we relocate to the parlour?'

As if he would be any less appealing standing in the parlour with his bare feet, muscled arms stretching the fabric of his shirt, and smouldering stare.

How do blue eyes smoulder? Shouldn't they be cool like a deep pond or stormy ocean?

She was getting distracted. Again. 'I would prefer you show me whatever it is that has you stealing my tray and luring me into your room so I can reclaim my hot chocolate and retire to my bed.'

'Luring you into my room? Shocking accusations! I am the Commissioner of Scotland Yard. I track down the evil villains thieving trays of hot chocolate; I don't lure innocent ladies into my room with those trays.'

I am not amused.

But the fizzing bubble of laughter trapped between her belly and throat begged to differ.

Edward wagged his finger at her like a scolding headmaster. 'Besides, you stormed in here of your own accord in pursuit of confectionery delights.'

Forcing her mouth to remain in a firm line, she put her hands on her hips in her best imitation of a scolding head-mistress. 'Which I never would have done if you weren't an evil, chocolate-thieving villain.'

For a moment, they stared at each other. While Edward's eyes danced with mischief, his face remained deadly serious. Ivy wasn't about to break first. It was an epic battle against the laughter threatening to defeat them both. Ivy didn't usually win battles, but she was determined to claim this victory.

The left corner of Edward's mouth twitched, then the right. He shook his head as a breathtaking smile changed him from stern commissioner to charming duke. 'You have me there.'

Ivy felt a surge of pride wash through her. She beat him.

What an unusual and addictive feeling. She quite liked winning. She might try doing it again.

Deciding to be gracious in her victory, she dropped her hands and clasped them behind her. 'What is it you wish to show me?'

He moved to his desk, waving her over and pulling out the chair for her. Ivy was achingly aware of his large, strong body just inches away from her as she carefully sat.

He leaned over her, pulling two notes into the circle of light cast by the lamp. Jamaican spice, soap, and the faintest hint of linseed enveloped her. Turning slightly, she inhaled, drawing his scent into her lungs and holding him there as something tightened in her centre, then slowly began to unfurl.

Edward clenched his hand into a fist. Almost as if he knew the strange effect he was having on her. Almost as if she might be having a similar effect on him.

He had rolled up his sleeves. She hadn't noticed before.

I was too distracted by his toes.

His forearms were covered in a dusting of black hair, but it didn't hide the movement of muscle and sinew. He leaned ever so slightly closer to her.

'This is the note you found in your pocket.' He relaxed his fist and nudged one of the notes. His low voice caused a resonating hum across her skin.

'Yes.' She was far too breathless.

'And here is the one we found in Thurston's pocket.' He placed the second piece of parchment next to the first. With one hand on the back of her chair and the other on the desk next to her, he bracketed her body with his own. She should feel trapped. Caged. Frightened. But she didn't. If she turned her head, their faces would be almost touching. For a wild moment, she nearly acted on impulse and closed the distance between them. Which was sheer madness.

Focus on the note.

Clearing her throat and wiping suddenly damp hands on her skirt, she bent her head to better see both missives. 'The writing isn't the same.'

'Exactly.' Edward tapped a long finger on the upward stroke of the letter 'D' from Ivy's note. 'Whoever wrote this has a light hand.'

Ivy picked up the second piece of parchment, holding it closer to better inspect the ink markings. 'And this is a much heavier pen stroke. Also...' She rubbed the paper between her thumb and finger, then did the same with the second one. 'My note is on thicker parchment.' She flipped both pages over. 'Even the seals are slightly different. This wax is much darker.' Offering them to Edward so he could look, his fingers brushed against hers as he took them.

He cleared his throat and straightened, moving away from her and the lamplight. He squinted valiantly at the seals. 'Yes. Very good, Lady Ivy.'

'Just Ivy.'

Edward's gaze was sharp. 'What?'

'I think we can dispense with formalities. I have seen your naked toes, after all.' Her attempt at levity failed the moment 'naked' escaped her lips.

No lady would ever utter such scandalous words. I've become a wanton.

She stood, nearly knocking the chair over in her haste. 'Well. Right. I should go.'

Spinning away, she lunged for the door, let herself into the hall, and rushed to her room. It wasn't until she slammed the door behind her and leaned against it, breathing as hard as a stallion at full gallop, she realised.

'Damnation! The hot chocolate.'

Oh God. He's going to know I forgot it. And that I was too much of a ninny to go back and get it. Perhaps I could wait until he is abed and sneak into his room.

Ivy slid to the floor and thunked her head against the door. The kitten crawled out from under her bed and pounced on her lap.

'Ridiculous plan, kitty.'

The solid wood supporting her suddenly disappeared, and she fell backwards onto the floor. Her upper half was lying in the hallway while her legs were still in her room. The kitten hissed, leapt from her belly, and skittered down the hall.

Edward stood above her, the tray of hot coffee in his hand. 'A kitten.'

Scrambling to her feet, her chignon irrevocably destroyed, cheeks flaming, skin no doubt blotching like strawberries squished on a porcelain plate, Ivy searched desperately for something to say. Anything that wouldn't make her sound like an utter cake. 'Err, yes. That is my kitten.'

'Did you fall? Are you well?'

'I'm fine. I was sitting on the floor already so...'

Because that's what any young lady does after nearly kissing a man in his bedroom. She scurries away and sits ever so demurely on her floor with a kitten purring on her belly.

'Ah. Well. You forgot something.'

'I, err, yes. My hot chocolate. Thank you.'

I am the biggest fool in all the land.

Edward tipped his head in the direction of her open door. 'Shall I just...?'

It would be petty of her to wrestle the tray away from him so he couldn't enter her room. After all, she'd been in his bedroom. What harm could come of letting him into hers if only to deposit the tray and then leave?

Ivy nodded her head in jerky movements and motioned to the desk. A much neater version than Edward's with her lists neatly stacked in organised piles.

'You can put it there.'

How odd to have a man in her room. Her earlier wonderings came back to haunt her.

I have an invited *visitor. Though really, I only asked him in to be polite. And get my chocolate. Not because I want him in my room.*

It was no use. She had always been dreadful at telling lies.

Good gracious. I do want him in my room.

The space seemed much smaller than moments before as she followed him to her desk. She didn't realise she was hovering until Edward turned around after depositing the tray and nearly crashed into her. His large hands gripped her arms to steady her.

Don't look up. If you look up, you'll be lost in those eyes. You'll stare at his mouth. He'll know. He'll know what you're thinking.

She looked up. And lost herself in his eyes. Stared at his firm lips. And saw the flash in his gaze the moment he knew. He knew what she was thinking.

'Ivy—'

'I think I'd like you to kiss me,' she blurted.

Edward took a deep breath, his gaze searching. 'Do you think it, or do you know?' He rubbed his thumb back and forth over her bicep, and even through the thin cotton sleeve of her dress, she felt the spark of friction.

'I know.' Tilting her chin up, she refused to break eye contact. She would not let fear stop her. Because greater than her fear was a desire to finally understand. To experience the sensation of Edward's lips pressing against her own.

'Well, thank God for that.'

Slowly, so she had ample time to pull back, Edward lowered his head closer to hers. He never looked away. In her limited experience of watching people kiss and be kissed, they always closed their eyes. But he was watching her so closely, Ivy's heart fluttered madly. His pupils dilated, nearly swallowing the dark-blue irises. His mouth hovered a moment away from hers.

'You smell like Jamaican spice.'

Oh, God. I said that. Out loud. Idiot!

He froze, the skin around his eyes crinkling in a smile. 'Do you like Jamaican spice?'

Ivy licked her lips. 'Yes. V-very much.'

'More than chocolate?' His breath skated over her lips like the echo of a kiss.

'More than chocolate.' She slid her hand up his rather rippling bicep and held firm to his granite shoulder.

He leaned down, but instead of pressing his mouth against hers, he brushed his lips lightly over her cheekbone. It felt like the graze of a moth's wing. Moving slowly, he feathered kisses over the corner of her eye, the curve of her jaw where it met her ear, the sensitive skin of her neck where her pulse beat madly, the tip of her nose, until she was simultaneously burning like a flame and melting into a puddle.

'Kiss me. Please!' It wasn't a request. It was a demand. She tightened her grip on his linen shirt. If he didn't take her mouth with his own immediately, she was quite certain her entire body would combust into flames.

'I am kissing you.'

Bastard!

Before she could pull away and unleash her venom on him

for being a heartless tease, he wrapped his long fingers around her neck, holding her still. His gaze consumed her. Ivy was certain the man could see beyond her shields, right into the hidden depths of her soul. Bending his head closer, he brushed his lips against hers.

Cripes. He's kissing me. I am being kissed.

She tingled from the soft sensation, but it wasn't enough. She wanted more.

Pushing up on her toes, Ivy's hands found their way over his strong shoulders, gripping his neck and pulling him closer.

12

Edward was drowning in a sea of glorious sweetness, and he wanted to dive deeper. When she asked – *told* – him to kiss her, he felt like a champion of old, claiming a hard-won victory. But he also knew he must use the utmost care. Ivy Cavendale was a dagger made of glass. Delicate, stunning, and infinitely dangerous. If she shattered, her jagged pieces would cut them both to ribbons.

But when she pressed her mouth more firmly against his and gripped his neck in her strong fingers, pulling him even closer, he was lost.

Ivy was vibrating with tension. 'More.'

He could give her more. He could give her everything.

Testing her desires and his own need, he flicked his tongue out, tracing the seam of her lips. Chocolate. She tasted of decadent, rich, bittersweet chocolate.

She inhaled sharply, and he pulled back. 'Too much?' He quirked his brow, forcing his desire to heel.

Her crystal-blue eyes were dazed with confused need. When

he expected her to pull away, she shook her head instead. 'No, I just didn't think you would... that is, I had no idea tongues were involved.'

Edward swallowed the laughter bubbling from his chest. 'You'll find tongues can be quite magical things. There's any number of ways one might use their tongue.'

Her eyes widened with unspoken questions. 'Truly?'

Edward brushed his finger along her hairline, marvelling at the beauty of her skin. 'Shall I tell you of all the things I wish to do with my tongue?'

She opened her wide mouth on a whispery inhalation. 'Umm...'

'I want to taste you. Right here.' He ran his thumb over a sensitive spot just behind her ear.

'You do?' Her bewilderment was dismantling the wall he'd built around his heart. A wall constructed to ensure he did not break his vow of living a single life. But while he might not merit the joy of connection, Ivy certainly did. And he so fervently wished to show her all the glories two people might share. If only for a little while.

'Will you allow it?'

He noted the moment her fear gave way to curiosity. 'I-I suppose. But...'

'We can stop whenever you choose.' No matter how far they travelled down this path, one word from her, one hitch in breath, one frozen muscle, and he would stop.

Be brave, Ivy. You are so much stronger than you think.

Her eyes held a world of racing thoughts he wished he could decipher. She blew out a breath. 'Fine.' She spoke as if agreeing to have her teeth removed or hair cut off.

'Fine?' He indulged temptation and inhaled her unique scent. 'I hope to make this far better than fine.'

She shrugged. 'I suppose we'll see.'

Edward raised his brows. 'A challenge? One thing you should know about me: I never back down from a challenge. It's the most assured way to get me to do something.'

'I can't imagine anything more challenging than making a tongue feel pleasurable.'

'Challenge accepted.' Kissing a line from the corner of her mouth to where her jaw met her neck, he nuzzled there a moment until he felt tension fall away from her muscles. When she once more gripped his neck, pulling him closer, he licked just behind her ear. She quivered in his arms. Sucking her soft skin into his mouth, he bit softly. She moaned, her lithe body rolling into him like a wave.

'Did I meet the challenge?' he asked, his lips brushing over the love bite.

'Yes.'

Yes. There might not be a more glorious word.

He took her lobe into his mouth and nibbled *just* hard enough to flirt with a sharp burst of pleasure.

'Oh, my,' she breathed.

Edward couldn't remember the last time he had been so overcome, so desperate to please. The women he usually entertained knew what they were about. It was a mutual meeting of needs between two experienced individuals. He focused on what he wished to get from the exchange, knowing the women did the same. It mattered to him that his partner found her own pleasure, but often, she knew exactly how to achieve her goal, and all that was required of Edward was to pay attention and follow her lead. It was akin to being given a map with an easily read key.

This was an entirely new experience. Ivy had no idea how her body reacted to pleasure. They were embarking on an unknown journey with no map at all, just instinct and a shared goal. This was a conversation full of twists, turns, and surprises. An adventure of discovery where his pleasure was intimately tied to Ivy's. This was connection on a level Edward had never before allowed himself to explore.

He might spend eternity in the fires of hell for claiming such pure sweetness when his life was full of ugly truths, but for a blessed moment, Edward didn't care. He pressed his mouth against Ivy's with more demand than before, brushing his lips over hers again and again until she gripped his hair and tugged. Her skin fairly hummed with need. He licked the seam of her mouth, and when she opened to him, he delved inside.

She tensed, but as he moved back, she followed him, not allowing the kiss to break. Edward slid his tongue over her teeth, sucking her top lip between his and biting softly.

Ivy growled. Actually growled. The sound skated along Edward's nerves, straight to his cock which filled with desperate demand. He slid his hands down to her hips and pulled her pelvis against his. The friction was glorious. Until every muscle in Ivy's body froze.

Edward immediately pulled back, shifting his hand to her neck and tilting her head so he could search her face. Her breath came in short gasps, her dilated eyes wide, her kiss-swollen lips parted. All potential signs of desire. All potential signs of fear. 'Too much?' he asked again.

This time, she bit her lip as her eyes filled with tears. She nodded. 'I'm sorry.'

'Don't apologise.' *I pushed her too far. Too fast. Idiot!* 'Never be sorry for telling me what you need. What you want or what you don't want. Especially what you don't want.'

'I just didn't realise... I didn't mean to do that to you. I shouldn't have... Father said that I was always tempting him.

Always making him want wicked things, do wicked things to himself.'

The surge of rage washing through Edward nearly eclipsed his control. But Ivy needed to feel safe. Giving in to his anger would not help her. So, he pushed his own feelings aside and focused on hers.

Gently squeezing her neck, he rubbed his thumb along her jawline. 'My body is responding because *I* want *you*. Not because you *made* me want you. A man's body is under his control. What a man does with it is determined by that man. Not the woman he desires.'

Ivy shook her head. 'But he said it doesn't work that way. A woman tempts the man and forces him to sin. Just as Eve ate the apple first, then tempted Adam.'

'Your father lied to you. Each person is responsible for their own choices, no matter who they are. You didn't make him do anything, Ivy. A little girl has no power to tempt her father. He was tempted because of his own evil sickness. You are *never* responsible for a man's desire, his actions, his sins. Those are his own.'

A fat tear escaped and rolled down Ivy's cheek. 'H-he told me my husband would take my body. It was his right. I would have no choice and whatever he wished to do – and Father delighted in describing all of the possible ways a man might break me, hurt me, control me – I would need to submit. Or be forced to submit. My body is a vessel for my husband's needs. His heirs. His pleasure.' She was choking on the words, gasping as though she couldn't draw air. 'That is my role as a wife. That is how the world works.'

But it shouldn't work this way. Not for Ivy. Not for any woman.

It was the same thinking that forced Philippa to give up her only love. That imprisoned every woman to a life where they had no control of their choices unless a man granted them the privilege of autonomy. And even then, society limited that autonomy.

It's unacceptable.

Edward acted on impulse, pulling her into a tight hug. 'So you have determined to never tie yourself to a husband. Because no one wants to sacrifice their freedom.' Her fine hair tickled his cheek as he held her, rubbing his hand up and down her back in smooth strokes.

'I can't. I would rather die.' Her body shook in heartbreaking sobs.

Edward desperately wished for the right words to soothe her. But there were none. So, he stayed silent and let her weep, trying to absorb her pain and make it his own.

When tears turned to sniffles and quaking became quivers, he pulled back. Her eyes were swollen, the tip of her nose turned red, and her cheeks splotched. He'd never seen a more beautiful, brave, brilliant woman.

'What do you need?'

She shook her head. 'I don't know.'

'Do you want to tell me what happened?'

'I never talk about him. I just want to forget him. Forget everything he said. Everything he did. He never touched me, but his words are here.' She smacked her head with the heel of her hand. 'He died, and I never even cried for him.'

'He doesn't deserve a single goddamned tear. Regardless of whether he touched you or not, he hurt you. Most horrifically.'

Ivy bit her lip and sniffed. 'What kind of a daughter doesn't grieve her father's death?'

'The kind who never had a father worthy of her. No one would fault you for dancing on the bastard's grave.' Edward took a breath, trying to pull his anger back. The last thing he wanted was to frighten Ivy. But the corner of her wide mouth tilted in a tremulous smile.

'I never thought about dancing on his grave.' A half-giggle, half-sob burst from her. Never was he prouder of his accomplishments than being able to make her laugh in this moment. 'Can you imagine?'

Edward nodded. 'Yes. I can.' Needing to change the subject before he did something really stupid, like pledging his life to making her laugh at least once every day, he stepped back, turning to the desk. 'Hot chocolate.' Picking up the pot, he turned. 'Would you like a cup?'

Ivy stared at him for a moment before her gaze dropped. 'That would be most kind.'

Ivy's room had as few furnishings as his own. She took two steps to her left and sat primly on the bed, her posture as proper as any lady taking tea in the most resplendent of parlours. Edward poured the rich, dark mixture into a cracked teacup and wished he could resurrect Lord Cavendale so he could rip him apart, one piece at a time. He turned and, with hands shaking, brought Ivy her cup of chocolate. 'I shall leave you to your solitude.' The last thing she needed was some brute of a man invading her space.

'No, stay. Please. Just for a bit. I... I don't want to be alone.'

Another brick in the wall he built crumbled. Then another. And another until the whole bloody fortification was falling around him.

'All right.' The only other seat in her room was the desk chair behind him, so he pulled it closer to the bed.

'Tell me something about yourself. Something funny. What scrapes did you get into as a boy?' Ivy sipped her chocolate and licked her top lip.

Edward swallowed the groan rumbling in his chest as he desperately wished to follow her example and lick her mouth.

This is not the time for me to be slobbering after her like some insatiable beast. She needs a distraction from the memories of her father.

He could provide her with that. For the next hour, he regaled her with tales of his youth. When he was only a boy of seven, he snuck out of the nursery with his sister to be midnight adventurers in the back garden of their country estate, only to be frightened off by a woodcock and caught by their nursemaid. 'Mrs Quimby was terrifying. My father felt strongly that children should be much like statues. Attractive. Silent. Still. Mrs Quimby endeavoured to make certain we accomplished that task.'

Ivy scrunched her face. 'That mustn't have been easy for you.'

Edward's smile faded. 'I rather think it was harder for Mrs Quimby than us. My father sacked her when he found Liza in the fountain diving for frogs.'

'Oh dear.' Ivy's eyes sparkled with mischief.

He forced his mind away from his sister. Even the pleasant memories turned painful, reminding him she was gone. Instead of lingering on old wounds that still bled, he told Ivy about a case he recently investigated. An earl was convinced his servant was stealing from him. After weeks of questioning the entire staff, a terrible storm blew through the countryside. The winds broke a bough from one of the lord's ancient oaks. A young groundsman discovered a cache of hidden treasures in a nest. Cufflinks, gold coins. Even a diamond ring. The real thief was a cunning magpie.

Ivy burst into laughter, covering her mouth. 'Did he apologise to the servant?'

Edward ran a hand over his jaw, scratching where the stubble was starting to itch. 'No.'

'Ah.' Ivy's lips hardened. 'Of course not. Why would he?'

'One thing I've learned through my work is that honourable titles rarely make honourable men.'

She nodded. 'But some men are good. Like you.' Ivy looked away from him, studying the pattern of her chipped teacup with an intensity worthy of an antiquity scholar deciphering Sanskrit.

Edward's stomach twisted. If only he were deserving of such high praise. 'No. I'm not. I've committed far worse crimes than the earl.'

Ivy caught him with her crystal-blue eyes. 'What crimes are you guilty of committing? Surely the Commissioner of Scotland Yard is above reproach.'

Exhaling a heavy sigh, Edward shook his head. 'No one is above reproach. But I shall not burden you with my sins.' The last thing he wanted was to change the way Ivy was looking at him. If she knew the truth of what he'd done, she would never be alone in a room with him again. And damn his selfish soul, he wasn't ready for that eventuality. 'It has been a long day. I will leave you to your rest.'

Standing from the desk chair, Edward carefully returned it to its proper place. Her desk was as neat and tidy as the woman who owned it. A drastic contrast to his own messy habits. Reading would approve of Ivy's commitment to organisation, something Edward had never mastered. But surely, she had a few messes tucked away somewhere. A drawer or cupboard full of odds and ends. Secret spaces of chaos he would love to explore. Picking up one of her lists, he couldn't stop the smile.

'Is this shopping list alphabetised?'

Ivy's cheeks grew pink, and the blush he loved bloomed on

her throat. 'No. Maybe. It helps to ensure I don't forget something.'

She stood and placed her cup on the tray, grabbing for the list as he quickly lifted it out of her reach. She tried again, lunging for him, her expression a mixture of determination and delight. He switched the list to his other hand behind his back. This time, when she tried to snatch it, she had to reach around his body, her face only inches from his own. He wrapped his arm around her waist to steady her as she stumbled, her body flush against his.

As swiftly as wind changing direction, the playful energy shifted. Ivy bit her lip, her eyes focusing on Edward's mouth. He felt her gaze like sun warming his skin. His body tightened. He knew she could feel his erection. Not wanting to repeat his earlier mistake, he immediately loosened his arm and stepped back.

'I don't want to frighten you, Ivy.' He couldn't stand to see the fear in her eyes. Not because of him or his stupid, optimistic cock. 'But just because my body is... reacting, it doesn't mean anything will happen. I swear it. Not without your permission.'

She stepped close enough to touch him, tracing the outline of his lips with her soft fingers. 'I don't want to be frightened. I hate it.' The vehemence in her words echoed through Edward. He would give *anything* to destroy her dread. But this wasn't his battle. It was hers. He couldn't face demons only she could see. But he could stand with her as she fought them. If she would allow it.

Stuffing the list in his pocket, he ran his hand down her arm in a stroke intending to comfort and pressed his forehead against hers. 'Sometimes, we have to face the fear. By doing so we discover it isn't what we thought at all. We light the lamp, and the shadows lose their power to haunt.'

Ivy shifted her head, her soft cheek brushing against his stubbled one. 'I wasn't frightened when we were kissing, or at least, not *very* frightened.'

'Because you are a woman of incredible courage.'

He could feel the apple of her cheek pressing against his own as she laughed. 'Hardly.'

Edward ran his hand over her silken hair. 'Most definitely.'

He was quite certain his body was going to explode with frustrated desire. But it was worth the glory of feeling Ivy's firm lips press softly against his jaw. 'I always thought kissing would be awful. And that was before I knew about tongues being involved. But when you licked me, it was... marvellous. Would I like licking you, I wonder?'

'Perhaps you should conduct an experiment.' He could hear the hope in his voice as he held his breath. Waiting. 'Lick away. See what you think.'

The velvet softness of her wet tongue on his neck created a corresponding sharp pleasure, tightening his spine. The sparking zing coalesced at the base of his back.

This is how I die. My heart will simply explode from beating too bloody hard.

'Hmmmm. I can understand the appeal.' Her words brushed over his throat, then her lips pressed against his thundering pulse.

Inspiration struck as his body balanced on the brink of combustion. 'Mayhap the rest will be similar.'

Pulling back, Ivy frowned. 'I don't understand.'

He felt the absence of her warmth but was also grateful for the separation. She was killing him in increments, and if he was going to keep his promise of not frightening her with the wild fantasies thundering through his mind, space was necessary. He let his hands fall to his side and took a step back.

'I went too fast earlier. When I pulled you against me, and you felt...' Bollocks. Now he was blushing. He couldn't very well say 'cock' in front of Ivy.

'Millie calls it a cock.'

Or I suppose I can just let Ivy say it for me.

Hearing the vulgar word slip from her perfect mouth, easy as you please, might be one of the more surreal moments Edward had experienced. He couldn't reflect on it because she was still talking, and he was desperate to hear what she might say next.

'I've heard other words for it.' She looked away for a moment. 'But I think cock is rather nice. I've always thought they were pretty birds. Much more glamourous than chickens.'

Edward refused to think about whom she had heard those other words from.

Her father.

That vile monster had no place here. Instead, he focused on how charming it was to hear Ivy describe 'cock' as a nice word because the barnyard animal it described was glamorous.

Fucking hell.

He could almost hear the last brick crumbling in the carefully constructed walls around his heart. It was impossible to isolate himself from this woman. Impossible to keep the vow he made so long ago. But perhaps he could find a loophole. He promised to remain alone, but that didn't mean he needed to avoid physical intimacy with Ivy. Even if he developed affection for her, she never needed to know. She had no desire for a husband, and Edward did not deserve a wife. Especially not one as fascinating as Ivy. If he fell, crashing into a thousand pieces upon landing, it would be a fitting consequence, and he would still be keeping his vow of solitude. In fact, the pain of having to do so would make it an even more appropriate punishment.

But I can still show her pleasure. She deserves to know the magic her body can achieve if she wishes to do so.

What an honour to be the one who might awaken her to the delights of two consenting people. It mattered little that he would be irrevocably ruined by Ivy because she would walk away from their time together knowing sexual pleasure was possible. Bringing her joy was worth whatever pain her imminent departure might cause him. And wouldn't Philippa delight in discovering Edward had fallen in love with someone he could never have? The poetic justice was stunning.

Steady on. I'm not in love with her.

Not yet. But Edward knew the signs. Even if it was a very long time ago, he remembered. Although this was not exactly the same. When he'd fallen in love with Philippa, it was the mad, obsessive passion of a puppy. This feeling was different. Deeper. Far more worrying.

Best not to think about it and focus on Ivy. Yes. Ignoring a problem always solves it.

'You like the word cock because you think the bird is pretty?' He tried to keep the humour from his voice and failed miserably.

Ivy seemed to realise he was laughing at her. 'Well, why not? It's certainly better than root or tackle.'

It was a shame Edward enjoyed using his tongue so much as he was about to swallow it. 'Where did you hear those words?' he sputtered like an offended dusty dowager.

Ivy shrugged. 'Millie and Hannah, mostly.'

Edward shook his head. 'Right. Well.' He ran his fingers through his hair and tried to gather his thoughts. 'What I'm trying to say is, you didn't think kissing would be enjoyable until you tried it. Perhaps it will be similar with other intimacies. If you are interested, that is. In more than kissing.'

Dear God. I am a bumbling idiot.

Tucking a strand of hair behind her ear, Ivy looked at her feet instead of him. 'You're right. I never wanted to kiss anyone before. I thought that part of me was broken. But...'

'But...' Edward encouraged.

She blew out a shaky breath. 'I find myself wondering, now. About... things... with you.'

He raised his brow, his lips twitched as all manner of illicit images flitted through his mind. 'Things?'

Ivy lifted a shoulder in a half-shrug. 'Millie, Hannah, and Penny give each other looks sometimes. As if they know a secret that I'm not privy to. I hate that. I hate feeling like I'm missing an integral part of myself. Like a limb that has been amputated.' She lifted her thumb to her mouth, biting the nail. 'Now I'm beginning to think that part of me wasn't amputated, but it's rather like a rose bush in winter, lying dormant.'

'And I am the spring sunshine, bringing it back to life?'

Ivy rolled her eyes. 'Men and their arrogance. You are hardly sunshine. And perhaps I am wrong entirely. Mayhap kissing is all I will ever want to do.'

'Shall we try another experiment then? To determine what you want.'

Ivy quirked her head. 'Experiment?'

'Your father told you all the ways a man can take from a woman. How sexual relationships can be an ugly extension of control and dominance. But it's also possible to give and receive a great deal of pleasure when both partners have equal power.'

Ivy's face paled at the mention of her father, but it was impossible to move forward without acknowledging how that man had distorted something that could be so beautiful.

Edward chose his words carefully, painfully aware of how important this decision could be for Ivy. 'In this situation between us, I propose you have total control. At least to start. Until you can trust me.'

She frowned. 'Total control of what?'

'Kissing. Touching my body. Letting me touch yours. Exploring any desires you might have.'

Her eyes widened. 'Touching each other... where?'

Clenching his hand into a fist, he beat back his lust with vicious determination. 'Wherever you wish. No part of me is off limits.'

'What if I freeze again?'

He shrugged. 'When you are frightened, we stop. Talk. Drink hot chocolate. Play whist. Practise shooting intruders. Whatever it is you need to do until the fear dissipates, and then we continue. If you wish.'

Ivy tapped her finger against her skirt. 'You believe if I face my fear of... intimacy... I might defeat it?'

Edward held his breath and nodded.

'I need to think about this. I've never wanted to explore,' she waved her hand between the two of them, 'whatever this is between us before.'

'And if you don't wish to now, we won't.'

Ivy puffed out a breath. 'I *do* like kissing.'

'And I very much like kissing you.' Edward snapped his mouth shut. He didn't want to pressure her. While he wanted to encourage her to face her demons so that she might vanquish them, it wasn't his place to tell Ivy how to heal from her wounds. Certainly not when the plan he recommended selfishly played into his own desires.

Ivy swallowed, the delicate column of her throat constricting as she tipped her chin up and pressed her lips together. 'I shall think on it.'

Edward nodded. 'Then I shall bid you goodnight.' Bowing

his head, he turned and walked from her room as every cell in his body screamed at him to stay.

When he reached his own door and undressed, he realised her list was still in his pocket. Pulling it out, he placed it on the desk next to the two notes from the Devil's Sons. Looking at the three pages together, he realised an odd similarity between Ivy's list and the note found on Lord Thurston.

'Bloody fucking hell.'

13

Ivy slept terribly. Her mind was too busy swirling around all the ideas Edward inspired. She entered the kitchen intent on making a strong cup of tea and organising her agenda for the day. There was much to be done for the upcoming ball. She had an idea she wanted to discuss with Olivia that would make the preparations even more fraught but might also ensure their donations increased.

Edward was already sitting at the table, two pieces of parchment sitting in front of him. He sipped his disgustingly bitter coffee from a teacup.

Ivy felt her face heat. She wasn't ready to re-enter their discussion from the night before, so she distracted him with another topic of conversation. 'I have an idea about the charity ball,' she spoke in a rush, hoping to divert any questions he might have about his proposed experiment.

Of kissing. And touching. And exploring each other.

Dear Lord!

Focus. Do not start drooling all over the kitchen counter.

Edward looked up from the notes, his dark brow raising in an unspoken question. The summer sun streaked through the window, turning his eyes an intriguing shade of indigo. There were streaks of silver at his temple, and his black hair shone like polished leather. Ivy desperately wished to test its texture against her fingers.

Grabbing the kettle and shaking it, she realised he must have refilled it for her. She lit the hob and looked over her shoulder at him. 'I think we should bring some of the children.'

Edward put down his coffee. 'To the ball?'

'Yes. Henry and Sarah would be the best candidates. It's easy to say no to an idea, but how could you possibly say no to Sarah's sweet face? Or Henry with his endearing smile? We need to show the beau monde these children are future contributing members of our society. Henry could make a fine footman or even officer for Scotland Yard. Sarah might be taking care of a peer's children one day. These are not just orphans. They are people the beau monde depend upon to keep their precious lives running smoothly.'

Edward leaned back in his chair and crossed his thick arms over an equally impressive muscular chest. She really should insist he wear a waistcoat and jacket at all times. The man was far too attractive.

'Play on their sympathies, then show the lords and ladies how it benefits them to give generously?'

Ivy took the wailing kettle off the hob. 'Exactly. You gave me the idea last night.' She turned to the teapot and half-filled it with boiling water to warm the porcelain before dumping it out, adding tea leaves, and refilling the pot.

'Did I?' She could hear the amusement in his voice and warmth bloomed in her chest.

Turning, she leaned her back against the counter and

crossed her arms over her chest, mimicking his pose. 'You did. When you spoke of how honourable titles rarely equate to honourable men. You are right. Most of the peers I know are motivated by their own selfish needs, so we show them how donating money to the orphanage benefits them, not the children.'

Edward's smile was infectious. 'You are a sneaky one, Lady Ivy.'

She grinned back. 'Thank you.'

Just as quickly as his smile appeared, it dissipated. He waved her over to the table next to him. 'I have had my own epiphany. I'd love your opinion on it. Look at these two notes.'

Ivy walked over to the table, her shoulder bumping against his as she bent to look at the two papers. 'That's my list from last night.'

Edward nodded.

She narrowed her gaze. 'And the note from Thurston's pocket.' Realisation dawned, and with it a growing sense of horror. 'Good God. It can't be.'

'I fear it is.' Edward's tone was grim.

She pointed to the first column. 'FH.' Then the next. 'LOA. AO. RS. ASO. Edward, those are the initials of orphanages throughout London. The Foundling Hospital in Bethnal Green. London Orphan Asylum, Alexandra Orphanage. Ragged Schools. And ours.' Ivy's hand was shaking, and Edward carefully took the note from her. 'They are making lists.' Bile rose in her throat. 'Of children.'

'I believe the first set of numbers are genders, the second are ages.'

'Oh God. One for boys, two for girls.' Tears threatened, but they would do no good against these bastards. The children didn't need a weeping woman full of horror. They needed a warrior ready with every weapon in her arsenal. 'We must do something, Edward. We must find the leaders of this group and destroy them. I have been a coward, letting Philippa, Hannah, Millie and Penny fight against these monsters while I stayed hidden in the shadows.'

Edward pushed his chair back and stood. 'You are no coward, Ivy. I saw you face off against one of these fiends myself. At the Widow's Ball, you could have stayed behind me while Thurston threatened me with a pistol, but you didn't.' He grabbed both of her shoulders and leaned down to look in her eyes. 'You stepped out of the shadows and defended me. Just as you defended these children the night he snuck through the bloody window.'

She shook free of his grip. 'But it's not enough.'

'It's not your responsibility to defeat the Devil's Sons, Ivy.'

'You're wrong. It is my responsibility. It is yours. It is all of ours. If we do not fight against these bastards, who will?'

He hissed out a breath and ran his hand through his hair.

Ivy felt the thrill of victory. She was right. He knew it. 'Exactly. We need to inform the others. Immediately.'

'All right.' Edward paced in a tight path between the kitchen table and the stove, then back again. 'I must go to Scotland Yard for several appointments or Reading will hunt me down and kill me, but I should be free by this afternoon. Can you leave the orphanage and meet at Philippa's?'

'I'm planning on tea at two with Olivia to discuss the ball and then I need to supervise the children for their chores. Could we invite everyone over this evening after the children are abed?'

'That all depends on whether you have sufficient supplies. Do you stock any port or brandy in this kitchen?' Edward made a show of opening cupboards and drawers.

Despite the seriousness of their situation, Ivy giggled. 'No. I don't think our budget extends to spirits.'

'Well, then. I shall have Reading send a runner to bring supplies from my townhouse. Lord knows we don't want to put the Prime Minister's men into the same war room as the Queen's Deadly Damsels without some liquid fortification.'

'So, it's settled? We'll invite Hannah and Killian, Millie and Drake, Penny and Liam and Philippa, of course. You should probably bring some whiskey as well.' How was this suddenly feeling like a party?

Because all my favourite people will be there. Including Edward. Especially Edward.

Oh no!

In a rather terrifying moment of clarity, Ivy realised her feelings for Edward had vastly surpassed polite acquaintances, eclipsed mere friendship, moved beyond someone with whom she might explore newly found physical desires, and delved into territory she never believed she would ever traverse. She couldn't even think the word, but it hovered on the edges of her mind like a mist.

Focus on the task at hand. Namely, finding these bastard Devil's Sons. Not twittering like a ninny over the Commissioner of Scotland Yard.

Edward drained his coffee cup, then took it back to the Belfast sink in the scullery where she heard him washing it out.

Oh my. He even cleans up after himself.

She allowed herself a moment to lean against the counter as her heart beat a mad tattoo.

I must pull myself together. There's no time for mooning about.

As he walked back into the kitchen, she straightened and poured tea into her cup.

'I shall take my leave. But I'll see you tonight, fortified with spirits and Reading. I would never say this in front of him, but he has quite the mind for investigations, and we need all the help we can get unless you object?'

Ivy shook her head. 'No. Please invite him. Should I ask Olivia to join us?'

Edward frowned, a line forming between his brows. A rogue desire to press her thumb there and smooth it away had her fingers twitching. 'Best not. Philippa is not a fan of Lady Smithwick's. For now, it's probably wise to keep the two of them apart.'

'I don't know why she's taken such a dislike to her.'

Something dark flashed in Edward's gaze. 'I might have an idea.' Before Ivy could ask him anything more, he glanced at the door. 'I should be going. I'll see you this evening.'

Her feet were moving before she could merit her actions. She gripped his forearm and pulled him close, pressing a kiss against his cheek.

What the bloody hell am I about?

Everything seemed to sharpen as she inhaled the scent of soap, coffee, and Jamaican spice. When she attempted to step back, he caught her around the waist, pulling her close. His hand wrapped around her neck, and she felt the heat of his lips hovering a breath away from hers. She tilted her chin, melting the distance as she pressed her mouth to Edward's. It began as a brushing of firm flesh against her own, but quickly, his fingers were tightening on her neck, his tongue delving deep. She opened to him, revelling in the silken sensation of his tongue tangling with hers as he tasted her. Confidence streaked through her. She sucked his bottom lip into her mouth, testing his flesh with her teeth. It was like untethering a wild animal. His hand moved from her neck to her hip, gripping hard enough for her to feel the bite, though he didn't pull her against him. Only this time, she wished he would.

Her blood pulsed through her veins, liquid fire, heating her skin and consuming any logical thought. She wanted more. Allowing herself the glory of exploration, she slipped her hand from his shoulder to his neck, then delved her fingers into his silky hair. Gripping the strands, she changed the angle of their kiss, plunging her tongue into his dark depths and tasting mint and coffee.

His hands were moving north again. One gripped her nape while the other bumped over her ribs. He palmed her corseted breast, and Ivy was quite certain her spirit left her body. She'd always felt mildly embarrassed about her chest. Hardly a shadow of her friend Millie's luscious curves. Barely large enough to fill the centre of her palm on the few occasions she had tested their weight. She sometimes felt like her body was trapped in the silhouette of a child. But when Edward rubbed his thumb over her hardened nipple, even through the layers of chemise, corset, and cotton, Ivy was caught in a conflagration of need.

'Oh!' She sounded like a panting animal, but her reaction seemed to further encourage Edward's efforts. He rubbed again, harder, and a corresponding spark of sensation lit between her legs.

Madness!

She didn't want it to stop.

Edward broke their kiss, his lips coasting along her jaw to her neck where he nuzzled and nipped, sucking the tender flesh into his hot, wet mouth.

Her gown was a simple summer day dress in a lovely soft green. It buttoned to the hollow of her throat. When she felt his kisses tracing along the lace trimming her neckline as his broad hand kneaded her overly sensitised breast, her heart hitched.

Edward froze.

No! I'm not so afraid. Don't stop.

But he pulled back, his hand retreating to her hips.

'Please, forgive me. You asked me last night for time to think, and I promised I would let you lead. Damn it.'

The hissed curse was her undoing. She understood shame on the deepest level. The last thing she wanted was for him to feel such a suffocating burden. Especially when she wanted this.

'You've nothing to apologise for. Last night, you asked me a question. I didn't think I was ready to give you an answer, but I am now.' Speaking the words solidified the truth in her heart and mind. Something about standing against the Devil's Sons, stepping into her power as she fought to defend the orphans under her care, made it easier to be brave in other parts of her life. Namely her sexuality. 'I want to explore... i-intimacy. With you.' Being brave didn't make it any less awkward to speak the words aloud. 'If we are going to war against the Devil's Sons, anything might happen, and I don't want to regret never knowing this part of myself.' Hearing the truth spill out of her own mouth before her mind knew the weight of it stunned her.

His fingers flexed against her hips, and she felt an urge to lean closer. His eyes, darker than the sky before a storm, widened. 'Are you sure?'

Plucking his right hand from her hip, she felt ever so bold as she pressed his callused knuckles against her lips. 'Quite.'

'Shall I come to you tonight? After our meeting?'

Her heart fluttered. But not in fear. In some strange cousin to that emotion, one that made her skin buzz and her stomach fizz. 'Yes.' Though she wasn't quite sure what she was agreeing to. She released his hand. 'What exactly shall we do? Tonight... when you come to me?' The words sounded impossibly scandalous.

Edward's lips quirked. 'What would you like to do?'

Oh dear. What do I want to do?

'Kissing, I think. And maybe more... touching. Perhaps I could try touching you this time. Do men like that? I mean, would *you* like that?' Because this wasn't about men. It was about Edward specifically. And Ivy. Just the two of them. And she *wanted* to bring him pleasure. Which was astounding. Her whole life, she thought physical relations were all about the man doing things to the woman. Unpleasant, painful, scary things the woman was forced to endure. But she was beginning to understand she could do things to Edward. Things that would bring him pleasure but would also grant her unexpected control. The very thought created a liquid heat to bloom between her thighs.

His jaw muscle jumped. Catching her hand in his own, he brushed his thumb over her wrist, spiking her heartbeat. 'I would like that very much. But this isn't about my pleasure, Ivy. It's about yours.'

She bit her lip. 'Perhaps it could be about *our* pleasure. Both of us. If it's all focused on me, I think I'll be too... aware.'

He exhaled through his nose, shaking his head slowly while his eyes never left hers. 'You are a wonder, Ivy Cavendale. So be it. Tonight will be for both of us. But you determine what we do and when we stop. On this we both agree. Yes?'

She nodded, assured that if they reached a point where her fear eclipsed her curiosity, he would stop. 'Yes.'

What a wonder. To trust a man to stop when I ask.

He lifted her hand to his lips and pressed a kiss against her palm, his teeth catching the fleshy heel, creating a pulse of heat in her most vulnerable of secret places. A part of her body she resolutely ignored unless she needed her chamber pot. If she refused to acknowledge its existence, it would stay hidden. And safe. Only now, the foundations of her understanding were shifting. Because with Edward, she already felt safe.

I must speak with Millie. Before tonight. I have questions.

And she couldn't very well ask Edward what they were supposed to do when he just gave that power to her. The very idea inspired a new wave of heat to rush through her. No doubt her skin was turning three different shades of crimson.

She watched Edward's gaze dip to her neck and knew he saw the splotchy patches. Pressing her hand against the stain, she tried to hide the evidence of her embarrassment. He gently gripped her wrist, pulling her hand away.

'Don't. Don't hide from me. One day, perhaps you'll show me how far that beautiful blush travels over you.' He pressed his lips together and dropped her wrist, as though wishing he could call back his words. But it was too late. She was already imagining it. Standing naked in front of Edward, letting his eyes roam wherever they chose as desire and innocence painted her skin in patterns of red and cream. She should be repulsed, but instead, the pulse in her cleft grew sharp. 'Forgive me.'

She shook her head. 'I don't think I will. Nor will I forget. The ideas you inspire, Edward.'

His pupils dilated as he took a careful step backwards. 'Then I shall take my leave and allow you privacy for your wonderings. Though, I do hope you'll share them with me later.'

Scandalous man!

'Farewell, Edward.'

Cutting a sharp bow, his eyes never left hers. The intensity of his gaze nearly burnt her to a crisp.

'Farewell for now, Ivy. Until tonight.' And with that, he turned and left.

Ivy picked up her teacup in shaky hands and listened to his footsteps. She waited until the front door shut before she abandoned her tea and raced to her room. It was imperative she dash off a missive to Millie. Immediately. With any luck, her friend could arrange to arrive before the others. Much needed to be discussed before their meeting, and very little of it concerned the investigation.

* * *

'I still remember the days when punctuality meant something.' Reading didn't look up from the report he was writing as Edward strode past and banged open the door to his office.

'I still remember the days when assistants assisted instead of buzzing away in my ear like an annoying little bee who has lost his honeypot.'

'Bees don't have honeypots. They have honeycombs.'

'They also have queens who expect them to complete the tasks they've been given, and that – although I owe you no explanation – is the cause for my tardiness this morning.'

That and a tryst in the kitchen with Ivy that had my blood so hot, I ordered a cold bath at my townhouse before dressing and coming into the office.

Edward still hadn't managed to adjust his morning schedule while sleeping at the orphanage, but the added hassle of returning to his townhouse to change back into his gentleman's clothes was worth the time and trouble if it meant Ivy was learning to trust him. Based on their conversation today, she might be feeling safe enough to take a terrifying leap. No price was too high for the immeasurable gift of her good faith.

But I'm certainly not going to share any of that with Reading. The man is impossible as it is. I can't imagine how miserable he would make my life if he knew how far I've taken things with Ivy. Or more importantly, how far I want to take them tonight.

Once he caught the scent of a secret, Reading was like a dog with a bone, relentlessly chewing until he reached the marrow of truth. So, Edward carefully guarded his expression.

'What exactly were you doing for the Queen this morning?' Reading looked up from his desk, placing his quill on the inkstand and shaking sand on the parchment to dry his carefully scribed words.

'Moving one step closer to catching the Wolf. I'm sure of it. But I can't explain this to you now. There is much to be done. If only I could find an assistant who spent less time worrying about my whereabouts and more time focusing on his work.'

Reading stared at him for a full five ticks of the clock.

Edward removed his coat. 'Nothing to say? That's not like you.'

'I'm trying to formulate an adequate response to such a load of tripe.'

Striding into his office, Edward felt a remarkable sense of well-being at besting Reading despite the damning evidence he and Ivy had uncovered.

The Devil's Sons were targeting orphanages. It made a horrible kind of sense. Originally, they coerced young women flooding into London from the country, looking for positions in grand houses. The young women would arrive for an interview, accept a cup of secretly drugged tea, and find themselves nailed into coffins and shipped across the Channel with no way to return. But so many of those women had parents, siblings, friends. People who would notice they were gone. Cause a fuss. Demand answers. Draw attention. Orphans didn't have anyone. With so many foundling houses overrun, children ran away or returned to the streets with frightening frequency. Overworked caregivers didn't have time to worry about missing orphans, much less search for them when so many new candidates were waiting for a bed. It was the perfect place to abduct children without anyone of importance paying the least attention.

'Until now,' Edward murmured to himself. He placed the file he had brought with him on the desk, flipped it open, and removed the two notes. One a list, the other a threat. One found in Thurston's pocket, the other in Ivy's. He placed them next to each other on his desk before pulling out a clean sheet of parchment to write up a new report for the Prime Minister telling him nothing, and a separate one for the Queen telling her everything.

He was interrupted from his work by a wide-eyed Reading. 'Sir, Lord High Chancellor Hardgrave, the Duke of Kerry, is here to see you.'

As Hardgrave walked into the office, the always unflappable Reading stared at him like a puppy might stare at a pork chop, or a child might look longingly at one of Gunter's freshly scooped ices.

Bloody hell. My secretary is in a right dither over the Lord High Chancellor.

Edward stood from his desk, tugging down his waistcoat and jacket sleeves. While the Prime Minister met with Edward from time to time for reports on the progress of various investigations and the overall activities of Scotland Yard, Edward rarely interacted with the Lord High Chancellor. He was one step below the Queen and had far more important matters to attend to than anything crossing Edward's desk.

So what the bloody hell is he doing here?

Lord High Chancellor Hardgrave shared the same colouring as his sister. His fair hair was cut neatly, his green eyes sharp with intelligence, and his stature impressive. However, aesthetics might be where the similarities ended. Where Olivia Smithwick displayed an innately gregarious personality, drawing the attention of crowds like moths to a flame, Lord Hardgrave was renowned for his work ethic and reticent personality. He was rarely seen at balls unless the Queen was in attendance. One stern look from him could wilt the wildest of debutantes, destroy the most devilish dandy, and silence every wagging-tongued widow in the beau monde. He was a force to be reckoned with. And he was currently in Edward's office.

'Lord High Chancellor, what an unexpected pleasure. Please sit.' Edward gestured to the chairs in front of his desk as he reclaimed his own seat. 'Reading, perhaps you could organise some tea. For Lord High Chancellor Hardgrave.'

Reading blinked three times and snapped his mouth shut as if he'd woken from a dream.

Most probably some fantasy about Hardgrave rowing down the Thames while Reading sits across from him, holding a striped parasol, reciting Shakespeare's Sonnet 108.

Edward long ago guessed the particular tastes of his assistant. But as homosexuality was illegal, and Edward had no desire to see his best employee and closest friend rotting in prison, or worse, hanging from a rope for the simple crime of loving a man instead of a woman, he let Reading's private matters stay just that. Private.

'Of course. How do you prefer your tea, Lord High Chancellor?' Reading gifted the man with his brightest smile.

Hardgrave waved away Reading's offer. 'Please, don't trouble yourself. I won't be here long.'

Reading bowed his head. 'Of course. Don't hesitate to give me a shout if you change your mind.'

Dear God. He's actually batting his eyes at the man.

'That will be all, Reading.' Edward's clipped tone revived Reading's naturally acerbic temperament as evidenced by the snippy look he shot Edward before turning and clipping out of the office. Edward noticed he didn't quite shut the door. The nosy parker was probably holding his breath with his ear to the crack.

Edward exhaled a calming breath. 'How can I be of assistance, Your Grace?'

Hardgrave tapped his fingers on his knee in a silent rhythm. 'I am hearing troubling reports, Commissioner Worthington.'

'Truly? May I inquire as to the nature of these reports?' Edward was no fool. He wouldn't tip his hand to anyone save the Queen. And Philippa, of course.

'A secret society of peers engaging in truly nefarious behaviour.' Hardgrave's green gaze cut into Edward like a broken bottle. 'If the reports are true, and word were to leak out to London at large, I shudder to think of the pandemonium it might cause amongst the rabble.'

'May I inquire as to where you received this information?'

'I would expect a man in your position to understand the importance of confidentiality amongst informants.' The Lord High Chancellor seemed equally inclined to keeping his cards as close to his chest as Edward.

Edward dipped his chin in a gesture of agreement. 'I am aware of a certain secret society of men engaging in the European flesh trade. They cater to a clientele whose tastes delve into the truly depraved.'

Flicking an invisible fleck of flint from his trousers, Hardgrave shifted in the chair. 'And what are you doing to find these men, Worthington?'

'We are pursuing every lead we have, Lord High Chancellor, with the utmost focus, I assure you.'

The man's gaze lowered to Edward's desk, catching on the notes sitting side by side. He leaned forward, snagging one of the pages before Edward could stop him.

'Is this one of your leads?' He flipped the page over, noting the seal before returning it to the desk in exchange for the other missive. 'Two notes from the same man. Who the bloody hell is the Wolf?'

Edward wasn't about to share his theory that the notes were decidedly *not* from the same man. 'We are working on that, Your Grace.'

Hardgrave made a rather undignified noise, followed by a filthy curse. 'Work faster, Worthington. It only takes a few carefully circulated rumours to spark a panic. The Queen has appointed me to lead her justice system, and by God, I will lead it with the utmost integrity. If there are members of her court committing such despicable crimes, you will find them and ensure they face justice. Do you understand?'

At five and forty, Hardgrave was young to hold such a powerful office, and it was clear he intended to impress the monarch who determined his future. Perhaps that was why he had such a fierce reputation. A combination of desperation and determination to impress was quite the motivator.

'I understand, Your Grace.'

Lord Chancellor stood, and Edward followed his lead. 'Keep me apprised of any new developments, Commissioner. And if there is any assistance you need, you've only to ask.'

Edward couldn't fathom what help he might ask of the Lord High Chancellor, but he nodded his assent, regardless.

Hardgrave spun and pushed the door open. It nearly slammed into Reading.

'Terribly sorry. I was just going to see if you hadn't reconsidered on the tea.'

Hardgrave looked from Reading to Edward. 'God's speed in your search, Commissioner.' He sidestepped a befuddled Reading and exited the office.

Reading rushed in, perching on the edge of the chair the Lord High Chancellor most recently vacated. 'What the devil was that about?'

'Devil indeed,' Edward muttered. 'I hope you don't have any appointments this afternoon.'

Reading leaned forward, his pencil-thin moustache glinting in the sunlight. 'Why is that?'

'We have a duchess to visit.'

14

Ivy's meeting with Olivia couldn't have gone better. Her friend was delighted with Ivy's plan to include Sarah and Henry at the charity ball, but that was nothing to her elation at hearing Philippa was willing to host the event.

'The grand Duchess of Dorsett agreeing to host a ball for orphans. Why, it will be the event of the summer season! The ladies in the Committee couldn't recollect the last time the duchess hosted even an afternoon tea at her mansion, let alone a dance. It's all thanks to you, Ivy. I know she never would have agreed to it had I asked.'

'I still don't understand why the two of you hold such animosity toward one another.'

Olivia only shrugged while looking closely at the lace on her glove. 'Chalk and cheese we are. Or mayhap diamonds and sapphires. Whatever it is, we don't mix. And I, for one, am glad of it. The last thing I need is to be trapped together with the insufferable Duchess of Dorsett.'

'She's not insufferable.' Ivy really liked Olivia. But she wouldn't allow her to speak ill of Philippa. Not when the duchess had given Ivy a chance to change herself. When Ivy went to Philippa after Millie's Yuletide wedding and asked to learn the skills of self-defence, Ivy never imagined Philippa would open her eyes to the power lying dormant within herself. Learning to wield a sword, throw a right hook, shoot a pistol, and grapple with someone larger and stronger than Ivy taught her something invaluable: she was far more powerful than she thought.

But Olivia taught her something as well. Offering Ivy the position of headmistress and entrusting the lives of seven and twenty children into Ivy's care was a gesture of faith that Ivy did not take for granted. Standing in the gap between her orphans and an intruder bent on hurting them took Philippa's lessons and Olivia's faith and combined them into action. She wasn't squaring off against a hypothetical opponent, but rather a real man intent on harming children entrusted to Ivy.

Both women played an integral role in moving Ivy from a place of weakness to strength, and yet Ivy would bet all her new-found confidence they would rather pull out their nails and soak their fingers in methylated spirits than stand next to one another at a ball.

I don't understand it.

But she hardly had time to consider the inner workings of Philippa's mind or the motivation of Olivia's dislike. After Olivia departed in a flurry of hugs and kisses, Ivy spent the remainder of the afternoon supervising the children in their chores and joining them for their supper. Sarah was not pleased to learn Ivy couldn't read to them before bed, but when she shared the news that both Sarah and Henry would be joining Ivy at the fancy ball full of wealthy lords and ladies and helping to divest these titled toffs of their extra coins to raise money for the orphanage, Sarah's attitude shifted. She and Henry helped corral twenty-seven very excited young people to their rooms a full half-hour before their usual bedtime with promises of an extra chapter being read the next night.

Ivy couldn't help smiling to herself at the sound of excited whispers emanating from Sarah's room as she walked down the eastern hall and descended the stairs to the entryway. Her timing was impeccable. A smart knock on the door alerted her to Millie's early arrival.

'I received your message. Are you well? What has happened?' Her oldest and best friend was a vision in cream and sage. Her linen gown was cut low in the front, displaying Millie's luscious figure to its best advantage, and the lighter fabric was perfect for a summer evening gathering with friends. Ivy marvelled at the twists and turns her life had taken. Never would she have imagined such a dashing and dynamic group of people all gathering because she asked them to join her. To plan an attack against a group of very dangerous lords. And the wonder of it all was that while fear was a subtle flavour, it didn't dominate the melange of emotions filling her.

Leading Millie into the parlour, she gestured to the some-what threadbare settee while she took the wing-back chair for herself. 'I am quite well. At least, I am not *un*well. More to the point, I find myself in a state of unusual disquiet.'

Millie's copper brows drew down in confusion. A coil of red hair broke free from her loose twist and curled charmingly against her freckled cheek. 'Disquiet?' She cocked her head and narrowed her eyes. 'Ivy, you are worrying me. Please, speak plainly. What has put you so out of sorts?'

Ivy fiddled with a frayed edge of upholstery where the fabric met the ornately carved wood. 'Edward.'

Millicent's brow rose so high, it nearly disappeared into her hairline. 'Edward?' Her tone conveyed a world of meaning while her lips twitched. 'Are we on such familiar terms with the Commissioner of Scotland Yard?'

'We might be,' Ivy hedged as her face grew warm.

'Ivy Cavendale! Tell me all. You must or I shall expire on this sad little settee.' Sweeping off the couch, she knelt in front of Ivy, completely heedless of the wrinkles being created in her gown. 'What is going on between you and the Commissioner of Scotland Yard?'

Ivy wanted to crawl under the table and never emerge. 'Nothing is going on. At least, not much more than a few kisses.' She was quite certain death by embarrassment was possible, and she would be the first victim.

'Kisses?' The word fairly exploded from Millie. 'You kissed him? Or did he kiss you? Let's hope you kissed each other. Ivy! This is most decidedly unexpected.' She waved a hand in front of her as tears filled her eyes. 'I wasn't sure you would ever want... Wait. Unless you didn't wish for him to kiss you.' Just as quickly as her eyes had lit with joy, they darkened with a much more deadly emotion. 'Did he force himself on you? Is he bullying you? Because Drake will cut that man's tackle off before you can boil the kettle for tea. And when he's done, I'll drag what's left of him into the garden for target practice with my throwing knives.' She gripped Ivy's hand so tightly, Ivy worried they might be fused for eternity. 'If he hurt you, Ivy, we will end him.'

Ivy's head started to spin. 'Good Lord, we aren't ending anyone. He didn't force me. Quite the opposite, actually.'

Millie loosened her grip. 'Truly? You actually wanted to kiss him? Only because you've always expressed a decided fear of such intimacies.'

Ivy shrugged. 'Yes, but I'm beginning to think some fears can only be defeated by facing them.'

'Ah.' Millie nodded slowly, though her mouth still turned down in a hesitant frown. 'And you think he is the right person to face your fears with?'

Exhaling a long breath, Ivy's voice only shook a little. 'I do.'

Millie's gaze never wavered. 'Have you told him? About your father?'

Ivy's throat grew tight. She had never been able to tell Millie the truth about her father, but she knew her friend suspected. It seemed a betrayal for her to have told Edward secrets she never shared with Millie. She nodded. 'I don't know why I told him. I should have told you first.'

'Ivy, I'm your best friend. You didn't have to tell me because I already knew. Mayhap not the details of what that bastard did, but you don't have to count the teeth on a tiger to imagine how easily it might rip someone asunder.'

'I always thought if I told you, the shame would be so great, it would swallow me whole. I couldn't bear the thought of you looking at me differently.' Something cruel and hard squeezed her ribs, making it impossible to take a breath.

'Oh, my sweet friend.' Millie pulled Ivy into a hug, fresh cotton and citrus enveloping Ivy in a scent as familiar and comforting as Millie herself. 'I will never see you as anything more or anything less than my fierce, beautiful, brave, and dearest friend.' It was an unexpected benediction. A granting of permission for Ivy to fall apart. So she did. Millie hummed softly, her hand patting Ivy's back like a mother soothing her child as Ivy let years of hidden pain surface like poison from a deep infection and spill out of her in a rush of tears.

Eventually, the storm passed. When Ivy pulled away, she felt lighter.

'I look a right mess.' Wiping tears from her cheek, she sniffed loudly.

'We can fix that.' Millie brought supplies with her. A bottle of crisp German Riesling and chocolate. She rushed to the kitchen and returned with a cool, wet cloth for Ivy's face and two mismatched glasses. 'I must say, it is rather interesting that you told *him* your secrets.'

Ivy held her glass up for Millie to pour and avoided her friend's eye contact. 'Perhaps he just happened to be in the right place at the right time.'

Snorting, Millie almost spilled wine as she filled her glass. 'Don't think you can lie to me, Ivy Cavendale. We've been friends for far too long. You trust him.'

I do. I trust him not to harm me.

'Should I not?'

Millie plunked the bottle on the table and sipped her wine. 'Philippa trusts him. Even if she doesn't like him. Oh! Maybe you can get him to spill that particular story. We've all wondered what their history might be.'

Ivy scrunched her nose. 'I'm not going to pilfer secrets from the man.'

'No. I don't suppose that would do given how important trust is between you. Right. So. You are going to face your fears with the Commissioner. How can I help?'

Sipping the sweet, fresh wine for courage, Ivy spilled the details of the previous night and more recent morning adventures. Tapping her nail against the chipped glass, she pursed her lips. 'My father told me how horrific it could be between a man and a woman. But it isn't that way for you. I want to know the beauty of it all. If I'm to lead this exploration between myself and Edward, I want to know all of the things we might explore.'

Millie refilled her glass, then Ivy's. Her eyes flashed with mischief. 'That is something I can do. Prepare yourself for an education in the divine.'

For the next hour, Millie was true to her word. When the other guests arrived, Ivy's imagination reeled. Her fear was no match for the burning curiosity Millie's detailed descriptions inspired. It was going to take all of Ivy's efforts to focus on their meeting and not what might happen once their guests left.

* * *

Edward tried to keep his focus on the conversation swirling around him, but he couldn't stop looking at Ivy. Every time she caught him staring, something flashed between them as he remembered their conversation from breakfast. He had been in a state of half-arousal for most of the evening, but he was also anxious. A strange amalgamation he hadn't felt since his first time with a woman. He wanted Ivy desperately, but he also understood how paramount it was not to push her beyond her boundaries. If he had to spend the next few weeks frigging himself to completion while reining in his impulse to bury his cock into Ivy's sweet cunny, so be it. Whatever she offered, he would shamelessly take, but not one inch more.

'If what you have discovered is true, I don't think Ivy announcing her decision to remain headmistress of the All Souls Orphanage will be enough to flush out the Wolf. The Devil's Sons can just turn to the other orphanages littered throughout London. If we want to force his hand, Ivy's announcement needs to be much more threatening to their operations.' Hannah was pacing next to the unlit fire. Killian stood near her and sipped the brandy he'd brought with him from a teacup. Ivy didn't have tumblers suitable, and Killian stated he cared little what vessel held the liquor so long as it did the job of not spilling all over him.

Philippa had claimed one of the wing-back chairs. Her dress, the colour of currents overlaid with sheer black organza, caught the lamplight and created a sheen like polished garnets. The same stone was sprinkled throughout her hair and wrapped around her neck in a waterfall. Even at a war gathering, Philippa was striking. But the only emotion she inspired in Edward now was warm affection and bone-deep respect. Every eye was drawn to her as she rubbed her finger against her thumb. 'I have a thought.'

'I'm sure you have more than one.' He couldn't help but bait her.

She glared at him, then turned her gaze to the larger group. 'The Devil's Sons is comprised of high-born members of the beau monde. As such, they have been raised believing value lies within titles and money.'

Drake and Millie sat together on the settee. The major general looked comically oversized on the small couch. 'How does that help us?'

Philippa rolled her eyes as though Drake were stupid. He, in turn, curled his lip. His scar made the expression terrifying, which was likely his intention. Two predators snarling at one another. 'It helps us because they don't believe anyone will make much of a fuss over a few missing orphans. But they are wrong. At the charity ball, we'll highlight how vulnerable these children are and lay out our plan to protect them. All of them. Not just the ones in this building.'

Silence covered the gathering.

'And how exactly are we going to do that?' Liam Renquist was one of the few members in their group who worked as closely with Philippa as Edward. While he had served in the Anglo-Afghan war with Killian and Drake, upon his return he accepted the Queen's secret request to join Philippa and Edward in their covert battle against corrupt members of the peerage.

His brothers-in-arms sided with the Prime Minister, fighting the same enemies with the differing goal of holding the men accountable through the House of Lords. A path Edward feared would hold no actual justice.

Liam's new wife, who caused quite the scandal when she ascended from maid to marchioness while serving in Liam's household, sat in the wing-back chair Liam stood next to. She gripped his arm and squeezed. 'I believe Philippa is about to tell us, darling.' Her quiet murmur pulled the marquess' focus away from Philippa. Edward didn't miss the look he gave his wife. It filled Edward with a sudden ache.

Gazing at the assembled group, he saw three fierce couples as united to each other as they were to this cause. He had always longed for that sense of belonging. To look at another and be known on such an elemental level. To embrace every part of someone. The ugliness. The beauty. The fear. The triumphs. And know that person did the same for him. It was a remarkable and rare gift being displayed so excessively in this parlour. A gift he knew he would never deserve.

Looking at Philippa, knowing he was responsible for taking that gift from her, regret nearly stole his breath. Because while he deserved to suffer a solitary life for the sins he committed, he wouldn't wish that for anyone else.

His gaze inevitably returned to Ivy. She perched directly across from him in the other kitchen chair. If he could play a part in teaching her the joy of physical connection, she might one day find the same kind of partnership her friends discovered with their spouses. And that would need to be enough for Edward, though the thought of letting anyone else take that place in Ivy's life made him want to rip out his worthless heart and throw it in the fire.

No more than I deserve.

A plain silk gown hid her beautiful skin from view. Would she let him remove her shield tonight? Might he finally trace the crimson blush with his fingers and tongue as it painted across her body? He was so lost in his imaginings, he almost missed Philippa's response.

'We are going to set up a task force led by the Commissioner of Scotland Yard himself to look into the state of London's orphanages, and Ivy is going to be the figurehead. A high-born lady with no children of her own, devoted to the cause of protecting our most vulnerable citizens.'

Because he was already staring at Ivy, he saw the colour drain from her face as her mouth fell open in a perfect 'O'.

'Pardon?' She glanced at him before refocusing on Philippa. 'That's impossible.'

Philippa raised a perfectly shaped black brow. 'Why? What is so impossible about a woman protecting children? It is the most natural thing in the world.'

'A woman like you, perhaps. Or Hannah as a fellow duchess. Millie or Penny would be grand in this role. Not me.'

'Why not you? You've done an admirable job of defending these children.' Millie added fuel to Philippa's fire.

'Which is why I should stay here. In my role as headmistress. If that won't flush out the Wolf, we'll have to think of another way to do it.'

Philippa tsked. Shifting irritably in her chair, she examined her nails. 'I just think you could do far more good working with Edward to protect *all* orphans rather than letting Lady Smithwick constrain you to only helping the seven and twenty children here.'

'Philippa, you must end this war against Olivia. She isn't constraining me.'

'And we aren't finding any solutions,' Millie added. 'Though,

I do think you would do a marvellous job working to protect the orphans, Ivy.'

'What about the proposition lacks appeal for you?' Penny asked.

Edward noted how Ivy's shoulders tightened. Her breathing was growing shallow and fast.

'Mayhap Ivy has her own reasons. Reasons she has no wish to share with all of us. It is late. Perhaps we should all retire to our respective homes and think on other solutions.' Edward couldn't sit silently while Ivy was being poked at by her friends.

Killian reached for his wife's hand. 'The hour is late. Let us retire. My best ideas always come after a good night's rest.' But the way he was looking at his wife promised anything but a restful evening.

Philippa audibly groaned. 'Try to control yourself, Killian. At least until the two of you are in your carriage.'

Drake shared a look with Millie that made the ache in Edward's chest pulse. Philippa rolled her eyes. 'Come, my lady. We should also seek our... slumber.'

Millie's cheeks grew pink as she swatted Drake's arm, but they both rose. Drake shook the gentlemen's hands, and Millie hugged Ivy, whispering something in her ear that had Ivy's neck splotching crimson and her eyes drifting over to Edward.

What the devil did she say?

'We should away as well.' Liam took Penny's hand, helping her rise.

'We'll think of something. Between the nine of us, surely we can come up with a plan that will force this wolf to come out from his den.' Penny's mouth drew into a determined line.

'The ten of us, Your Grace.' Reading was hunched over a small table, scribbling down notes. He looked up from the parchment and gave the group a hesitant smile. 'I'm rather good at finding secrets. I shall put my total focus on discovering this wolf and thinking of ways to trap him.'

'Good man.' Philippa rose with the grace of a falcon ascending in flight. 'I suppose our evening is at its end. Edward, I would like a word with you before I leave.'

Her dismissal of the others couldn't have been clearer. Hugs, handshakes, and well wishes were shared as the three couples and Reading took their leave. When only Ivy, Philippa, and Edward were left, an awkward silence descended.

'Right. Well, then. I shall just...' Ivy twisted her fingers together and began to walk toward the door, but Philippa stopped her with a gentle hand on Ivy's arm.

'I don't mean to push you, Ivy. I know you wish to stay in the shadows. But when I look at you, I see a powerful woman with the skills and abilities to change this world for the better. I don't want fear to stop you from achieving your goals.'

'Is this my goal, Philippa? Or is it yours?'

Brava, Ivy! Standing up to Philippa. Not many have the courage to do something so frightening.

Philippa pressed her crimson lips together. 'You are right. Perhaps this is my goal. But will you think on it, see if it might also become yours?'

Ivy blinked, swallowed, and finally tipped her chin in the smallest nod. 'I appreciate your faith in me, Philippa. And I will consider it. Goodnight.' When she turned to Edward, her crystal eyes carried secrets he was desperate to uncover. 'Worthington.' He didn't miss that she wasn't wishing him goodnight. Because they would be seeing one another very soon. If Philippa would hurry up and spit out whatever it was she needed to tell him.

As soon as Ivy shut the parlour door behind her, Philippa pulled her fan from some hidden fold in her skirts and thwacked it against her hand. 'I have been thinking about your request.'

Edward quirked his brow. 'What request is that?'

'You asked if we could become friends. I told you to protect Ivy and we would see. Well. I've reached a decision.'

It felt like months since his conversation with Philippa in his office, but it all came rushing back. He dreaded her response. 'And?'

'I would not be opposed to a friendship with you. And as a friend, I have some advice.'

Edward forced his lips to refrain from twitching in a smile.

Of course, Philippa will not agree to friendship unless it serves her purposes. Well, what harm can a little advice do?

More than he thought.

'Tell Ivy.'

His heart froze along with every muscle in his body. 'What are you talking about?'

Philippa thwacked her fan once more, an irritated lioness flicking her tail. 'I'm not a fool, Edward. Nor am I blind. It's obvious the two of you share some kind of... understanding. I don't know why I am cursed to be surrounded by idiots constantly succumbing to Cupid's arrow, but in this instance, I cannot be upset. Ivy deserves love. More than most, I'd wager.'

'But I do not, Philippa. Not after what I did.' His voice broke.

'You are a man, Edward. You make mistakes like any other man. One stupid decision does not warrant a lifetime of punishment.'

Anger rallied against his grief. 'I rather think it does when that decision ends in someone's death.'

She walked over to him, lifted her hand, and slapped him hard. The shock of it stunned him. He placed his hand over his cheek, not sure how to react. It was only a fraction of what he deserved, and yet he never expected the duchess to lower herself to such a display of emotion.

'Snap out of your self-pity, Edward. You acted selfishly, yes. But I know you did not intend for it to end as it did. Until recently, I only thought of my own suffering, but I am capable of growth too, Edward. I have realised your loss was just as great as mine. You deserve love just as we all do. And I see that love in you every time you look at Ivy. As much as it pains me to pay you a compliment, you would be a good partner for her in this life. Tell her. She will understand, and perhaps that understanding will help you.'

'Help me to what?'

'Forgive yourself. Finally. Move forward with your life. Be happy.'

'What about you, Philippa?'

Philippa's smile shone as fragile as glass. 'Oh, don't worry about me. I have Stokes waiting at home for me. Finding new and interesting ways to annoy him brings me endless joy.'

'What about happiness? Love?'

Philippa's bottom lip quivered, and her cobalt eyes sparkled with unshed tears. 'Not all of us were meant for love that lasts a lifetime. Some of us only have it for a moment. But the pain of losing it doesn't diminish the glory.'

Taking a huge risk of losing his hand entirely, Edward reached over and squeezed Philippa's forearm in a gesture of comfort he hoped she would receive. 'You deserve so much more than a moment, Philippa.'

'What we deserve and what we receive rarely balance, Edward. As someone who has lost love, it is an affront to my very being to watch another person – even if that person is you – refuse such a gift.' Lifting her free hand, Edward flinched. Philippa smiled as she placed it gently against the cheek still red from her slap. 'We are friends now. As your friend, I insist you stop behaving like a complete imbecile.' Patting him just hard enough to reignite the sharp sting in his cheek, she blinked away her earlier emotion. 'Goodnight, Edward. I shall see myself out.' She turned and swept out of the parlour, leaving in her wake the scent of jasmine and frankincense.

Edward was asking Ivy to face her fears, but was he brave enough to face his own?

I suppose it is time to find out.

15

Ivy had made a list. It wasn't very long – only a few items from her talk with Millie – and she hadn't time to alphabetise it, but it sat on her desk, and she stared at it with wide eyes. Could she actually do this? Did she *want* to do this?

Yes. And if it becomes too much, he will stop. He will wait.

The truth of that gave her courage. Courage swiftly transformed into complete anxiety when Edward knocked on her door. Because it had to be him on the other side. No one else was knocking for Ivy. She didn't want anyone else knocking.

Standing, she brushed her hand over her dress, strode to the door, opened it before she could change her mind, and promptly lost all power of speech.

Good gracious, he is handsome.

His black hair showed evidence of recently being disturbed, no doubt by running his fingers through it. Eyes so dark they could have been black were hooded and hidden in the hall's shadows. His firm jaw looked rough with stubble. He had removed his jacket and cravat. His shirt showed a V of skin at his throat.

Ivy tried to swallow.

'May I come in?' Edward's low voice created a buzz in her belly echoing over her skin.

Words were too difficult with all the butterflies swarming from her stomach to her throat. Instead, she nodded and stepped back, granting him entrance to her inner sanctum.

Edward moved with carefully controlled grace as if he might spook Ivy. As if she might run.

If I did run, would he chase me?

And why did the thought of Edward pursuing her create an illicit thrill down her spine?

What might he do if he caught me?

More ideas to add to her list.

His sharp gaze took in the neatly made bed, the hook holding Ivy's nightgown and wrap, her neat desk. The list.

Dear Lord. The list. I should have hidden it.

He stepped closer and picked up the parchment.

'Wait, don't.' Ivy took a jolting step forward, but it was too late. Pulling out the glasses she found so appealing, he perched them on his nose. His wicked lips tilted in a knowing smile as he looked from what was in his hands to Ivy. The flare of desire she saw in his eyes froze her to the floor.

Bloody hell.

Heat rose from her chest up her throat and over her cheeks.

'You've made a list.'

Well, there's no getting out of this now. In for a penny, in for a pound.

Ivy thrust her chin out and schooled her expression to remain calm. 'I have.'

'There are only three items on this list. And one is in Latin.'

It was quite possible Ivy's embarrassment would run so hotly through her body, she would melt into a puddle, thus ending this awkward conversation.

'Are you unfamiliar with L-Latin?' Her voice came out as a high-pitched squeak.

Edward took off his glasses and tapped them against the parchment while his gaze burned through her. 'Quite the contrary. Latin is one of my favourite languages. Only, this word begins with a "c". It should be at the top of your list, but it's at the bottom.'

'I didn't have time to alphabetise it.'

Edward's firm mouth parted. 'Ah. Of course.' He returned his attention to the parchment. 'Kissing. Touching. And then...' Edward folded the parchment and placed it carefully onto the desk with his glasses. 'Perhaps we should start at the top.'

Ivy blinked rapidly. 'Yes. All right.'

'Kissing.' His gaze shifted from her lips to her breasts, to lower still before returning to her eyes. 'Where would you like me to kiss you, Ivy?'

Where, indeed.

Directing their explorations seemed like a grand way to maintain control, but now, in the moment, she felt overwhelmed. Tapping her finger against her skirt, she focused on the V of skin peeking from Edward's shirt. Tears threatened. Not from fear, but frustration. After speaking with Millie, she had a much more vivid view of what might happen between a man and a woman, but she had no idea how to communicate her desires to Edward.

'Ivy, I can leave right now. Or we can sit and talk. Nothing need happen tonight if you do not wish it.'

Frustration slipped into anger as she watched his desire fade into concern. He misunderstood her hesitance. It wasn't that she didn't want him; it was that she wanted more than she could articulate. 'I don't want you to leave. I'm not some fragile thing, Edward. I don't wish to be treated like I might break.'

Clenching his jaw and exhaling through his teeth, Edward crossed his arms over his chest. 'All right. What do you want, then?'

'I don't know!' She bit her lip as a tear escaped and tracked down her cheek. 'I want more. That's all I know.'

'What about your list?'

Ivy shook her head. 'There's only those three things because I can't... Millie explained what can happen, but I don't know how it would actually work.' She waved between the two of them. 'With real people. Not that Millie isn't a real person. Or Drake. That's not what I'm saying.'

Edward grabbed her flailing hand and pulled her a step closer, pressing a kiss against her palm. 'You haven't done any of those things, so how can you know what you might like?'

'Yes. Exactly.' Relief eased some of her roiling emotions as she dashed the tear away with the back of her free hand. 'I know you wish to give me control, and I want that. But I also want to learn what pleases me. What pleases you. I can't direct you in areas where I have no expertise. I need a teacher, Edward, and you are the only man I trust to do the job.'

Edward exhaled a shaky breath. 'You trust me?'

Something fell into place within her, a sense of rightness that solidified her decision. 'I do.'

He shook his head, his mouth parting and his eyes sparking with an emotion she couldn't name. Wonder, perhaps. Awe. It was overwhelming to have Edward look at her so intensely. She almost stepped away.

'Right.' He nodded his head, his expression shuttered once more. Pulling her closer, he stopped when their bodies were a breath apart. Before Ivy could retreat, he gripped her waist, holding her steady. 'I propose an amendment to our earlier plan.'

Ivy was distracted from his words by the bite of strong fingers flexing against her hip. Wet heat bloomed between her thighs.

Letting go of her hand, he trailed his fingers up her arm, tangling them in her hair as he gripped her neck. Tipping her chin up, his words whispered against her lips. 'The headmistress shall become the pupil. We will address each item on your list, but as your teacher, I will make additions as needed. I shall take the lead, but you always have the reins. You will stop me if you feel frightened or overwhelmed. But I won't stop unless you tell me to do so.'

He knew she wasn't a porcelain doll who might shatter at the least provocation. She was strong and resilient. Powerful and profound. But she was also fragile and frightened by her past. Some miracle of fate had brought her a man who understood the dichotomy of her soul.

'So, if I tense up, or can't find the right words, you won't think it's because I'm afraid?'

'Exactly. I won't assume just because you are feeling apprehensive or nervous that you wish to end our explorations. But if you say "stop", I always will. Teaching you pleasure is my greatest honour, but I would never forgive myself if you walked away from this hurt in any way. Are you amenable to this plan?'

Yes!

It was a brilliant suggestion that alleviated the pressure of making all the choices while still giving her ultimate control. Her heart cracked and something warm and sweet filled her chest. 'I am.' Tilting her chin a fraction higher, she pressed her mouth against his, sealing their deal with a kiss and granting him permission to lead them on this adventure.

She thought he would continue kissing her, but he stepped back three paces and started unbuttoning his waistcoat. 'You were looking at my throat earlier. Were you wishing to see more?'

The man is a mind reader.

'Yes.' It was a bold statement, and she felt the power of owning her desire. She *did* want to see more of him, and she wouldn't pretend otherwise.

I want to see all of him.

'Have you ever seen a naked man before?' As he spoke, Edward removed his waistcoat and draped it over the one chair in her room. Before she could answer, he began on the buttons holding his linen shirt closed.

If a fire broke out in the orphanage, Ivy wasn't sure she could tear herself away from this moment. Edward undid the last button halfway down his shirt and waited.

'No.'

'Do you want to see me?'

'Yes,' she breathed.

Reaching behind him, he gripped the back of his shirt and, in a fluid movement, pulled the linen over his head, letting it drop next to the waistcoat on the back of the chair.

His body was an homage to the beauty of the male form. Thick arm muscles bunched and shifted as he rubbed one hand over his chest. Ivy followed his fingers. He brushed them over flat, dark nipples. His stomach was divided into six defined ridges of hardened flesh. Hipbones jutted out, and a V of ridged muscle on either side of his abdomen disappeared into low-slung breeches. A defined bulge grew even larger where the placket of his breeches strained against three small buttons. His large hand swept lower, blatantly rubbing the evidence of his arousal. He hissed out a breath.

She never imagined looking at a man's naked torso would cause so many sensations to spark to life. Her skin felt tight, her nipples constricting into two sharp points. Her heart was thudding so hard, she felt the pulse in her fingertips. Tingling turned to a hollow ache between her thighs.

'Touch me, Ivy.' True to his word, he was directing her. Instead of sparking fear or fury, his command came as a relief. Because she wanted to touch him, and his words gave her permission.

Taking an unsteady step forward, she let her fingers explore the silk and steel of hard muscles covered in smooth skin. His light sprinkling of black chest hair crinkled, and when she scraped a nail over the disc of his nipple, he groaned. Her eyes flew to his face. The raw need hardening his mouth, tightening his jaw, flashing in the dark-blue depths of his gaze humbled Ivy. She caused such ravenous hunger in this powerful man, and yet he held it in check. For her.

What a marvellous thought.

On a muttered curse, he delved his hand into her hair, gripping her neck and pulling her close. His kiss was a claiming as he plunged his tongue into her mouth. She welcomed the invasion. Giving her hands free rein, she rubbed down his chest and over the ridges of his belly, delighting as his stomach muscles clenched beneath her fingers. Scraping teeth over his bottom lip, she swallowed his growl and revelled in the friction of her stays pressing against her hardened nipples as he pulled her hands from between their bodies and crushed her tightly to his chest. His mouth nibbled along her jaw to her neck where she felt the bite of teeth before he soothed the same spot with sweet, sucking kisses.

She was dissolving into him, losing herself when he pulled

back and moved his hands to her waist. 'Turn around.' He pivoted her so she faced away from him.

'What are you doing?' It felt strangely vulnerable to give him her back.

'Do you want me to stop?' Her hair had fallen from its pins and cascaded behind her. He lifted it, and cool air rushed over the back of her neck before his warm breath caused her to shiver in need. He pressed open-mouthed kisses on her sensitive nape. She was melting once more.

'No.' If he stopped, she might spontaneously combust in the middle of her room.

Nipping her shoulder, his sharp teeth were dulled by her dress.

Tugging on her hips, he pulled her with him as he took a step backwards, then another. Sitting on the chair, he drew her onto his lap, her back to his chest, her head falling onto his shoulder, giving him free access to her neck and throat. His steel shaft pressed insistently against her bottom, and she lifted her hips.

'I don't want to hurt you.'

He pulled her firmly back in place. 'You won't. Trust me. It feels amazing.' He ground her against him and groaned. 'But this isn't for me.'

Ivy wasn't sure if he said that to her, or himself. She opened her mouth to ask why this couldn't be for him, but he was nuzzling her neck. He bit her softly, then sucked the sensitive flesh. Ivy moaned as blood rushed to the surface in a wash of heat.

She didn't realise his hands were busy bunching up her skirt until the night air wound around her ankles and up her calves, causing her thighs to tremble. She should stop him.

But why? I want this. He wants this. Why can't we share this magic together, just for tonight?

'Have you touched yourself before?'

Ivy's thoughts froze. The very idea was shocking.

'Because you are going to touch yourself now, Ivy. You are going to show me what you want. What you like.'

She couldn't possibly. Tensing to stand, he shifted his arm to wrap diagonally over her torso, clamping her tightly against him. His other hand stopped tugging up her skirt. For a moment, they sat together, breaths coming hard, bodies tight with need. 'Do you want me to stop? You need only say.'

She arched against him but didn't speak the word.

'Or do you want to touch yourself, Ivy? Do you want to see how glorious it feels? To discover how much pleasure your body can experience?'

Well, when he puts it that way, only a fool would refuse.

Ivy was no fool. 'Yes,' she moaned.

His dark laugh rumbled against her back. 'Oh, no. That won't do. You must be specific, or I won't know. Tell me you want to touch yourself. Tell me you want to feel the wet heat of your quim as you finger that sweet little nub hiding beneath all your layers.'

She could barely make sense of his words, let alone repeat them. 'I don't...'

'Tell me, Ivy.'

The command in his tone was impossible to refuse. 'I want to touch myself.'

'Yes,' he hissed as though her words brought him acute pleasure. Releasing his grip on her torso, Edward took her hand, tangling their fingers together so the back of her hand pressed against his palm. His other hand continued gathering her skirt, encouraging her to lift her hips so he could bunch the cotton around her waist. She peeked down and saw her pale thighs glowing in the lamplight.

Oh dear Lord.

Her thatch of maiden hair, dark blonde and coarse, caught the lamplight. If he looked down now, he would see her. Completely bare. The idea of it created a new wave of heat to crash through her body.

'Hook your foot around my calf.' His gravelled command meant she would have to lift her thigh and shift her legs apart. 'Now.'

Before she could fully process his request, her leg was already moving. Following his orders was oddly freeing. She didn't have to think about what she wanted. And if she froze, he froze with her. Waiting for a signal to move forward or retreat. He was giving her control without the pressure of directing their game.

'Now the other foot.'

As she complied, he shifted his thighs further apart. Her legs moved with his, and cool air kissed the wet heat of her cleft.

'Oh my God.' Just the contrast of cold and hot created a sharp, tingling pulse at the apex of her slit.

'Yes, darling. Don't think about anything else except what you are feeling.'

He covered her hand with his and moved them both over her thigh. She felt the sensation of her smooth skin beneath her fingers, the soft crinkle of her pubic hair, and then silky, wet heat.

'You are so wet, Ivy. Your cunny is making such sweet nectar. I'm going to lick and suck and taste you as you come apart for me. But not yet. Not until you beg me for my tongue.'

Sweet heavens!

Millicent had explained cunnilingus to Ivy, but the whole

thing seemed like an embarrassing and hardly enjoyable act for either participant. She only wrote it on her list because it seemed so improbable. Until those devilish words spilled from Edward's lips and all Ivy could think about was his hot tongue licking where her fingers tickled against skin so sensitised, she feared she might scream.

Guiding her finger through her slit, Edward's thumb grazed over her mound as he slid her index finger through plush folds. Ivy's body arched like an electric current ran through her when the pad of her finger grazed against a magical cluster of nerves. Burning, sweet pleasure pulsed from that small point, zinging through her blood, sparking over her skin, sending a thousand spiralling tingles to every pulse point.

'What is happening?'

'That's your clitoris.'

'Millie said there was a spot...'

'Millie was right. Find your rhythm. See what feels good. Rub it, pinch it, flick it. What do you like?' He withdrew his hand, giving her total control. Gripping her hip instead, he rubbed his thumb back and forth in a mesmerising pattern. But not nearly as fascinating as the pattern she was establishing. Tight little circles, long slides up and down, toying with her aching entrance before bringing the sweet wetness back to coat the tight bundle of nerves currently consuming her.

She focused on the sensation, chasing something elusive, just on the edges of her consciousness as Edward whispered encouragement in her ear.

'Yes, sweet Ivy. Just like that. Don't be afraid.'

As she neared the precipice, she held her breath. Something gorgeous and shimmering was just there, a promise away. Millie told her about this pinnacle, this incandescent moment, but she couldn't imagine the power of it.

'Don't stop. You are so close. Let go, Ivy.' His lips brushed her ear, his voice drowning out any doubts rising from her memories. This was nothing like the fearful images her father created in her mind. This was stunning and fierce. Beautiful and wild.

Edward's free hand palmed her breast. Clever fingers found her hard nipple and pinched her, the sensation muted by layers of cotton and stays. But it was enough.

With a final tight circle, she imploded, sweet glory pulsing through her with each heartbeat. Edward covered her hand once more, flattening her palm and rubbing hard against her clitoris, grinding out the glorious sensations until she was quite certain her spirit left her body and joined the cosmos.

Moments passed. Or minutes. Or millennia. It was hard to say, but as she came back to herself, something had changed.

I have changed.

Like a wave cresting or a bird rising from the misty fields, she was reborn. She was still Ivy but different somehow. What magic she held within herself! To finally understand the secret looks exchanged between her friends and their partners, to realise engaging in physical intimacy could be a transformative experience of pure joy. It changed everything. And now she knew, she wanted to feel it again.

'That was unimaginable.'

'You are well?'

'I am very well.' Ivy felt a bubble of delight fizz up from her chest and expand her ribs. As she shifted to face Edward, the insistent pulse of his hard cock beneath her bottom highlighted an important fact.

Edward had sated her hunger, but his needs were still unmet. She shifted, and he groaned. Carefully trying to avoid his rather swollen appendage, she stood, letting her skirts fall back around her ankles. Turning to face him, her eyes travelled inevitably south of his face and caught at the waistline of his breech.

Millie explained that if a man did not release his seed, it could be painful for him, though she was quick to reassure Ivy that it wasn't her responsibility to relieve a man unless she wished to do so. Seeing Edward's rigid body, every muscle tight with unmet need, his eyes still wild even as he tried to force his lips into an easy smile, she knew what she wanted.

Dropping to her knees, she gripped the heel of his boot and began to tug.

'What are you doing?' Edward's alarmed voice would have been amusing in any other circumstance.

'I'm taking off your boots.' She freed his first foot, threw the boot behind her, and moved on to the second.

'Why?' He reached down to stop her, but she brushed off his hands.

'Because we aren't done.' With his second boot in her hand, she rocked back on her heels and let her gaze linger on the outline of his hard, turgid cock. She wanted to see it. The appendage her father had told her would cause such unmitigated pain. She wanted to know what Edward's penis looked like and decide for herself whether it was something she should fear.

'Ivy, this is all new to you. Perhaps this was far enough for tonight.'

'I haven't said stop yet.' Struggling to her feet, she took a step back, giving him space to also rise. 'I want to see you. All of you.'

Edward raised an eyebrow. 'I don't want to frighten you.'

She rolled her eyes. 'I have faced off against an intruder, shot a man in the shoulder, and helped you track down a criminal. They may have all been the same man, but still. I'm not some weak-kneed ninny. You won't frighten me.'

His eyes glinted in a look that *should have* frightened her. 'All right. I shall show you all of me, but only if you show me your blush. Everywhere it stains your skin.'

Devious devil! He thinks I'll back down. He's wrong.

'You first.' One good threat was worth another.

Raising a dark brow, he bit his lip and Ivy desperately wanted to lick him. Just there where his teeth dug into the firm flesh of his mouth. 'I'll hold you to that, Ivy. If I take these off,' his finger hovered over the buttons of his placket, 'then you remove your dress, stays, and shift. Swear it.'

God, she loved it when he demanded things from her. Which made absolutely no sense, but somehow his rough command empowered her. She could grant him this boon or deny him. Either way, he would honour her choice.

'I swear it.' She nodded at his pants. 'Quit stalling, Commissioner.'

He shook his head. 'Wicked woman.' Slowly, Edward flicked open the three buttons holding his placard in place. His erection bobbed free, and Ivy was certain all the air had been sucked from her room. Untying the drawstring around his waist, he pushed down his breeches, stepping free of them. In a gesture hinting at unexpected self-consciousness, he rubbed both hands up and down the outside of his hips.

Millie had tried to describe the male appendage to Ivy, but her words couldn't encompass the truth of it. The hard ridge of flesh was bulbous at the top, a hood of skin pulling back from the glistening, reddish tip. The shaft was tight and pulsing, jutting upward. A slit at the tip of it beaded with a creamy pearl. The entire thing was far too large to ever fit inside Ivy, and all her father's threats re-emerged.

'How could that possibly...' Ivy swallowed and tried to find words to finish her sentence.

'Fit inside you?' Edward passed a hand over his cock, hissing a breath as he did. 'When you reached your climax, your channel flooded with fluid. It helps to ease my way. I know there is pain for a woman the first time, but there can be pleasure as well. There will be pleasure if you wish to go that far.'

As much as she wanted more, she wasn't sure she was ready for *that* much more just yet.

'Is that the only way to ease your... er... situation?'

'No. I can stroke myself to release.'

'What else?' Millie described how a woman could take a man into her mouth and bring him relief that way. She assured Ivy the experience could be quite empowering. Ivy wasn't sure how, but Millie had never lied to Ivy. After everything she had just experienced, she was willing to try. 'Can I bring you to climax with my mouth?' The very idea should repulse her, but staring at the cream leaking from him, her mouth watered.

Edward's cock jerked in response to her words as he clenched his hands into fists. 'You don't want to do that, Ivy.'

His words were like a gauntlet being thrown. Ivy agreed to let him take the lead, but she would be damned if she let him tell her what she did and did not want. Stretching her mouth in a smile, she licked the corner. 'I haven't said stop, Edward. You promised we would do everything on the list.'

'This wasn't on the list. If you want me to lick your sweet cunny, I will happily oblige.'

That gave her pause as Ivy imagined his dark head between her thighs, his strong tongue rasping over her newly discovered bundle of nerves, his lips pressing kisses to her cleft.

Oh my!

No. I won't be distracted. He is clearly in pain. I want to bring him relief.

And if Millie was right, Ivy wanted to know the kind of

empowerment controlling Edward's pleasure in such a raw moment could bring her.

'Well, it's my list so I can add to it whenever I like. And I'm adding this. Now.'

Something dark and dangerous snapped in his eyes. A beast straining against the chains of control. 'Are you certain?'

Ivy spent her entire life fearing everything a man might take away from her. Overpowering her body, stealing her autonomy, and forcing her submission. But fear held no sway here because Edward refused to take anything from her that she did not freely offer. And he had already given her a moment of incandescent beauty. She wanted to return the favour. Give him something in return.

'Tell me what to do.'

16

Her words shifted something in Edward. While she wanted to be commanded, he shouldn't agree to this request. Just imagining her mouth wrapping around his cock was a fantasy he couldn't possibly deserve. He must convince her to see reason.

'Not all women enjoy this. I don't want you to do something you find unpleasant.'

'You promised you would let me take the reins. That you wouldn't stop until I told you. I want to do this.'

Edward was doing his best to be a good man. An honourable man. But he could only resist so much temptation. Listening to Ivy repeatedly demand to take him in her perfect mouth pushed him beyond his limits.

If I am going to burn eternally for my sins, I might as well take this memory with me to hell.

Hardening his expression to one of complete command, he straightened his shoulders and gripped his raging cock. He couldn't remember the last time he'd been this hard. Just brushing his palm over the tight skin nearly caused him to break. But he vowed to maintain control. He wouldn't rush her, and he wouldn't embarrass himself. Despite what she asked, this act could overwhelm even an experienced partner. If she pulled back, asked him to stop, he would honour her command, even if it shattered the very foundations of his soul.

'Take off your dress.' If they were going to do this, he was going to hold her to the promise she made. He refused to leave her room without seeing every inch of her creamy skin.

Ivy's hands shook, and he almost backed down, but she pressed her wide mouth into a determined line. The confidence he saw flashing in her eyes encouraged Edward to stay the course. She wanted this.

Thank God for that.

Turning, she presented her back to Edward once more. 'Will you unbutton me?' She had no lady's maid and was probably used to managing her dresses alone, but her request nearly undid him. Now *his* hands shook, though thankfully, she couldn't see his fingers as he fumbled with the buttons. As the edges of her dress parted, revealing her pale shoulder, Edward couldn't stop from bending forward and pressing a kiss to her shoulder blade just above her stays.

Ivy swayed toward him, but he steadied her and stepped back. 'Turn around, Ivy.'

She did as he asked. Her crystal eyes were almost swallowed by black pupils as her chest rose and fell with quick breaths. Edward let his gaze roam. 'Take. Off. The. Dress. Now.' While he was a man used to leading, he had never displayed such dominance with any of his previous partners. But something about Ivy's permission to teach her called to a darker desire within him. Her response fanned that flame into a conflagration as she shrugged out of her dress and let it pool at her feet.

She stood in her stays and shift. The blush he so desperately wished to map over the contours of her body splashed across her clavicles, spreading over the pale skin of her chest before disappearing into the thin cotton shift. Her stays were laced tight, pressing her small breasts up like two sweet offerings peeking from the low cut of her shift.

Edward didn't think it possible to become more aroused, but his body hardened further, and he stifled a groan of need. He would *not* spill his seed like some untried youth. Biting the inside of his cheek hard enough to taste iron, he exhaled a long breath. 'Now the stays.'

Reaching behind her, she pulled a few times on the laces, then tugged. The stays loosened, and Ivy shimmied the padded cotton down her body, bending over to step free. Her shift gaped at the neck, and he caught the mesmerising glimpse of dark-pink nipples.

I want to taste them. Lick and suck those sweet buds until she screams my name.

His desire roughened his words. 'Your shift. Take it off.' He needed to see her bared to him more than he needed his next breath.

Ivy pulled one arm free, then the other. He saw the quiver in her bottom lip, but he also saw her chin thrust forward as she let the shift slither down her body.

'Fucking beautiful.' His words were not gentle, but neither was the emotion he felt. And her quick smile was a benediction.

Her breasts were perfect. Small, firm mounds tipped with dark-pink nipples straining toward him. Strawberry splotches painted her skin in a masterpiece of cream and crimson. Her lean torso and long limbs highlighted Ivy's strength and athleticism no doubt honed by Philippa's training.

I want to feel her legs wrapped around me while she rides me into oblivion.

He could spend the rest of his life staring at her. 'Touch your breasts, Ivy. Show me what feels good.'

'I thought I was going to—'

'Now,' he growled, feeling feral with need. But still he watched her for signs of fear.

Her crystal gaze flashed with temper instead.

Good. Push back if you wish. Tell me to leave. Tell me I don't deserve this moment.

Because Edward was balancing on a razor edge. If he could keep the focus on Ivy, her needs, her pleasure, he could allow himself this moment. But if she made this about him, he would have to stop her. Tell her the truth. Wait for her judgement and inevitably retreat back into isolation. And goddamn it. He wasn't ready to walk away. Not yet.

Lifting gracefully shaped hands, Ivy tentatively touched her breasts. Her eyes widened with discovery as she toyed with her nipples. When she pinched one between her thumb and forefinger, rolling the bud until she hissed and curled in on herself, Edward knew he'd passed the point of retreat. Only her request to stop would turn him back now.

'Come here.' He reached his hand out and Ivy blinked heavy lids. Lost to her own pleasure, it took a moment before she responded, stepping forward on unsteady feet.

'Do you still wish to take me in your mouth, or would you rather I suck, nibble, and bite those sweet nipples of yours until you reach another crisis?'

Her lips formed a perfect pout that he was desperate to dismantle with kisses. 'You're trying to distract me. I told you what I wanted.'

Unable to resist temptation, Edward bent his head and sucked a perfect nipple into his mouth, swirling his tongue around the puckered flesh, sucking hard enough to make her gasp. She was so responsive, he knew he could make her come just by playing with her breasts. And God, did he want to make her fly apart. To claim her next orgasm as his own.

He pulled back just far enough for his lips to brush over the tightened bud as he spoke. 'Are you quite certain?' Blowing cool air on the now wet flesh, Edward savoured Ivy's lean body shuddering in his arms. A corresponding burn of pleasure coalesced at the base of his spine. He could feel his balls tightening as his cock pulsed again. One stiff wind and he would be jetting his seed.

'Yes.' Her answer was the low keen of a woman drowning in desire.

'Yes, what? Tell me Ivy. What do you want?'

'I want to take you in my mouth.'

Damnation!

He didn't want her to do this. This act was focused on his pleasure, not hers, and he wanted tonight to only be about Ivy. But some women also enjoyed sucking a man to completion. Mayhap she was one of those fabled few. It mattered not. Despite Edward's resolve to ignore his own pleasure for hers, he was no match for her determination.

What man could resist such a request?

Certainly not Edward. Harnessing his frustration against his own weak will, he clenched his jaw and stepped away from her perfect body. Looking around the room, his eyes fell on her pillow. He strode to the bed, grabbed the pillow, returned to Ivy and dropped it on the ground between them. 'On your knees.' Maybe she would come to her senses. Tell him to stop. For a woman who experienced trauma in her past, this couldn't be something she wanted.

But she dropped to her knees in front of him, looking up expectantly. 'Now what?'

She had never seen a cock before, let alone touched one, and Edward was going to have her sucking him like a courtesan. He was a bastard, but she refused to be swayed. So he would find a way to make this good for her.

Stepping closer, his cock jutted in front of him. Her eyes grew wide, and he thought she would pull back. But instead, she reached out, gripping his hot length in her clever hands.

'It's so hard. Is it always this way?'

Edward thought of ice-cold water, spiders in his hair, writing reports, anything to distract him from the bliss of her soft fingers gripping his aching flesh. 'No. Only when a man is aroused. Ivy, many women don't enjoy doing this. There are other ways I can find release.'

She leaned forward and before he could force another word from his mouth, she pressed her lips against the sensitive tip of his cock in a chaste kiss. The bead of cum glistening there now painted her lips. Flicking her tongue out to taste his seed, Edward was quite certain his body would explode. She wrinkled her nose, but did not pull away. 'Tell me what to do.' Her wide eyes looked at him with total trust.

I won't last. There is no way I can last. I must last.

'Suck me into your mouth as deep as you can. If you gag, pull back.' He took her hand and gripped the root. 'You can stop whenever you want to, Ivy.'

She refocused on his cock, leaning forward and opening her mouth. Watching her lips stretch over his engorged flesh was the most erotic image Edward had ever seen. When her hot, wet mouth encased him and she tentatively sucked, Edward couldn't stop his hips from thrusting forward. He tightened his hand around hers, forcing her to grip him hard, and pulling up and down the length of his staff in rough motions. She caught his rhythm, matching her mouth to their hands. Her tongue ran along the underside of his cock, hitting a sensitive spot where the head met his shaft. He wasn't going to last. Pulling free of her, he kept her hand on him as he stroked hard. He couldn't look away from their joined hands around his steel shaft as the sweet burning joy built to a crescendo. Jets of seed pulsed from him, coating Ivy's chest and belly, painting her with his essence as pleasure echoed through his body in ever-expanding circles.

Her eyes widened, locked on to his cock, but she didn't pull free of his grasp and when he released her hand, she kept pumping until he gripped her wrist, stopping her.

He was panting like a man running from his demons. And maybe he was. 'I'm sorry.' He'd pushed too far, lost to his own needs instead of ensuring she found pleasure in the moment. Desperately looking for a cloth, he settled on his shirt and snagged it from the chair. Grasping Ivy's hand, he carefully helped her stand. She still hadn't said anything, blinking like a dazed woman recovering from a fainting spell.

Edward tried to remain focused on cleaning her, but it was impossible not to note her swollen nipples, her ragged breaths, her sweet lips darkened to ripe berries. Catching his hand, she stilled his movement. He didn't want to look at her, couldn't bear to see shame or disgust or – *God damn me to hell* – fear in her eyes. But he refused to be a coward. Lifting his eyes, he held his breath and met her crystal gaze.

'That was... astounding.' Her face wasn't full of anger or fear, but rather an astonishing kind of knowledge. 'I did that to you.' She shook her head. 'I made you come apart.' Ivy pressed his palm against the valley between her breasts. 'Do you feel my heart? How can sucking you make me ache here?' She slid his hand down her tight belly to cup her mound. 'Burn here?'

'Giving someone else pleasure can increase your own.' *If you care for them. If their experience is more important than your own.*

He curled his middle finger, splitting her outer lips and dipping into her molten core. She shuddered before pulling his hand away.

'I think we should stop.'

Immediately, Edward stepped back. 'Of course.'

Ivy walked to the peg holding her nightgown and wrap. She pulled the flannel robe around her, hugging herself. 'For now.' She spoke the word quietly, her eyes focused on his knees before she flicked them up to his face.

He held on to those two words with the same desperation a man might hold on to the rope keeping him from a deadly fall. 'For now?'

Her blush darkened over her neck and Edward wanted to pull the robe open to watch it transform her skin but busied his hands instead with re-donning his breeches.

'I was hoping we might finish the list. Maybe add more to it? Tomorrow night, perhaps? If you are agreeable to that plan.'

Edward would be agreeable to any plan involving Ivy's naked body joined with his. Buttoning and tying his breeches, he tried to keep his expression from showing his exuberance. 'I don't believe I have any other pressing matters.'

Ivy raised a pale brow. 'Well, as long as your calendar remains free, then.'

He took a step closer, pulled her into his arms and pressed a lingering kiss against her mouth, inhaling her scent, memorising her flavour. 'Nothing could keep me from you.'

He meant to say, nothing could keep him from meeting with her tomorrow night. But as the words slipped free, the truth of them resonated in his chest. Nothing could keep him away from Ivy. Tomorrow. The next day. Forever. Whether he deserved her or not. Whether she wanted him or pushed him away. The trajectory of his life was permanently altered. She was now true north to his internal compass.

Dear God. I love her.

Dear God. I need to leave.

In a shattering moment of self-realisation, Edward came to a painful truth. He could refuse Ivy nothing. If she asked him to stay with her, forever, he would. Which was impossible. He couldn't betray his oath. If he came to Ivy the next night, it would never be enough. He would come back again and again and again. Philippa told him to tell Ivy the truth, but she was finally wrong. If Ivy heard his worst sin and still accepted him, or even worse, if she fell in love with him despite his crimes, there would be no force in nature that might stop Edward from staying with Ivy forever. Even the promise he made so many years ago to remain alone. A punishment he very much deserved to endure. He was a fool to believe he was strong enough to resist Ivy's pull. If he didn't walk away now, he would break his vow and lose his last shred of honour. So instead, he must break his promise to teach Ivy pleasure.

She ran her fingers along his jaw. 'Goodnight, Edward.'

'Goodnight, Ivy.'

But what he really meant was goodbye.

* * *

Twelve days had passed since Ivy's first night with Edward. The ball was only two days away. He had been planning to join her the evening after their encounter, but Sarah fell ill, and Ivy spent the next several days tending to the poor girl and hoping none of the other children displayed symptoms. Scarlet fever was a constant fear in the orphanages, but it wasn't the only illness that could steal lives. Luckily, Sarah never developed the bright-red rash or swollen neck indicative of the frightening malaise. She recovered from her cold with relative ease, but then Philippa descended.

The duchess insisted they tour other orphanages to determine exactly how dire the situation might be for the children. After seeing ten different foundling homes in seven days, it became clear to Ivy it was dire indeed. Much needed to be done for the parentless youth of London. Institutions varied wildly in quality of food and cleanliness. Access to schooling was limited or non-existent, and the overall health and safety of the children was questionable at best. It was clear to see how a brotherhood like the Devil's Sons could so easily infiltrate the disorganised institutions and steal children with no fear of repercussions. It was also clear that someone needed to be standing up for these innocents.

When speaking with various individuals responsible for running the homes, Ivy found most were just as harried and overwhelmed as she felt. Struggling for resources, inundated with more children than beds to house them, and battling against distrust and misgivings from orphans who had only ever seen the ugliest life had to offer felt like an impossible task. Many of the patrons were just fighting to survive. But a few of the men who only deigned to speak with her because the duchess stood by her side were less than forthcoming. One glance at Philippa confirmed her suspicions. These men were profiting from the money being donated while the children under their care were suffering. It was enough to make Ivy's blood boil, and to convince her Philippa might be right. Mayhap she could do more good working to improve all the orphanages instead of just hers. But she was loath to admit this to the duchess. Philippa was far too comfortable being right.

Probably because it happens so frequently.

And if she did fall in line with Philippa's plans, she would be working closely with Edward for the foreseeable future. Just the thought caused an alarming thud in her chest and warm tingles in all the places his mouth had touched her those twelve long nights ago.

She would need to move back with her aunt and allow a new headmistress to take over the orphanage to focus her efforts on the task force. While helping Edward ensure London's orphanages provided safe, healthy, caring environments would come without income or even recognition – after all, a woman could hardly be expected to publicly take on such a role – Ivy could be frugal with her spending and live off the inheritance from her father. Knowing she would be impacting the lives of so many was humbling and something she very much hoped she could accomplish. It would be worth living with Aunt Gertrude indefinitely.

As Ivy sat down at her desk to make notes of what still needed to be accomplished before the charity ball, she couldn't stop her mind from wandering back and remembering what it felt like to sit in that exact chair, only with Edward beneath her.

Why hasn't he returned?

The first few nights away from Edward, she had been focused on Sarah, mopping her brow, holding her when the nightmares came, letting her cuddle the kitten whom Sarah insisted on naming D'Artagnan. After several frightening nights, Sarah began to fare better, and Ivy returned to her room, although D'Artagnan did not. He had found himself a much more adoring human to keep him happy with cuddles, stolen snacks from the kitchen, and endless ear scratches. And his absence only highlighted her loneliness.

While Ivy's days had been busy, her nights were decidedly quiet without even a purring kitten to keep her company. As she thought back on her early mornings and late evenings, she realised, Edward had been avoiding her. Though he still slept at the orphanage, he often ran out the door just as she came down to break her fast, not returning until well after Ivy sought her bed.

'Why?' It was an excellent question. No one in her room could give an adequate answer, as she was the only one there. But she knew where she might find a man who could.

Already in her nightgown, Ivy took the wrapper from the peg next to her bed. She padded in bare feet down the hall, pausing when a soft cough came from Henry's room. After several moments of silence, Ivy continued her sojourn to the first door in the hallway. Edward's door.

Her nerves jangled like chains on a carriage, but she would not be deterred. They had a deal, and he wasn't fulfilling his portion. She deserved to know why. 'Put your shoulders back. Straighten your spine. Don't be a silly ninny.' Clearing her throat, she lifted her hand and knocked smartly on the door, then cringed at the loud sound, looking down the hallway to ensure no sleeping children had been disturbed.

The door flew open, and Edward stood in his breeches and linen shirt. He swiped off his glasses and shoved them in his pocket. His feet were bare. That detail caused another thud in her chest as her breasts became unaccountably heavy. It seemed implausible their meagre weight could increase for no reason other than Edward's bare feet, and yet they did. Her nipples constricted into tingling buds and warmth unfurled in her belly.

What kind of crazed woman turns into a puddle over naked toes?

The Ivy-kind of crazed woman. Blinking hard, she pulled her focus back to Edward's face. His dark eyes were hooded, his cheeks unshaven, and his usually neat hair needed a trim. 'Are you well?'

Because you don't look well. You look haunted.

Though she wasn't about to say that aloud. What if he was ill? What if Sarah's cold had transferred to Edward? That would explain his unwillingness to visit her room these past few nights.

I am terrible to hope illness upon someone as a favourable alternative to being rejected.

But there it was. She felt rejected. Because Edward had not sought her out after their life-altering evening together.

At least, it was life-altering for me. Mayhap it was just a normal Tuesday evening for Edward Worthington. Bastard.

'I am fine. Just tired. It has been a busy week.'

In all her years of fearing men, she never imagined she might be hurt by a man avoiding her. In fact, avoidance had always been something she worked to achieve. If men didn't want her, they couldn't take from her. They couldn't hurt her. But this rejection was altogether different. It did hurt.

Because I do want him. Most ardently.

But even more than wanting, she *missed* him. She had grown to enjoy their mornings together discussing what tasks they must complete each day. Edward's mind fascinated Ivy, and she enjoyed listening to him talk through a problem. Even more, she loved that he listened to her, sought out her opinion, appreciated her input. Before Edward, the only men she knew were her father and brothers and her relationship with them could hardly be construed as pleasant. Her father considered Ivy a commodity he owned and could sell to a future husband. Her older brother treated her like a nuisance to be endured at formal functions. Even her younger brother, who she'd been closest to before he left for the war and never returned, thought of her more as an affectionate pet than a fully fledged human. Never in her nine and twenty years had she imagined becoming friends with a man. Yet, of all the confusing and conflicting emotions Edward inspired within Ivy, the warm affection of friendship was the most surprising. And now he was giving her the cold shoulder. She wished to know why.

Deciding to take the offence, Ivy strolled into his room and spun, her hand on her hip. 'I thought you were a man of your word, but you reneged on our deal.'

His dark-blue eyes deepened to midnight skies and he stepped closer to her. 'That is a serious accusation to make about a gentleman.'

For the first time since meeting him, Ivy was reminded that Lord Edward Worthington, Commissioner of Scotland Yard, Duke of Landbourne, was a dangerous man. She took a half-step back before stopping herself. Because she also remembered that she was an equally dangerous woman.

'I'm not accusing you. I'm simply stating a fact. You said nothing could keep you from me. Twelve days have passed. Twelve nights, and it would seem nothing *has* kept you from me. Nothing has occurred and you have stayed away. Explain yourself, sir.' The thrill of a fight zinged through her. God, it felt good to confront this big, powerful, deadly man and know she could hold her own.

'Explain myself? Do you really want my explanation, Ivy?' Something dark and hard flashed in his eyes and Ivy wasn't sure. What if she was the reason he stayed away?

But facing the truth was better than living in fear of it. 'Is it because of me? Did I do something wrong?' Ivy was unschooled in the ways of intimacy and Edward surely felt the tedium of trying to navigate the treacherous bog of her past trauma.

No doubt, he had been with many women, all far more sophisticated and knowledgeable than her. All eager to engage in unimaginable naughtiness. It couldn't be very thrilling to try and school a woman in bed sport when his time was spent avoiding anything that might frighten her.

She was mildly shocked when he stepped forward and dove his fingers into her hair, gripping her waist with his other hand. He held her head steady as he leaned closer. Leather, coffee and mint infiltrated her senses. 'You did everything right. I promised I would make this only about your needs. Your wants. But then I had you on your knees sucking me so fucking sweetly. You make me want what I cannot have.' As if to prove his point, he pressed his mouth against hers in a punishing kiss. Licking the seam of her lips insistently, Ivy opened for him. His tongue plunged into her depths, and she tangled with him in a frantic battle for control. Slipping her hand under his shirt, she traced her fingers up his stomach muscles, pressing her thumb against the flat disc of his nipple.

His body hardened and she swallowed his groan. But instead of deepening their kiss, touching her, commanding Ivy to do something decidedly wicked, Edward did the worst possible thing. He froze. Ivy recognised his reaction.

Oh God. He's frightened. What could possibly scare Edward?

She pulled away instantly, letting her hand fall from his body. 'What's wrong?'

Taking an unsteady step back, Edward ran his finger through his hair, tugging hard on the strands and looking everywhere but at Ivy. 'We must talk.'

This is bad. Really bad. Who hurt you, Edward? And where are they now so I may destroy them?

The need to strike, maim, and systematically dismantle whoever had created such fear in him shocked Ivy, but she leaned into the violent emotions. Because when it came to protecting those she cared about, Ivy was beginning to realise she was a force with whom one did not trifle.

'Sit.' He gestured to the bed.

Pulling her wrapper tight around her, Ivy sat on the edge of the mattress, her muscles tense and ready. Edward grabbed the chair from his desk and sat opposite her, resting his forearms on his splayed legs. His gaze stayed fixed on the wooden floor between them.

'Tell me, Edward.' No matter how bad it was, she needed to know.

Her heart thumped painfully.

Damnation.

'I've done something terrible, Ivy. Something I can never undo.'

'What?' She ached to reach out to him, but the distance was too great.

'I killed my sister.'

Everything warm and soft within Ivy froze solid.

He couldn't look at Ivy. Couldn't bear to see her crystal eyes, so full of warmth and heat and desire, shift to fear and mistrust and loathing. Because of course she would hate him when he told her the truth. Just as he hated himself. But it was time. It was time to tell Ivy about Liza.

He exhaled a shaky breath and forced his mouth to form words. 'Before I tell you, I must ask for your promise to keep certain things confidential. While my own reputation is hardly worthy of protecting, this story involved someone we both know. Someone who might be hurt were certain facts made public.'

Ivy straightened her spine and looked down her nose at Edward, every inch a duke's daughter in her pious outrage. 'I hope you know me well enough to trust my discretion, Worthington.'

'I do trust you, Ivy. Implicitly.'

She hmphed out a breath. 'I should hope so.'

God, she is marvellous.

Which made the next part of his story even harder to tell.

Because he would lose any respect or devotion Ivy might feel for him. But it must be done.

'My sister was only two years younger than me. Being so close in age, we grew up in each other's pocket. To everyone else, she was Elizabeth, but to her closest friends – me and Philippa – she was Liza. Our father's country estate abutted Philippa's land and as children, the three of us spent most of our lives seeking each other out. Running through the fields, riding ponies, swimming in the lake that separated our properties. Liza trailed along behind me like a duckling behind her mama. Drove me mad. But Philippa didn't mind. She claimed our games were always better with three.' Edward smiled at the memories and wished he could end his story there, but once started, he found he couldn't stop. 'The summer before I was sent to Eton, we planned an escape. The three of us were going to sneak into the gypsy caravans and go on a grand adventure. Father found us sneaking into the stables one night, pillowcases stuffed with food. He thrashed me properly and I couldn't leave my room for a week. Poor Liza was beside herself with guilt and any thoughts we had of escaping our predetermined futures died that night. I went off to Eton and Liza stayed in the country with Philippa.

'How I missed them that first year. I'd never spent much time with boys my age and after months of unique torture only young men seem capable of, I longed to return home. When term finally ended, I raced back to the country, desperate for the comfort of the only two people who truly understood me. Philippa, Liza, and I fell back into our easy friendship as though no time had passed. But as I spent more time away with the boys at Eton, listening to them brag about their escapades, talk about the women they would bed or wed, my feelings for Philippa shifted. She was my closest friend and the only woman I could imagine spending my life with.'

'You fell in love with her.'

Hearing Ivy speak the words out loud only reminded Edward what a foolish lad he'd been. His dry laugh was bitter with self-loathing. 'I thought I was in love. But what does a twenty-year-old pup know of love? That summer, I had it all planned out. I would confess my undying devotion to Philippa and when I inherited my father's title and lands, we would invite Liza to come and live with us.

'She had been out in society for four years by then, but resolutely rejected any interested suitors, much to the frustration of my father. Liza had long professed to me her desire to remain single, and I convinced Father not to force her into a match too soon. Not until she had time to find the right man. But once Philippa and I wed, we could extend an invitation for Liza to stay with us, and she need never marry if she didn't wish it. In that moment, I felt so goddamned generous. The benevolent older brother providing his sister with sanctuary.'

'Philippa agreed to marry you?' Ivy's shocked gasp forced his gaze to her face and, if the story weren't so tragic, he would have laughed at her wide-eyed expression of disbelief.

'She never got the chance to give me an answer because I never asked. Fate spared me what would surely have been an unforgettable rejection.'

'Ah.' Ivy nodded, as though she understood. But she didn't. Not yet.

'I was young and stupid and caught up in the first flash of desire, bright and consuming in its newness.' He shook his head in disgust at his own hubris. 'Such a fool! I was so lost in my obsession, I failed to see what was right in front of me.'

'What?' Ivy leaned forward, her bright eyes focused on him, lips parted. Even in the depths of his darkest memories, her beauty distracted him for a moment. But he needed to continue. To tell her everything and be done with it.

'Philippa and Liza. They were mad for each other. They'd been falling in love for years. Certainly longer than I'd been in love with Philippa. And unlike my flash of passion, I believe their love ran deep.'

'Goodness. Philippa and your sister? That must have been quite a shock for you, Edward.'

The last thing he deserved was her sympathy. 'It shouldn't have been. If I'd only opened my eyes to see the truth instead of the fantasy I conjured.'

Ivy scooted back on his bed, bending her legs and wrapping her arms around them. Her pink toes peeked out from her white linen nightgown, and she rested her chin on her knees. 'How did you find out? Did Philippa tell you?'

Edward could still remember the moment he discovered them. 'No. I found them. One afternoon, we were all meant to go riding. The girls weren't in the house, so I went out to the stables to look for them. Philippa had Liza trapped against the stall. At first, I thought they were just being silly, but then I saw her kissing Liza. And Liza kissed her back.'

'Oh, my.' Ivy huffed out a breath and he wondered if she was trying to imagine it. Edward's memory of that moment was burned into his mind. Warm sunlight filtered through the barn door. Sweet hay tickled his nose, and the sounds of feminine laughter drew him deeper into the barn. Philippa was wearing one of her scandalous split skirts. Her leg was pressed between Liza's more traditional riding habit. One hand was buried in Liza's chestnut hair and the other gripped his sister's waist. Philippa whispered something in Liza's ear and her smile lit up the barn. But Edward didn't see the love shimmering between them. He only saw betrayal.

'I was so lost in my own anger and jealousy, I went straight to my father.'

'You didn't confront them?'

'No. I'm not sure they even knew I was there until later. My father was furious. He stormed out to the barn and caught them, dragging Liza back to the house and forcing a footman to escort Philippa home. He'd never hit Liza before that day, but he was determined to beat the devil out of her. That's what he told her as he thrashed her to ribbons.'

'Oh, God.'

Warm droplets were tracking down his cheek as he remembered Liza's horrified screams. 'He locked her in her room then went to Philippa's father and told him what happened. Both men determined it was time to find husbands for their daughters. And Father didn't waste a moment. Within the week, he informed Liza a marriage had been arranged between her and one of his friends, a man whose first two wives died, one from scarlet fever, the other in childbirth.'

'No! How could he marry his daughter to one of his friends?'

'Because he wanted to punish her. But Liza refused. She told him she wouldn't speak the vows, and if the man married her anyway, she would run away. Father never took well to threats. He told her she would either marry his friend or be committed to a sanatorium. Her mind was unwell. Why else would she pursue an unnatural relationship with Philippa? At least, that is what Father thought. He determined she would either cure herself by marrying, or he would cure her by sending her to bedlam.'

Ivy tightened her grip around her legs and shook her head. 'Are all fathers so cruel, or just ours?'

A weight Edward didn't realise he'd been carrying cracked. With such a simple question, Ivy managed the impossible. She made Edward feel validated. Understood. Like he wasn't alone. Like mayhap this wasn't all his fault.

She continued before he could answer her question. Which was fortunate as he had no answer to give. 'Poor Liza. And poor Philippa. What happened?'

Edward wished he could forget. He had never told anyone of the last night he saw Liza. Not even Philippa. But the words spilled from him like hot, sticky tar.

'I waited until the house was quiet and I snuck into her room. She was sitting at her desk writing a letter. To Philippa, I presume, but it felt like an intrusion to ask. I'll never forget that conversation.'

The years disappeared and while he stared at a stain on the floor, he saw his sister with her chestnut hair tied in a loose braid, her eyes haunted, her hand holding a quill. The lamplight flickered.

'What's done is done, Edward. My fate is sealed.' Liza's voice was too calm, her eyes devoid of their mischievous spark.

'I did not mean for him to send you away. You must know. I wasn't thinking. We can still get you out. I've sent word to Philippa. We'll sneak you through the servants' hall and out the kitchen. She is to meet you in the western woods. You can flee from there together.' When at first it pained him to think of Philippa with anyone else, now he would happily suffer such heartbreak to save his sister from the hell their father planned.

'To where, Edward?' Her doused fire flared up again as anger brought life to her features. 'Two young women with no money, no protection, no future. It's madness. I will not see Philippa's life ruined. Her father is going to send her to Europe, to a finishing school instead of making her marry right away. She might yet persuade him to let her remain single. But Father will never be swayed. He hates me, Edward. I saw the rage seething in him when

I told him how much I love her.' Liza's voice broke as tears tracked down her pale cheeks.

Edward desperately wished to disagree with her. But he feared she was right. 'If you won't leave with Philippa, at least consider his proposal. Marriage might not be so bad. Bridgemore is old and in bad health. You may only need to endure for a few years.' Even to his own ears, the argument was horrific. Edward couldn't imagine suffering a moment of Bridgemore's hungers, let alone years. But surely it was better than bedlam.

'Listen to yourself, Edward. I would rather rot in a sanitorium than submit to any man, especially a man like Bridgemore. If it comes down to it, I shall throw myself from the roof first.' Her voice was resonant with defiance.

'Don't, Liza! Don't even say the words.'

'Death is not always the worst fate, Edward.'

'Bedlam might be.' He couldn't let her be taken to the sanitorium. He'd heard the horror stories and read the ghastly accounts of ice baths, restraints, beatings and starvation. His sister did not belong in a house for the insane. 'You must consider marriage, Liza.'

'No, Edward, I mustn't. If my freedom is going to be taken away, I will at least control this one last decision.'

If only she had known the horrors that awaited her. If only Edward could have seen into the future. He would have forced her to make a different choice.

'I can never forgive myself for what I've done to you.' Edward's whispered words hung between them and when he would have welcomed her rage, instead, she offered him something far more devastating.

'Punishing yourself does not ease my sorrows, Edward. You are my brother. I would not wish misery upon you, not ever. I love you.'

She loved him when he was the very worst kind of brother. The very worst kind of man.

'She died in the sanitorium several months later.' Edward closed his eyes as his heart ripped in two once more. But this pain belonged to him. He earned it. It was his to carry. Leaning into the heart of his suffering, he forced himself to continue. 'They found her in her room. She'd used her bed sheets to—' He couldn't speak the words.

He heard Ivy moving, the bed springs creaked, and then her warm hands covered his. Gripping his fingers, she pulled him from his seat. She wrapped her arms around him and held him close. 'I am so very sorry, Edward.'

He shouldn't have accepted her comfort; he didn't deserve it. But instead of stepping away, his body curled around hers for one precious moment and he let himself sink into his grief. 'Liza never would have killed herself if I hadn't acted in a fit of petty jealousy.' He spoke the harsh words against Ivy's soft skin and felt her shudder. 'Her blood is on my hands. So is Philippa's eternal heartache. In one fucking moment, I destroyed the two women I loved the most.' Rage seeped in, granting him the strength to do what he should have from the start. Pushing Ivy away, he turned, unable to face her. 'I don't deserve comfort from anyone, least of all you.'

The floorboard creaked as she stepped closer. Edward stiffened when her hands wound under his arms, wrapping across his chest, and pulling his back to her front. The soft pressure of her lips on his shoulder nearly shattered his control. 'Why not me?'

She was everything he wanted and nothing he deserved. 'Because I love you, Ivy.' The words ripped from him, and she froze when they stabbed into her. Because his love was a terrifying blade that cleaved. His love destroyed the object of its affection. His love was abject destruction. 'My love is a curse, Ivy. A jealous, angry thing. I swore the day Liza died I would never let myself ruin anyone else the way I ruined them. But I couldn't even keep that promise. And now you stand here in my room, offering me consolation. How can I possibly allow myself to be with you when she met her end alone?' His heart beat at a mad pace.

Pulling free, he spun to face her. To look into her eyes and show her the ugly face of his sins. She took a step back, her hands in front of her like a groom trying to calm a wild horse.

Good. You should be afraid.

Because he felt wild. He felt unhinged. He needed to convince her how undeserving he was of her love. His vow was cracking, and it would shatter if she didn't leave immediately. 'You want to know why I didn't come to you twelve days ago? Why I can't even look at you without wanting to tear my heart from my chest? Why I stay away when every part of me burns to touch you, taste you, show you all the ways your body can fly apart? Because I don't fucking deserve you, Ivy. You need someone so much better than me.'

'I don't want anyone else, Edward.'

'More fool you! Get out, Ivy. Now.'

But the stubborn woman refused to move. She just stood there. Staring at him.

Fine. If she won't leave, I will.

He moved to the door, but she was faster, stepping in front of him and blocking his way.

'No. I'm not going anywhere. Neither are you.' Putting her hand flat against his chest, she held steady as he leaned closer.

'You can't stop me.'

She slid her hand up to his neck, pulling his head down to hers. 'Watch me.' Her lips were warm and sweet and perfect as she pressed them against his. With a groan of frustrated desire, Edward put one hand on the door next to her head and gripped her hip with his other. She pushed too far. Too hard. But he was going to push back.

'You still want me? Even now? After everything I told you?' He spoke into the shell of her ear before sucking the lobe into his mouth, biting hard enough for her to hiss. But his rough actions were like pouring oil onto a flame. Ivy's hands dove under his shirt, her nails dragging across his heated skin, her thumb flicking his nipple. His cock grew hard, and his thoughts scattered like stones over ice.

'I still want you.' She arched her body against him. Edward was raw and crazed and desperate to feel anything other than the pain threatening to consume him. Her touch was light in his darkness and Edward lost the battle he had been fighting for so long.

I won't break the promise I made to Liza, but neither will I break the promise I made to Ivy. I will show her how good it can be between two people. And then I will leave.

He was making a deal with the Devil for the price of his soul, but Ivy was worth the cost.

Pulling her wrapper and nightgown down both shoulders, he stopped at her waist, holding the material against the door so her hands were trapped, and her perfect breasts were bare to him. 'Then you shall have me and live to regret it. Tell me to stop, Ivy.'

Holding his gaze, she bit her lip and slowly shook her head. 'Don't stop.'

* * *

Ivy's heart broke for Edward even as her body burned. To have experienced such incredible loss and then to blame himself for his sister's death. He was so very mistaken. It wasn't his fault Liza died. His father forced her hand. Society and its twisted view of love certainly contributed. Edward was only guilty of acting like a young fool. Yet he mercilessly punished himself for his mistake. It was a marvel he hadn't imploded.

He needs comfort. But he won't accept it. So, I shall give him what he will take. Pleasure, and when he is too sated to refuse me, I will give him what he needs.

Because she cared for Edward. Deeply. And when a friend was hurting, Ivy would do everything in her power to offer them sanctuary.

In the midst of his many staggering confessions, Ivy hadn't forgotten the one pertaining to her.

He loves me. Edward Worthington loves me.

This gave her pause. She liked Edward. Respected him. Admired him.

I trust him.

But did she love him? It was too much to consider. Not when his tongue was swirling over her taut nipple and sparks of pure glory were jolting through her veins, pooling in that magical place at the apex of her thighs.

Stop thinking. Just feel. Think later.

Excellent suggestions. Ivy was determined to follow her own advice.

She tried to lift her hands free. She wanted to touch him. Explore his body. Sink her hands into his thick hair. But he growled, pulling away from her breast and glaring at her with his dark eyes. 'Don't. Tonight is for you.'

'Touching you *is* for me. I *want* to touch you.'

His firm lips pressed into a hard line as he shook his head. 'Don't think about me. Just what you're feeling. Your father told you a man would only take. Tonight, I want to show you how much a man can give. But you must let me.'

He can give, but he won't receive. Stubborn fool.

But Ivy knew something Edward did not. She learned it through her friendship with Millie. Through her mentorship with Philippa. Through her time with the orphans. Love was a wondrous thing. Much like powdered sugar. Even when you thought you were only sprinkling it on others, you ended up covered in the sweetness yourself. If Edward believed giving her love would stop him from receiving it, fine. She would add it to the list of all the things he was wrong about. Because in giving her love, he would inevitably receive it himself.

'All right. Tell me what to do.'

Edward clenched his jaw, and she ached to run her fingers over the twitching muscles. But she would honour his request. For now.

In one violent tug, he pulled her nightgown and shift all the way down her body, helping her step free. 'Put your hands behind your back.' She did as he asked, crossing her wrists over each other and pressing them against the small of her back. He gripped her hips and pushed her pelvis against the door, trapping her hands between her body and the wood. 'Spread your legs.'

Heat washed over her at the illicit command, but she slowly moved her thighs apart.

Edward's fingers traced over the blush rushing across her chest. His thumb brushed over her puckered nipple and Ivy moaned as her cunny began to weep. He was watching her with such intensity, Ivy was sure he could count the scars upon her soul. Brushing over her nipple again, his pupils dilated as she bit her lip. 'So sensitive.' He circled again, then dipped his head, taking the other into his mouth and sucking hard.

'Damnation!' An invisible cord linking her nipple to her clitoris pulled tight. Ivy saw stars. Teeth scraped over the sensitive tip of her breast, and she was quite certain something inside her shattered as intimate muscles clenched.

'I need to taste you.' Edward dropped to his knees, trailing kisses down her belly. Before Ivy could process his words, his nose nuzzled against the hair covering her mons.

'I don't think—'

'Exactly. Don't think. Just feel, Ivy.' He dipped his head lower. When his tongue split her lips in a silky swipe of velvet heat, Ivy's legs buckled. But Edward was ready for her. Holding her hip against the door with one hand, he gripped her right thigh and pulled it over his left shoulder, then followed with her left leg over his right.

Dear heavens. I am sitting on Edward's shoulders. And my quim is right in front of his mou...

Ivy lost focus as Edward gripped the globes of her bottom in his strong hands, kneading one, then other. He licked along her inner thigh, biting the sensitive skin and making her nearly jump out of his hands.

'Don't move.'

Easy for him to say. I'm not biting his...

His tongue delved into her cleft and Ivy may have screamed.

'Cover your mouth with your hand.'

She pulled one hand free from where it pressed against the door and slapped it over her lips, moaning as his tongue flicked, his mouth sucked, his teeth scraped. He left no part of her untouched. Nibbling the frilled edges, plunging his thick tongue into her aching channel, licking the cluster of nerves, but never long enough. He was toying with her and Ivy was too lost to complain. All she knew was she wanted more. She wanted everything.

'I want you to...' She had no words, but she tilted her pelvis, riding his face. 'I want...'

'Fly apart for me, Ivy. Let me taste your climax.' His tongue circled her clit again, and again, and again. Then he caught the bud between his teeth and bit down just hard enough to shatter her world.

Ivy screamed his name into her hand as her body pulsed and her core flooded. He lapped her like a cat in cream. Slowly, the ecstasy ebbed to a lazy, liquid heat.

Putting one leg on the floor, then the other, Edward rose from the ground, kissing his way up her body until he pulled her hand away from her mouth and pressed his lips against hers. She could taste herself on his tongue. An aftershock of pleasure rolled through her body. Her core still ached in an empty echo of need.

I still want more.

Reaching between them, Ivy fumbled with his falls but couldn't manage the buttons. In desperation, she rubbed her flat palm over the bulging ridge. 'I want...' She squeezed, unsure how to make her need clear. Wishing for better words. Never in her life had Ivy imagined she would want a man to plunder her body. But never before had she imagined a man like Edward. He wasn't some faceless husband intent on taking his pleasure at the cost of Ivy's control. He wasn't interested in forcing her to submit. He was a man who devoted his life to justice. Who punished himself for crimes he hadn't committed. Who chatted with her over coffee and laughed when she retold stories of the children's antics. He was her friend. And she wanted him to become her lover.

'Do you want this...' He put his hand over hers, rubbing her palm over his trapped cock, then let go and twisted his wrist, his fingers trailing through her still wet core, pushing one finger slowly inside her. 'Here?'

Yes! Exactly. That is precisely where I want you.

Closing her eyes and focusing on the rough rasp of his finger pressing inside her body, Ivy nodded.

Stepping back, he took her hand and led her to the bed. She started to climb up, but he tightened his grip. 'Wait.' Letting her hand go, Edward quickly undressed, and Ivy let her gaze wander unheeded over his beautiful body. He climbed onto the bed, moving back so he sat against the headboard. His cock jutted up from the nest of black curls, the tip weeping with a pearly bead that made Ivy's mouth water. He was like a feast laid out, waiting for her. And she almost lost her nerve. 'Come here.'

Why is it that his orders make this so much easier?

It was a question for another time. Ivy crawled on the bed totally nude and mostly confident. When she reached him, Edward took her thigh and eased it over his hip.

What is he doing?

She kept her knees tight to his sides because if she widened them, her pelvis would drop, and she risked impaling herself. This wasn't right. She was supposed to be on the bottom. He would push her legs wide and thrust inside her and Ivy would lay still and let him. But this was nothing like that at all.

'I'm not sure what...'

Gripping her hips, Edward slowly pulled her down. His cock slipped through her folds, not entering her, but dragging over her clitoris in a silky slide of sensation.

'Oh. My. Heavens.'

'Just like that, Ivy. Ride me until you find your rhythm.'

'Are you not meant to, er... enter me?' Though the idea of his large appendage fitting inside her body seemed impossible and the rubbing was shockingly pleasant.

'Not until you're ready.'

Of course. Not until I'm ready. How the blazes am I supposed to know when I'm ready?

'Ride me.'

She did as he commanded, shifting her hips, changing the angle until each drag over his steel length grazed along her cluster of nerves. She had always been a good horsewoman, and the motion was not dissimilar. So she posted, cantered, and finally galloped, chasing another climax. So close to the shining pinnacle but not. Quite. There.

Edward's hands covered her breasts, pinching her nipples in tandem, kneading the delicate flesh until she screamed.

'Now, Ivy.' Edward gripped her hips, lifting her and tilting his pelvis until his blunt head pressed into her aching entrance. Slowly, he pulled her down over him, filling her. The sensation of being stretched to bursting overwhelmed her.

He reached a point and paused. 'I'm sorry.'

Sorry for what? This is glorious.

Gripping her hips, Edward thrust up and sharp pain lanced through her.

'He will spear you with his prick. You will scream, Ivy. But he won't stop. He'll never stop.'

An old panic reawakened. Her father's insidious whisper filled her mind. Her lungs froze. The pleasure suffusing her body only moments before faded like mist and in its place was suffocating fear.

'Stop!'

18

Edward stopped. He started to lift her off him, but she grabbed his hands, halting him.

'No. Don't move.' She could hear the sob in her words and wanted to disappear. Hide away. Find the darkest shadow and make it her home. She shut her eyes, unable to look at him.

'I won't.' Edward slid his hand up her side over her shoulder to her spine. He ran his fingers up and down in soothing strokes. 'Look at me, Ivy.'

Squeezing her eyes tighter, she shook her head. Ivy was lost in the darkness.

'Look at me.' His soft, deep voice vibrated in her heart.

Slowly, she opened her eyes.

'Tell me what feels good.'

She tried to think about his words. Focus on something other than the searing heat of invasion. 'I don't know what...'

'Don't think about the pain. Think about breath in your lungs. Cool air on your skin.'

'Your hand on my back.'

'Yes, darling! My hand on your back.' He continued rubbing.

His other hand slipped up her side until he cupped her breast and kneaded slowly. 'What else?'

'Th-that's good.' She arched her back as he leaned close and pressed a sweet kiss against her nipple.

As Edward continued to rain soft kisses over her chest, Ivy realised the shock of invasion wasn't nearly as painful as the fear of her father's words. And her father was wrong. Edward did stop.

'Stay here, with me. It's just us. You and me.' As Edward crooned the words his hand kept stroking up and down her back. His other hand slipped back down, gripping her hip. 'You're safe, Ivy.'

The panic ebbed with every stroke of his hand. When his thumb inched closer to her slit, traced the seam where their bodies met, desire reawakened. The burn of fullness shifted. Pleasure painted the edges of pain as her channel stretched around him. She took a shuddering breath and tensed her inner muscles.

A white arc of sizzling sweetness zinged through her. She clenched again, chasing the lightning, and Edward bit his lip. His hand stuttered on her back.

What a wonder.

She could make him react just from... She tightened once more and watched his pupils blow wide.

Fascinating.

Edward found her clitoris, pulsing and swollen. He rubbed the pad of his thumb in soft circles and Ivy clamped around his cock harder as echoes of pleasure became a keening cry of sweet need.

'God, woman. You are killing me.'

'Tell me what to do.'

'Ride me, Ivy. Just as you were before.'

She could do that. Tilting her pelvis, she lifted up, the drag of his thick shaft through her aching channel made easier by the wetness she provided. She slid down, grinding herself against his thumb, taking more of him into her. Up again. Down harder. She bottomed out and something sharp and bright came to life.

Fingers dug into her bottom, urging her on. Faster. Deeper. Closer. Flesh slapped flesh, sweat trickled down her spine. He reared up, fastening his hot mouth over her nipple, sucking hard, nipping with sharp teeth as he thrust up with his hips, hitting that bright spot again. And again. And again.

Waves of stunning glory washed through her as she flew apart. Wrapping her arms around him, she held tight, riding him over the cliff's edge. Moments later, he pulled free, his cock painting ribbons of white over his belly and chest.

Ivy collapsed on top of him, uncaring of the sticky mess. Replete. Exhausted. Sore. Sated. Complete.

* * *

They didn't talk and the silence felt sacred. A soundless sanctuary.

Edward took a towel from the washbasin next to his bed and cleaned his body. Rinsing it in the shallow bowl, he came back to the bed and gently moved her legs apart, wiping the blood from her thighs. There wasn't much. She'd bled more when she fell and scraped her knee. She'd always imagined rivers of blood and endless pain. But after the first shock, it had been nothing like her frightened imaginings. It was beautiful.

Ivy felt strangely raw. Not her skin. Not inside where she pulsed still with a memory of their joining. But in her chest. In the vast, unmappable topography of her soul. She was supposed to be comforting him, but perhaps comfort was like love. Impossible to offer without also receiving in equal measure.

He lay on his back and pulled her onto his chest. She could hear his heart thumping a soothing rhythm as he dragged the blanket over them. Ivy breathed in his scent of coffee and mint, her eyes drifting closed. She couldn't remember feeling so safe.

When next her eyes opened, sunlight streamed through the window, and she was alone. A note lay on the pillow next to her.

Ivy, I'm sorry. You deserve better.

'Bastard!'

* * *

'So you just left?' Philippa sat in her front parlour, a steaming cup of tea in her hand and a scowl pulling down her crimson lips.

'What else should I have done? You, of all people, know the depths of my sins, Philippa. I'm the last person who deserves a woman as sweet, brave, and courageous as Ivy.'

'Good God. You sound as dramatic as a young miss at her first ball. Should I ring for Stokes to bring you some smelling salts?' She took a sip of tea before placing the dish on the table in front of her.

Edward's sharp laugh was devoid of any joy. He sat across from her in a velvet wing-back chair, but his frustration made it impossible to remain still. His leg bounced up and down in a manic beat. 'I thought you would take a little joy in my suffering. After everything I've done to you, it must be satisfying.'

Philippa rubbed her thumb and forefinger in endless circles.

'One would think. But no. I find no joy in your pain, Edward. Unlike some people, age has granted me wisdom.'

'The great Duchess of Dorsett admits to ageing? Mayhap I do need smelling salts.'

Her eyebrow took wing as she leaned forward. 'I admit no such thing. I'm merely explaining why my intelligence far surpasses your own.'

'Ah. Well. Never mind, then. Proving your superiority to me is nothing new.'

'Exactly. But I do have something new to share.'

Edward felt a sense of dread wash through him. 'I'm not sure I'm up to hearing it.' He tried to keep his voice light, but his jest fell short.

Philippa tsked. 'Brace yourself.'

Edward took a deep breath, exhaled, and nodded for her to proceed.

'I forgive you, Edward. Not for Liza's death. And not for what I was forced to endure.'

'Because those are unforgivable crimes.'

'No. Because those are not your crimes to carry. I forgive you for telling your father.'

Edward shook his head. The sting of tears threatened as he rejected her words.

Philippa stood and walked to him, crouching down in a shocking display of improper posture and forcing him to meet her gaze. 'I forgive you, Edward, for the crime of acting like exactly what you were. A stupid boy full of pride. But I have come to realise that is the *only* crime of which you are guilty. The same as every other young lad in London.'

He wouldn't accept her words. If he let go of his self-hatred, if he accepted Liza's death was not his to carry, then he would lose that burden and, in doing so, lose part of Liza. It made no sense, but holding his guilt felt like holding her memory. 'No. It was my fault.'

Philippa covered the hand he fisted on the armrest of his chair. 'It was not. And it's time for you to let it go, Edward.'

Bowing his head, Edward allowed the tears to fall. 'What if I can't?'

'You must.'

'I'm so sorry, Philippa.'

She squeezed his hand. 'So am I, Edward. But the truth is, everything that occurred after you went to your father in a silly fit of jealousy was beyond your control.'

'But if I hadn't said anything—'

'Liza would have told your father herself. She was bound and determined to profess our love, even when I warned her of the consequences. And if I was able to convince her to stay quiet, someone else would have discovered us. We were hardly discreet. Just as full of blind confidence as you in our false faith that love would conquer all.'

Philippa's words slowly sunk into his mind, fracturing long-held beliefs and seismically shifting his understanding of truth. He could imagine Liza striding up to their father, her heart-shaped face full of defiance, declaring her love for Philippa. And their father's reaction would have been the same. He still would have demanded Liza marry the man of his choosing or be banished to bedlam. If what Philippa said was true, Liza's fate was inescapable, and Edward was just the pawn who brought it to fruition.

'So you see, Edward, your actions only hurried along events that were destined to occur.'

As the weight of guilt lifted, the ache of grief rushed in. 'I miss her. Every day.'

'Every moment. Yes. I know. But she would never want you to live like this.'

He lifted his head and stared into Philippa's cobalt eyes. It was strangely like looking in a mirror. 'What about you?'

Philippa pulled back and rose to her feet, her face hardening into the lines of a woman in complete control. 'We aren't discussing me. We are talking about you. And what an utter mess you've made with Ivy because of this ridiculous martyr mentality. No one likes a sad sack, you know.' Turning, her blackberry silk skirts swished around her legs. She tucked a non-existent loose hair back into her intricately coiled twist. Looking over her shoulder, she speared Edward with a scathing glare. 'Punishing yourself for the rest of your life is very melodramatic of you. Rather Gothic, if you ask me. I expect better from the Commissioner of Scotland Yard.'

Edward leaned back in his chair and took his first deep breath in forever. Perhaps Philippa was right.

Of course she is. She's always right, the bloody harridan.

He would never stop missing Liza. Never stop grieving her. Never stop wondering what life would be like if she was still present. But mayhap it was time to forgive himself. To finally do as his sister asked and not live a life of lonely misery.

'She isn't the only person I miss, Philippa.'

In lieu of a response, Philippa pulled a fan from her pocket and scratched her nail over one of the jewels.

'I miss you. The friendship we shared once so long ago. If you are asking me to forgive myself, then I am asking you to let me back into your life. We are the only two people who really knew Liza. Can we not start there and rebuild our friendship?'

Philippa's shoulders tightened. 'You ask too much.'

'I'm just following your example, Philippa.'

'As painful as it is for me to admit, there are times – seldom and fleeting though they may be – when I also miss your friendship, but I don't know if I have room in my busy schedule for anyone else.'

Standing, Edward crossed the distance between them and gripped her hand in his. 'What about old friends who are sometimes prone to be melodramatic sad sacks?'

She sniffed. 'Perhaps.'

It was as close as Edward would get to her agreement. 'Thank you, Philippa.' His voice cracked with a dangerous cocktail of grief, love, and hope.

She pulled from his grasp. 'Don't become maudlin. I can't abide blubbering fools. We have a charity ball tonight and much to be done in the meantime. Namely, tucking your tail between your legs and devising an apology speech for Ivy to rival all others. Think of what you said here and then improve it by one thousand.'

'Ah. There is the duchess I've grown to cherish.'

'Fix this with Ivy so we can refocus on our mission. It's time to capture a wolf.'

Philippa pulled the decorative rope to summon Stokes. After waiting several seconds, she pulled again. Harder.

Eventually, the door creaked open, and Stokes slowly entered, his back ramrod straight. His eyes focused on the floor three feet to the left of Philippa. 'Yes, Your Grace.'

'Fetch me my writing supplies, Stokes.'

The butler shifted his gaze to the writing desk tucked in the corner. He tipped his chin. 'You mean, those writing supplies?'

Philippa rolled her eyes. 'Don't be a fool. Those are for formal letters. This is just a little note to invite Ivy to take advantage of my lady's maid and dress for the ball here instead of at the orphanage.'

'You wish me to fetch informal stationery?'

Philippa looked at Edward and shook her head sadly. 'Poor old stodger. He's getting a bit...' She looped a finger in circles next to her temple before refocusing on the butler. 'Should I use smaller sentences? Is that the problem? Or just shout louder? Ink. Quill. Parchment.'

'Of course, Your Grace.' Stokes strode sedately over to the writing desk, pulled out a fresh piece of parchment, dropped it on the floor, and trod on it. He bent, pinched the corner, and walked over to Philippa, holding out the slightly crumpled paper. 'Casual notepaper, Your Grace.'

'I sometimes wonder what life might be like without you, Stokes, but such fantasies are too good to ever be true.'

'Certainly, Your Grace.'

Curling her lip like she had just eaten an unripe strawberry, Philippa rolled her eyes. 'I'm sure there's something you should be doing to prepare for tonight, Stokes.'

'Yes, Your Grace. I *was* doing important work. But then you summoned me.'

'Well, that was certainly a waste of everyone's time, wasn't it?'

'Of course, Your Grace.' Inclining his head in a regal bow, he turned and left as slowly as he arrived.

'One day.'

'Yes, yes. You'll sack him. I know.' Edward failed to hide his smile. While danger awaited only a few hours away as they prepared to draw out the Wolf, for the first time in forever, he felt a sense of hope.

* * *

Ivy must have lost her mind. She never should have agreed to let Philippa's incredibly talented lady's maid dress her for the ball. Delacroix was like a military general, pulling, tugging, pinning, twisting. But the effects were astounding. Her fair hair was twisted into a sleek knot at her crown. Wisps spilled out like a waterfall of silvery blonde around her face. Rubies were clipped strategically to look like clusters of roses. Looking at herself in the full-length glass, Ivy was lost for words.

Her dress – another Madame Collette miracle – was crimson red. A colour Ivy would never choose. It drew far too much attention. And the cut of her neckline was two sneezes away from being completely indecent. Delacroix had done some magic with Ivy's corset. While she was fairly confident her ribs were broken, she no longer resembled a flat plank of wood.

'One of the advantages to small breasts is much more plunging necklines. You look marvellous, Ivy.' Millie stood on one side of her as Hannah came from behind with a wickedly sharp dagger.

'Here, put this in the pocket. Do you have a pistol?'

Ivy nodded. 'Yes.' She patted one side of her skirt and slipped the dagger into the other side. 'I don't know what to say to Edward.'

'Tell him he's being a right blockhead. If that doesn't work, drag him to Philippa's back parlour and show him exactly what he'll be giving up if he doesn't pull his head out of his arse.' Penny stood behind Ivy.

When Ivy arrived at Philippa's after receiving her note, she expected her mentor would be there. She did not expect to see Millie, Hannah, and Penny with their own maids, all crowded into Philippa's private suite of rooms. Apparently, Philippa had extended her invitation to all the Queen's Deadly Damsels. Ivy spent the afternoon letting Delacroix work her magic while she poured her heartache out to her friends. They had much advice to give, ranging from cutting off his bollocks – *thank you, Hannah* – kidnapping him and stealing away to a cottage in the woods until he came to his senses – *wonderful idea, Millie, though I don't have any spare cottages at the moment* – and now dragging him to an empty room during a charity ball and accosting the man – *interesting tactic, Penny, but requiring a mite more confidence than I currently claim.*

There was a knock on the door, and Philippa's butler, a portly man with the posture of a military commander, stepped inside. 'Lord Drake, Lord Killian, and Lord Reynard have arrived.'

Millie pinched her cheeks in the mirror and pressed her lips together. 'We should go down. The guests will be arriving any minute. Don't be nervous, Ivy. We're all here to support you. Just stand up there in front of the entire beau monde and convince those self-absorbed, horrible prigs to give a fig about orphans. Then, wait for the Wolf to emerge. Simple as a Sunday pudding.'

Ivy felt ill. 'Yes. Well. I've always hated pudding.'

Hannah squeezed her arm. 'You'll do grand, Ivy. Try imagining everyone with peacock feathers coming out of their noses.'

'Or that no one is wearing trousers, but they all have chicken legs,' Penny added helpfully.

As the women rustled to the door in layers of silk, crinoline, and lace, Philippa approached from where she had been staring out of a large window to the grounds beneath. 'Ivy, may I have a word before we descend?'

Millie was at the door and paused, turning back to them. 'Is anything amiss?'

Philippa waved her on. 'No, I just need a private moment with Ivy.'

'Right. We'll see you down there.' With a little wave, she hurried after Hannah and Penny.

Ivy's belly dropped as she looked at her mentor. Philippa's sharp gaze, usually so direct, seemed to land on every object in the room except for Ivy. 'What is wrong, Philippa? You look... anxious. And you never look anxious.'

'I want you to be careful tonight, Ivy. Remember your training. And if there is any unforeseen trouble, stay calm. Trust your instincts. And don't hesitate to strike if you're given an opportunity.'

In the flurry of activity leading up to the ball, it was easy for Ivy to forget the inherent danger. But members of the Devil's Sons would be leading ladies around the dance floor, sipping on the ratafia, smoking their cheroots, and watching. Always watching as Ivy took centre stage and threw down her gauntlet. Instead of fear, Ivy felt a defiant pulse of anger course through her. *Good. Let them watch.* Let them hear her words and know their brotherhood was under attack. Ivy had no intention of losing this war. They should fear her.

'I won't hesitate, Philippa. You have trained me well. I'm ready.'

'I would speak to you about another issue.'

Ivy nodded as Philippa flicked open her fan and examined the jewelled patterns.

'Edward came to see me today.'

Every muscle in Ivy's body tightened. The pulse in her neck beat hard against her skin. 'Did he?' She tried to remain nonchalant, but the words emerged as a squeak.

'He did. I know he spoke to you of Liza.'

Ivy's heart dropped with heavy grief for her friend. 'I am so sorry for your loss, Philippa. I can't imagine how painful it is for you.'

Philippa gently closed the fan and caught Ivy's gaze in the mirror's reflection. Love. Devastation. Grief. They all swirled in varying shades of sapphire, cobalt, and indigo. Philippa blinked, and her eyes cleared, but the pain did not. 'Losing one's partner is an agony I wouldn't wish on anyone. And never experiencing the kind of love I was blessed to know – even if it was only for a short time – is not something I would wish for you, Ivy. Edward is a good man, and he loves you, but he is also an idiot. Luckily, he is less stupid now than he used to be. He shouldn't have left you this morning. But sometimes, our own demons chase so close behind, the only option we have is to flee. At least for a time. A feeling you are most familiar with, and therefore best able to understand, I think.'

As usual, Philippa was correct. Ivy did understand the need to run at times. But if he was running away, how could they move forward? 'What should I do, Philippa?'

'While I credit Hannah, Millie, and Penny for giving sound advice, I think an honest conversation might be the best route. Lay out your cards, Ivy. Tell him what you want. Ask what he wants in return. What he is capable of giving.'

I never know what I want.

But for the first time in her life, it wasn't true.

I want Edward.

And she wasn't about to let a little fear stand in the way of claiming him.

'Thank you, Philippa. Your advice is sound as always. I wonder if you would take some from me.'

Philippa raised a black brow. 'You have found your courage. Rarely does someone dare give me advice. Except Stokes, perhaps, but that man lives to vex me. Please.' She nodded her head, granting Ivy permission.

'I can't imagine how painful it must be to lose someone you loved so deeply. But I don't believe opening your heart again to the possibility of a new love dishonours what you shared with Liza.'

Philippa's eyes flashed, and Ivy nearly retreated. But this was too important to back down. She turned to face the duchess and gripped both of her shoulders. The jewels sewn into Philippa's deep purple gown dug into Ivy's fingers. 'Liza would want you to find happiness again, Philippa.'

Philippa tried to pull back, but Ivy refused to loosen her grip. 'If circumstances were reversed, would you wish her to remain alone for the rest of her days? Denied the comforts of companionship? Never again experiencing the beauty of loving and being loved?'

Philippa swallowed. She turned her head to look over Ivy's shoulder. Ivy squeezed Philippa's shoulders. 'I know it is easier to remain in the shadows. Believe me. I've spent years safely tucked away. But it's a half-life, Philippa. And you deserve more than that.'

Clearing her throat, Philippa met Ivy's gaze. 'I find receiving advice is far less enjoyable than giving it.'

Despite the weight of their conversation, the danger they would soon face, the impending conversation Ivy needed to have with Edward, a giggle bubbled up from her belly, and she let it burst free. 'Very true. I shall endeavour to keep my advice to a very minimum henceforth.'

'Thank you, Ivy. I will consider your words.'

Ivy let her hands drop free and brushed them over the softness of her silk skirts. 'Shall we?'

'We shall.' Philippa led them out of her rooms and into the fray.

19

Edward generally avoided balls. They were crowded, smelly, exhausting affairs requiring him to wear his least comfortable suit, stiffest boots, and tightest cravat. He'd much rather have been riding his favourite gelding in the mews, or drinking whiskey in his library, or feasting on Ivy's body in some shadowy alcove. A body he'd spent most of the evening watching with unabashed desire.

Ivy was brilliant. She moved through the guests like a sleek ship cutting through waves, engaging in conversations with lords and ladies, even dancing with a few dandies. Her face was a serene mask of charm, and while he'd noticed her finger tapping away at her skirts more than once, no one would ever guess the shy wallflower was anything less than a consummate host.

Edward kept his distance, watching the people around Ivy, focused on anyone who might look suspicious, but outside of a young man's hand slipping lower than it should during a waltz, he'd seen nothing alarming. And Edward couldn't stay away from her any longer.

Her back was turned to him as she spoke with Olivia. Lady

Smithwick was stunning in an ivory gown of gossamer fabric that captured the candlelight and shimmered pearl pink, icy blue, and pale green, constantly changing as she moved. It clung to her curves and highlighted the woman's pale skin and hair. She looked like an ice queen descended from the high mountains and drew appreciative glances from more than one titled lord. Her husband spent much of the evening hovering over her like a jealous dog guarding a bone. Edward couldn't imagine their union brought either of them much joy, yet Lord Smithwick wasn't about to relinquish his possession.

'Commissioner Worthington.' Lord Percival Smithwick nodded curtly before his gaze swiftly returned to his wife.

Warm satisfaction flowed through Edward's blood as Ivy turned sharply, her lips parting on an inhaled breath. The blush painted her skin, and his body leaned closer in an unspoken question.

Will you accept me? Will you accept my imperfect love?

'Commissioner, I was hoping you might join us. How are you enjoying the evening?' Lady Olivia's warm greeting was the perfect foil to her husband's cold reception.

Edward forced himself to turn to the elegant lady who helped mastermind the charity ball.

'Quite the turnout, Lady Olivia. Even your brother has graced us with his presence. I thought he only attended events when the Queen was present. Dare we hope Her Royal Highness might surprise us with a visit?'

Lord Smithwick put a possessive hand on Olivia's arm, tugging her closer to him. 'Doubtful. The Lord High Chancellor is a loyal brother, and his presence here is a credit to the devotion he has to his sister. He's always wanted the best for you, hasn't he, Olivia?'

Something ugly passed between the couple. A message Edward couldn't decipher, but one he noted.

Shifting slightly so her shoulder turned away from Lord Smithwick, she regained some of the space he'd sought to shrink. Olivia smiled at Edward. 'Indeed. My brother cares a great deal for me. I'm sure his presence here has helped convince others to give generously. We've already raised more money than we expected.' She tipped her chin at the chest set up on a table in front of the unlit hearth. The massive fireplace was large enough to fit five men standing shoulder to shoulder. Edward followed her gaze and saw young Henry standing next to the chest with Sarah on the other side. His thin shoulders were thrown back, chest puffed out as he guarded the donations with a fierce scowl on his young face. Sarah was watching the ladies on the dance floor, her eyes wide with wonder. She looked charming in a dress of white with pink lace trim. 'It looks like you chose the right guards for the donations.' Edward smiled across the ballroom at the lad whose cheeks flushed crimson at the recognition, then winked at Sarah, who burst into a giggle, pressing her hand over her mouth.

Olivia laughed. 'He insisted on it and who could pass by sweet little Sarah and not be tempted to give generously? Don't worry, I've commandeered some of your fine officers to ensure the children and the money are safe.'

Standing behind Henry and Sarah were three constables in the unmistakable blue coat and brass buttons of the Metropolitan Police. Edward didn't recognise them, but with a police force boasting several thousand, it wasn't surprising. The men were scanning the crowd. Edward took comfort in knowing any thief would have to get through three grown men before they faced off against Henry and Sarah.

Edward turned his focus to Ivy and willed his voice to

remain steady. 'You are looking especially lovely this evening, Lady Cavendale.' He couldn't stop himself from taking in all her stunning beauty. He knew his gaze lingered far too long to be considered polite, but he didn't care.

'As are you, Worthington.' Ivy's lips curled at the corners. 'Are you ready?'

Edward cocked his head. 'For what?'

'Our announcement. You didn't think I would stand in front of all these people alone, did you?'

Actually, he hadn't given any thought to how they would announce their task force. A glaring oversight. His mind had been so distracted by thoughts of Ivy, he hadn't even considered that he would need to speak in front of the entire beau monde. His mouth became dry as the desert, and all words fled his mind.

The orchestra struck up a waltz. In a fit of panic, Edward extended his hand to Ivy. 'First, a dance?'

Ivy bowed and took his hand. He led her to the crowded dance floor and settled his fingers around her waist. Her lean, powerful body was like an anchor holding him steady in a stormy sea. As the cello and violins swept them away, Edward felt the unfamiliar flutter of nerves in his belly.

'I owe you an apology, Ivy.'

She spun out from him then swirled back into his arms. 'Indeed. I woke to an empty bed this morning.'

He blinked, cursing his own cowardice. 'I thought it would be best to leave you alone.'

'No.' Ivy squeezed his shoulder. 'You thought it would be best to remain alone. There is a difference.'

He swallowed his quick response. Because she was right. Guiding them in a flurry of intricate steps, he manoeuvred them close to the wall of windows looking out on Philippa's gardens.

Honeysuckle, roses, and hyacinth sweetened the air as a summer breeze wafted through the window. There was a French door propped open to let in the night air. Slipping Ivy's hand from his shoulder, he interlaced their fingers and tugged her onto the veranda.

'Commissioner Worthington, you shall create a scandal at our charity ball.'

'I don't care. I will not have this conversation with the beau monde watching.' He pulled her to the corner of the marble porch and spun to face her. 'I am a flawed man, Ivy. And you are right. I meant to remain alone. I thought it a fitting punishment for my crimes.'

'Edward, you are not responsible for Liza's death.'

He nodded. 'I know that now. In my head.' He tapped his temple. 'But it still doesn't feel that way in here.' Moving his hand to his heart, he flattened his palm against his jacket and felt the wild beat. 'But I'm endeavouring to convince my heart to catch up with my head.'

She covered his hand with her own. 'Would you like some company whilst you persuade yourself to accept that I love you, Edward?'

Her words broke his last shield like shattering glass. Lifting their joint hands, he pressed a kiss to her palm. 'You love me?' It was more than he could hope for. The familiar whisper of unworthiness wound through his thoughts, reminding him of every reason he was undeserving. 'I don't—'

Her hand flew through the air, connecting with his cheek in a stinging smack. He was shocked into silence. It was the second time in as many days a beautiful woman had slapped him.

Ivy rubbed where her hand left a red mark. 'Cease telling me you don't deserve my love. In fact, the next time you profess your unworthiness, I shall do worse.'

Like dousing a sleeping person with cold water, her promise cleared away the mists of his past and awakened something new within Edward. Hope for the future. 'I must confess, I find myself wondering exactly what kind of punishment you might exact upon me.'

Ivy pulled his head down and pressed her lips against his. Her tongue darted out to test the seam of his mouth. When he opened to her, she plunged in, exploring his depths. He grew hard and needy in an instant.

'Have you ever tupped fully clothed outside a crowded ballroom?' It was a wicked proposition and impossibly dangerous. Anyone could discover them. But Edward didn't give a flaming fig.

'Oh yes. All the time,' she quipped. When he ran his finger along her plunging neckline, she shuddered. 'We need to speak to the guests, Edward. Remember?'

'We will. In a moment.' He bent his head to follow the trail his fingers took with his tongue, nuzzling the sweet rise of her left breast, then her right.

Ivy's hands were in his hair, tugging. 'You are impossible.'

'And yet, you still love me.' Just saying the words breathed life into his creaky soul.

His thumb breached the boundary of silk hiding her sweet nipple from him. She moaned, her forehead resting on his shoulder. He leaned closer, kissing her neck, tasting the salty sweetness of her skin.

'I do. I love you. And I promise we shall finish this. Later.' When she pushed him away, Edward reluctantly submitted.

'Fine.' He felt like a schoolboy being denied a sweet. But a treat deferred only became more delicious when it was finally consumed. 'But I shall hold you to that promise, Ivy Cavendale.'

'I would expect nothing less of the honourable Commissioner Edward Worthington.' She winked, and Edward fell a little further in love.

I shall always be falling. Ever deeper.

His heart beat a wild tattoo as she took his hand and led him back to the ballroom.

* * *

Ivy strode on shaky legs to the table holding the chest of donated money. Nodding at Olivia, her friend hurried to where the musicians were playing and whispered instructions. Their song ceased instantly. Couples on the dance floor pulled apart, looking around to find the disturbance.

Philippa cut through the crowd to stand next to Ivy. Edward flanked her other side, and her gaze sought out Millie, Hannah, and Penny. They were filtered throughout the crowd. Drake stood close to Millie, his hand on her hip as he kept a watchful eye on the crush. No doubt his scarred visage helped to scare off any potential threats.

Hannah's hand was in her pocket. Killian was behind her, his suit jacket not quite hiding a pistol-sized bulge.

Penny and Liam were on the dance floor. She turned to face Ivy, her back against her husband's chest. He kept his hands on her shoulders, pulling her close as Penny gave Ivy a reassuring smile and plucky wink.

The moment was unaccountably surreal. She'd spent endless hours training in the ballroom. Philippa must have had her servants working from dawn until the dead of night to remove the training paraphernalia. Wooden dummies, sandbags, targets, and countless weapons ranging from swords, pistols, throwing knives, and cudgels were usually spread across the parquet, but now the walls were swathed in purple and yellow silk. There wasn't a weapon in sight, though Ivy guessed plenty were hidden amongst silken skirts and suit jackets. The floor was packed with some of the wealthiest and oldest titles in Queen Victoria's realm. What might these grand lords and ladies think if they saw this ballroom a week before?

Summer blooms covered the tables. Beeswax candelabras flickered, and the three chandeliers highlighted a ceiling painted with a breathtaking rendition of Artemis during a hunt. She held her bow aloft, an arrow notched and ready. Nymphs frolicked in the trees, and a stag walked by her side begging the question, exactly what – or perhaps whom – was she hunting?

Evil men.

Ivy took courage from the fresco. Before she could lose her nerve, she raised her voice to address the crowd. 'If I could have everyone's attention, please.'

Hundreds of eyes turned to Ivy, and her stomach twisted in a nauseating roll.

Oh dear God. I am going to be ill in front of the entire beau monde.

A warm hand pressed against the small of her back. With no one behind them, Edward's gesture was hidden from view, but Ivy felt his encouragement fill her with strength. Her gaze flicked to Henry. The lad nodded at Ivy, stiffening his already straight spine, a proud sentinel protecting the money that would change so many lives. Sarah's wide smile lit her face, and in a terrifying moment, Ivy realised what a beauty she would one day become. Her undefined future was another reminder of how important this moment was for all of them.

'The Duchess of Dorsett has so kindly hosted this ball to raise money for our most vulnerable.' Ivy spent the next few minutes describing the harrowing fate of so many innocent children orphaned by illness, poverty, or violent crime. She spoke of the tenacity, skill, and enterprise these young people could achieve. The roles they could play in contributing to the betterment of society, industry, and service. The danger of neglecting hundreds of young lives who, without the chance of honest industry, might turn to far more unsavoury pursuits. Or become prey to an ugly underbelly of crime. Her nerves fell away as she became more impassioned. 'It is our responsibility to protect these children, provide them with education, skills, and training to become contributing members of the realm, and ensure no corrupt forces are preying on our most innocent, vulnerable citizens. Your donations tonight will help us with this most important mission. And further, Commissioner Worthington has agreed to create a task force focused on ensuring the health and safety of all our orphans.' Ivy looked to Edward as a ripple of whispered comments rolled through the crowd.

'Lady Cavendale is right. Scotland Yard's primary purpose is to prevent crime. To that end, we will be keeping a watchful eye on our orphanages to ensure each child housed within has the opportunity to achieve a bright future.'

'And to aid in this most important work, I shall be stepping down as headmistress of All Souls Orphanage to focus my work on supporting this task force and its most important mission. Rest in the comfort of knowing your contributions tonight will be put to good use. If any man wishes to harm our children, they will need to contend with me.'

'And the full force of Scotland Yard.' Edward's deep voice boomed through the quiet crowd.

'And Queen Victoria herself.' A new voice rang out. The crowd swung their collective gaze to the other side of the room. The Lord High Chancellor stood next to his sister. He cut a striking figure with his height and solid stature made even greater by contrast to his sister's petite form.

Ivy reached down, surreptitiously gripping Edward's hand

and squeezing. The Lord High Chancellor's endorsement was an unexpected boon. When Millie started clapping, the crowd caught on, soon creating a thunder of support that only dissipated when Olivia instructed the musicians to play a lively reel.

Ivy and Edward made their way to the children as a rush of lords and ladies swarmed the orphans to drop more money in the chest.

'You were right brilliant.' Henry's eyes shone as he looked at Ivy.

'You aren't going to be our headmistress any longer?' Fingers pulled on Ivy's dress as Sarah's chin wobbled.

'No, silly. She was just saying that to the crowd. You aren't leaving us, are you, Miss Ivy?'

Damnation. I should have thought to speak with them before this. Idiot.

Ivy took Sarah's hand into her own and squeezed. 'I am so sorry. I should have told you before. But I will still come visit. I promise. Every week.'

A fat tear rolled down Sarah's now splotchy cheek. 'But it won't be the same. Who will read stories to us at night? And protect us from men sneaking in the window? Who will take care of me if I get sick again?' Her quavering voice rose higher with each word.

'I don't want a new headmistress. What if she smells of fish oil? Or beats us if we don't get our chores done fast enough?' Henry turned to Edward. 'She can't leave. You've got to make her stay.'

Edward put his hand on Henry's shoulder. 'I can't make her do anything, nor would I ever try. But I promise we shall find the right headmistress. Someone with nary a hint of fish oil.'

'Who will read to you every night,' Ivy agreed, the heartbreak of Sarah making her want to take back everything she said about supporting the task force and rush to her small little room at the orphanage. 'We promise.'

Sarah covered her face, her thin shoulders shaking with sobs. Ivy pulled her into a hug and looked helplessly at Edward. This was supposed to be a moment of triumph, but she felt terrible.

Olivia swept through the crowd, joining the tragic quartet. 'What on earth is wrong?'

'The children didn't realise I would be leaving my post.'

'You can't leave.' Henry's face grew red, his eyes suspiciously bright. 'You must stop saying it. Please.'

Help! Ivy mouthed to Olivia.

The fair beauty nodded her head. Taking Sarah's and Henry's hands in each of hers, she spread her lips in a bright smile. 'Why don't you both come with me? Cook has far too many puddings and will need some help eating them up. You've done such a wonderful job tonight, you deserve a special reward. You'll feel loads better once you've had something to eat, and then we can discuss what to do about Miss Ivy. Trust me, darlings, all will be well.' Pulling the children along, she swept out of the ballroom.

'I feel awful.' Ivy wanted to lean into Edward, but there were too many eyes on them.

'So do I. We should have spoken with them first.'

'It was stupid of me not to think of their shock.'

Edward clenched his jaw. 'Stupid of us both. It's only been a short time, but I've grown very fond of those two. All of the children at the orphanage. We'll think of something. Some way to reassure them. But now, let us join the others at the refreshment table and see if our little speech drummed up any suspicious behaviour. There will be time enough to focus on the children once we've captured the Wolf.'

What kind of person had she become when the prospect of flushing out evil lords bent on horrific crimes improved her mood?

I'm no longer hiding in the shadows.

Nor did she want to remain alone. An idea was germinating.

What if I asked Worthington to marry me? And if he agreed, would he also be willing to take on Henry and Sarah?

It was a revelation of thought. To even imagine not only binding herself to a man for the rest of her days but adopting two children on the cusp of adulthood. Was it madness?

I don't care. I'm not going to hide from what I want any more out of fear.

The seed of her idea propagated and grew like a vine, unfurling in her mind with endless possibilities. Providing the love and security she never experienced to two young people who had only known heartache and hardship would be a joy she could barely imagine. Guiding Sarah through the gauntlet of high society. Helping Edward mentor Henry and finding a vocation he would enjoy. What richness the two children would bring into her life. It was a shining dream, but was it one she could achieve?

It doesn't have to hinge on Edward marrying me. I can do this on my own if I must. Mayhap I won't be able to adopt the children, but I can hire them to work in my household if that is the only option available. If he rejects me, at least I know where I stand. I shall ask him tonight. When we are back at the orphanage. And I'm naked in his bed. Or he is naked in mine.

Some might think using her body as a tool to increase the odds of wooing him might be dishonourable, but she was going to use every weapon in her arsenal to fight for a future with Edward and the children. The thought of him refusing her was painful enough to have Ivy catching her breath as they walked around the edges of the ballroom.

'Are you well?' He gripped her elbow, squeezing tight.

'Quite. It's just these stupid slippers.'

Millie had a cup of ratafia ready for Ivy when they arrived at the refreshment table. Killian sidled up to Edward and handed him a flask.

'You'll thank me later.'

Philippa joined them. Her sharp gaze landed on the flask. Faster than an adder's strike, she snatched it from Edward, unscrewed the top and took a long swallow. 'Not bad, Killian.' Re-capping the decanter, she tucked it into her pocket.

'Hey!' Edward's mock outrage was the perfect comedic relief.

'I assume you will return that later?' Killian asked.

Philippa raised a brow and smiled. 'I've found assumptions to be rather dangerous things. Rarely do they come out the way we wish.'

Ivy cleared her throat. 'Has anyone heard anything suspicious? Any whispers when I gave my speech?'

The group took turns recounting information they'd gleaned while dancing and mingling, but outside of a countess embarking on an affair with her footman, an earl marrying an American heiress with bad teeth and a large bank account, and a certain young debutante who might be in an interesting condition with a man lacking a title but flush with money from his work in shipping, there were no rumblings of the Devil's Sons.

'Well, we may not have flushed out our prey, but we've certainly done some wonderful work for the orphans.' Ivy tried to put a favourable light on their efforts.

'We aren't done yet. Not by half. Focusing on orphanages is a great way to put pressure on the Devil's Sons.' Edward's hand found its way back to Ivy's waist. 'Eventually, they'll slip up. We need to increase our watch on the docks. If we can catch them moving the children—'

'But capturing the laymen won't stop the leaders. We need to find the Wolf. I thought tonight would be the catalyst.' Philippa thwacked her fan, then narrowed her gaze. 'Your friend is coming to join us.' She turned away as Olivia approached.

'Lady Winterbourne, I never got the chance to thank you for hosting our ball. You've helped make this a wild success.' Olivia's smile looked strained, her eyes straying from Philippa to Ivy. Something was wrong. Ivy could see it in the fine lines bracketing Olivia's lips.

'I did it for Ivy. And the children, of course.'

'Of course. Heaven knows you wouldn't trouble yourself to help me. I would wager you wouldn't deign to spill your wine on me if my dress were alight.'

'I don't drink wine.' Philippa stretched her mouth. 'And I certainly wouldn't waste good whiskey as it would likely only intensify the conflagration.'

Olivia narrowed her eyes. 'Indeed.' She turned to Ivy. 'May I speak with you privately? There's a small issue.'

'Can we assist?' Millie's voluptuous figure and wild red curls were set off in a gown the colour of burned caramel. Drake's eyes kept wandering to her neckline every few moments, and Ivy was certain she'd heard him growl something indecent in Millie's ear not moments before.

'Thank you, but no. It's just a small issue brought up by some ladies from the Committee.' Olivia linked her arm through Ivy's and tugged. 'We shan't be long.'

Ivy felt Edward's fingers dragging across the silk of her dress as she walked away. She gave him what she hoped was a smouldering look. Based on the flush crawling from his neck to his cheeks, it worked.

Now, if only I could get him to growl naughty things in my ear.

She hid a secret smile as Olivia swept them out of the ballroom and down a corridor toward the library. Instead of entering the large room replete with floor-to-ceiling shelves, a rolling staircase, and a collection of first-edition books many said rivalled that of the Queen herself, Olivia kept walking.

'Where are we going? What is amiss, Olivia?'

Olivia paused. Tears shone in her green eyes. 'Oh, Ivy, I'm so sorry. It's all my fault.'

A thrill of alarm washed through her.

'Tell me at once.'

'It's the children. They've gone missing. I took them to the kitchen for a treat and told them I'd be back once I checked on the chest. I asked Percival to take it to the study to count out our donations. I thought we could announce it at the end, a grand cap to our successful evening, but when I returned to collect the children from the kitchen, they were gone. Cook had no idea where they went.'

They were so upset about me leaving. Dear God. What if they ran away?

Visions of Henry running into street toughs or Sarah begging for scraps of food on a dirty street corner in Whitechapel filled Ivy with a familiar feeling. Fear. But this was not the freezing, cover-your-head-and-hide-in-the-shadows kind of fear. This had sharp edges and claws. This had teeth and strength and rage. This was feral, a fierce, demanding action.

'Where have you looked? We can start in the kitchen and search every room. I'll get the others. We'll split up and comb the gardens as well.'

Olivia shook her head. Looping a loose strand of hair around her finger, she coiled it and tugged. 'I already checked the kitchen. Why don't we try some of the closer rooms together? If we don't find them, we'll get help. This is the last thing we need the guests to discover.'

Because she had no time to argue, Ivy agreed.

They made quick work of the servants' hall, pantry, and scullery.

'They aren't here.' Panic was making Ivy ill. What if they weren't on the property? What if they were walking the streets together in the dark? All alone.

'What about the stables? When I left the kitchen, Cook was talking about some kittens that had just been born in the stables.' Olivia looked a little wild-eyed. Her pale skin was almost white. She fidgeted with a button on her gown until the thing popped off, but Olivia didn't seem to notice. 'I'm so sorry I let this happen.'

'It isn't your fault. If Sarah discovered there are kittens in the stables, I've no doubt that's where we'll find them.' Ivy infused more confidence into her voice than she actually felt. After this, they would need to get the others. Philippa's house was far too palatial for two people to search every nook and cranny. Even if the guests were disturbed, finding the children took precedence.

Rushing back through the kitchen, they took the back door to the mews. Even across the cobblestone yard, Ivy could see lamplight flickering in the stables. With so many guests arriving by carriage, it was no wonder the stable boys were up and about, helping direct the traffic, finding places for groomsmen to park their carriages while they waited for the ball to end. Keeping Philippa's horses calm amidst so much activity. But when she followed the yellow light past several stalls, no rushing men were about. The nicker of a horse and stomp of a hoof comforted Ivy. Stepping into the centre of the stables, she saw two figures sitting together on the hay. Rushing forward, Ivy almost reached them when she realised something was wrong.

They weren't moving. Their hands and feet were tied together, and they'd both been gagged.

The distinctive sound of a gun being cocked stopped Ivy cold.

'Lady Ivy Cavendale. Finally, I can remove the thorn you have become in my side.' Lord Percival Smithwick stepped from the shadows of a stall near the children. His pistol was pointed directly at Sarah's blonde head.

Olivia's husband is the Wolf?

It made sense. He was at the Widow's Ball when young Thurston was given his note. He was aware of the happenings at the orphanage with his wife heading up the syndicate funding the venture. He was the bloody brother-in-law to the Lord High Chancellor. There was no telling what secrets he took back to the Devil's Sons after sharing port and cigars with his wife's brother. With a few carefully crafted questions, he could easily be one step ahead of them.

Turning, she yelled a warning to Olivia. 'Run! Get the others.'

But as her friend careened into the stable, she stumbled to a stop, staring at her husband.

Ivy moved in front of Olivia. Slipping a hand into her pocket, she palmed the pistol and held it behind her back. She couldn't draw on Smithwick. Not when he was so close to the children. But if she could get the gun to Olivia, distract him, draw him closer to her, and get him to point his gun at Ivy, then Olivia could take the shot. Even if she missed, the report of the gun would draw attention, and Ivy might be able to take advantage of Smithwick's surprise.

'What are you doing, Smithwick? Put the gun down.' Backing up another step, she felt Olivia's skirt tickling the back of her knuckles.

The slimy toad threw his head back and laughed a high-pitched, shrieking sort of sound. 'No. I don't think I will.'

Olivia's warm hand covered hers. She took the gun from Ivy.

Huzzah! Now I just need to get him away from the children.

Putting her hands in front of her, she started moving slowly closer to Smithwick. 'You don't want to do this. Hurting these children helps no one.'

'That's where you're wrong, you stupid little fool. We have orders to fill, and you have put a dent in our production. These two will go some way in helping to restore our good faith with some very wealthy customers.'

Oily sickness coated her stomach. What kind of monster described children as product?

Sarah started to sob, tears tracking down her face and getting caught on the rag tied around her mouth.

Ivy mustered a smile. 'Don't worry, darling. No one is going to hurt you. I'll keep you safe. I promise.'

Olivia made a strangled sound behind her as Ivy took another step closer to Smithwick.

'The promise of a woman.' He laughed again. 'About as useful as a bouquet of roses on the battlefield. Don't you agree, Olivia?'

Ivy didn't want him looking at Olivia. He might see the gun she was valiantly trying to hide in her skirts. Ivy needed his attention firmly focused on her. 'What do you hope to achieve tonight, Smithwick?' If she could get between him and the children, protect them with the shield of her body, Olivia might be able to get off a shot before Smithwick could fire his own weapon.

'Just one more step in our plan, Lady Cavendale. You see, we can't have a certain commissioner poking his big nose into our business. Certain members of the peerage, myself included, would have a bit of mud on our faces if that happened. Imagine if the beau monde were to discover how many dirty little street rats disappear every day, all on order from the Devil's Sons.'

'I rather think you'd have a noose around your neck.' Ivy sidestepped closer to Smithwick and the children, angling her body to keep him directly in her line of sight. She had a dagger in her pocket and while she wasn't as adept at throwing knives as Millie, she wasn't half-bad. If Olivia couldn't shoot her husband – which was a deuced difficult thing for anyone to do, let alone an untrained woman like Olivia – then Ivy would use the dagger as plan B. She doubted they would have time for any other plans.

'Then you have no idea how many lords are on our payroll, Lady Cavendale. Trust me, no member of the Devil's Sons will ever hang. A member of the peerage being trotted out of Newgate and executed in front of the rabble? Can you imagine?'

She was already doing so with Smithwick claiming centre stage in the scene she envisioned.

'You will be held accountable for your crimes.' She was close enough now. Picking up her skirts, she rushed forward. *'Now, Olivia!'* Reaching the children, she wrapped her arms around both of them, covering them with her body, closing her eyes and waiting for the deafening report of her pistol.

Instead, Smithwick's high-pitched laughter sent a thrill of alarm down her spine. Opening her eyes, she turned to Olivia.

Her friend held the pistol in a shaking hand, but it wasn't pointed at Smithwick. It was pointed at Ivy.

20

Edward's feet hurt and he was desperate to loosen his cravat. He wondered how long it might take Ivy to deal with whatever problem the Committee of Concerned Ladies for Community Betterment was having. Mayhap they could leave the ball within the next half-hour. He was desperate to enlighten Ivy on the finer points of lovemaking in a carriage. All the bouncing caused by cobblestones could be quite... invigorating. Just imagining her sitting backward on his lap, her skirts around her waist, his hard length penetrating deeper with every rut they jolted over. He would direct the driver to take the long route back to Islington.

'Right. That's it. I shall just go find her myself,' he muttered to no one in particular. As he was winding through the thinning crowds, a servant approached him with a sealed note.

'For you, Commissioner Worthington.' The servant held out the missive, his head bowed.

As soon as Edward took the note, the man disappeared back into the crowd. Glancing down, Edward's stomach dropped.

The head of a crow. The body of a wolf. The tail of a snake.

Ripping the note open, his hands began to shake.

Ivy is in danger. Go to the stables.

He should alert the others, but glancing around, he couldn't see any of them. They may have left already. Hannah and Killian had said something about needing to end the evening early. The last he saw of Millie and Drake, the couple were making their way to the entry. He hadn't the time or patience to try and locate Penny and Liam.

He turned and fled the ballroom, nearly knocking Philippa over in his haste.

'What is wrong?' Philippa gripped his arm, holding him steady when he needed to run.

'Ivy. Stables.' He shoved the note into Philippa's hand then wrenched free, his feet flying across the polished floor toward the kitchen. It was the fastest route to the stables. The fastest route to Ivy.

* * *

'I'm so, so sorry, Ivy. I had no choice.' Olivia's beautiful eyes were red-rimmed and swollen. She bit her lip so hard, Ivy nearly winced. Her sweet friend looked absolutely miserable, and she would have felt awful for her.

Except she's pointing a bloody gun at my chest.

'You are part of this?' It was impossible.

Damnation! Philippa was right again. *She told me not to trust Olivia.*

Rage swept through her blood and Ivy forgot to be afraid. She spent her whole life fearing men like Smithwick. Men like her father. His smug smile, the triumph flashing in his eyes.

The confidence that no mere woman could ever upset his plans. But to think, in the end, she'd been betrayed by her friend.

Olivia was wrong. There was *always* a choice. And Ivy chose to resist. If she died tonight, it would be fighting, not cowering in fear. But she would also do what she could to free her children.

Olivia had made poor use of the weapon Ivy slipped her. She had no doubt Sarah and Henry would do much better. As she stood, she snuck her hand into her other pocket, took the dagger and cut a hole in the lining so the weapon could fall to the floor beneath her skirts. She toed the thing behind her, feeling it bump into Henry's leg. His small gasp was all the confirmation she needed. If they could cut their bonds, they could run. Ivy just needed to give them a chance.

'Of course she is part of this. She is my wife, to command as I please, aren't you, dear?' The cold glint in Smithwick's eyes left no doubt as to the kind of cruelty he exacted upon his wife.

She almost felt sorry for Olivia. Almost.

'You promised nothing would happen to the children, Percy. You said we would let them go.'

'Don't call me that. You know I hate when you call me that. And what do you know of promises kept? You promised to love, honour, and obey your husband. How long did that promise last? Months? Weeks? Not even days. One broken promise deserves another. We have quotas to fill, Olivia.'

Olivia pressed a hand over her mouth. Her wide gaze flicked from Ivy back to Smithwick. 'I can't...'

'You know what is at stake if you do not.'

Ivy saw the horror fill Olivia's eyes. Whatever threat Smithwick held over her, it was a powerful one. Perhaps Olivia had less choice than Ivy assumed.

'Take the children to the carriage waiting in the mews. Some of my men will be there to pick up the delivery, then hurry back here, wife. I'll need help getting rid of her body.'

He's talking about me. My body.

Sarah's sobs grew louder and more frantic.

'What good does killing me do, Smithwick? Worthington won't stand for it. He'll hunt you down like a rabid dog.' She needed more time to think. To find an opening. To create an opportunity for the children to escape.

'He won't have a reason to. That's why we must get rid of your body, Lady Cavendale. No body, no crime. And the note he finds in your reticule, the one you so helpfully left with your coat upon arrival, will confirm his worst suspicions.'

Ivy cocked her head. 'I don't understand.'

'Of course you don't. A woman's delicate brain couldn't possibly be strong enough to hold the plans men create. Your dear friend Olivia here was kind enough to forge a letter from your lover. It's already been placed in your bag awaiting discovery.'

Edward? But I haven't told Olivia about Edward.

'Not a real man, of course. Who would want to seduce a cold plank of wood like yourself? But no one need know that. According to his letter, the two of you were plotting to steal the money from this charity event and escape to the Americas. When Commissioner Worthington finds the money gone and you with it, convincing him to abandon his task force and track down a thieving bitch who betrayed him will be easier than convincing Olivia here to follow the commands of her husband. By the by, aren't you supposed to be taking those children to the mews?' He raised a brow at Olivia.

Olivia brushed past Ivy. 'I am so sorry,' she whispered.

But her apology only increased Ivy's fury. 'What good does that do? Don't be sorry. Be better. Fight with me,' she hissed.

Olivia wouldn't meet her gaze as she awkwardly tucked the gun under her arm, knelt beside Henry and untied his feet. Then Sarah's. Ivy wished she could bash Olivia over the head and knock some sense into the woman.

'Come along, children.' Olivia spoke the same way she'd done when inviting them to the kitchen for pudding. 'Upsy-daisy.' She stood, grabbing the gun in one shaky hand, then reached down to help Henry up, but pulled back her arm as if she'd been bit. A crimson stain soaked through the sleeve of her gown. She looked rather dumbfounded at the wound. 'He c-cut me.'

Henry lunged for her again, his eyes wild, his lips pulled back in a snarl. This was the boy who'd spent years on the streets, fighting for his survival. 'Get away from us,' he screamed, brandishing the dagger as he put his body between Olivia and Sarah.

Smithwick swung his gun around. He cocked the pistol. The weapon was pointed at Henry. He was going to shoot the boy.

With a feral war cry, Ivy launched herself at Smithwick. He didn't have time to retrain his weapon before Ivy was on him. The force of her attack toppled them over and she landed on top of Smithwick. Gripping him tightly between her thighs, she scrabbled for the gun. Grabbing his wrist, she slammed his hand against the cobblestones once. Twice. Three times until he lost his grip. The weapon fell free and Ivy dove for it.

Sharp pain nearly stole her breath as he gripped her hair, wrenching her back. But not before she grabbed the pistol.

'Not so fast, you skinny little bitch.' He was in an awkward position on the floor, his hand twisted in her hair, but she ignored the pain.

While he surpassed her in strength, Ivy fought with wild abandon. She couldn't fire the gun at such close quarters, but there was more than one way to subdue an adversary. Thrusting her elbow behind her into his ribs, air exploded from him as he lost his grip on her hair. Twisting her torso, she arced the pistol through the air, using it as a cudgel against his cheekbone. The hard metal cut into his skin, opening a wide gash that spewed blood. She fisted her other hand and slammed it into his throat, revelling in his choked gasp. Scrambling to her feet, she kicked him with all her might, aiming for his soft belly. Curling into a foetal position, one hand pressed against his gushing cheek, the other trying to protect his middle, Ivy kicked him again. His high-pitched scream was like music.

Ivy stood over him, the pistol held tightly in her hands. One flick of her finger and it would be done. Smithwick would be dead.

'Ivy, don't pull the trigger.' Edward's voice was like a shock wave through her system.

Edward's heart was in his throat and his legs had cinder blocks attached because they were too heavy to move. Every cell in his body wanted to run to Ivy. Hold her in his arms. Convince himself that she was safe, and well. She was magnificent standing over the snivelling weasel. But he dare not take a step closer. She was balancing on the brink of a madness he knew well. One false move and Ivy might fall.

'Philippa, find Olivia. She went that way.' Edward pointed to the back of the stables. The fair-haired beauty had made a run for it the moment Edward skidded into the stable, right before Ivy slammed her fist into Smithwick's throat. Olivia's bright hair and iridescent dress would help Philippa hunt the woman down in the darkness.

With a swift nod, Philippa pulled a pistol from her skirt and quickly disappeared into the shadows.

He forced his gaze away from Ivy to the children. 'Henry, Sarah, come behind me. Yes, that's it.'

Henry helped Sarah to her feet, the dagger still held in one hand. They skirted the edge of the stables and then cut across the short distance in the centre to huddle behind Edward.

Returning his gaze to Ivy and Smithwick, Edward put his hand on Henry's shoulder and held the boy's gaze, willing some of his strength into the lad. 'Take Sarah to the kitchens. Find the butler, Stokes. Tell him what has occurred and that we need to locate Lord Killian, Lord Drake, and Lord Renquist and their wives. If they've left the ball, he can send a runner to their houses. They are needed here. Immediately.'

'Yes, sir.' The boy's voice wavered.

'Good lad.'

When Henry reached for Sarah's hand, she pulled away, her eyes on Ivy.

'I won't leave her.' The girl's voice wavered, but she thrust her chin out in an expression reminding Edward of Philippa.

'She wants you to be safe. I'm here. I'll protect her, Sarah. You can trust me. Right now, you must go with Henry.'

She blinked and pressed her lips together. For a terrifying moment, Edward thought she would refuse him. He had no idea what he would do if she did.

'You promise she'll be okay?' Sarah asked.

Edward nodded. 'I do.'

'Fine. But I'm not holding his hand.' She huffed, glaring at Henry's hand as though it were diseased. Instead, she strode past him out of the stable. Henry gave a long-suffering sigh and hurried after her.

With the children safe, Edward could give all his attention to Ivy.

'He's the Wolf, Edward.' Ivy's hand shook, her finger tightening on the trigger. Smithwick curled into a smaller ball, his arms over his head as if they might deflect a bullet. 'He was going to sell Henry and Sarah. He was going to kill me and try to make it look like I ran away with the money.' Her voice was too calm. Devoid of inflection.

'She's lying.' Smithwick peeked from under his own arm. His desperate gaze found Edward. Tears, blood, and snot streaked over his dirty face. 'She's gone mad. She admitted her plan to me. She was going to run away with her lover.' Spittle sprayed from his mouth. 'You must believe me.'

'Lying coward!' Ivy kicked him again, and he tightened back into a ball, groaning in pain.

'Given that I am her lover, and we have no intentions of going anywhere, I'm inclined to believe the lady.' Edward understood Ivy's struggle. He wouldn't mind putting a bullet in the man himself. He certainly deserved such punishment for his crimes. But Edward had a better idea. 'Ivy, he is not worth the stain his blood would leave on your soul. He can't hurt the children. Step away from him.'

'I don't mind a few stains.'

'Fair, but he's more valuable to us alive.'

Ivy looked at Edward. 'How?'

She was fierce and fearsome and if he wasn't already in love with her, this would seal his fate. She wouldn't follow his lead without first understanding his reasoning. A fair deal, as he would do the same thing in her shoes. 'A few nights in Newgate might loosen his tongue to share the secrets of his brotherhood. And if it does not, seeing which men in the House of Lords push to release him from his sentence will give us just as much information. If they are even willing to risk exposing themselves to save this worthless maggot.'

Ivy turned her head back to Smithwick. 'He says he won't hang. He says he'll be released.'

'Then we'll find him again. Do you hear me, Smithwick? If

you are released, you better be prepared to run, because we will find you.'

Smithwick's response was a garbled sob.

Ivy kicked him again, Edward guessed she hit his kidney by the way Smithwick howled. But her grip on the gun loosened and he knew reason had eclipsed revenge. 'Fine. We shall let him live long enough to know what it feels like to have a noose around his neck.'

Edward breathed a sigh of relief, then found some rope. Ivy kept her gun trained on Smithwick while Edward tied his hands and feet tight enough to cut off circulation. When he was certain the weeping lord was securely bound, he stood and walked to Ivy, wrapping his fingers around her pistol's muzzle. 'I think we can put this down, now.'

Holding her arm stiff, her eyes resolutely trained on Smithwick, she didn't move. Edward gently cupped her cheek and shifted her to face him. 'You were stunning.'

* * *

Ivy blinked and tried to make sense of Edward's words. It was like waking from a horrible nightmare. But the keening sobs from Smithwick were far too real to be a dream. She would have killed him. Without thought or question. He threatened Henry and Sarah, and she would have pulled the trigger to ensure their safety. In a moment fraught with terror, she hadn't felt fear, just a strange, resolute calm. But now, all the horror seeped in to chase away the rage.

Dropping the pistol, she collapsed into Edward. 'I would have shot him. I *wanted* to do it.'

'I know. And I wouldn't have blamed you for it, but this way is better, Ivy. I swear it.'

Edward wrapped his strong arms around her, pulling her tight against his chest and she sank into him, her body shaking. 'I'm quite cold.'

'It's shock. It will pass. Just stay right here. With me.' Edward rocked her back and forth and she burrowed deeper into his coat, inhaling coffee, mint, and man.

She could have easily died this night and never again felt the glory of being held. Never again known the beauty of falling asleep with her head on Edward's chest, the rhythm of his heart carrying her into dreams. They had only shared one night together and it wasn't enough. It would never be enough. If today was any measure of the danger they might face moving forward, she didn't want to waste any more time.

'We should marry. Immediately.' She spoke against the rough fabric of his coat.

Edward pulled back, his eyes searching her face. 'You are still in shock. You don't know what you are saying.'

Ivy lifted her hand to trail a finger down his cheek. 'I know exactly what I'm saying.' She brushed her thumb over his lip, his pupils blew wide. 'Edward Worthington, Commissioner of Scotland Yard, Duke of Landbourne, you are the only man I could ever imagine sharing my life with, and you are the only man I can't imagine this life without. Will you marry me?'

Edward blew out a breath. For a terrifying moment, she thought he would refuse her. After all, they never spoke of marriage or commitment. This had been about pleasure and exploration. But he loved her. He said it himself. And she loved him.

Drat. Did I tell him that bit? I can't remember. No wonder the men do this part. It's bloody awful.

'If I forgot to mention, I do love you. I love you very much and, er, that would be one of the reasons I think we should marry.'

The ghost of a smile tilted Edwards firm lips into a crescent. 'Really? And what would the other reasons be? Shall we write a list?'

Ivy couldn't stop her grin as her cheeks heated. 'Will you marry me, Edward?'

He pulled her back into his arms, pressing a sweet kiss against her lips. 'It would be my greatest honour, Ivy.'

'Oh, one more thing.'

Edward nuzzled her neck. 'Yes?'

'I wish to adopt Sarah and Henry.'

Edward froze and Ivy's heart stalled right along with him. If he refused her this, she wasn't sure how they would move forward. 'You mean we.'

Ivy frowned. 'What?'

'I'm not sure you understood what you were proposing earlier. If we marry, then we agree to make our decisions together. You are not adopting Sarah and Henry.'

'Why ever not?' Her newly awakened anger bubbled forth. She would fight him on this point if she must.

'Because *we* are adopting them. Together.'

She took a moment to absorb the details of his face, the scent of the stables, even the sound of Smithwick weeping at her feet. Because this was *the* moment when everything changed. The quintessential strike in her timeline of before and after. 'Truly?' Joy could sometimes hurt like the sweetest ache.

Edward nodded, tugging her back to him for a searing kiss.

Smithwick's desperate sobs ruined the moment. Ivy reluctantly pulled away. 'I suppose we should deal with him. And find Philippa and Olivia.' She still hadn't processed her friend's betrayal.

'I suppose we should. But later. Later, we will celebrate. I can get a special licence. We can be married by next week if you wish.'

If *she* wished. What a marvellous thought. After everything her father told her, all the ways marriage would ensure her captivity, her subservience, her forced submission, to know this union would be based on her wishes was miraculous. But still, not quite right.

'If *we* wish. Didn't you just say? We make our decisions together.'

'What a lucky man I am to have such a brilliant fiancée. Let me try again. Do we wish to marry next week?'

Ivy's heart overflowed. 'We do.'

Three weeks later

'I cannot believe no one can locate Olivia. Do you think she left England entirely? Maybe returned to Europe, or took a vessel to the Americas?' Ivy had been Lady Ivy Worthington for two weeks, but still, it felt like a dream. She stretched in Edward's large bed, *our large bed,* not missing her narrow mattress in the orphanage one tiny bit.

'I have no idea.' Edward lay next to her with the sheet barely covering his very aroused appendage. Flipping her over so she was on her belly, he pulled her nightgown up and began trailing kisses along her spine.

'I am worried about Philippa.' Ivy tried to keep her focus on the conversation, but whirls of sweet ecstasy were spinning over her skin from the centre of each hot kiss.

'So am I. But I was rather hoping we could discuss this later.'

Edward palmed her bare arse and squeezed hard enough to make Ivy moan.

'It's just, no one has ever knocked Philippa out, have they?'

'No one except Olivia,' Edward agreed, his teeth scraping over her shoulder blade before he bit hard enough to make her desperate for more.

'I still can't credit it.' Ivy's words were rather breathless, but she pushed forward. 'Philippa raced after her in the stables, came around a corner, and wham! Olivia hit her with my gun. Knocked Philippa out cold. It's hard to know if her obsession with finding Olivia is due to Philippa's passion for justice, or a very bruised ego.'

Edward slapped her arse with the flat of his palm. The sting resonated in her nipples. 'You know the children will be banging on our door soon, wanting to break our fast together. And we promised Sarah we would let her try riding the new pony after that. We have a very limited moment to engage in all manner of delightful wickedness and you want to ruin that with conversations we could have any. Other. Time.'

Ivy arched her back, knowing the move would lift her buttocks. Edward growled as she smiled into the pillow. 'Of course, my love. We can discuss this later.'

'Good.' Edward used his thigh to push her legs apart, pulling her hips higher so her knees dug into the mattress. He ran his hands along her sides, bumping over her ribs to cup her breasts. She gasped as he squeezed and pinched her mercilessly.

'I can't believe Lord Smithwick was killed in prison. Do you think the Devil's Sons orchestrated his murder?'

Edward groaned, pulling his hands away from her breasts and holding her hips steady. 'Remember when we determined our decisions should always be made together? Well, if we can't come to an agreement that pillow talk does not include Olivia,

Philippa or, for God's sake, the murder of certain prisoners, then I may have to override some of your decisions.' He smacked her arse again, harder.

Ivy squealed into the pillow. She loved it when he was a little rough. 'We certainly wouldn't want that.'

Spreading her cheeks, he brushed his thumb over her back entrance before delving into her wet folds.

'God! I want you. Now.'

'Then you shall have me,' Edward growled as he thrust into her channel from behind, the pressure creating a spark of sensation across her clitoris.

'I do so love when we make decisions together,' she gasped.

'As do I, sweet Ivy.' He pulled back only to plunge again, deeper.

'Don't stop,' Ivy demanded.

Don't stop loving me. Don't stop being with me. Don't stop sharing this life with me.

'Never. I swear it.'

And just as she trusted him with her heart, body, and soul, she knew this was a promise he would always keep.

* * *

MORE FROM DARCY McGUIRE

The previous book in The Queen's Deadly Damsels series from Darcy McGuire, *The Confessions of a Lady*, is available to order now here:

www.mybook.to/ConfessionsLadyBackAd

ACKNOWLEDGEMENTS

I would like to thank all of the many women in my life who have supported me. First and foremost, my mom, Mari, for being such a shining example of both the strength and softness required to be a woman. My grandmother, Jessie, who turns 100 this year and has exemplified love, acceptance, and resiliency every moment of her life. My two girls, Makielah and Meguire, who have never been afraid to boldly stand in their authentic selves. My mother-in-law, Charlene, for accepting me into her heart and family with all the love and none of the judgement. My sisters-in-law Charla and Elizabeth for encompassing all the facets of sisterhood. My niece, Emily, for fiercely advocating for others while she walks her own path with grace and honour. My tribe of gorgeous friends who stand with me through the storms and remind me dancing in the rain can be just as much fun as dancing in the sun. The amazing women of Boldwood who have helped turn my dream into a reality including my editor, Megan Haslam, and my copy editor, Emily Reader. And my talented agent, Katie Reed, and Andrea Hurst for taking a chance on me and championing my efforts every step of the way. Women have an incredible talent for changing the world through the action of love. I'm so honoured to be a part of such a vibrant, proud, powerful community of people.

ABOUT THE AUTHOR

Darcy McGuire is a high school counsellor who grew up in the wilds of New Zealand but happily settled in the Pacific Northwest. In between dodging territorial geese, gathering duck eggs, taking the dog for long walks, Darcy loves writing about fierce female protagonists who may dodge daggers and bullets but never seem to escape Cupid's Arrow.

Sign up to Darcy McGuire's mailing list for news, competitions and updates on future books.

Follow Darcy on social media here:

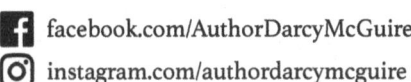 facebook.com/AuthorDarcyMcGuire

instagram.com/authordarcymcguire

ALSO BY DARCY MCGUIRE

The Queen's Deadly Damsels

The Secret Life of a Lady

A Lady's Lesson in Scandal

The Confessions of a Lady

A Most Unlikely Lady

You're cordially invited to

The Scandal Sheet

The home of swoon-worthy historical romance from the Regency to the Victorian era!

Warning: may contain spice 🌶

Sign up to the newsletter
https://bit.ly/thescandalsheet

Boldwood

Boldwood Books is an award-winning fiction publishing company seeking out the best stories from around the world.

Find out more at www.boldwoodbooks.com

Join our reader community for brilliant books, competitions and offers!

Follow us
@BoldwoodBooks
@TheBoldBookClub

Sign up to our weekly deals newsletter

https://bit.ly/BoldwoodBNewsletter